CW01626908

When the soul of an old house meets the house of a new soul, the magic begins!

HOUSE *of* DREAMS

MARK STIBBE

BOOKLAB

First published 2023 by Bella Books UK, a Pawprint/Imprint of BookLab

www.thebooklab.co.uk

British Library Cataloguing in Publication Data. A catalogue record for this book is available from the British Library.

ISBN: 978-1-3999-5813-4

Cover design by Esther Kotecha

Printed in the UK

Dedication

This is book is dedicated to the memory of John 'Sharpy' Parkin, my oldest friend.

Moonlight can play odd tricks upon the fancy, even upon a dreamer's fancy. As I stood there, hushed and still, I could swear that the house was not an empty shell but lived and breathed as it had lived before.

Daphne Du Maurier, *Rebecca*

Contents

1

THE HOUSE

The healing began with an old cob wall, ten feet tall, and a yearning to know what lay behind it.

It was early morning and Tony Lawson was driving towards Stonehenge. He was approaching what was once called the Village of the Five Trees when he noticed two stacks of chimneys and several dormer windows peeping above a tall wall on his left. Without giving it a second's thought, he left the main road and entered the village. He never paused to ask why.

After a few missed turns, he found the lane adjacent to the house whose roof he had glimpsed. A 'For Sale' sign stood at an angle beside the gate to the property. The board looked jaded, and its letters faded. The green wood of the gate also needed a fresh coat of paint. The place seemed deserted.

Tony lowered the front windows of his car and winced at the ice-cold air. He leaned to his left, unbuckled his seatbelt, and strained his eyes to catch a glimpse of what kind of house was hidden by the tall wall with its tiny, tiled roof running all the way along the top. Rubbing his gloved hands, he observed a thin plaque embedded in the wall. Its gilded letters said, 'The Old Rectory.'

He closed the windows and parked opposite the green gates. He briefly checked his appearance in the rear-view mirror. Taking out a comb, he made sure every loose strand of his silvery hair was in place, including his close-cut beard.

Tony was just about to walk over to the gates when his phone rang. He looked down and saw the name Wendy. He stayed in his seat, taking advantage of the warmth.

"I've just sent you a file," Wendy said, her voice calm, her tone sombre. "It's your divorce papers."

Tony sighed.

"I'm sorry, Tony."

"It's okay."

"Do you need to stop?"

"I've literally just parked."

"If you've got time, maybe skim-read them now. You're due at Harley Street later at 4pm. You could talk it through with Shree if you need to process it."

"I'll maybe do that."

"If you need me, Tony, just call. I'm in the office. I'll drop what I'm doing, as always."

"Thanks, Wendy."

Tony ended the call and opened the file.

Each page felt like a punch.

There was a letter from Renée's solicitor.

A raft of county court papers with his case number.

Then one word in bold and capitalised.

Dissolution.

Tony sighed again.

Like a monastery, he thought.

As he glanced through the pages, his eyes locked on a paragraph in which Renée had formed the statement of case. The lined box enclosed a summary that was terse, cold, and clinical.

Prioritised his work.

Sense of exclusion.

Distress.

Emotionally detached throughout.

Distress (again).

He thrust his phone back in his pocket and sat back in the seat. Closing his eyes, he shook his head. It was not so much the terminal nature of the language that rocked him. It was his surprise that three decades of his imperfections, none of which he could deny, had been reduced to a charge that took just seconds to read.

Tony opened his eyes. Leaning to his left again, he looked at the old wall and the beaten-up gates. He dismissed the melancholy as if he was brushing snowflakes from his shoulders. Stepping out of his vehicle, he smoothed out his suit jacket and jeans before crossing the lane. He paused only to study a carved engraving of a horse on the wall. *The signature of the original builder*, he surmised.

He opened the gates.

Before him, there was a gravel drive.

It was flanked by holly bushes.

He walked ten more paces before he saw the house.

The façade was made of banded brick and covered with flinted stones. It had two main storeys, with a large attic above. The front door, whose top half was glazed, stood beneath a stone-framed window with a date carved in

Roman numerals - 1530. Either side of the door, there were four more windows, two on each floor. To Tony, it was his dream house. Grand, but not too grand.

He took out his phone. His voice broke the silence that hung like a spell in the garden.

"Wendy, I'm going to text you the address of a house. Can you check it's still for sale? And please find out anything you can about its history. It must have been Tudor originally, but it looks as if it was rebuilt after that, maybe in the eighteenth century."

While Wendy got to work, he peered through the two windows in the upper part of the front door. The ground floor was empty. No dressers, tables, paintings, lamps. No movement either. Not a soul. The place looked uninhabited.

He walked around the side of the house and found some outbuildings, one of which seemed to have been a Victorian laundry room. He proceeded to some larger buildings that had clearly been stables. In one of them, he found the remains of what looked like a Tudor bread oven. Beyond them, there was a walled garden. Unkempt. Wild. Unloved. A bit like the house.

Tony wandered back and then stood looking at the lawn in front of the rectory. There was an apple tree in his eyeline at the edge of the uncut grass. Yew trees stood beyond that, dishevelled and forlorn. The house and grounds were in a dire state, but there was a patina of serenity and antiquity within its mystic boundaries.

As he walked onto the gravel, the stones crunching under his heels, Wendy rang back.

"It's still for sale. Been on the market four years. It needs a lot of work by the look of the photos."

"Anything about its history?"

"Your instincts were right. It was originally a Tudor hunting lodge. Owned by King Henry VIII..."

"That makes sense," Tony interrupted. "His coat of arms is carved into the stone above the front door."

Wendy continued. "It was burned down in the early 1700s but restored by the then rector Thomas Stephens. The Queen Anne style is still visible, although it was given a big refurb by a gentleman called Lord Portman 150 years ago."

"That would account for the Victorian vibe," Tony said.

"Do you like it?"

"I love it."

"It might be good for you..."

"What?"

"Getting away from that great big box in Chelsea. There are so many memories there."

"True," Tony said, before adding, "And then there's the small matter of my stalker."

Wendy said, "Perhaps the best reason of all."

"But can I afford it?"

"You can, as it happens."

"Even after Renée's asset stripping?"

"Yes."

"Please arrange a viewing then."

The call ended.

Tony turned and stared back at the house. His eyes were drawn to the garden to the left.

Something seemed to move.

A figure.

Tony rubbed his eyes.

Nothing.

Shadows, he thought.

He would have stayed there longer, but the cold was biting harder, and he was trespassing.

When he reached the gates, they were shut.

Someone, or something, must have closed them.

Pushing them open, he paused and took one last glimpse of the house. His eyes were drawn again to the lawn. There was something about that stretch of grass. Something emanating from the wet soil. The house was soaked in it. Not just history. Mystery too.

Maybe it was the sacred residue of all the clerics who had prayed in the Old Rectory. Or maybe something older still, woven into the tapestry of the house's genesis.

He could not tell.

One thing he did know.

He would be back.

2

THE COUNSELLOR

Shortly before 4pm, Tony drove beneath the hanging Christmas lights of London towards Harley Street. Twenty minutes later, Shree was opposite him in a small chair with soft grey arms. Tony sat on a cream-coloured couch, his feet resting on a purple rug that stretched from his side of the room to hers. A standard lamp radiated with a modest light on his right. A red candle, encircled by fake green holly, flickered on the glass coffee table between them.

Shree repositioned the cushion towards the top of her back and then took her notebook and pen from a small table beside her chair. "How are you, Tony?"

"Been better."

Her deep brown eyes seemed to widen.

She waited.

Tony said, "My divorce was finalised today."

He reached down into an old leather briefcase and pulled out a folder. Withdrawing the documents, he turned to a dog-eared page. He paused to read something.

Shree waited again.

He lifted a sheet.

"It's her final crushing verdict."

"And what does it say?"

"That I was emotionally disengaged and that she was a victim of a total lack of empathy."

He forced the papers back into the loose-leaf file and dropped them back into the briefcase.

"How does that make you feel?" Shree asked.

"Well, that's my problem, isn't it? Apparently, I don't."

Tony sat back and looked up at the magnolia ceiling. He seemed to be examining it for any imperfections.

"You've been decorating," he muttered.

"Tony!"

"Sorry," he mumbled.

He leaned forward. "You asked me how it made me feel... the truth is, it unsettled me ... a lot, actually ... I know I need to take responsibility for all this, but it made me think of myself as ..."

He tried to look away from those eyes.

He surrendered. "As a failure."

He brought his hands to beneath his chin and clasped them, almost as if he was praying. "Ten years at bloody boarding school..." he said, his voice almost a whisper.

"What about them?"

"Taught me not to feel."

Shree scribbled on her pad.

"You never felt anything at school?"

"Only when I did something well."

"Like what?"

"Excelling at sports, or in an essay."

"I've seen this before in ex-boarders," Shree said.

"Seen what?"

"This desperate striving to achieve, this longing to feel valued by making a success of yourself."

Tony shuffled his feet.

Shree asked, "Why did the papers upset you?"

"I suppose it's because I've always worked my socks off to succeed in my work, my book writing, my speaking engagements, my media work, everything related to my job, and... I suppose ... I did manage to do quite well in those public roles."

"That's an understatement," Shree said.

"But none of that mattered when I read that today."

Tony sipped some water.

"Why?"

"Because it's the first time in my life I've felt like I failed."

"At anything?"

"No, of course not."

"But you said it was the first time."

"I mean at something important."

Tony took another sip.

"What does it matter if my books, talks, and podcasts have been successes if I've failed where it really matters?"

Another sip.

"I felt guilty when I saw that."

"Guilty?"

Shree glanced down at her notepad. Her straight black silky hair was so long the ends touched the paper. "And yet you just said when you read the papers, you saw yourself as a failure."

"So?"

"So, you're a writer, Tony. Words matter."

"Sorry," he said. "I'm not thinking clearly."

"Listen, Tony. There are two feelings you're experiencing. You feel guilty because of what you've done, or not done, in your marriage. But you also feel ashamed about what you think that makes you. Guilt is connected to what we do. Shame is connected to who we are. You feel guilty because you've failed. But you feel shame because you've labelled yourself as a failure."

"And this is important because?"

"Because it's good news, Tony."

"It doesn't feel like it."

"You just said 'feel' again. For someone who's convinced they've shut down, I'd say you feel a lot."

"Maybe ..."

"There's no 'maybe' about it. And what's hopeful is the fact that you're speaking to me for the first time in ten years about shame. You've never acknowledged that before."

Shree's dark, round face seemed to glow.

"Shame is what you felt today, not just guilt. And shame is what you've been trying to bury ever since you were abandoned as a boy. That's the part of your soul that needs to heal."

Tony raised his eyes.

"I suppose so."

Shree waited, then asked, "Have you been dreaming?"

"Nothing significant, not for ages." Tony looked away and added, "It's a bit ironic, isn't it?"

"What is?"

"An expert on dreams not dreaming."

Shree carried her notebook and pen to a small desk. She

placed it on the tabletop and then turned. "There's buried trauma in that soul of yours," she said. "But remember what I always say... Where's there's buried trauma, there's often..."

"Buried treasure," Tony said.

"Exactly."

Tony stood. Shree, who was a foot shorter, looked up at him.

"Are you going to take it easy this evening?"

"I'm doing some research about a house."

"A new home?"

"Maybe."

"London?"

"No, the West Country."

"That might be good for you."

"Wendy thinks so too."

Shree led him towards the door.

"Are you doing that podcast with Hugh tomorrow?"

"I am. It's the last one before Christmas."

Shree took his arm and stopped.

"And are you with anyone Christmas Day?"

"No."

"Will you be all right?"

He nodded.

"Text me if you need a chat."

"I won't be disturbing you and Aya. Isn't it your first Christmas together?"

"It is. But she would understand."

"Thanks, Shree, but I wouldn't dream of it."

"Dream away if you want to," she said.

Tony left the office and headed through reception. Walking

outside the building, he spied a Christmas tree through the window of a nearby house, pulsating with coloured lights.

He opened the door of his R8, turned on the ignition, and started to make his way through the traffic.

A familiar festive song had just begun on the radio.

"It'll be lonely this Christmas."

He shook his head.

He turned off the song before heading back in silence to his big box in Chelsea.

And that night, he dreamed.

3

A DREAM

In his dream, Tony was back at the Old Rectory, standing near the gate, looking at the lawn. His eyes were drawn to the space where he thought he had seen something on his visit.

It was then that he noticed her.

A woman in a long grey Tudor dress, such as a maid might wear, with a ring of iron keys hanging from her pinched waist. She was standing near the apple tree, staring up above the front door of the house, at the ancient window with the stone surround.

She seemed to sense Tony's presence.

Later, it would not be the white ribbons holding her red hair that struck him as strange, nor her lack of protection against the cold. It would be her choreography. Touching the hem on both sides of her dress, she curtseyed, her eyes never leaving his.

When she reached the lowest point, her hands stretched out towards the grass. It was almost balletic. If it had not been for the grey modesty of her attire, he would have called it regal.

In his dream, Tony wondered how he was meant to respond to such a noble gesture. He considered making a bow, but in the end all he managed was a wave.

The woman smiled, took the keys in her hand, then disappeared into thin air.

Tony ran down the drive.

He shouted, "Hey!"

Paced over the patch of grass where she had stood.

Knelt.

Felt the turf.

There was no sign of her.

He spoke to the earth.

"Where are you?"

Silence.

Not even a breath of air.

He spoke again.

"What is your name?"

Silence again.

Not even a rustling of boughs and leaves.

Then he bent as low to the ground as he could and whispered, "What do you want from me?"

There was a gust of wind from the direction of the apple tree facing him. It was so strong that it almost caused him to topple over onto the damp soil beneath him.

Tony struggled to his feet, the smell of the wet grass still filling his nostrils, the dampness of the soil on his knees.

The wind ceased.

He looked around the garden.

He searched for her among the yews and hedgerows

before doing a sweep of the more open spaces.

There was no sign of the ghost.

He returned to the gate.

Looked back.

There was a golden glint in the windows of the house as the dying sunlight kissed the unwashed panes.

The place seemed both empty and yet inhabited.

Dead and alive.

When Tony woke with a start, he was alert.

His mind racing.

He reached for his dream journal underneath the bedside lamp next to him.

He took hold of his pen.

The last entry had been over three years ago.

He began to scribble down his feelings first.

Wonder.

No, awe.

Mystery.

Yearning.

A visceral yearning.

Still gnawing.

Still calling out for something.

I have no idea what.

Not once did he say "fear."

Or "terror".

This was his world, after all.

Tony next wrote a description of his dream. As soon as the nib of his Mont Blanc fountain pen struck the page, it was as if something took hold of both it and him.

Although he had some measure of control, when he had finished, he wrote a single word.

Automatic.

He sat up.

For several minutes, or what felt like several minutes, he pondered these things in his heart.

As his eyelids began to grow heavy again, he wrote one more sentence in his journal.

Who is she, this ghost in the garden?

4

THE PODCAST

When Tony arrived at his studio the next morning, the elation of having dreamed again had put a new spring in his step.

"Hugh is ten minutes out," Wendy said as he entered the green room. "Tim's ready to go live as soon as he arrives. He just wants you to film a quick intro first."

Tony nodded and headed through a padded door into the recording studio. He sat and put on his headphones. Tim counted down with his fingers.

Tony's voice was low and rich. "Welcome to the Royal Road podcast. I'm really excited to introduce our special guest today, Hugh Ullman, one of the stars of the new Christmas film, *The Snow King* – a film that's taking the world by storm."

Tim raised his hand. He checked what he had filmed, then gestured for Tony to continue.

"Hugh asked to come on the show to seek advice about a recurring dream. I for one can't wait to hear more! As Freud said, the interpretation of dreams is the royal road, the *via regia*, to the knowledge of the unconscious. I'm looking forward to travelling down that magical road with another guest."

Tim ran a playback.

He smiled.

"That's perfect, Tony. I'll have the main theme from Hugh's film playing beneath that."

Tony was about to head back to the green room when Wendy escorted Hugh into the studio. He was dressed in a checked shirt, bright green cardigan, and red cords.

"Good morning, Santa!" Tony said.

Hugh looked confused. "Oh, you mean the colours."

"Green and red, Hugh. And that new beard...it's very white!

"The movie," he said with a wink.

Wendy showed him to his chair and gave him an espresso.

"Cosy place you've got here," Hugh said.

Tim gave him some headphones. "We go live in two minutes. There's a clock just there."

Tony said, "You've seen the format, I'm sure. You share your recurring dream, I try to interpret it, with the help of our viewers, and then you respond at the end."

"Perfect," he said.

When the clock reached zero, Tim ran the intro and provided the Elgar-like score of *The Snow King* as a lush and resonant underlay to Tony's equally lush and resonant voice.

"Hugh, great to have you on the show. I'm one of millions who love *The Snow King*. Can you reveal exclusively on the Royal Road if there's going to be a sequel?"

"I can't. But what I can do is reveal what I've been dreaming about. I'm hoping you can help me."

Tony smiled and said, "Fire away."

"I've been having this for a while. On and off. Not every night. Maybe once a month. Two months, perhaps. It always follows the same sequence, always takes place in the same setting."

He took a deep breath.

"I'm standing in the attic of a house. Not a country house or a mansion. A detached house, the lower half red brick, the upper half white wood. I think it's near the sea."

"Any idea where?"

"No."

Tony gestured for him to continue.

"I can hear someone or something humming a tune. It's always the same tune. Coming from downstairs. I head down to the next floor and search the four bedrooms and the communal bathroom. There's no sign of the singer."

"But you can still hear the song."

"Not a song, a tune."

Tony scribbled some notes on a pad.

"I explore the ground floor rooms. Everything is furnished 1940s. There are black-and-white photos everywhere. I seem to recognise it all. And yet at the same time, I have no idea where I am, and I haven't a clue who it is I'm seeing in the photos."

Hugh reached for his espresso.

He took a sip.

"I head into the hallway and open the old blue door to the cellar. I walk down a steep flight of rickety wooden stairs and step onto the cold stone floor below. The cellar is completely empty. No boxes. No shelves. No wine racks or bottles. Empty. Save, that is, for one thing. The one humming the tune."

"And who's that?"

"Not who. What. There, in the corner, is a fish. It's pale and grey. Almost ghostly. The tune is coming from its protruding lips. One eye is looking at me intently."

"Are you scared?"

"No."

"That's a pretty surreal image," Tony said, "even by the standards set by this podcast."

"Can you help me?"

"Well, let's have a go. Just remember, there's three stages to our process. The first stage is narration. You've just done that for us. Thank you for describing the dream so clearly."

Hugh nodded.

"The second is interpretation. Here we need to decode any possible symbolism in the dream, both in its audio as well as visual contents. So, then, let's start with the visual aspects of your recurring dream. And we'll begin with the house."

Tony opened a folder and began to read.

"Jung taught that houses often have two storeys in dreams. The upper floor symbolises the conscious mind, the lower floor the subconscious. Beneath the lower floor, there are two further levels - the cellar and the cave. These represent even deeper levels of the subconscious and, according to Jung, these have to do with our past, often going back to ancient times."

"Makes sense," Hugh said.

"What you're seeing in your recurring dream is therefore

an invitation to make a journey from your conscious mind right down into the deepest levels of your subconscious, and this invitation comes in the form of a tune sung by a fish."

"Unreal, isn't it?" Hugh said.

"It may appear that way, but let's press on. When you reach the underground level, the cellar, you see and hear a fish. Is it always the same kind of fish?"

"Yes."

"Can you describe it?"

"It's a flatfish."

"Let's find some pictures."

Tony searched on his laptop and started a slideshow on the screen in the studio, describing each picture for his listeners.

Five photos in, Hugh cried, "That's it!"

Tony smiled. "That's a member of the sole family. Does that ring any bells for you, Hugh?"

He shook his head.

"Remember, dreams often revel in puns and wordplays."

"Oh, you mean soul!"

Tony continued. "Did your family come from Kent?"

"Why do you ask?"

"Well, did they?"

Hugh looked down at his shoes. "I've never spoken about this publicly before..." his voice was quieter now. "I was adopted as a baby. Recently, I've been researching my biological parents. They lived in Kent. That was the county of my birth."

"And was Dover the town where you were born?"

"How did you know?"

"Because the fish in your dreams is a Dover Sole."

Hugh looked startled.

"Listen, Hugh. I know it sounds strange, but you need to explore your soul, because ... well... sometimes we need to understand our history before we can solidify our identity."

Hugh nodded.

"And that," I said, "leads to the third stage of the process, activation. There's always something to apply, to action, to do. In your case, you have a choice. You can stay in the upper storey of the house, living out of the conscious mind, or you can go down into the cellar and explore who you really are."

Hugh smiled. "That's pretty insightful."

"We're not done just yet! We've only looked at the visual content. What about the audio? What about the tune the fish is humming? Are you able to sing or hum that tune to us?"

Hugh laughed. "There's a reason I never get invited to do musicals! I'm almost tone deaf."

"Give it a try," Tony said.

Hugh started to whistle. It was not altogether tuneless. Here and there, Tony recognised a familiar riff. So did the fans watching the podcast. Some of them spotted it too. Tony wrote a note to Tim to line it up to play when Hugh had finished.

When he stopped whistling, Hugh said, "I'm sorry, Tony. That was all over the place."

"I don't agree. Listen to this."

Tim pressed play.

There was a familiar strings intro.

Then the unmistakable voice of Vera Lynn.

There'll be bluebirds over
The white cliffs of Dover
Tomorrow
Just you wait and see

There'll be love and laughter
And peace ever after
Tomorrow
When the world is free

By the time the track was done, Hugh was holding back the tears.

"Tomorrow, when the world is free," Tony repeated. "Freedom is on the way, Hugh."

"And peace ever after," he said, wiping his eyes.

Tony waited for his guest to compose himself.

"Are you alright?"

Hugh nodded. Then he spoke again. "The one thing I know about my birth mother was her Christian name."

He paused.

"It was Vera."

A longer pause this time.

At the end of it, Tony said, "You know, Hugh, the Dover Sole is regarded by many chefs as the finest of all fish."

Hugh nodded.

"There's a message in that, Hugh."

"There really is," he said, his voice faltering.

Tim starting the countdown.

Tony spoke. "We'll be back in the New Year with more celebrity guests sharing their dreams. In the meantime, it just remains for me to thank our guest today, Hugh Ullman."

As the music played, Tony and Hugh left the studio.

"The numbers are off the charts," Wendy said as they entered the green room. "And the feedback's just stunning."

"Thank you so much, Hugh," Tony said.

"I'm the one who should thank you."

"No need," Tony said as the two men embraced. "To be perfectly honest with you, I'm going through the same kind of process myself. So, I was right there with you."

Hugh smiled. "Well, Tony, as my fellow Scousers would say, you'll never walk alone."

"In that case," Tony said. "I'll meet you on the royal road."

5

THE NEIGHBOUR

After a long lunch with Hugh – Dover Sole, of course - Tony returned to Chelsea. It was dark when he stepped out of the car. The streetlamps illuminated the street but not the first twenty metres of the alleyway that led from the road to the front courtyard of his modern mansion. This was set back from the road, concealed by a row of tall, terraced, red-bricked houses. He had to navigate a communal path before the security lights on his property were motion-activated. The one lamp that lit up this neighbourhood path seemed to be broken. He felt his way along the pathway using a metal railing.

Six metres before he reached his paved garden, Tony saw a shape in the gloom ahead. It was a man. He was wearing a long dark cloak and had a stick in his hand.

Tony stopped.

Fetching his phone, he switched on the torch and shone it in the direction of the intruder. As soon as he saw the familiar black beret, he knew who it was.

"You're trespassing, Maul," he said.

The man chuckled.

"It's not a nice feeling, is it, Tony? Having someone walking all over your property."

"What the hell are you talking about?"

"You know exactly what I'm talking about. You used my intellectual property. You stole my ideas. Used them in the book that made you famous. Made you rich. You owe me."

"I owe you nothing," Tony said.

Maul was not for budging.

"At the very least, you owe me half the royalties and my name on the cover of the book."

Tony laughed, prompting dogs in the neighbourhood to start barking. "You're delusional," he said. "You know full well I'd written the first draft of my book before I even met you. In fact, I didn't even know who you were by the time I submitted it. None of your ideas are in that book, or anything else I've written!"

Maul raised his cane and pointed the tip towards him. "You're a bloody liar!"

More barking.

"Put that down," Tony said.

"Or what?"

"Or I'll have you arrested for trespass."

"Trespass?" he said. "This path is shared and public ground. You do not own it. Any more than you own the IP for that book. Go ahead. Call the police."

Somehow Maul had discovered the truth about the path. The ground on which Tony was standing was not his property. And he had positioned himself in the space where the lights and cameras could reveal and record him.

Tony tried a different tack.

"Look, Matt. I know you've fallen on hard times. But trying to cheat me out of my royalties and reputation isn't the answer. If you'd come to me as the friend you once were, I would have helped you. Still would if you just told the truth."

"I don't want your pity or your charity," the intruder spat, his saliva cascading onto the ground.

Just then, Tony's phone died.

The darkness was thick.

Really thick.

Panic began to rise.

Tony was about to run when he heard the backdoor of the end-terrace house behind him.

He turned to see his neighbour standing on a well-lit threshold. He was holding his mobile phone.

The neighbour squinted in Maul's direction. "Who's that? Do you want me to call the police, Tony?"

"He's threatening me!" Tony shouted.

"I'll phone 999," he said, pressing on his screen and then lifting the handset to his ear.

As Tony's head was still turned, Maul pushed past him and headed out towards the road.

"This isn't the last of this!" he shouted. "You'll be hearing from my lawyers!"

And then he was gone.

Tony's breathing now became loud and erratic.

Sweat glistened on his brow.

His neighbour took hold of his arm.

"Come in," he said.

Tony followed into the kitchen.

"Let me take a look at you."

The neighbour fetched a black case from the hallway and brought it to the table where Tony was sitting.

"Unbutton your shirt, please."

He drew a stethoscope out of the bag and pressed the disc-shaped resonator to Tony's chest. It was cold.

"Hmmm," he said.

"Hmmm what?"

He took out a blood pressure monitor, wrapped the clasp around my upper arm, and took several readings.

"Your BP is high, and your heart is racing," he said.

"It's not surprising though is it?"

"No, it is not. He seemed like a very angry man. What's his problem?"

"He's gaslighting me."

Tony sighed as his neighbour parted the Velcro and put the monitor back in his bag.

"I didn't know you were a doctor, Rakesh."

Rakesh smiled. "It's sad, isn't it? We live just a few feet apart, and we have never been in each other's homes."

"It's kind of you to help me."

"I want to give you some medicine," Rakesh said.

"No, it's all right. I'm okay."

"But I insist."

Rakesh returned a moment later with a bottle.

"Here!"

Tony looked at the label. "That's a very expensive Bourbon."

"Like I said. It's very good medicine."

He poured the golden liquid into two tumblers.

"I will keep an eye out for you," Rakesh said. "If he comes

back, I'll give him a piece of my mind."

"That's very kind, but I'd keep clear of him."

"Ah, but my name is Rakesh."

"So?"

"So, Rakesh means Lord of the Night!"

"I'll drink to that," Tony said.

The tumblers chimed.

"Thank you for your hospitality."

Rakesh smiled. "In my religion, welcoming guests is one of the five duties of every householder."

"But you didn't invite me."

"That's the whole point."

"What do you mean?"

"The Sanskrit word for guest is *athithi*. It means 'without time.' You could translate it as 'without notice.' If the guest isn't someone who calls without time, they're not a guest."

"That's fascinating."

Rakesh looked at Tony and continued. "What's the point of owning a nice home if you're not going to have an open door. That's the main purpose of working hard and buying a house like this, or a house like yours. To provide hospitality."

Tony drained the glass.

Rakesh lifted the bottle. "Here, have some more!"

Tony shook his head.

"Some food, then."

"I had a big lunch."

"Okay, then."

Tony made to leave.

"My turn next time," he said.

6

THE LAWYER

The next morning Tony took a cab to his lawyer's offices. When he arrived, he sat on a black plastic sofa and cast his eyes over the abstract paintings on the walls. When the receptionist brought him an espresso, he walked to the huge windows and gazed at the people scurrying about their business in the plaza far below.

He drained his tiny cream cup and headed back to reception. Today, the white walls and the high ceilings seemed cold and distant. A fake plant gave a splash of colour, but even that could not redeem the bland minimalism of the vast and unpoetic space. Maybe it was the contrast with the Old Rectory, but the steel-beamed edifice was lacking in memory, resistant to intimacy.

"Sorry to keep you waiting, Tony."

Yinka was wearing a tailored, pin-striped suit. He was fifty, like Tony, but his ebony skin was flawless.

"Looking good, Yinka," Tony said.

Yinka led Tony to the boardroom. Tony took a seat one

side of the long glass table. Yinka sat opposite.

"How can I help you?"

"It's Matt Maul," Tony replied. "I think he's about to come after me with a claim."

"Go on."

"He was waiting for me outside my house last night. He said he was going to contact his lawyers."

Yinka looked concerned.

"What's his beef with you?" he asked.

"He claims I stole some of the ideas in my first book, *Dreamers*, from him."

"And did you?"

"Of course not. The first draft was written before I even knew Maul existed, and well before I made the catastrophic error of allowing him to become a friend."

"What about the premise for your book? Did you ever share that with him verbally before it was published?"

"I invited him and his girlfriend to dinner a few times with myself and Renée. He and I talked about what we were both writing. I probably wasn't as guarded as I should have been. The wine was flowing rather freely whenever we met."

Yinka asked, "Do you have any emails, drafts of the book, on your computer? Especially ones that predate your first meetings with Maul - anything with a digital footprint?"

"You're talking about a paper trail."

He nodded.

"That's where I have a problem. I have dissociative amnesia disorder. Nothing to worry about. I'm having therapy. But one of the side effects is that I've completely forgotten the basics when it comes to my computer skills."

"What about asking Renée for help?"

"Things are a bit frosty."

"But didn't she work for you?"

Tony nodded.

"If she can retrieve the relevant documents, then that will potentially weaken his case."

Yinka poured a glass of cold sparkling water for his client. "Why's he doing this to you, Tony?"

"He was a successful author once," he replied, "But he was better at self-promotion than he was at writing."

"You mean he conned people."

"Yes. Even his name is fake. His real name is Michalis Oikonomou. Changed it to Matt Maul because he thought it sounded and looked better. But it was all part of his BS."

"What happened to him?"

"In the end, his agent refused to rep him, and his publishers cut their losses."

"But that still doesn't answer why he's targeting you."

"I really have no explanation. I've always been kind to him. But he thinks the world owes him a good living. He wears his entitlement as shamelessly as that stupid beret."

Tony took a gulp of fizzy water. Too fast. Coughing and spluttering, he dabbed his lips with a wadge of scented tissues from a lilac, rectangular box on the table.

"I'll get Nadiya onto this," Yinka said. "She's one of our partners and an expert in media cases. Nobody better. She's involved in these sorts of disputes all the time."

"Thank you."

Tony put his head in his hands.

Yinka removed his glasses. "I'm concerned about you, Tony. You look tired. Stressed. Not yourself."

"Thank you, Yinka, truly, but you're my dispute lawyer

not my counsellor."

"I'm also your friend."

Tony wiped the last drops lurking in his short beard. "It's the divorce. I'm not feeling myself."

"And Maul senses it," Yinka said.

Tony nodded.

"I'll ask Nadiya to be at the ready. She's just the right person to give Maul a run for his money."

Yinka walked around to Tony's side of the table.

"I'm concerned that he's been waiting outside your house," he said, placing his hand on Tony's shoulder. "Your home should be a safe place. Maybe you need to get away for a bit."

Tony sighed. His voice was soft now. "I've got my eyes on a new pad well away from the city."

"Conducive for writing?"

"Yep."

"How long is it since you last wrote a book?"

"Too long. I've been a little ... distracted."

"Well, maybe you should take some time out."

Tony thanked Yinka and left. As he walked out onto the plaza below, a text came through from Wendy.

The Old Rec. Viewing arranged for this Saturday. 11.00am. Hope that's okay?

Tony replied with a thumbs up.

He hailed a cab and sat back into the seat. Leaning back, he closed his eyes and thought of the house in the Village of the Five Trees. His safe house. Beyond Maul's reach.

He had made up his mind. If he liked what he saw inside the property, it would be his.

7

THE VIEWING

Three days later, Tony drove to the Old Rectory. When he arrived, he sat and looked at the gardens, half expecting to see the ghost. She was not there. Or she was there, but he did not see her.

Tony walked to the front door and rang the bell.

A suited woman appeared.

"Mister Lawson?"

He nodded.

"My name is Ms Macready. Let me show you around."

Ms Macready led him through the hallway into the living room. His eyes were drawn to the windows. He walked over and paused for a minute gazing at the gardens.

She said, "There's a Ha-Ha."

Tony smiled.

As they turned back into the dusty room, she said, "It was originally built in 1530, as a Tudor manor house. There are still parts that date from then, as you can see - windows, an archway, a wall. But much was destroyed by a great fire at the beginning of the eighteenth century. It was shortly after that when this was built, incorporating the surviving parts of the manor house."

Tony paused in front of the stone fireplace, imagining who else had stared at the burning grate.

"I'd like to know more," he said. "A house as old as this always has an energy. You can sense the presence of those who have lived here over the years. It's almost ... tangible."

"The historian is the one you need."

"Historian?"

"He has lived in these parts for as long as anyone can remember. I can email you his contact details. He knows everything about this house and its history."

She stopped and looked at Tony. "I recognise you," she said. "You're *the* Tony Lawson, aren't you? You write about dreams. And you were in that recent film..."

"*The Dream Ticket*," he said with a sigh. "It wasn't great. Let's just leave it at that."

He looked down at the floor.

She laughed. More loudly than the comment had ever warranted. And she blushed.

"Can I just ask..."

Tony had heard those four words a thousand times. He loved being on stages where he could talk to thousands without ever feeling drained, but he always feared the lines of people wanting to ask questions after he came down from his talks.

"Can I just ask you about a recurring dream?"

"Go on."

"It's always about a white stag at night-time. The stag tries to cross a road from one part of the woods to another.

A Range Rover appears. The creature is caught in the headlights. It is paralysed, too scared to move. Then I wake up."

"Always before you know what happens?"

She nodded.

"Have you read *Watership Down*?"

The woman looked confused.

"All of us have fears, but the rabbits in *Watership Down* have a special kind of terror, when caught in the headlights, when they cannot move. They have a word for it. Stephen King uses it in his novel *The Stand* as well."

She was struggling to understand.

"It's the word *tharn*."

Tears flooded her eyes.

"Tharn is my ex-husband's surname."

"And he drives a Range Rover?"

"Drove," she said. "He had to sell it and give me half the money during the divorce."

"Forgive me for asking, and don't answer if it's too much, but did he .... did he harm you?"

The tears were running down her face.

She nodded.

Tony waited till she had composed herself.

"There are three reactions to abuse," he said. "They are flight, fright, and fight. You don't need to resort to any of them. He has no legal hold over you, other than what you allow him."

The woman started to wipe her tears.

"No more *tharn*."

His words were soft, but they were firm.

"And never forget, the white stag is a symbol of royalty.

You must be very honoured for it to cross your path."

"Thank you," she said. Then, "Sorry. I expect people do this to you all the time."

Tony smiled.

After they had toured every empty room on both floors, they returned to the hallway.

"The prospectus says this is an auction sale. When is that?"

"January 6th."

Tony cursed.

"Is there a problem?"

"Can my assistant, Wendy, bid instead of me?"

"Of course."

Tony walked to the front door.

He said, "Don't forget the historian's details."

She nodded.

They said their goodbyes.

Tony sat in his car.

Waiting for the heater to clear the windscreen.

As the mist cleared, he shuddered.

She was there!

The maid from his dream.

Her red hair tied in white ribbons.

The white linen partlet over her neck.

Grey woollen kirtle.

White smock.

Keys hanging from her waist.

There was a smile on her pale and freckled face.

And a shining in her eyes.

Tony wanted to get out of the car and run over to her, but he seemed frozen to his seat.

As he watched, eyes wide with wonder, he saw her do again what she had done before.

The curtsey.

She swept one foot behind her and bent her knees outwards while holding the hems of her dress away from her body. This time it seemed a deeper and more elaborate gesture, more like one performed by a lady in waiting at court.

No sooner had her hand swept across the surface of the grass, as before, than she disappeared, leaving no trace of her presence, other than a mesmerizing memory.

As Tony regained mobility, he took hold of the steering wheel and turned the car towards the gates, heading for the road back to his modern mansion in Chelsea.

He knew he would dream again that night.

8

A DREAM

That night in his dream, Tony found himself at the beginnings of the Old Rectory, at the time of its Tudor origins.

He saw three people, two men and a woman, dressed in simple work attire. They referred to each other as brother and sister and were working with intense speed and synergy. They measured a plot of the ground that Tony could tell from the contours nearby was the earth on which the Old Rectory now stood. With the help of some labourers, they cordoned off the area after digging the foundations. They planted timber posts in small steps around the periphery and together hoisted a wooden frame into place. They added one floor at a time. Right up to the last minute, one of the two brothers – who Tony took to be a carpenter – was sawing at the bones of this skeleton made of oak. The edges could not have been straighter.

The tall, thin chimneys were next. They seemed to be made of moulded bricks and had three-leafed clovers carved into them. The flues and fireplaces, hand-carved by the carpenter, were added. His skills seemed to extend to stone, not just wood.

When all the timber of the house's frame had been painted in tar, the three instructed the workers to cover the timber structure with skin. They covered every gap between the posts in wattle panelling. They added daub. After that had dried, they created an unblemished white-and-black façade. All this happened at great speed. To Tony's mind, it was like watching something in fast-forward mode, even though he was, in truth, witnessing a rewind.

This high tempo applied to their building of the steep pitched roof using crude, clay tiles, as well as the filling of the many casement window frames with minute glass panes, all held together by lead in the shapes of triangles, squares, diamonds, and lozenges.

The scene then switched to the interior.

The three siblings and their helpers covered the downstairs walls with tapestries depicting Easter scenes from the Gospels. These were embroidered in gold, green, red, and dark brown. They then created plasterwork murals of thistles and pomegranates.

Upstairs, the carpenter constructed four-poster beds and his sister added hangings of velvet and brocade. Heavy oak chests, whose lids bore the same crest, rested on plaited rush mats.

They built a fine library with oak-panelled walls, adding hundreds of books in calf and Moroccan leather. Beyond the library they constructed a chapel with a Bible on a simple, wooden lectern. Tony saw the open page. It was the English translation William Tyndale published in 1526. The sister paused in front of the book and prayed. "Lord, open the eyes of the King of England."

Down in the cellars, they built ovens and stoves before bringing in iron cauldrons and a spit for meat. The carpenter set up shelves and his sister filled them with pots of herbs and spices. Tony could smell basil and coriander, even in his dream.

After the interior was finished, it was time for the gardens. Here the sister, the gardener, took the lead. She created knots arranged in a cruciform shape. He overheard the older brother, who seemed to be the architect, saying that even John Chapman, the most famous gardener in England, would have been proud. There was hyssop and lavender, thrift and marjoram, savoy and thyme in one quarter, and primroses, violets, sweet Williams, and pink roses in the other. The sister, the gardener, named them as she sowed the seeds. No sooner were the seeds in the earth than the stems and leaves grew out of the soil.

Here and there, she planted apple trees. She also named these as she went. "Green custard, pippin, and winter queening." These too grew at surreal speed. Where there were ancient mounds, she turned these into mounts, fashioning them into roosting places adorned with white thorn and hazel. When she had completed this part of the garden, she turned to her brothers. She clapped and laughed.

While the brothers built a wall to surround the private garden, she began her final project. With the help of a group of gardeners, she planted yew trees to form a pathway around the perimeter of the garden, each corner marked by the same tree in boxes.

When the three siblings had finished, they set up timber

posts with a carved lion on top of each, painted in gold. On top of these creatures, they attached a small flag with the Tudor rose, fluttering in the breeze. Between each of these posts, they established a network of green wooden rails to prevent visitors from straying from the gravel pathways onto the beds of flowers and herbs.

All this took no time.

No time at all.

Once she had finished, the sister sighed and turned with a smile to her brothers.

She curtsied and said, "To paradise right well comparable."

They laughed.

"Right well comparable," they replied.

When Tony awoke, he took his dream journal from the bedside table and began to write.

9

THE HISTORIAN

After his dream, Tony was impatient to meet the historian Ms Macready had mentioned. The next space in his diary was the following weekend. By Saturday morning, his curiosity had intensified. He had arranged to meet the historian at midday.

After a four-hour drive, Tony passed through the green gates and pulled into the gravel driveway. As soon as he stepped out of the car, he caught a glimpse of someone at the old Tudor window above the front door. Whoever it was, they were watching for his arrival, standing just beyond the stone ledge the other side of the glass. When Tony drew closer, he observed an elderly man dressed entirely in black. He had a full head of grey, straggly hair and a long nose that seemed to extend like an anteater's snout.

When the front door opened, the man stretched out his hand. "Mister Lawson," he said.

"And you are?"

"I am the historian."

"Do you have a name?"

"You can call me Con."

As he entered the bare vestibule, Tony said, "I don't recognise your accent. "Where are you from?"

"Germany, but I worked in Zurich much of my life. It's been a very long time since I was there. I've been living near here. Walking distance from this grand old house."

The historian paused and waited for a response.

"It is very grand," Tony replied.

Con led Tony into the sitting room where a team of decorators had long ago left a set of wooden stools in a corner. They sat together, almost nose-to-nose. As the sunlight poured into the room, Tony thought again what a peaceful place it was to rest and recover, to think and write. It was a house fit for a dreamer.

"Ms Macready tells me you're an author," the historian said.

"I am, yes."

"This house has often been occupied by people who wrote books," he said. "For five hundred years, it has been a haven for those who enjoy solitude and whose calling is the pen."

"She mentioned something about that."

"Did she mention that the first person to truly own this house, after its builders, was a female author?"

"She did not."

"She was the first woman ever to have her own name on the cover of her book."

"Who was that?"

"Queen Catherine."

"As in King Henry VIII?"

"The same."

"How did she come to live here?"

"The King gave it to her as a wedding gift."

"This was her own home?"

"After the King died, she stayed in a house in London, another in Hansworth, and this one here, her favourite."

"How do you know she lived here?"

"The evidence is everywhere."

Tony searched the room and frowned.

"Not so much in this room," he said, "But around the property. In the village too, provided you have eyes to see."

Tony was still confused.

"Consider the name of the walk that takes you around the garden. What's it called?"

"No idea."

"It's called the Queen's Walk. Queen Catherine used to take exercise by walking it when she was staying here. And tell me, Tony, what was her surname, the sixth Queen?"

Tony dragged the names of the queens from somewhere within a memory from his schooldays.

"Parr," he answered. "Queen Catherine Parr."

Tony's eyes widened.

"Parr Lane! In the village!"

"I told you there were signs."

"So, you're saying that the original house was once owned by a Queen of England?"

"Her feet walked across this same ground."

The hairs on the back of Tony's neck began to bristle.

"And you say she was the first woman to have her own name on a book cover?"

The historian nodded.

"I didn't even know she had written a book."

"Four, to be precise," he said.

Con stood and walked to the windows overlooking the lawns at what was now the back of the house, their grass protected from the sheep by the invisible Ha-Ha. He looked beyond the fields to a hill topped by a cluster of trees.

"She met here with her soulmate, the love of her life. Sir Thomas Seymour. A dashing seafarer. A tall, handsome man with a fine beard and blazing blue eyes."

"I thought she was married to the King," Tony said as he came and joined him at the windows.

"She was a devout woman," he said, "so she did not consort with him while married to Henry. She was all set to marry Thomas before the king set his affections upon her. After the King died, Queen Catherine reignited her passion for Thomas. They had trysts here, far from the madding crowd in London."

"Sounds romantic," Tony said.

He sighed. "It was. But it was not easy for them. People can be very censorious. Especially English people. You love it when people rise, but you love it even more when they fall, no?"

"Why did people disapprove if she was a widow? If her marriage was over, she was free to love again."

He answered, "It was not considered seemly for her to marry so soon after the king's death."

"That's sad."

"It is, but they found happiness for a while at this secluded house, away from the city."

"Was that when she wrote her books?"

"She wrote while she was married to the king, and she wrote after he had died. Her books were immensely popular.

They helped many people believe in God without needing to buy divine favour from the priests with their indulgences."

"She was a freedom fighter, then."

"With her pen, yes. Not only for those who wanted a simple faith, but for women whose voices were unheard."

"She sounds inspiring."

"I have always been an admirer," he said.

He turned away from the window and led Tony out of the room into the hall, his buckled black shoes tapping the surface of the flagstone floor. Before he opened the front door, he said, "There have been many writers who have lived here, including the Reverend Charles Kingsley, author of *The Water Babies*."

"My mother read it to me when I was a child," Tony said.

The historian smiled. He drew a golden pocket watch from his black waistcoat. Lifting it, he stared at the face and the hands, then raised his eyebrows, as if he was late for something.

As Tony grasped the handle, he looked out onto the grass. "When I came here before, I saw a woman on the lawn, near that apple tree, dressed in simple Tudor fare. She curtseyed and then disappeared. Would you know anything about her?"

"Ah, you've seen her."

"Who is she?"

The old man squinted.

"The question you need to ask is *where*, not who."

"She's on the lawn, that's where she is."

"Exactly. And what's there?"

"I don't know."

"Then I'll tell you. The old kitchens are there. Buried in

the earth beneath the grass."

"Why are they so important?"

"Perhaps another time," the historian replied.

Placing his watch back in his pocket, he said goodbye.

Tony stood outside the house, looking at the gardens.

What was it about the woman?

What was so important about the kitchens?

What about the historian, come to mention it?

This was a house with only two storeys, but it told many tales.

10

A DREAM

That night, Tony dreamed again. He dreamed that he was back in time at the house's Tudor beginnings. It seemed to be a warm summer evening and he saw many villagers walking into the gardens. The three siblings were welcoming them to a sumptuous feast. As the flames in a makeshift pit began to rise, the flesh of an enormous hog sizzled on a spit above a freshly dug pit. There were lute players and drummers playing joyful music. The three began to dance. Their movements were elegant and synchronised.

When they finished, everyone applauded.

As the fire in the pit diminished, ten maids clothed in grey-and-white dresses emerged from the house carrying freshly baked bread and flagons of cider. They walked in a procession. Each had simple white ribbons tied to their hair.

Before dinner was served, the sister invited the guests to walk along the tiled pathway flanked by the many Yew trees she had planted. Some of the children ran as far as the nearby hill, its slope and summit decorated by clusters of trees - oak, beach, and silver birch. Others ran to a nearby maze, one of the most intricate and elaborate Tony had ever seen. They tried to outdo each other in finding a way out of the complex system of corridors and dead ends. They all had to be helped by the sister to find the way; she behaved as if she had been the one who had designed and built it.

Back in the grounds of the house, there was the sound of laughter everywhere, and compliments for the work which the three, with the help of the labourers, had completed.

"What perfect lines!"

"And those windows!"

Another man called the house "enchanted".

One even remarked that the house looked as he imagined "The Father's house must look, the one where there are many rooms, the one we shall inhabit when all our troubles fade."

Even in his dream, Tony could see the bonds that connected them in a strong and vibrant community.

Just then, a frowning priest entered the garden. He was short and had a belly as pronounced as his air of entitlement.

The younger brother saw him.

"May I help you?" he asked.

The priest looked disgruntled. He replied, "I am Father Thomas Trotteswell from Tarrant Hinton. My care of souls extends to this village." The priest was looking past the carpenter, distracted by the sizzling hog. He turned back to the carpenter and announced, "I am here to bless this new house."

"Did you help us build it?"

Trotteswell's chubby cheeks reddened.

He said, "A priest has higher matters to occupy his time

than manual labour."

The carpenter asked, "Was the Saviour not a craftsman – a skilled worker in wood and stone?"

Trotteswell stood his ground. "It is right and proper that I give a benediction over this house."

"But it is already blessed."

"By whom?"

"By the hands of those who have built it."

The priest said, "These simple folk are not ordained."

The carpenter shook his head. "Does not the Apostle Peter speak of the priesthood of all believers?"

Trotteswell countered. "There is only one priesthood!"

"Yes," the carpenter cried, "And we are a part of it!"

The sound of music stopped.

The villagers stared with wide eyes, as if they were spectators at a joust.

"You are enemies of the ancient and hallowed faith," Trotteswell protested, his voice spitting like the pig.

The carpenter stifled a laugh. He said, "We are enemies only to those who stand in the way of poor, common people experiencing God's rich and uncommon love."

The priest said, "You are a liar. You are not of the true faith nor of the one true church!"

The carpenter parried the blow and thrust at the priest. "The sure ground of God remaineth and hath this seal," he replied. "The Lord knoweth those who are his."

"What translation is this?"

The carpenter smiled. "The people's translation."

Trotteswell pushed out his chest and pulled his girth inwards. "This is not the end of the matter."

As he stormed out, the two other siblings, who had been

keeping watch a stone's throw away, approached.

The architect looked at them both and said, "He will be back. His house in Tarrant Hinton is far inferior. I can tell by his eyes that he is greedy to possess our home."

The sister said, "He is a serpent in our Eden."

The three held each other for a moment. Then, aware of the bystanders, they turned back to the fire and gave thanks for the hog that had given its life.

And Tony awakened, feeling hungry.

11

THE ACCUSER

Two weeks before Christmas, Tony was invited to give an interview on the Shelton Show. Sitting under the studio lights, waiting for it to begin, he was daydreaming about the house, wondering what further trouble it had encountered after the priest had left.

Fiona Shelton, his host, sat next to him. She had worked her way up from being a news anchor in a regional TV network and was now the lead interviewer with the BBC. In her late thirties, she already had three prestigious coups to her name. The most famous was a home secretary whose shady soul she had prised open with the precision of a surgeon. It was a masterpiece, up there with Frost's incisions into the open calloused heart of President Richard Nixon. Whether they liked her or not, people respected her. Tony did too.

"You're going to be great," Fiona said. "There are millions of people wanting to learn about the real Tony. Members of the public will be dying to ask you questions later."

"Oh good," he said with a sigh.

They both smiled.

"I'm looking forward to hearing what you have to say," Fiona added. "Dreams are intriguing."

He nodded.

The countdown began.

Clapping followed.

Fiona switched from personal to professional and began her introduction to the programme.

Tony heard snatches of what she said.

"Nation's most popular dream therapist... in many ways a pioneer of dream therapy ... author of *Dreamers* ... had a cameo role in the now cult classic *The Dream Ticket...* "

He winced at that.

And more.

Turning to Tony, Fiona asked, "Let's go back to the beginning, to when you were eight years old. How did losing both your parents influence what you do today?"

There was a gasp.

Tony was not a rugby fan, but he knew from friends who enjoyed the game what he had just received. When a rugby player threw the ball to someone and they were about to be crunched by an opponent, it was called 'a hospital pass.' It was guaranteed to hurt, sometimes so badly that you had to be taken off the field of play. Tony knew that Fiona wanted him to last the whole show, but this was unexpected. He felt its impact in his solar plexus.

"Erm... well..." he stammered.

Seeing his hesitation, Fiona changed her tone. She became more empathetic. Less clinical.

"I mean, Tony, the trauma must have been terrible. I'm so

sorry you went through that. What I'm asking is this," her voice was soft. "How much did reverie play a part in your resilience?"

Tony was again disoriented. The brilliance of the second question was as startling as the unexpectedness of the first. No one had ever thought of asking him this before, not even his therapist, who he was sure would be watching.

"It was crucial," he replied.

"Can you unpack that a little?"

"I think I responded as any child would to sudden and severe trauma. I began to dissociate. Unable to escape in my body, I began to escape in my mind. I began to daydream, and as I began to dream in the day, this seemed to unlock something in my subconscious during the night as well."

"You took refuge in dreams," Fiona said.

"It led to me become a student of them."

"At eight?"

"From eight onwards. I read everything I could find on the subject in my old school library. Everything related to dreams. Anything I could lay my hands on."

"What school was this?"

"I attended a minor prep school in Berkshire. My parents had left money in a trust. My uncle, my mother's brother, made sure that I was looked after in the school holidays."

"So, you not only had to endure bereavement, but also being sent away to boarding school."

"It was hard, but the books helped. I devoured them. Books became my world. Especially books about dreams, about the fantastical, about myths too. And I guess I found comfort and escape in what I read, as well as in what I dreamed."

"So then, reverie really was a key to your resilience."

"It was, yes."

"Did you have a favourite author when you were a boy?"

"I did."

She paused, waiting for an answer.

"Edgar Allan Poe."

She raised her eyebrows and smiled. "Rather macabre, wouldn't you say? Didn't he write about murder, drug addiction, depression, suicide, and even being buried alive?"

"He was the first great horror story writer," Tony said.

"And the inventor of the detective story," she added.

He nodded.

"What was it about him that fascinated you?"

"Dreams. He was intrigued by them. He thought that life was a dream within a dream, to quote the title of one of his poems. I'm sure Christopher Nolan's film *Inception* ultimately owes a debt to this insight, a film about dreams within dreams."

Fiona began to recite, "All that we see or seem is but a dream within a dream."

Tony took a sip of water.

He then said, "Don't forget he ends with the same thought as a question, not an assertion. Is *all* that we see or seem but a dream within a dream? Poe did not deal in shallow certainties. He lived in the shadowlands of ambiguity and mystery. Ever since I was eight, that's where I have lived as well..."

"So, for you, dreaming leads to recovery?"

"What Poe called visions in the dark night and waking dreams have helped me, although I would use the word resilience rather than recovery." Tony bowed his head. Then he added, "I do believe in the therapeutic power of dreams."

"Are you in therapy?"

"Is anyone *not* these days?"

Laughter from the audience.

"If you want me to quote Poe," he continued, "I'd say I'm waiting for what he called that holy dream that will cheer me like a lovely beam, this lonely spirit guiding."

"Are you a lonely spirit?"

"I'm divorced."

"Friends?"

"I sometimes find it hard trusting people."

"But you still take comfort in your dreams?"

"I do."

"What are you dreaming about these days?"

Tony laughed. "You're beginning to sound like my therapist. I'm going to pass on that one, except to say that I currently have a rich dream life, and I'm more hopeful than I have been for many years that I'm going to find my way home."

Fiona smiled. "That's fair. You've been very honest. Let's press onto other topics."

And, true to her word, she did.

Until at last, with nearly sixty minutes elapsed, she returned to the subject with which she had begun.

"Any last thoughts about dreams, Tony?"

"Maybe a poem of Poe's," he said.

Fiona waited for him to continue.

"In the poem I love, Poe longs to return to the time when he was a boy, before the cold reality of waking life afflicted him. He yearns for a time when he dreamed of what he called living light. And he wonders if, when we die, we enter a dream state that parallels and transcends that childhood state of reverie."

"Do you believe there's an afterlife, Tony?"

"There was a mystical longing in Poe's poetry."

"But what about you?"

"I think we all have such longings, if we're honest."

There was a pause.

Tony watched the motes of dust in the lights. He heard a suppressed cough from the audience.

He broke the quiet with Poe's lines.

Oh! That my young life were a lasting dream!

My spirit not awakening, till the beam

Of an Eternity should bring the morrow.

After that, the audience applauded.

Tony wanted to slink away, out of the light, back into the shadows, away to his minimalist house. But questions had been promised, and he could not leave just yet.

On and on they went, for another hour, Fiona reading out the names of each of the questioners and introducing the topic of the pre-prepared questions. Until, that is, the very last.

"A Mister Maul," I think it is. "You have a question about Tony's bestselling book."

As a light spotted him, he rose.

A beret covering his scalp.

Tony shuddered.

How did he get in here?

How did he get to ask the last question?

"Mister Lawson," Maul said," in a tone as calm as it was condescending. "I overheard a man at my private club yesterday, saying that the ideas for your first book were the intellectual property of another writer. Is that true?"

Fiona looked confused. She turned and whispered, "That's not the question on my card."

Tony waved his hand.

Maul asked, "Do you not think it would be honourable and ethical to give credit to that person and grant him substantial compensation from the huge royalties the book earned?"

There were murmurs as he sat.

Tony leaned forward. "Edgar Allan Poe faced false accusations too. They came from a man who had once been a friend of his, but who deceived, bribed, manipulated, and defamed him to such a point that Poe was driven to drink and died on the streets of Baltimore. This man, Rufus Griswold by name, stopped at nothing to ruin Poe's reputation, even deceiving Poe's mother to hand over priceless papers and manuscripts belonging to Poe himself."

Tony paused.

Then he concluded. "It seems to me to be the price that dreamers must often pay, the assaults of those who seek to rob and kill. To quote Michele Obama, when they go low, we go high."

Applause.

Rage on the accuser's face.

End credits.

Music.

And then Tony was away.

All the way home in his limousine, Tony looked over his shoulder at the cars behind, trying to see any sign of the man with the black beret, but the headlights were too dazzling.

When, at last, the driver dropped him outside his house,

Tony hurried inside. He drank a shot of bourbon while he stared at the images from his wall-mounted cameras outside, checking there were no intruders in the passageway.

By the time he had drained his drink, he had made his decision. He ran downstairs carrying nothing but his dream journal. Within seconds, he was heading out of London towards the southwest.

When he entered the drive of the Old Rectory, there were no lights on in the neighbouring houses. He switched off his headlights and sat staring out of the front window, at the lawn where the girl in the bonnet had appeared. He started to relax.

He leaned his head back against the rest and adjusted his seat to allow him to recline. As he stared at the shadow of the house, he was transported in his memory to his school days. He could see the oak-panelled walls of the school library. He was standing there, aged ten, finding a story by Poe. *The Fall of the House of Usher*. He was staring wide-eyed at the illustrations. Devouring the words.

Usher's house had seemed to be alive. At one with its owner. The crack in its front wall an outward expression of the fractures in the deranged owner's soul. Tony was determined not to repeat this story. The cracks in his soul would not destroy him. He would be restored. And the Old Rectory, that would be restored too.

Tony marvelled at the synchronicity between his sensitivities and the house's sentience. It was providence, this meeting of two presences. One five decades old with human skin. The other five centuries with a hide of brick and stone.

Tony looked at his watch.

1.00am.

He was safe here.

Away from the capital.

The silence calmed him.

The darkness enfolded him.

There, beneath the watchful windows of the house he was coming to love, he closed his eyes.

He was doing what he had always done.

Finding resilience in reverie.

12

A DREAM

As Tony slept in his car, he saw in his dream the people of the Village of the Five Trees waiting for the sister to open the gates to the Tudor house. The three siblings had now added an open-sided barn behind the house to hold meetings for those who wanted to hear the Bible read and taught in their own tongue. Humble labourers, along with their wives and children, seemed to have deserted the priest, his church, and his Masses. They had come to the house instead.

The sister opened the gates and the people gathered in the barn, removing their hats, sitting in a semicircle on haybales. A wooden lectern with ornately engraved angels' wings stood in the centre. Tony took these to be the work of the carpenter. After prayers were offered, the carpenter walked to the rustic pulpit and opened Tyndale's Bible – the same book Tony had seen before in the private chapel in the house.

Before he spoke, the gardener – or the Beloved Sister, as people now seemed to be calling her – handed out straw, ribbons, and flax to the children, encouraging them to create and play while her brother spoke. They were to listen with their ears while they made ponies and people with their hands. She told them there was a prize for the best strawman, straw dog, or straw horse.

The younger brother then started to speak. "As you all know full well, I am a carpenter and builder by trade, and it is for that reason I have a special concern for creating strong houses. In every home that I, and my beloved brother and sister, have built, we have started by the making of firm foundations."

He stretched out his hand and pointed at the house. "See, there, our dwelling, our home! When we started working on our dream house, we began by digging a large rectangle in the earth, filling it with stone, ensuring that it was solid. Without a good foundation, a building will fall when it is shaken."

There was a murmur as the people nodded, looking at each other, acknowledging the truth of it.

"So, what is the foundation for our faith?"

The people all knew the answer.

"This is what the Apostle Paul writes in his Second Epistle to the Corinthians. He declares, 'For other foundation can no man lay than that which is laid which is Jesus Christ'."

The people bowed. The children stopped their weaving, nodding towards the ground. Even in Tony's dream state, the holy innocence of their reverence moved him.

The carpenter continued. "The Apostle Paul tells us that the man who builds his life on this hallowed ground is a wise builder. Are you wise builders, beloved friends?"

There were some in the barn who started shifting on the

bales, looking down at the straw-strewn earth, pondering their own plight and the condition of their souls.

"We all fall short," the carpenter said, "but we all have access to the kindness of God as well."

Tony saw one or two weeping.

"In this great house we built," he said, looking with devotion towards the magnificent building again. "The foundation is made of stone. There is an archway of stone, a wall of stone, hearths of stone. Do you know what that means?"

He paused, as if he had just seen something.

"It means that if a fire breaks out, the stonework will remain. The wood and wattle will disappear, but there is something that will survive the flames forever. The same is true for us. There is something that lives on. Our faith in him who gave his life for us."

He was staring beyond his listeners now.

"The fire shall try every man's work," he concluded, his voice softer now, his head beginning to bow. "When the fire comes, we must ensure that our faith is unshakeable."

As his words trailed away, a new sound emerged.

The adults saw what the carpenter had observed.

Trotteswell, in ceremonial regalia, was entering the grounds, followed by a bishop, a small flock of black and grey friars, and a troop of armoured soldiers carrying bristling pikes.

As the priest approached the carpenter, some of the children clung to their mothers and began to cry.

"You are arrested on suspicion of heresy," the priest declared. Two of the soldiers seized the preacher. Another two the English Bible. The last two the lectern.

As they manhandled the carpenter, he looked at the people with tears in his eyes.

The gardener cried, "This is an unlawful arrest. My brother has done nothing save tell the truth."

"No, Mary!" the carpenter shouted.

She fell silent.

The architect protested. "If you are taking our brother, then take us too!" He offered his hands to be bound.

"This warrant of arrest is only for him," Trotteswell said. "But this royal order is for all of you."

A lawyer then read from a scroll. "This house and its gardens are hereby requisitioned by the Crown. From this day forth, this property and all its furnishings shall be the possession of His Majesty King Henry VIII under the stewardship of Father Thomas Trotteswell."

As the lawyer stepped back, the priest looked at the architect and the gardener. He said, "You have not escaped punishment either. The house is no longer yours. I am to be its keeper."

The architect started to complain, but he was silenced with a slap from one of the soldier's gloved hands. His sister took a handkerchief and wiped the blood from his nose.

After the carpenter had been dragged away, the bishop marched into the centre and unrolled another scroll.

"By the authority of God, the Father Almighty, and of the blessed Virgin Mary, of Saint Peter and Paul, and of the holy saints, we excommunicate, we utterly curse and ban, commit and deliver to the devil of hell, all you who have been gathering in this place." He paused to take a breath. "Excommunicated are you as perpetual malefactors and schismatics." He fixed his gaze upon the villagers and said,

"We give you utterly to the power of the fiend, now and forever."

The bishop departed, his retinue with him.

"What will happen to the carpenter?" someone asked.

A man lowered his hat. "He will be questioned and tortured in the bishop's prison, but he will not recant. There will a writ of execution from London. A pyre will be set up in the town square by order of the county sheriff..." The man struggled to continue. "His work will be tried in the fire, but it will not be found wanting."

Even as he said these words, the scene changed.

Tony saw the town square.

The architect covering his eyes.

The gardener sobbing.

A smell of smoke.

Burning flesh.

A crowd jeering.

And the carpenter in the centre of it all.

Fixed to a wooden post.

His body twisting.

His life extinguished in a fire that was fuelled by the raw materials of his own trade.

When Tony awakened, he was shaking.

13

THE REMEMBERING

Tony was relieved that his next session with Shree fell so soon after his dream. Even though it was not normal procedure, Shree suggested they meet at the Old Rectory. She asked him to bring his dream journal.

When she arrived, she joined Tony in his car. They both sat and stared at the house.

Shree broke the silence. "Do you know this book?"

She showed him a paperback in pristine condition. *The Poetics of Space* by Gaston Blanchard.

"I've heard of it, but not read it."

"It's a gift. I think you'll find it interesting."

"That's kind of you."

Shree opened it. "Blanchard believed that houses aren't just material boxes. There's something spiritual about them too."

"Spiritual?"

"Listen to this," she said, turning the pages. "He writes, 'If I were asked to name the chief benefit of the house, I should say: the house shelters daydreaming, the house protects the dreamer, the house allows one to dream in peace.' Doesn't that sound spiritual?"

"I'd love to be able to dream in peace."

"He also wrote that the soul is a house, and the house is a soul. What do you make of that?"

"This house behaves like it has a soul. Every time I come here, that same night I have a dream. The dream's always about some incident in its history. Last night, it turned into a nightmare."

"Tell me."

"I saw the original Tudor house and its grounds being invaded, and one of the three people who built it being arrested and taken away to be burned at the stake."

"What for?"

"For preaching that everyone could find their way to God, without the interference of corrupt and controlling clergy."

"Okay, so the Tudor version of this house belonged to supporters of the Protestant Reformation."

"Yes, including Queen Catherine Parr."

"Then it is, in every sense, a spiritual location, or what Blanchard would have called a poetic space."

"You don't know the half of it. I've even seen a ghost here."

"Where?"

Tony pointed to the lawn. "Over there!"

"What form did it take?"

Tony described the maid.

And the curtsy.

"That is fascinating," Shree said.

"How so?"

"There seems to me to be some sort of synchronicity happening. The past of the house, and yours, are aligning. And the house seems to be speaking to you. My wife Aya would love this."

"Really?"

"Yes. She's a disciple of Marie Kondo. She believes that houses are sacred spaces and that we should greet our houses, and even thank them. It's a practice rooted in Shintoism."

"I'm not familiar with Shintoism, but I'm sympathetic to the sentiment."

"It's a beautiful idea," she said.

Tony asked, "Why do you think this is happening to me? Why this house? Why now?"

"Symbiosis," she said.

"What do you mean?"

"This house seems to me to have something traumatic in its past, as do you, and both you and it are in desperate need of remembering what's happened. You need each other."

"I don't understand."

Shree said, "Where's there's buried trauma..."

Tony finished her maxim. "There's buried treasure."

"Exactly."

"Are you saying that the house is suffering from dissociative amnesia, like I am?"

"I don't know."

"What *are* you saying then?"

"I'm saying that I think perhaps there's buried trauma in both you and the house. The soul of your house needs you, and the house of your soul needs it."

"That's a professional psychological view, is it?"

Shree laughed. Then she handed Tony the book and said,

"You'll find Blanchard was a phenomenologist more than a psychologist. In fact, he was quite critical of psychology."

"Then why are you sharing it?"

"Because sometimes our search for meaning takes us into terrain that is mystical, magical, miraculous even, and phenomenology is better suited to that enquiry than psychology."

Tony frowned.

"May I see your writeup of your dreams?" she asked.

Tony handed her his journal.

She spent ten minutes reading through the four dreams he had recorded. Then she closed the journal and turned to him. "There's something very revealing going on."

"You don't say!"

"I do say. If you look carefully at what you've written, it feels to me like you're being told a very vivid story. The characters are alive. Their words are lifelike too. How are you remembering everything so precisely and, dare I say it, accurately?"

Tony looked ahead at the façade of the house. "Something happens when I start writing," he said. "It's not just that I'm reliving the dream. I also seem to understand the things I'm reliving, even though I have no recollection of ever learning them."

"Like the theological arguments?"

"Yes, and other things too."

"That's very interesting."

"It's as if I know things I've never been taught."

"Anamnesis," Shree muttered.

"Pardon?

"Sorry, Tony. It's a term from the writings of Plato, and

others. Socrates believed that true knowledge is not so much about learning something new as remembering something old."

"In a past life, you mean."

"Not necessarily. It could be familial memories. DNA. Who knows? It's a mystery. All I know for sure is that you're plumbing the depths of it in these dreams."

Tony sighed. "Am I going mad?"

"No."

"Then what?"

"You're suffering from a form of amnesia, Tony. Not about everything. Yours is localised. Confined to a period of your past when you experienced a severe trauma as a boy." She returned the journal. "The dreams you're having and recording, these seem to have something to do with remembering."

"My stuff? Or the house's stuff?"

"Both."

Tony shook his head.

"Don't be anxious, Tony. It's all about what Proust called the remembrance of things past. When you visit the house, it seems to stimulate memories. The house provides triggers. These have something to do with your healing."

"For my amnesia?"

"Yes. Your soul's prescription for amnesia seems to be a rather unusual form of anamnesis."

"In that case," Tony said. "I can expect to remember more things in a dream tonight, after being here again."

Shree looked at her watch.

"Time's up?" Tony asked.

She nodded.

"Just relax and go with this, Tony."

"I'll try."

Shree left the car.

After she had driven out of the gates, Tony started reading the book Shree had given him. He paused at one long and luminous sentence, basking in its beams. "Memories of the outside world will never have the same tonality as those of home and, by recalling these memories, we add to our store of dreams; we are never real historians, but always near poets, and our emotion is perhaps nothing but an expression of a poetry that was lost."

Tony was on a mission now. It was time to rediscover the poetry he had lost.

14

A DREAM

In his dream that night, Tony saw Henry VIII entering the house. He came limping like a beggar not striding like a colossus, wearing a cap not a crown. He used a stick to support his frame. And what a frame! He was as wide as he was tall.

The king sat and looked above the fire in the hall, his eyes drawn to the head of a red deer mounted on the wall. The poor creature had a startled look, its deep brown eyes locked in shock and fear after an arrow had penetrated its heart. Yet, even with the imminence of its own demise, the animal looked regal, dignified, and brave. Its antlers were crooked and sharp, like a crown of thorns.

"We shall have such sport today!" the king cried.

"Let the hunt begin!" the king cried.

The king turned to the master of the lodge. "Mister Morris, have there been any more sightings of the white hart?"

The man, a priest, said, "The other night..."

"Where? Speak! Where?"

"Not half a mile from here."

"Give the details to Sir Antony Denny," the king said, gesturing to the gentleman by his side.

The king took a swig of wine and asked, "Where is the breeder?"

A pale old man with bushy white sideburns and a bald scalp was ushered into the king's presence.

"What have you for me?"

The man presented a sweet-faced greyhound. It was tall and slender with a long sharp snout. Tony could tell by the purple, studded collar that he was a gift for the king.

The dog wagged his short tale, sniffed at the king's leg for a moment, then settled at his feet.

"I shall call him Rex!" the king exclaimed. "Rex Canorum, King of the Dogs!"

The king looked between the dog's back legs.

"This one will not be siring another pup," he cried.

Even in his dream, Tony thought that the princely hound was not alone in that regard.

After the breeder departed, one of the servants retrieved the king's cape and the monarch hobbled outside to the edge of the grounds. There Tony saw a mound of earth with a small turret of wood built on top. In the turret, which was covered with a wooden roof and some foliage, there was a seat. The king was helped up a ladder onto his makeshift throne. Below him, stood four men with crossbows and arrows, ready to hand the loaded weapons when commanded.

The hounds and beaters went to work and soon a fallow deer broke out of the woodland. In its frightened mind, all it saw was what looked like a tree, but as it drew near, the king fired an arrow. It missed, but the hiss of it alarmed the beast.

"Another!" the king shouted.

One of the men, halfway up the mound, passed up a loaded crossbow and the king shot again, taking care to avoid his new greyhound herding the doomed creature towards his master. This time the arrow was true. The four-bladed tip hit its target with a shrill whistle and a sickening thud.

The deer faltered.

Its front legs buckled.

Blood seeped from the wound in its chest.

Denny exclaimed, "Good shot, your majesty!"

The hound was upon the deer now, fixing it to the ground, making sure not to pierce its hide with his teeth. The deer struggled, twitched, then died. There was a cheer as the king descended from the small tower. He was so excited by his kill that he had, for a moment, forgotten the pain in his leg. He raised his crossbow, a wide grin on his red face, a proud glint in his fierce eyes.

"Tomorrow!" he shouted. "We will hunt the white stag!"

There was a cheer.

Then the king motioned for quiet.

"It was in a vale near here," he said, wiping some sweat from his face, "that my ancestor, King Henry III, stumbled upon a white stag. He chased the white hart down but, when he looked the noble creature in the eye, he spared it." The king clasped his hands. "When I aim at the white hart, I will not show such weakness. There will be no mercy, and tomorrow night, I will host the feast of feasts."

In the dream, the scene now changed.

Tony found himself in a candle-lit interior.

The king's bedchamber.

Tony could smell something foul.

The king ordered Sir Anthony Denny to take the bandages off his ulcers. The sight of the pustulant mess turned Tony's stomach. That was not all. By dawn's first light, the king had struggled out of bed twice to use the royal pot. Denny emptied it both times.

The scene changed again.

Exterior.

The king, wearing a cap with an enamelled badge depicting St George slaying the dragon, climbed back into his turret. The courtiers and beaters walked the fields, hills, and woods, trying to coax deer towards the tower.

There was no sign of the white stag.

The king was furious when the sport ended.

There was another scene change.

Back to the drive.

Outside the front of the house.

Tony saw the king staring out of his carriage, his bad leg propped up on a cushioned stool.

The king saw something glowing in the trees.

Rex, the greyhound, stirred from his slumber and sat bolt upright next to his master.

The dog sensed it.

As did Tony.

The white hart.

The king scowled.

The dog growled.

"Look there!" he shouted to Mister Morris, who was standing next to the stationary vehicle. "A thousand curses! That creature is as elusive as King Arthur said it was."

"As elusive as the Holy Ghost," Morris muttered.

"What's that?"

The priest said, "No one knows where he comes from or where he is going." He made the sign of the cross on his chest. "He is as elusive as the Holy Ghost."

The king frowned. He fiddled for a moment with his stiff and jewel-studded collar. Then he turned to Denny who was sitting next to him. "I will not be hunting here anymore. Give this house to the Queen. It can be her country retreat."

"I'll have the lawyers draw up the papers," Denny replied.

The king barked an order to the coachman and slammed shut the window of his carriage.

The entourage pulled away from the gates of the house. As they departed, Tony saw the white hart standing at the edge of the woods nearby. It was noble beyond all nobility, majestic beyond all majesty, and it had survived. This king, the most powerful man in England, had been powerless to hunt and kill it – as powerless as he was to cure his seeping and purulent ulcers.

Thus, the foul-smelling monarch left.

While the white stag remained.

There would be no feast of feasts that night.

And no new antlers on the walls.

15

THE EX

After Tony sent her a text, Renée agreed to meet him at his local coffee shop on the morning of Christmas Eve. Wrapping his scarf around his face and pulling the flaps of his hat over his ears, he headed to the café, sat at a table, and listened to the Christmas carols.

After ten minutes, he was starting to feel his face blush with the heat, so he removed his hat and draped his coat over the top of his chair. He took the scarf from his face and braced himself for some greetings. But none were forthcoming. Maybe it was the Christmas cheer, but everyone was focussed on each other. The young couple next to Tony seemed oblivious that he was even there. They were staring into each other's eyes. Tony remembered how it was with Renée at the beginning. They had seen eye-to-eye just as these two did.

As Tony was reminiscing, she entered.

"I haven't got long," she said. "What do you want?"

"Let me get these."

"I said I haven't got long."

The couple broke from gazing at each other and cast a glance in Tony's direction. He wanted to say that he had registered the tension too. That he had lived with it for twenty years.

"The usual, then," he said, his initial politeness giving way to a more unfeeling tone.

Renée marched to the counter and ordered their drinks. Tony heard her telling an aproned boy to bring the coffees to the table. The poor lad was not used to such bossiness. He seemed to cower. Tony could not blame him. Renée was a formidable sight. She was wearing her black, two-piece suit. Jacket and skirt. Her black shoes were as shiny as those worn on parade by a drill sergeant.

Blushing a little, the lad nodded.

"Have you come from the office?" Tony asked as she returned and made to sit at the table.

"No, I haven't."

"A funeral then."

"Don't be stupid, Tony."

The couple cast another glance towards them, then started to prepare for their evacuation.

"You said in your text this is about money," she said. "This had better be worth my time."

"It's about Maul," Tony said.

She raised her eyebrows.

"He's a twat," she said.

At least we agree on something, Tony thought.

"He's arguing that he gave me the main ideas for my first book during dinners at our house."

"I don't remember that."

"That's because it didn't happen. I had the first draft written well before I met him."

She said, "Don't say I didn't warn you about him. That said, I don't think he's got a leg to stand on."

"All the same, he's threatening me. He accosted me outside the house a week or so ago. He accused me of intellectual property theft. Suggested the same thing on live TV."

Renée's expression changed from aloof to anxious. Tony knew this would happen. If there was one thing guaranteed to turn her from cold to concerned it was the subject of money. Especially money that she might either be due or denied.

"Don't let him succeed, Tony. He's a greedy, feckless little shit. He doesn't deserve any of the royalties."

Tony took a sip of coffee and nodded.

"How are you going to stop him?" she asked.

"With your help."

The concern morphed back into coldness.

"You're asking me to clear up yet another one of your messes? I told you I was done with that."

Tony stared at her pale forehead. There were lines. Ones he had not seen before. The scars of worry. Signs of age. And the roots in her hairline were showing the tiniest traces of grey, despite the skills and the dye of her ever-patient hairdresser.

"It's in your interests, Renée. If he gets royalties from my book, that will impact how much you get from me."

The coldness turned back into concern.

"I'll help if I can."

Tony took a sip of his coffee.

"This part is a bit embarrassing," he said.

She frowned.

"I have been diagnosed with dissociative amnesia disorder. I'm receiving help for it, but one of the symptoms is forgetting basic skills in relation to work."

No reaction.

"Obviously, most of my work is done using my computer, both writing and speaking. And it's my computer skills that seem to have deserted me. I know there must be a paper trail that supports my defence, but I can't for the life of me ..."

"It's okay. I'll do it," she interrupted. Her tone was patronising – one that she had adopted since their wedding day, speaking to him as if she was the exasperated parent, he the helpless child. "But I want to make one thing clear."

"And what's that?"

"This is the very last time."

Unless there's money at stake, Tony thought.

"Have the laptop sent over," she said, speaking to Tony as she had to the frightened barista.

The couple next to them hurried away.

"I have it here," Tony said, removing the laptop from his case and handing it to her. He added, "I didn't think you'd want me bringing it over to your new apartment."

Just then, a man sat down at the table next to them. He was well over six feet. Taller than Tony by several inches. Thin. Completely bald. Finely trimmed grey beard. Olive skin. Kind eyes. Almost avuncular. Suit and tie. Cashmere coat. Smart. Very smart.

Renée changed the moment she saw him.

Leaning over, she kissed him on the lips.

"This is Nick," she said.

Her eyes seemed to be shimmering. Just as they had in

the months after she and Tony had got engaged, until the wedding. Tony felt for the man. He had no idea what lay in store for him.

"Can you take this laptop for me, darling?" she said, passing Nick the black case.

He smiled.

"I'll need to spend some time on it after Christmas. I hope you don't mind, sweetheart."

He nodded and stood.

Renée took his arm.

She left without a nod or a goodbye.

Once they were gone, Tony breathed a sigh of relief, sat back in his chair, and drained the dregs of his festive coffee.

He was starting to daydream about the Old Rectory when his reverie was interrupted.

"All right, Tony?" a man two tables away said.

Tony nodded.

"Was that the trouble and strife?"

"Used to be."

"Looks like you've dodged a bullet there, mate."

Tony chuckled.

"More like a missile."

The man laughed.

As the sound of muted Christmas carols continued to fill the coffee shop, Tony inhaled the bitter aroma of coffee beans and the sweet scent of cinnamon rolls.

Then he donned his hat and coat.

He said goodbye to the barista, thanked him for the coffee, and walked to the door.

As he stepped onto the snow-powdered street, he could just make out behind him the first lines of an old familiar carol about the journey of the Magi. As the choir sang about the star that drew them, it occurred to him that these ancient astrologers had travelled hundreds of miles on lurching camels to Bethlehem.

What kind of power drew them to the dwelling? What otherworldly presence met them there? Tony possessed an Audi R8, capable of travelling several hundred miles in a matter of hours. They had lumbering beasts that must have taken months, maybe years, leaving their backsides numb.

Tony shook his head.

He hailed a cab and headed back to Chelsea, his heart filled with images of men dressed like Arabian knights crossing vast deserts, following a strange light to a house faraway.

They were dreamers.

But their focus was the future.

His was the past.

He would find his way, just as they had.

16

THE BATHTUB

It was a cheeky request but after Christmas Ms Macready agreed to it without hesitation. "Is it all right if I have a look round the interior of the Old Rectory with a friend of mine? She's a designer. I'd like to get some initial thoughts about the extent and costs of the work ahead, if I succeed at the auction."

Ms Macready replied that she would be in the drive waiting for them the following Saturday at 2pm.

It was a grey morning when Ella arrived at Tony's London house. She was wearing tortoise-shell glasses and a woollen cap to cover her bald head. They set off for the Old Rectory and, on the way, Tony talked about the village and the house, describing the layout of the interior, the plan of the gardens, all three acres of them.

"It was originally called the Village of the Five Trees in Anglo-Saxon times," he said.

"What a beautiful name," Ella said.

Tony smiled. "The village was known for five horse

chestnut trees. Only one of them still stands. It's in the garden of the Old Rectory and it's gigantic."

"Brilliant!" Ella cried.

"Rooks nest in its branches and, according to Ms Macready, when the wind blows hard, the tree yields a constant supply of kindling for the open fireplaces in the house."

Tony turned onto the road to Blandford Forum.

"The walled gardens must have been stunning at one time," he said. "There's an abundance of trees. Lime. Oak. Silver beach. Copper beach. Blue cedar. And there's even a Ha-Ha, with a path up to some woodland in the fields beyond. In the springtime, white flowers appear everywhere. It's really... well... almost sacred."

"When I was growing up in Northern Ireland," Ella said. "I often dreamed of secret gardens."

"This house has a bit of magic about it too," Tony said. "It was given as a wedding gift to Catherine Parr..."

"Ah! The Queen who survived..."

"Indeed," Tony said.

"And not just one husband," Ella said. "But four! The most married of all of England's queens!"

"Yes, and her legacy lives on in the village. Parr Lane. Parr Grove. And there's a path known as the Queen's Walk. It used to run from the terrace outside the living room window around the garden, which was in the 1530s much larger than now. Originally, it was a yew-tree walk, although not many yews remain."

"We can restore that," Ella said.

"That's what I hoped you'd say. I would love the Queen's Walk returned to its former glory. Yew trees should line the walk and the path should be clearly marked."

"I love the vision," she said.

They had joined the A354 and were drawing near to the village when Tony pointed out the window.

"See the top of that copper beach tree?"

Ella nodded.

"That's the garden of the Old Rectory. You can see the chimneys and dormer windows from here."

Tony drove into the village and showed Ella various roads, named after the Queen of course, before heading through the gates into the drive. Ms Macready was waiting for them.

Once they were inside, Tony turned to Ella and said, "This was originally a Tudor hunting lodge. It was destroyed by fire in the early 1700s, then further altered in the middle of the 19th century. I want to recreate the Victorian vibe."

Even as he said this, Ella became hyper-focused. Beginning with the living room, or "the drawing room" as she called it, she started scribbling in her notebook.

"This wall," she said. "We should knock it down."

The wall in question separated the drawing room from a space which the prospectus described as the music room, but which was in fact a redundant passageway.

"It will make the drawing room much bigger, although you'll have to put up with a fireplace that's slightly off centre. Are you prepared to tolerate that?"

"Of course."

Ella continued to scribble.

"We could have mahogany furniture in here. And shelves, creating a library, full of old books."

On she went, striding through every room of the ground floor. Upstairs, she repeated the exercise, with excited comments about four-poster beds and mahogany chests, until Ms Macready took them up another staircase into a large attic with studded beams.

"The beams are Tudor," Ms Macready said.

The entire garret was empty save for one unexpected object at the far end. An old, roll-topped bathtub. Although it needed re-enamelling, its white paint had stood the test of time.

"Victorian," Ella said. "They made them sturdy and practical in those days. See the cast-iron? Not just durable, but perfect for retaining the heat of the water as well."

"What's it doing here?" Tony asked.

"I have no idea," Ms Macready said.

"I'll ask Con, then."

"Con?" Ella asked.

"The historian."

"Do you want to keep the bath?"

"Of course."

"Then you mustn't skimp on antique taps."

Ella headed back across the wooden boards, the sound of her slingback heels echoing throughout the loft. Tony told Ms Macready to go downstairs while he took one last look. He remembered something Blanchard had said about attics representing the rational and cellars the irrational part of the mind. "Up near the roof, all our thoughts are clear," he had written. He was right. There was nothing chaotic or mysterious up there. Nothing except the bathtub.

Joining the others outside the front door, Tony directed Ella's attention to the stonework.

"See the date? It says 1530." He pointed to a shield carved in the stonework. "And there, the crown, garter, dragon, and greyhound supporters, and the rose and portcullis?"

"I see them."

"King Henry VIII."

"I love the greyhound," she said.

"Me too. Always have. In fact, I'd love to own one in the future. Imagine walking one on this land, where the King allowed his greyhounds to run."

"I can see it, Ella said.

Tony smiled.

They said goodbye to Ms Macready and got back into Tony's car. On the way out of the drive, Tony glanced at the lawn. There was no sign of the ghost in the garden.

On the road back to London, Tony said, "As long as no one else offers silly money, the house should be mine in the New Year. How long do you think it would take for you to work your magic?"

"Allow nine months."

Tony gasped.

"Tony, I'm going to have to employ old-school builders and decorators who specialise in old houses. Craftsmen who know what cornices are, what they should look like."

"Do you know anyone?"

"Of course. There's a company run by a wonderful old chap. I can sound him out now if you seriously think the house will be yours. But it won't be cheap. It's skilled work."

"Please do," Tony said.

"It's a big project, Tony..."

Tony was silent for several minutes. Then he turned to her. "I want to ask a serious question. Are you strong enough to do this?"

She nodded. "My chemo's finished. This will take my

mind off things. It'll be a labour of love, mind you."

"I'm in love," Tony said. The words were out of his mouth before he even thought about it. "I love every inch of the grounds. Every room. Every nook, cranny, corner, and crevice. I love the attic. And I'm sure I'm going to love the cellar."

"That's beautiful," she said.

"The house feels timeless to me," he agreed. "Everything about it seems to outlive us."

"Even the old bathtub," she said.

"Even the old bathtub," he repeated.

17

A DREAM

That night, in his dream, Tony saw the house in Victorian times. A young man dressed as a clergyman was arriving at the front door. A maid wished him good morning.

"It is a good morning, Jane." There was the hint of a stammer in an otherwise clear and commanding voice. "I do not think I have ever seen the Downs look so beautiful."

As she took his hat, stick, and gloves, he asked, "How is the cleaning progressing?"

Shaking her head, she said, "If you'll pardon my bluntness, Mister Kingsley, but Dr Wyndham has been the most careless of men. It is forty years since he was appointed Rector, and he has not spent a single night here. Now all is wrack and ruin."

"Just take one room at a time," the clergyman said. "As long as the bathroom is ready first."

"It is ready, sir."

She led him up the stairs to one of the chambers where, unlike the rest, the walls were papered, the woodwork whitened. Tony could almost smell the fresh paint.

In the centre of the room lay a large white bath.

"It is magnificent!" he said.

"It arrived from London yesterday, sir."

"And everything is fitted?"

She nodded.

Then she sighed.

"What is it, Jane?"

"The villagers."

"What of them?"

"They have been talking."

"What about?"

"They all say the same thing, that they wish you were the Rector and not just the Curate, and that Dr Wyndham would stop this pretence and resign his living."

Mister Kingsley replied, "I'm not sure the good folks in Eversley will support the idea of me staying. And as for Fanny..."

The front door opened. A young woman dashed over the threshold, calling out to her husband.

"Charles! Are you here?"

"Fanny! Darling!"

They embraced at the threshold. Their kiss was long, deep, sensuous. Jane, who was standing at the top of the stairs looking at them, blushed and turned away.

"It is four months to the day since our wedding," Fanny said as she held him. "Every day is bliss."

"Every night as well," he added.

They laughed.

Jane's cheeks reddened.

There was another knock on the front door and the ruby-faced maid rushed downstairs.

"Can I help you?" she said.

A man and a boy were standing outside. The man was dressed in plain and tattered clothes. When he grinned, at least half his teeth were missing, and the other half stained beyond all recovery. The boy, no more than six-years old, was dressed as a chimney sweep. He was holding a brush. His face and hands were covered in soot. Light rain was falling on the child's head. It would have taken a long and thunderous downpour to have shifted even a modicum of the dirt from his locks or a hint of the grime from his skin.

"Come in!" Fanny said. She looked at her husband. "It's all right, Charles. I asked them to come."

She led them to the fireplaces and flues of the house. At each one, she repeated the same refrain about forty years of neglect.

"This will take all day," the master sweep said with a greedy look. "It will cost you more."

"No matter," she said. "If someone doesn't look after this house, it will surely fall. There is already a case to be made to the Archdeacon against Dr Wyndham."

"On what charge?" the master sweep asked, his eyes lighting up at the thought of a man of the cloth on trial.

"Dilapidation."

"De lap what?"

"A Rector can be taken to ecclesiastical court if he allows his rectory to fall into a state of disrepair."

The Curate, hearing this, entered the room and interjected. "Neglecting your house is like neglecting your wife," he said. "It is a sin against marriage and against nature itself."

The master sweep looked sceptical while the boy looked inquisitive. The master slapped the child, knocking his hat to the floor. A puff of soot ascended from the fallen cap.

The older man struck him again.

"Enough!" the Curate shouted. "There is no need to berate or strike him. Treat him well, sir."

Another sneer.

Another growl.

"Go to it, boy!" the master sweep barked.

The boy walked to the hearth. His gait betrayed a limp caused by the contortions of his body, still in the process of forming. His ankles and knees seemed to pain him.

Using his back, legs, and elbows, he shimmied up the flue.

There was the sound of frantic movement.

Piles of dirt and dust fell into the hearth.

The boy shouted. "There's too much soot!"

He cried out in pain.

"I'm stuck!"

He was wedged in a narrow section of the flue.

"You fool!" the master sweep shouted. He approached the grate and intended to light a fire to force the boy down, but the Curate stood in his way while Fanny moved behind him. She bowed low to avoid hitting her head on the stone. She reached up for the boy's feet and started to manoeuvre him from side to side.

"Try to keep calm," she said.

Several moments later, the boy fell into the fireplace, accompanied by a cloud of soot.

The boy sobbed, then hugged his rescuer.

"You're safe, now," she said.

"Bravo, darling!" the Curate said, kissing the smudges on

her creamy skin. She laughed at his blackened lips.

The Curate turned to the master sweep. “He must have the rest of the day off,” he said.

“He is allowed one day off a year.”

“Then let it be today.”

“Mayday is the allotted day.”

“I will compensate you,” the Curate said.

He removed a coin from his pocket and gave it to the man. “You can go. But the boy can stay.”

When the master sweep had left, the Curate looked at the maid and said, “Please run the bath, Jane.”

“Has it arrived?” his wife asked.

“It’s upstairs.”

Fanny took the boy’s hand. “What’s your name?”

“Tom, Miss.”

“Well, then, Tom. You’re about to christen our new bath?”

“Miss?”

“You’ll see!”

As they entered the bathroom, the boy’s eyes opened wide. He covered his mouth with his grubby hands, stifling his cry of amazement at the sight of the white roll-topped tub with the shiny brass taps. In his young mind, he must have imagined he had entered a palace in London, or a stately home in the country.

When Jane finished running the bath, Fanny asked her to wash his clothes. She saw her maid’s frown. “If they are beyond redemption,” she said, “we will find new ones.”

Jane nodded and left.

Fanny tested the temperature with her elbow then invited the boy to step into the tub. His body was white, save for his face, neck, arms, and hands. They were as black as a raven's feathers.

The boy splashed the water with his hands.

Then laughed.

He submerged, then surfaced with a splutter. His eyelids, sore from months of soot, were red.

Charles, when he entered, saw the boy revelling in his liquid world. "I think he is well and truly baptised."

Fanny chuckled.

She washed the boy, making sure that every stain and smudge was lifted from his skin, every trace of ash from his hair. When he stood to be rubbed with a warm clean towel, the water swaying about his feet was browner than the dark floorboards.

"Thank you, Miss," he said. Then he added, "I am normally allowed only one bath a year."

Jane brought fresh clothes and dressed him.

"Please clean the bath and pour a fresh one," Fanny said.

While Jane set to work, Fanny took Tom downstairs and fed him in the kitchen. Her husband spread some fresh bread with jam made from wild strawberries.

"Do many live like you, Tom?" he asked.

"What do you mean, sir?"

"With no choice but to risk getting stuck up a chimney to earn a few pennies and a day off once a year."

"I don't get any pennies, sir."

"The master doesn't pay you?"

"No, sir. Sweeps don't get paid."

"That is outrageous!"

"It is how most of us live," the boy said, his voice more matter of fact than sad.

Soon after, it was time for the boy to leave.

"Thank you for rescuing me, Miss," he said. Then, turning to the Curate, "And for letting me use your new bath, sir."

The Curate replied, "Never forget, Tom. If you remember to wash your body, your soul will be all right."

"I'll try to remember, sir."

While Jane took the boy home, the couple headed upstairs, stripped, and climbed into the bath. They sat facing each other, the hot water causing beads of sweat to moisten their brows.

"We must fight this injustice," Charles said.

"What have you in mind, Charles?"

"We must give the rest of our lives to helping these children." He rubbed some dirt from his lips. "I will never believe that a man has a real love for the good and the beautiful except he attacks the evil and the disgusting the moment he sees it. Children are dying in crowded, roofless cottages without clean water."

Fanny looked down at the water and said, "A dying child is one of the most dreadful sights in the world."

She looked up again and gazed into his eyes. "Darling," she said, leaning forward and taking his freshly washed face in her hands. "I have something to tell you."

"What is it?"

"I want a child."

Hearing this, the Curate splashed the water as the boy had done.

Fanny laughed.

When he calmed down, she turned and leaned against him, her back to his front. He started to wash her, lathering his hands with soap, caressing and cleaning her body. He said,

"Our child's begetting will be the most delicious moment of our lives."

As she closed her eyes, he whispered something while inhaling the scent of her glossy brown hair.

She turned - her eyes filled with desire.

"What was that my love?"

He said it again.

Louder.

"We shall have a water baby."

Fanny was the one splashing now.

18

THE LIST

Two days after his visit with Ella to the Old Rectory, and just under a week before the auction, Tony sent a text to the historian asking if he was free to meet.

Tony's mobile vibrated two minutes later.

It was Con.

Meet me outside the lynch-gate to St Peter's Church? I want to show you something.

The message ended with a smiley face.

What is it about old people and emojis? Tony thought.

Tony stopped the car and typed a reply.

"I'll be there in four hours."

Without thinking, he added a smiley face.

When Tony arrived, Con was standing outside the old gate in a long black coat and a floppy cap.

"I'm intrigued," Tony said.

Con's nose had either grown a little longer or Tony had just failed to gauge its full length the last time they had met. It looked so like a big bird's bill that Tony looked beneath the old man's chin to see if there was a gular pouch hiding a supply of water.

"This is St. Peter's Church," Con said, pointing beyond the gate. "It's at least 1200 years old. Along with the Old Rectory, it was upgraded by Lord Portman in the 1870s."

He opened the gate and they started to walk down the churchyard path. Pointing to a tree, he said, "That came from the seedling of a two-thousand-year-old yew."

He stopped and turned to face Tony. "A place like this can give you a sense of the mystery of time, no?"

Tony nodded.

"The original church was built in Anglo-Saxon times and was made of wood," he said. "It was replaced by the stone church 1200 years ago. The perpendicular tower was added two hundred years later. So, you could say that like the yew tree, it survives."

The historian took a ring of black, iron keys from a side coat pocket and opened the door just as the sun began to break through the clouds. They walked through the vestibule into the nave. Tony's eyes were drawn to the painted east windows.

Noticing his gaze, the historian said, "the left and right panels depict scenes from the life of St Peter, after whom this church has been named. They cover his entire spiritual journey, from being called by the Saviour to being crucified upside down in Rome."

"Upside down?"

"Yes. Peter did not count himself worthy to be crucified in the same manner as his Lord. He made his request, and the Romans granted it. He died a very courageous death."

Con led Tony to the organ and pointed to something on

the wall to its right. It was a list of the incumbents who had served at St Peter's since the thirteenth century.

"This is what I wanted to show you," the historian said.

"It's a rollcall of vicars," Tony observed.

"Rectors, not vicars."

"What's the difference?"

"The difference is in how, historically, they were paid. Vicars were paid a small stipend by the Church whereas rectors were entitled to the rents and tithes of the parish."

"Rectors were paid more?"

"They were comfortable, yes, especially if they found ways of making a profit from the land."

"Why are you showing me this?"

"Partly because the fine house you want to buy is an Old Rectory not an Old Vicarage."

"And?"

"And because the list on this wall tells you far more than you may realise about the rectors who lived here."

"What do you mean?"

"First of all, please to note that some of the rectors from the Tudor Age onwards were writers."

"I don't recognise any of them," Tony said.

"See here, 1722, Christopher Pitt. He was a famous poet in his day. He published a popular translation of Virgil's Aeneid in 1740. He was a friend of Alexander Pope."

"That is impressive."

"The next rector George Bingham, wrote books, including a biography of Dorset's most famous historian, John Hutchens, who includes details of this village, church, and rectory."

He next pointed to Thomas Wyndham.

"Wyndham was rector for nearly sixty years but never lived in the house which is why it became so dilapidated. It was Lord Portland who renovated it after years of neglect."

"Was Wyndham a writer?"

"No, too lazy, but several of his curates were."

"Curates?"

"Junior clergy, ones who hadn't yet become rectors or vicars but who served as apprentices as part of their preparation. Several of Bingham's curates became published authors."

The historian looked at Tony with a smile. "You have discovered the bathtub in the attic, no?"

Tony nodded.

"It belonged to the novelist Charles Kingsley, who later, after his short spell as curate here in 1844, became famous for writing the children's book, *The Water Babies*."

"I know."

Tony told Con about his dream.

"He seems to have liked a bath," Tony concluded.

"Yes, he was, shall we say, *obsessed* with washing. He had a bath every day. The bath in your attic was his."

"Then he was a bit of a water baby himself."

The historian nodded. It was a joke he had either heard or made before. Many times.

"It's an impressive list," Tony said.

Con said, "I want you to remember what Charles Kingsley said. 'Still the race of hero spirits pass, the lamp from hand to hand.' You're a writer, like them. So, pass the lamp."

"I am no hero spirit," Tony said.

Con pointed to the list again.

"Take a look at this."

His finger landed on the year 1547. "It says John Elmer," he said. "But this is only half true."

"How so?"

The Old Rectory was originally a Tudor manor house and hunting lodge, as you know. It was given as a wedding present to Queen Catherine Parr, his sixth wife."

"In what year?"

"The year of our Lord, 1546."

"According to the list," Tony said, "that's the year John Elmer became rector."

"No. Someone else was made rector in 1547 and he lived in your house with his wife and servants for several years, serving this parish very faithfully and commendably."

"Who?"

"His name was John Parkhurst. He was chaplain to Queen Catherine Parr. She gave the house to him just before she died in 1547, after giving birth to her only child."

"Why isn't he on this list?"

"Why do you think?"

"Because it was a secret?"

"Precisely."

"What kind of a secret?"

The historian smiled.

Then he tapped his long nose.

"Let me get this right," Tony said. "Queen Catherine Parr was given the Tudor mansion by Henry VIII, and she allowed her chaplain to live in it, and he was appointed the rector."

"Yes, in 1547." He repeated, "1547" as he began to walk down the nave towards the door.

Tony followed him up the path behind the church and

through the graveyard. They paused at an old, unmarked gravestone in one corner of the cemetery. It stood all on its own in neglected, uncultivated ground. Rectangular. Flat, unlike the upright headstones. It looked so blighted with moss and dirt that whatever words had been written there had, at least to Tony's eyes, long since disappeared.

Con saw him studying the marble stone and said, "God knows who's buried in that grave."

Tony said, "This place seems to be full of secrets."

Con led him out of the churchyard. He turned towards the Old Rectory. "Do you want to see it before you go?"

"I do."

They headed into the drive and stood on the lawn.

"It's an extraordinary thing, no?"

"What is?"

"That the greatest female author of the Tudor Age, Queen Catherine Parr, lived and wrote here."

"It really is."

"And that she let her chaplain live in it, a man who also had a gift for writing. In his case, not works of religious devotion, like the Queen's, but books of Latin verse."

"Latin?"

"Yes, it was very popular at the time."

"Is that why the Queen chose him?"

The historian replied, "When King Henry VIII and Queen Catherine Parr visited Oxford in 1543, John Parkhurst wrote Latin verses in honour of their visit. The king was very taken with his words and with him as a man. He suggested that Catherine should appoint him as her private chaplain, so she did."

"So, Parkhurst was a famous writer too."

"He published thousands of lines of Latin verse. They came out in a book in 1573 entitled *Ludicra*, meaning "playthings," "sources of fun," or "games." He was one of the best of these poets."

The historian turned to Tony. His dark eyes seemed to dig deep into his soul as he spoke.

"This house is looking for someone who understands and respects its past. You are a writer, Tony. This is what the house was born into and what the house yearns for now. If you buy it, will you honour that history and continue its legacy?"

Tony replied. "It is a fine place to dream and write."

"Yes, it is. Dr Samuel Johnson once visited the parish and the Rectory. Do you know what he said about it?"

Tony shook his head.

"He described it as a place very pleasing by its situation."

"He was right," Tony said.

"But do you know why he said that?"

"I don't."

"He was talking about Christopher Pitt, the rector who spent a lot of his time writing very popular books while he lived in the Rectory. He said that Pitt loved living here because it is a place, I quote, 'likely to excite the imagination'."

"It is strangely therapeutic," Tony said.

"It is indeed."

They walked out of the drive and back towards Tony's car. As he opened the door, Tony paused to say goodbye.

The historian was leaning over the top of the lynch-gate, gazing at the church and grounds. "A kind of glory lingers still," he murmured.

"Sorry, what?"

"It was written by William Ewart, the curate who lived in the Old Rectory after Charles Kingsley. The poem is called 'The Village Choir'. He was talking about the afterglow when the choir finished chanting at evensong." Con took a deep breath before reciting. "An echo, till God comes, survives the music made by good men's lives."

With that, he looked at his watch, opened the gate, and headed towards the church door.

As Tony began the journey back to London, all he could think of was the absent name in the rollcall of rectors.

Why was John Parkhurst not mentioned?

What was the big secret?

Time would tell, he reassured himself.

Time would tell.

19

A DREAM

Although he was dreaming, Tony felt the majesty of the queen's entrance. When she walked across the threshold to the ancient Tudor lodge – a gift from the king himself - she stopped, her blue-grey eyes drinking in her new surroundings.

The Queen smiled.

The house seemed to smile back.

Tall and pale-faced, Catherine Parr was dressed in a long robe of crimson cloth. Her sleeves were made of golden satin and trimmed with velvet. Her hair was auburn, her headdress studded with diamonds that twinkled in the light of the hall.

She turned to check that her ladies in waiting had hold of her two yards of train before entering the hallway.

"It's perfect!" she said.

She composed herself, looked back at her ladies, and spotted her chaplain at the door.

"Please offer a benediction, Mister Parkhurst," she said,

her tone now pious and serious. She knelt and closed her eyes. Her ladies followed suit.

The bearded chaplain, the only one standing, raised his right hand and uttered a blessing for the windows and doors, consecrating every part of the house from the garret to the cellar. Tony could almost sense the warm trembling of it all. The stones and timbers of the house seemed to vibrate with an otherworldly pleasure.

As he finished with the sign of the cross, the kind-faced cleric said "Amen," and everyone repeated the word. The echo of it rose through the rafters towards the heavens.

The Queen stood, her retinue rising with her. She continued her inspection of the house, crossing every one of the thresholds, both upstairs and downstairs, until she settled on a smaller room upstairs, one with a view of the gardens.

"This will be my study," she said.

"Majesty?" the nearest of her ladies enquired.

"My writing room, Jane. It has such a fine stone window frame. Make this chamber ready."

The ladies hurried to fetch some baggage from outside. On their return, they positioned the Queen's dark oak desk beneath the windowsill and set her quill pen at the ready. The candle flames shimmered as the women left.

Only the chaplain remained. He wore a black cap and gown, which in different circumstances might have appeared funereal and sad. But he was far from that.

"Majesty," he said, his voice soft. "This house will make an island of peace in a sea of turmoil. These tranquil halls will be a great aid to your writing. Are you pleased with them?"

"I am, John. And I am grateful to the King. It is a most

generous and thoughtful gift."

"And what is your Majesty intending to write here?"

"A book."

"On what subject?"

"*The Lamentation of a Sinner.*"

"A most holy theme, your Majesty."

"Our lives are like a house," the Queen said. "We need each day to inspect the rooms to brush away the dust and dirt. Tomorrow, my sweet ladies will clean this lodge from top to bottom, removing anything that might grieve the Spirit. But tonight, I will purge the house of my soul from all impurities as well."

"A most apt picture, your Majesty."

"It is a common comparison. Do you not remember what St Augustine wrote?"

"I confess, I do not."

The Queen touched her two crucifixes. "My soul is like a house, small for you to enter, but I pray you to enlarge it. It is in ruins, but I ask you to remake it. It contains much that you will not be pleased to see. This I know and do not hide."

The chaplain smiled. Then he asked, "Is there anything you wish to confess, your Majesty?"

"Something has been weighing on my conscience."

The chaplain waited.

The Queen sighed.

"I lied to the king."

"Majesty?"

"John, you know the main reason I married the king, other than my sense of duty, was to seize the opportunity to share the faith of the Reformers to inspire him to rid this country of dead and false religion once and for all."

The chaplain nodded.

"And you know that I conversed with the king, for an entire evening, urging him to put his faith in the merits of Christ's passion, not in popes and priests."

The chaplain nodded again.

"That conversation was overheard," the Queen whispered.

"By whom, Majesty?"

"The Bishop of Winchester."

"Stephen Gardener?"

"The same."

It was the chaplain's turn to sigh.

"The bishop took exception at me, a wife, teaching her husband. That was bad enough for him. But worse still, he is a defender of the lifeless piety that we abhor. He complained to the king that I had no authority to act thus and that I should be punished."

The Queen's fair skin became ashen.

"The king summoned me to ask questions of me, ones designed to expose my intentions. Gardener was to hide in the shadows and overhear the conversation." She inhaled so deeply that it shook her slender frame. "If I had continued to talk to the king as I had, Gardener would have been witness, juror, judge, and executioner, and I would have been just another Queen who lost her head."

She grasped the diamond-encrusted jewel around her neck and held it in her pale fingers.

"What happened, Majesty?"

The Queen's tone was grave.

"A faithful friend in the court told me what was going to happen in the king's chambers, and I changed my stratagem. Instead of trying to instruct His Majesty, I bowed to his superior state as king, and to his greater wisdom as my husband."

"Did you succeed?"

"It took all night, but I did. His Majesty was most relieved and gratified. He believed me when I said that I had not intended to instruct him, but that I, an admirer of his peerless knowledge, had merely been eager to study at his feet."

The Queen allowed herself a smile.

"Gardener was beside himself with rage, especially so on the morrow, when men arrived to arrest me, and the king sent them packing with a harsh rebuke and a slap about the head."

The chaplain smiled too. Then he frowned and asked, "Why has this vexed you so?"

"I lied," she whispered. "And my lie came from fear, a fear of sharing the same fate as Queen Anne and my namesake. I am a sinner, John. There is no other word for it."

She paused as a breeze caught the flame of the candle on her writing desk. Then she said, "If I had been living in the full assurance that I was loved by God, then I would not have been afraid of the king. Does perfect love not cast out fear?"

There was silence.

The chaplain waited again.

"I have been living with a great sadness of soul ever since. I am a daughter of the King of kings and yet I behaved as if my faith is dead, and I am a slave again to fear."

The Queen knelt.

Crestfallen.

"I should have given my life for the true Gospel of Christ," she said. "Other women have been far braver. Look at Anne Askins. She finished her race well. I did not."

"Your race is different."

"Is it, John?"

"It is. Martyrdom is a calling, not a choice."

"Then what is my calling?"

"To write books, your Majesty."

"That does not seem so great a sacrifice."

The chaplain said, "There are those who are called to write in blood, like St. Peter, and then there are those who are called to write in ink, like St. John. Both pay a price."

He came and stood before her as she remained kneeling. He said, "*The Lamentation of a Sinner* will be a celebration of lively and feeling faith. Your words, forged in the fire of repentance, will have the sharpness of a newly fashioned blade."

The Queen bowed. "We are all tired of dead, human, historical faith and knowledge", she said. "It is time for a religion of the heart, not just the head."

Then she prayed a childlike prayer to the High King of Heaven, confessing her failings, asking for forgiveness as a daughter would of her trusted and most loving Father.

The chaplain uttered absolution, assuring her that her sins had been cast as far from her as the east is from the west.

She stood.

Her fair skin was radiant again, as were her blue-grey eyes.

"Thank you, John."

He bowed.

"I will start writing now."

At that, he left.

She sat at her desk, took her quill pen, and dipped it in the inkpot. Bending over the page, she paused before she began to write. The flame at her candle was strong and upright now, not faltering and flickering as it had been before.

"Most loving Father," she prayed, "Let your great charity burn and flame in my soul and let your abundant and affectionate love be forever printed on my heart."

No sooner had she finished than her nib was on the paper, scratching at the parchment, the ink flowing even as her thoughts began to pour from her heart, not in some predetermined and contrived design, but as a series of heartfelt meditations.

As she wrote, peace poured over her.

Tony sensed it too.

And when he woke, he wrote a record of his dream. And the nib of his pen raced across the pages of his journal.

20

THE AUCTION

New Year's Eve dragged for Tony, and so did New Year's Day. He could not wait for the auction, an event that coincided with a longstanding commitment to take his godson Jimmy to their favourite chateau for a slap-up meal. They were booked to travel at the exact time of the bidding. Tony had considered postponing, but Jimmy looked forward to their days together. They were an annual tradition - an immovable feast. Postponing it was not something Tony was prepared to contemplate. It would be like cancelling Christmas.

When Tony discovered the double booking, he thought about changing the timing of their journey, but that proved impossible too. Their lunch was a four-course meal. The timings of both their arrival and meal were inflexible. They had been planned by Wendy with military precision. The day with Jimmy would go ahead. Tony would have to trust that all would be well at the auction.

When Tony met Jimmy in Folkestone, the boy looked taller and leaner than he had the same time a year before. He also wore a more anxious expression. But when he saw his godfather, the furrows left his forehead and the life returned to his eyes.

"Hello, favourite godson," Tony said.

"I'm you're *only* godson," Jimmy said.

"So? That makes you even more special."

Tony drove to the Channel Tunnel. Once onboard, they stood beside the car as the carriage doors drew shut.

"How's it going at school?" Tony asked.

The anxiety returned to Jimmy's face.

"You know I've moved, don't you?"

"Yes, your dad sent me an email. He informed me that he's sent you to a boarding school."

"Yeah. Great thirteenth birthday present, wasn't it?"

Tony frowned.

"I've been struggling," Jimmy said.

"What with?"

"I'm homesick."

Tony placed his hand on the boy's shoulder. He said nothing. He wanted to hug him, to tell him it was going to be okay. But his godson was already releasing his grip. He knew why too. He had started to believe the age-old lie, the lie believed by countless boarders, the lie that said he wasn't worthy of love, of being at home.

Tony changed the subject.

"Here," he said, whipping a glossy folder out of his black leather bag. "Take a look at this."

He handed him a prospectus.

"What is it?"

"My new home, hopefully."

Beginning to rally, Jimmy said, "Nice pad!"

The boy began to study the photos of the Old Rectory. He took his time. Pouring over each room and the gardens. He read the potted history of the house. Raising his eyebrows, he said, "It was owned once by Queen Catherine Parr. That's sick!"

"Very sick."

"Bit different from your place in Chelsea."

Tony laughed.

"Our tastes change when we grow older," he said. "When I was a boy, I hated sprouts. I used to shout 'No greens' to my parents. They never took any notice, of course. But today I love them. Can't get enough of them when I have a Sunday roast. I can't think why I didn't like them when I was younger."

Jimmy smiled and said, "Remind me never to share a room with you after a carvery."

They both laughed.

"How much is it?" Jimmy asked.

"Two and a half million."

"Holy shit!"

"Jimmy!"

"Sorry."

Tony smiled.

"When's the auction?"

"Right now."

"Are you kidding? Why aren't you there?"

"You come first, Jimmy. I've left the bidding in Wendy's very capable hands. I'll find out what's happened when we're out the other side. If it's meant to be, it'll happen."

"Can't you keep in touch by phone?"

"I've tried, but there's no signal."

Jimmy tried his phone.

"I can't get one either."

"Don't worry about it!"

"Do you think you'll get it?"

"It's a funny thing," Tony answered. "I woke up this morning with a strong hunch that I should raise the budget by 120k. I messaged Wendy to tell her my new ceiling."

Jimmy's jaw dropped. "Now I'm really impatient," he cried. "I really want you to win."

Twenty minutes later, they were driving out of the terminal and onto the motorway when Tony's phone rang. It was Wendy. "What's the news?" Tony asked.

"It's yours, Tony!"

Jimmy cheered.

Tony's heart missed a beat.

"It's a good job you raised the budget," Wendy said. "Someone came in at the last minute. The extra 120k threw him off. That was a good shout on your part!"

Tony thanked Wendy and told her to contact him when she needed his signatures.

Jimmy said, "I want to come and stay there."

"Of course. But you'll have to wait a bit. I'm having the whole place done up, including the gardens. It's going to take about nine months before its habitable."

"Next Christmas, then!"

"Great idea!"

Jimmy clapped.

Two hours later, they were sitting in the restaurant of an old chateau. Conversation turned once again to Jimmy's move to boarding school. He was serious throughout, until a plate arrived with roast venison, runner beans, sprouts, and potatoes.

"Look, godfather! Greens!"

The sprouts brought the smile back to both their faces.

Six hours later they were back in England and parked outside the entrance to Folkestone Central railway station.

"Safe journey," Tony said as he gave Jimmy a hug.

This time, Jimmy would not let Tony go.

Tony whispered, "I'm always here for you. And you can come and stay at Christmas. And after that. I want you to treat my new place as a home from home."

"Thank you, godfather," he said.

And then he was away.

Tony, meanwhile, drove back to London. His thoughts were torn between concern for Jimmy and excitement about his new property. He couldn't believe what had happened at the auction. Yes, the Old Rectory was in a desperate state, but already the dilapidated house felt more like home than his shiny pad in Chelsea.

21

THE CIDER

In the following days, Tony sent texts to his godson until the boy's answers stopped – a sign that he had undergone the painful re-entry into the strict and timetabled regimen of his boarding house. By then, Wendy had finalised the legal paperwork and paid for the new home in full. After a brief call with Tony, she also set a budget for Ella to start work on the house and gardens. Only when Tony applied his signature to all the documents, and the funds had been transferred, did it truly hit him. He, Tony Lawson, was the latest steward of a house that had stood for five centuries, a house that once belonged to Queen Catherine Parr. He could not remember being this energised since he was a boy.

As the January days wore on, Tony started daydreaming about the many rooms in his new home. One room seemed to loom large and often in his imagination - a room on the second floor whose stone-framed window looked onto the lawn. The window in this room was, to Tony's mind, spectacular. Situated above the front door of the house, it was one of the surviving Tudor features of the property. It was arched. On the exterior of the house, the stonework still bore in Roman numerals the date of the construction of the manor house - 1530. Ever since his first visit to the Old Rectory, Tony's eyes had been drawn to it. He had often imagined Queen Catherine Parr standing beneath it.

Tony had studied the window and observed that it was made of stone, both the surrounds and the mullions. There were, in fact, three windows side by side, like a triptych. Each window was made up of six panes. These, Ms Macready had assured him, were from Tudor times. Each square pane was surrounded by a leaden frame. The hinged windows, held in place by their ancient latches, opened outwards, as was the Tudor custom when it came to casement windows.

Above the three windows, there was a hooded stone arch with three patterns. At the top, there was a single diamond-like shape. Underneath, on either side, there was a floral pattern made up of five leaves. Each of these carved gaps in the stone – the diamond and the leaves – were filled with the glass used by the original builders, the three that Tony had seen in his dreams.

As he thought about this window, and indeed the room into which it ushered in the sunlight, he remembered the one possession that he still had from the distant days of his childhood. It had survived both the long season of his trauma, his years away at boarding school, and the decades of adult life leading right up to the present: his father's desk - a dark mahogany pedestal desk with a green leather top. It had brass handles on each of the three drawers in both pedestals, and on the long drawer beneath the top. Tony had inherited it from his father, as his father had from his own father.

This desk stood in a bedroom in his Chelsea home, covered by a bedsheet, along with other items of furniture and boxes of possessions collected over the years. It had been undisturbed while Tony had lived in London, a period of fifteen years. He had not removed the dustsheet during that entire time. He could not bring himself to look at the old desk, knowing that it would trigger some synapse in his brain and release images of the golden age before his trauma.

But today was different.

Elated by the prospect of the new property, he decided to lift the sheet and take a tape to the desk. He measured its height, width, and depth and then came to a decision. The upstairs room with the Tudor window would become its new home. If it fitted beneath the windowsill, he would have it repolished and it could stand beneath the antique panes. In this place of welcome solitude, Tony hoped that he would come to write again, resting his laptop on the same surface used by his father and his forebears, while gazing at the trees and the lawns when he needed to let his mind wander.

That afternoon, Tony drove to the Old Rectory and, tape measure in hand, met Ms Macready.

"Congratulations!" she cried. "I'm thrilled you won and that the house is yours. You must be delighted."

"Thank you."

Tony climbed the stairs and entered the room with the Tudor window. It was a glorious January day. The sun was shining in a cloudless sky. The room seemed to be almost transfigured by the light shining through the panes. He stood enchanted for several seconds, unable to do anything except stare.

"You okay, Tony?"

"I am, yes."

In truth, Tony was under the house's spell. Light was pouring into his mind even as it was flooding the room.

He said, "It's amazing to think that so many gifted writers would almost certainly have looked through this same window, staring out upon these gardens."

"I'm told that the inscription outside says this was originally a prayer room," she replied.

"Told by whom?"

"The historian. Speaking of which, he asked if he could leave you a gift. It's downstairs."

Ms Macready made to go downstairs, but Tony asked her not to fetch the old man's gift just yet.

"Could you help me with this before you go?" he asked.

They extended the tape.

"It's perfect."

Ms Macready looked confused.

"My father's desk. It'll fit beneath the sill. I want to start writing a book here. It's the perfect spot."

She smiled and then asked to be excused. "I need to check the old cob wall outside," she said. "I was told there was some damage last week during the storm."

Tony looked at his surroundings. This would make an ideal study. It had been a prayer room in Tudor times. His father's desk would have to suffice today as a makeshift altar.

As Tony scanned the room, his eyes were drawn back to the window. Without thinking, he lifted himself onto the sill and sat with his back to the right-hand side of the stone surround, looking down onto the gravel drive to his left and centre, onto the grass lawn off to his right, the lawn where the ghost had curtseyed.

Only when he was perched on the sill did it strike him how strange it was that he had performed this act. This did not cause him to move. Nor did any concern for the antique window make him leave the sill. It had stood for five centuries; it would tolerate his burden for a few minutes while Ms Macready, who was marching the length of the wall outside, completed her inspection.

As he sat and gazed at the stones on the drive, Tony was captivated by a memory. He was at his prep school, aged eight. It was his first day and he was staring at his parent's car in the drive - a VW campervan. Two-toned - sky blue and white. His mother was in the passenger seat and his father was about to enter the driver's door. He turned, looked up at the window, and saw Tony waving. There were tears pouring down the young Tony's face. His dad could sense it. He frowned, then, managing his own grief, he smiled and mouthed the words, "We'll be back." His dad blew him a kiss. Young Tony blew one back. Then the car pulled out of the drive, the tyres crunching the stones.

"We'll be back," his father had said.

But his parents had never returned.

They had lied.

Even after the accident, Tony had often waited, staring out of the same upstairs window at school.

And now, over forty years later, here he was sitting on the sill, just as he had done for many months when he was a boy. The weather outside seemed to sense it. There was rain on the windowpanes and tears in his eyes. The sun had disappeared.

Tony slid from the cold ledge, wiped his face, and walked downstairs just as Ms Macready returned.

"Here it is," she said, removing a white cotton cloth covering something on the floor.

It was a glass bottle.

Old and brown, with a screw top.

About a litre.

Full.

And a glass goblet.

"I think he meant for you to open it now," she said. "To celebrate your success at the auction."

"What is it?"

She removed a postcard leaning against the back of the bottle. It had a picture of a Tudor lady on the front and some scribbled handwriting on the back.

She passed it to me.

"Queen Catherine Parr," Tony said.

"The painting?"

"Yes. By someone called Master John."

"Her red hair is stunning."

"Auburn," Tony said.

"It's cider," she said. "An old, local recipe. Dating back to Victorian times. Claims it's what true cider should taste like. Not like the sparkling, champagne drink people buy today."

Tony opened the bottle.

The scent of apple was unmistakable.

He poured some of it into the glass.

Golden.

Shimmering.

He sipped from the goblet.

It was not fizzy, just as the Professor had warned, but rich, deep, fruity, and strong.

Very strong.

A strange warmth trickled down his throat into his stomach – a warmth that not only calmed his body but soothed his soul like balm, turning the sadness he had felt at the window upstairs into a serenity, an equilibrium, there in the hallway.

"Would you like to try it?" Tony asked.

"No, no. The historian left me with strict instructions that it was for your lips alone. I don't want to cross him. He is a very sweet old man. Very helpful with the sale of this property."

"Helpful?"

"Yes, I probably shouldn't tell you this, but he made it very clear from the start he was keen for you to buy it. Said you were an ideal fit, you were. Being a writer and all."

"You've met him then?"

"Never in person. He's sent a few emails and I spoke with him once on the phone."

"You've never actually seen him?"

"No. Why do you ask?"

Tony remembered the old man's strange appearance again, but he held back from describing him.

She said, "I'm sorry if you think he's stuck his nose..."

Tony spluttered.

"Did I say something?"

He screwed the cap back onto the bottle and made to leave, the cider in one hand, the goblet in the other.

Outside, Ms Macready locked the front door. "Here," she said, handing over a ring with a set of keys. "These are yours. I'd shake your hand, but it looks like they're full. I have a feeling you and the Old Rectory will be very happy."

Tony smiled at the old, iron keys.

After one last look at the window, then the lawn, Tony travelled back to London through the pelting rain. When he arrived at his house, he made himself some dinner, watched some videos about the Tudor age, then headed to bed with a glass of Con's elixir.

Once again, the golden liquid soothed him.

Within no time, his soul was in a state of cider-induced tranquillity.

And soon, very soon, he was fast asleep.

Dreaming again.

22

A DREAM

In his dream, Tony was no longer in Tudor times. He was looking at the Victorian house, and he was watching events unfold in his garden at what looked like harvest time.

A well-upholstered rector with a round, ruby face, appeared. He was looking at the trees. They were heavy with apples. A few were already on the ground, their light green surfaces wizened by wasps. He picked up an unblighted specimen and sank his teeth into it. He murmured approval as the juice spread down from his thick lower lip across his dimply chin.

He turned to a man next to him. "These stubbards are perfect, Mister Rivers. They will make fine cider."

The man nodded. "Bobby dazzlers they are, Rector."

The rector turned from the garden towards the house. He frowned. "The old place is looking glum."

Mister Rivers said, "That Mister Wyndham..."

"Doctor Wyndham, if you please."

The man continued, "Doctor Wyndham..." he tipped

his hat with mock reverence. "He spent all his time by the sea at Melcombe Regis, he did, hobnobbing with the king. He didn't spend a single night in the Rectory. Left it all gabberd."

The rector nodded. "I've approached Lord Portman to ask him if he will help restore it."

Mister Rivers said, "Doctor Wyndham left the house in the same poor state as the souls in his parish. He never cared for us. Have you heard what he did one Christmas, Rector?"

"I have not."

"He told one of his curates to ban the old mince pie."

"What, pray, was the old mince pie?"

"A Christmas tradition in our village, sir. I mean, that chitter-faced man was already unpopular for not living in the parish, but when he decided to do away with the old mince pie, he could not have been hated more, the blow poke."

"You still haven't told me what it is."

"A tradition."

"You said that already."

"At Christmas."

"You said that too."

"Sorry, sir. The first rector appointed by Queen Catherine Parr, may she rest in peace, started giving a quart of cider and a crusty pie filled with mince to every soul in the parish. Mister John Parkhurst was his name if my memory serves me."

"A capital display of generosity," the rector said.

"That was the problem."

"What do you mean?"

"Doctor Wyndham objected to money being spent

wastefully, as he saw it, when it could have gone to help the poor. At the next tithe-day supper, a farmer by the name of Billy Frampton asked the curate whether the rector was planning to follow through on his plan. The curate replied that he was."

The rector shook his head.

"He told the curate to tell the rector that he did not care a brass button for his penny-loaf ways and stormed off to his farm, where he collected a bundle of banknotes, then headed to the pub. He told the landlord to give everyone a quart of cider and a mince pie on Christmas Eve. And he gave him the money."

The rector chuckled.

"That's not the end of it, neither. Come Christmas Eve, old Billy offered up a toast." Mister Rivers cleared his throat. "To the Queen, God bless her! May she send more pigs and less parsons."

The rector roared with laughter.

"Doctor Wyndham never crossed the parish boundary into our village, not even when he resigned the living last summer, when you, Mister Bury, arrived soon after."

The Rector nodded. "1862," he said. "My annus mirabilis."

"Pardon?"

"My wonderful year."

"Not that wonderful, Rector. You arrived too late to harvest the apples. They were already lying rotten on the ground."

"Not this year, Mister Rivers. Tell the labourers to gather the harvest. We are going to make a fine cider."

Men and women started to pour into the grounds carrying

wicker baskets. They sang harvest songs as they collected the fruit and took it to the loft of the Rectory.

After all the apples had been gathered in, Mister Rivers said, "The barrels are ready, sir."

He led the rector to a barn with uncovered sides and wooden casks stacked high at one end of the roofed building. The rector bent low and sniffed at them.

"Mister Rivers, you give me your word that these barrels were used only for spirits."

"For whisky, sir."

"Good," the rector said. "If these casks have been used for beer, the cider will be weak. But if they have been used for whisky, the cider will be stronger than ale."

"And better tasting," Mister Rivers said.

"I am partial to both," the rector muttered.

"Just so long as you don't drink ale after cider," Mister Rivers said. "Cider upon beer is very good cheer."

Their murmurs of agreement were interrupted by a loud rumbling the far side of the barn.

"The crusher has started," Mister Rivers said.

The rector made his way to a four-wheeled engine releasing steam into the sky. The labourers who had carried the fresh apples to the attic in the house had now brought down apples that had been growing mellow over several weeks. The workers fed the older apples onto racks where they were crushed to pulp, their precious liquid flowing into vast tubs. The men then filled the whisky barrels with it, their voices whistling old Dorset tunes that could be heard above the chug-chug-chug of the engine and the sound of belts and pulleys.

When all the apples had been through the press, the rector

gave permission for the men to bring their own apples and barrels. This was their reward for the hard work. One by one, their apples passed through the machine. One by one, the workers helped each other to pour the liquid into their own barrels. One by one they tasted the fruit of their own trees and their own labours.

The women now lay wooden tables. Everyone fell silent as the rector pronounced a benediction over the year's harvest, gave thanks for the gift of cider, and blessed the mutton pies they were about to receive. They waited as pints of cider were brought in pewter mugs and plates of mutton pie were laid in front of them.

As darkness fell, torches were lit. Then the dancing and music began. The air was rich with the odour of the squab pies made by the rector's wife.

"I have something for you, my handsome," she said. Her face was red from the kitchens. "I meant to give it you earlier today, but I forgot, what with all the preparations."

She wiped both her hands on her frilly apron, making sure that every trace of grease and gravy had gone. She took a brown paper package from the pouch at the front of her pinny. It was held together by a piece of string with a bow knot.

"What is it, Anne?"

"Something you've wanted since he started publishing parts of it in the *Macmillan Magazine*."

He looked confused.

"Here," she said.

He opened the package.

It was a book.

With a navy, Morocco cover.

Geometric patterns in gilt on the spine and front.

Marbled endpapers.

The title and author's name in gold.

The Water Babies.

Kingsley.

The rector gasped.

"You didn't!"

"Oh yes, I did!"

He cried, "It is a very handsome copy. 350 pages! With several illustrations by Mister Paton. Published London, by Macmillan and Company, 1863."

He handed the volume back to his wife who returned it, like a Roo, into her pouch.

"You are the apple of my eye," the rector said.

"Given the number of apples that have caught your fancy today," his wife said, "I take that as a compliment."

They both laughed.

The rector turned to the gardener. "Did you meet him?"

"Who, sir?"

"Kingsley. He was here twenty years ago."

"I did, sir. He wasn't here long. My wife Jane was his maid of works. She could tell you a few stories."

"I'm sure she could, Mister Rivers," the rector's wife said. "But that's all in the past."

"Fond of a bath, he was," Mister Rivers continued.

"You'll be saying things about us one day," Anne said.

"Only good things, if today is anything to go by."

The rector tapped his nose. "Perhaps it's time to instigate a new annual tradition."

"What's that?" Mister Rivers asked.

"One that might offer a modicum of redemption for

Doctor Wyndham's misplaced frugality."

Mister Rivers frowned.

"We shall call it 'the old mutton pie'," the rector cried.

"That would be most welcome, sir."

The rector and his wife walked into the house while the music continued to play outside.

As they watched from the window, Anne asked, "What are we going to do with all the money from the sale of this cider?"

"I have thought of that. It would not be right to keep it. We can have both this annual custom and be charitable as well, contrary to what Dr Wyndham claimed."

She chuckled

"We should take up Kingsley's cause," the rector said. "The use of children in the cleaning of our chimneys is a vile and terrible injustice. Let us push for a bill in Parliament and set up a fund for supporting children rescued from this dreadful slavery."

Enlivened by this vision, they walked upstairs to the Tudor window. "It does my soul good to see this, William."

As they beamed at the dancing villagers on the lawns, and the children frolicking in the orchards, neither saw what Tony saw in his dream. The three had appeared. Dancing amid the guests. Their arms interlinked. Their faces bright and alive.

Just as it was in the beginning.

23

THE CLAIM

When his alarm went off, Tony rose with a contentment deeper than anything he had known in years. The goblet lay empty beside him on the table. He could still detect the scent of apples. He turned to his phone. There was an email about Matt Maul. His peace deserted him, and the familiar frown returned.

Later that day, Tony met Yinka in the same boardroom as before. This time, he was Yinka's last appointment. The lights of London glowed and flickered outside the huge windows.

When Yinka came in, he was carrying two books. He put them sunny-side-up on the table. He pointed to one of them and asked, "Do you remember Dan Brown's, *The Da Vinci Code*?"

"Of course."

Tony picked up the paperback and glanced at the back cover blurb to check the details of the story.

"Do you also recall it was the centre of a copyright

infringement case that went to the high court?"

"Yes, I do. Wasn't there another book published before Brown's that was quite similar?"

"Yes, this one." Yinka pointed to the other paperback entitled *Holy Blood, Holy Grail*. "The two authors made the same claims Brown makes later in *The Da Vinci Code*."

"Ah yes, that's right."

Yinka said, "The two authors, the plaintiffs that is, took it to trial, but the judge ruled against them."

"So, they lost."

"They did and they didn't."

"What do you mean?"

"The case generated a lot of publicity, as you can imagine, and the sales of both books rocketed as a result. There are some who believe that the claimants knew they would likely lose, and their legal team too, but they figured that the astronomical increase in royalties would more than cover the court costs."

"Were they right?"

"Well, I'm quite sure they sold a lot more copies than if they'd kept quiet or given up on the claim."

"What's that quote about bad publicity?"

Yinka smiled and answered, "There's no such thing as bad publicity, supposedly a PT Barnum saying, but I'm afraid there's no documentary evidence he said it."

At the mention of documents, Tony frowned. "I'm guessing there's a reason you're mentioning Dan Brown."

"There is. I have done some research into this case. In the end, the judge ruled against the claim because Brown had not stolen what they had written. In other words, he may have relied on their *ideas*, but he didn't steal their *words*."

Yinka placed the two books side by side again.

"The case simply confirmed what every reasonable person knows that authors borrow ideas all the time. That's a given. But just because you use an idea that another author has explored doesn't mean you have broken the law."

"So, when does it become criminal?"

"When you use another author's words without permission or proper accreditation."

"Let me get this right," Tony said. "Even if Maul was right, which he isn't, that I used ideas he spoke about at dinner, and did so without accrediting him, then he hasn't got a leg to stand on because those ideas were not written down by him in a book."

"Or a letter, email, text, whatever," Yinka said.

Tony shook his head. "It's lucky I have a digital paper trail somewhere on my computer."

"On that issue, have you got anywhere with Renée?"

"She's taken my laptop to see if she can piece it all together. I have a feeling she may not be quick."

"We do need that footprint," Yinka said.

"Will it silence him?"

"Not necessarily."

"Tell me that's not true."

"Tony, copyright law is complex. These sorts of cases are argued all the time. Most are settled out of court because the costs of going to trial often run into millions."

"Hang on. If it's the documentation of ideas that's protected in law, not the ideas themselves, then I really don't see how Maul has got any kind of case against me."

Yinka said, "There's an old saying among lawyers. Where there's a hit, there's always a writ."

"What on earth does that mean?"

"It means that when a book like yours becomes a hit and spends 128 weeks ..."

"129!" I interjected.

"129 weeks in the bestseller lists," he continued. "Then it can be deemed a hit. And when something's a hit, there's often someone who makes a claim about copyright infringement. In former times, this was described as issuing a writ."

"I would have been better off not writing it at all."

"I'm afraid, Tony, this is the dark side of human nature, what in my Catholic upbringing would have been called the deadly sins. Your former friend is exhibiting at least two."

"Envy," Tony said.

"And greed," Yinka added.

"What about sloth?" Tony asked. "I mean, he's lazy and wants everything for doing nothing."

"Perhaps, yes. And you could even add wrath."

"So, he's guilty of four out of seven."

Yinka nodded.

"What do you advise?"

"You have two options. You can fight this and take it to the High Court. If you win, he'll have to pay much of your costs. But you need to realise this will consume enormous time, energy, money, and you may take a hit in terms of reputation."

"And the other option?"

"You settle before it gets to court, and you get Maul to agree to a confidentiality clause."

The glass door opened.

"You remember Nadiya?"

Tony stood and they shook hands.

"Sorry we have to meet under such difficult and stressful circumstances, Mister Lawson..."

"Please call me Tony."

"Nadiya will be working with you," Yinka said. "Along with her junior, Hamish Carmichael."

Hamish was half Nadiya's age. He looked fresh out of university. His pale face was smooth and hairless.

Tony shook his hand too.

They all sat.

Nadiya opened a folder and pushed a letter over to Tony's side of the table. It only took a few seconds for Tony to realise that the letter was from Maul's legal team.

Nadiya said, "As you can see, Tony, Maul's legal team have brought a case against you for allegedly stealing the ideas of your book *Dreamers* from the plaintiff."

Tony laughed. When he composed himself, he said "I understand he needs to have written something for me to have broken copyright law, something physical like a document."

Nadiya looked at Yinka and then back at Tony. "That is certainly part of the defence that we will build," she said. "However, you need to know that the law is moving in this area. It isn't static. Maul may also try to argue that you have stolen intellectual property that he created, rather than copy some document or other."

Yinka looked at Tony and said, "You see why most cases get settled out of court."

"But that would be grossly unfair," Tony said.

Yinka said, "Sometimes, we need to make a distinction between what's fair and unfair and what's legal and illegal.

The Law, I'm afraid, is sometimes more concerned with the latter."

"What are you going to do?" Tony asked Nadiya.

"I'm going to tell them that *Dreamers* is your IP and then I'm going to tell them to back off."

"Will that work?"

"No, but it will delay things. The more we push back, the higher the costs will be for the plaintiff, and the longer that goes on, the more desperate he may become."

"On costs," Tony said. "What's your rate?"

"£900 an hour. If we win, you'll get about 70-80% back."

"How long could this go on?"

"At least six months," Nadiya said. "If it goes to trial, we're probably talking 12 to 18 months."

Tony groaned.

"What are your instructions, Tony?" she asked.

"Accelerate the process. Don't procrastinate. I want this sorted as soon as possible. I'm going to be in the States for the next six months doing some TV work in New York. I'd appreciate it if we could resolve this by the summer when I return."

Tony stood and shook Nadiya's hand. "While I'm away, can you and I conduct our meetings virtually?"

"Of course."

Tony said goodbye.

Yinka then escorted him to the elevators.

"What would you do in my situation?" Tony asked.

"I make a point of never answering that question. However, growing up in Nigeria, I used to hear my dad saying something to people who had been wronged."

"What was that?"

Yinka smiled. The smooth round surface of his dark forehead seemed to be glowing as he spoke. He said, "If you fill your mouth with a razor, you will spit blood."

With that, the doors closed.

The serenity Tony had enjoyed that morning had gone.

He needed another glass of Con's cider.

24

THE CONTRALTO

After his meeting with his lawyers, Tony was determined to escape to the country. At lunchtime the next day, he checked his security cameras and left home. He drove out of the city as fast as the traffic and the speed cameras allowed.

Arriving in Salisbury, he paused at a camping shop and bought a camp bed, sleeping bag, and camping stove. He then went to a supermarket for some supplies. When he arrived at the Old Rectory, he had everything he needed for an overnight stay.

Tony took the keys and opened the front door. He now had free access to his dream house any time he wanted. He was the new custodian of its mysteries.

Tony knew it would be one week before the team of gardeners and decorators descended on the house and grounds, all of them overseen by Ella, his site manager and old friend. This was his last chance to stay in the house before they all arrived, and before his impending trip to the States to do a long stint of late-night TV shows in New York.

A window of opportunity had opened. Tony had climbed through it and was now walking through every room of the house.

He decided to count the number of fireplaces.

There were twenty-one in total.

Four were still operational. One in the drawing room. One in the dining room. One in a bedroom. One in a small room that would act as a snug or a den just off the large kitchen.

He proceeded outside and found some dry kindling and logs in a small outhouse that had once functioned as a Victorian laundry room. He lit a fire in the grate in the drawing room and set up his camp bed and sleeping bag, using the light from the roaring fire. He ignited the stove and started to heat a pan of tomato soup, accompanied by some old songs from a favourite playlist on his smartphone, amplified by a separate wireless speaker.

He was about to spread a slice of bread with butter when he heard a knock at the front door. The last thing he was expecting was a visitor. Had Maul somehow followed him?

On high alert, Tony switched off the stove and took his torch. Heading out of the drawing room, he shone the light to his right, onto the window of the upper part of the front door.

He breathed a sigh of relief.

It was not Maul.

It was Con.

He opened the door.

"How did you know I was here?"

"I saw a light in the window as I was passing and thought it wise to investigate."

"Would you like to come in?"

Con nodded, withdrew his black cloth cap, and stepped over the threshold into the hallway.

"When is the restoration to begin?"

"In a few days."

Con smiled. He said, "I suppose you're taking advantage of the quiet before the storm."

"Something like that."

Tony ushered Con into the drawing room. "I'm sorry. The electricity's off. We'll have to rough it."

"That will not be a problem," Con said.

Tony drew up two stray stools. They sat in front of the fire while Tony gave the soup a stir.

"That music..." Con said.

"What about it?"

"The singer is Clara Butt, the contralto from the early 1900s. It was said there was gold in her throat. But you do surprise me, Tony. She surely is too old-fashioned for you, no?"

"Not at all. Her songs have good memories for me. These ones are recordings of gramophone records I used to listen to in happier times when I was a boy."

Con withdrew a small bottle from his overcoat pocket and poured its contents into the metal canteen on the floor.

"More of your cider?"

"Have you finished the last bottle I gave you?"

"I have."

Tony took a sip.

Within seconds, the pounding headache he had been enduring since early morning disappeared.

He began to relax.

"Better?" Con asked.

"Much."

"Tell me more about your affection for Dame Clara's songs," he said. "What is the story?"

"My grandfather. On my father's side."

"What about him?"

"He heard Clara Butt perform in her first concert in the Royal Albert Hall. He was enchanted by her voice. Went on to see her at every concert he could, until he volunteered to fight in the First World War. Even then, he got to hear her again."

"Really? How so?"

"She sang once to the troops. He was one of the lucky ones who heard her. He would whistle the songs and remember her voice in the trenches. The beauty of it, he said, was an antidote to the ugliness of the Western Front."

"I see," Con said.

As the sweet, smooth liquid continued to work its magic throughout his body and soul, a new song from the list began to play. The logs burned in the hearth and they both listened in silence, captivated by Clara's singing. It was a recording of her singing the old spiritual, 'Deep River.' Her voice was plangent yet hopeful, full of desire, yet with an assurance of fulfilment. When the crackling of the recording finished, Tony switched off the playlist. He and Con sat in silence, lingering in the longing, resting awhile in the harmonious intrusion of the past into the present.

"She came here, you know," Con said.

"What?"

"Dame Clara. She visited this house."

"When?"

"When James Hussey was the Rector, at the beginning of

the twentieth century."

"James Hussey?"

"The grandfather of Marmaduke Hussey, who became chairman of the BBC. Marmaduke's father grew up in this Rectory. Once again, this house yields its secrets, no?"

"It really does."

Con poured some more cider into the canteen. When the last drop had fallen, he said, "Dame Clara sang in this house. She did so for free, saying that it was part of her divine duty."

"How do you know?"

"The event was documented."

"Who by?"

"One of James Hussey's daughters."

"I wish I had been there," Tony said.

"You will be," Con said with a smile. Then he added, "Allow me to tell you something interesting about Marmaduke Hussey, James Hussey's grandson."

"Yes?"

"He wrote and published a memoir. In it, he talked about visiting this very house for the first time very late in his life. He had been travelling all over the world and never felt he belonged anywhere, not until he came to visit this house."

"I can relate to that," Tony whispered.

Con nodded.

He continued. "Marmaduke, or 'Dukey' as his family and friends knew him, went to the church here. He found a hassock with his grandfather's name embroidered on it. He knelt on it. The moment moved him deeply. Connecting, earthing, grounding him with his forebears. With a sense of home."

"Did he come to this house?"

"In his memoir, he said he did, yes. He slept in the upstairs room, the one with the Tudor window. This was the one his father had occupied when he was a boy. Dukey imagined his dad growing up there. That moved him very deeply too."

"I'm sure."

"It was the only time he said he felt a sense of homecoming, here in the Old Rectory."

Tony gazed at the hissing wood in the hearth, lost in his own history of rootlessness. Then, remembering the tomato soup, he said, "Would you like some?"

Con lifted his long nose at a slight angle and then took out his golden timepiece. "It is most kind of you," he said, checking the hour. "But I must be away. It has been good to see you again. I do hope all goes well with the restoration."

Tony escorted him out into the hall.

"When will you be back?" Con asked, putting his limp cap over his white, curly hair.

"I'm away for a long while now," Tony said. "I have a lot of work on in the States. TV mostly."

"In America?"

"Yes, New York."

Con chuckled.

"What's funny?"

"Dame Clara sang at Carnegie Hall," he said. "Life is full of such strange moments of alignment, no?"

"I'm coming to think they are."

"I hope it goes well for you over there, and I look forward to seeing you when you return."

With that, the old man turned his face towards the drive and stepped out into the cold.

Tony returned to his soup and buttered bread. The food,

along with the cider he had now finished, left him content and sleepy. As the charred timber in the grate emitted a fading light, he removed his shoes before turning in for the night.

Tony lay down on the camp bed and climbed into his sleeping bag. Resting his head on a makeshift pillow, he stared out the window and up at the night sky. The thin slice of the moon cast a pale light upon the drawing room. Tony imagined the ghosts of past rectors and their families warming their hands before the hearth. How they must have taken solace in the house and in each other. The village had been isolated in James Hussey's time, accessed not by roads in any modern sense but by tracks of dirt covered in stones trampled by horses and carts. The village had a church, a few farms, some stables, a post office, a tavern, and that was about it. About sixty souls lived here. The church and the Rectory were the heart of it all. A warm, beating heart.

The Rectory was a safe house for people then, and it was a safe house for Tony. Far away from London, hidden from the avaricious eyes of Matt Maul, the Old Rectory was his haven. Tony welcomed the isolation. And although the roads were far better than they had been in Hussey's day, he was glad they were smooth because it meant that he could access the house without discomfort.

He closed his eyes.

Switching on his playlist again, Tony set the sleep timer for thirty minutes and began to listen to Dame Clara singing 'Abide with Me.'

He did not make it beyond the first verse.

He was fast asleep.

At one with the house, and the house with him.

25

A DREAM

Tony now dreamed of his house in Victorian times. A woman had just arrived at the threshold. She had a diamond star brooch pinioned to the front of her wavy black hair, and a similar jewel, with twelve shafts of light emanating from it, on a golden necklace.

Once inside, she stood at the entrance to the drawing room on her left and the dining room on her right, giving the many souls crammed in the house a chance of seeing and hearing her, including those sitting all the way up the stairs, and the servants crowded on the landing. Her dark eyes looked at everyone and a smile broke out on her pretty face. The bearded rector, James Hussey, came and stood next to her. Even though he was tall, she made him look diminutive.

The rector's eleven children watched with wide eyes and open mouths at their Amazonian guest. They were whispering about her on the stairs, comparing her to a mermaid.

The rector spoke. "To our esteemed patrons Lord and

Lady Portman, and all our guests, I extend a warm welcome. Those of you who have been at evensong have heard something beyond all normal powers of description. In the place of our choristers, our guest sang the choral parts of our service. If Jenny Lind is the Swedish Nightingale, Clara Butt is the English Songbird."

Many nodded.

The rector continued. "This evening, we welcome a very distinguished guest to the Rectory. She is the most famous singer in England and her name is known and respected throughout the world – a world she has travelled and toured for some years now, along with her husband, Mister Kennerley Rumford, whom we also welcome, as her accompanist on the piano."

The rector paused.

"Ladies and gentlemen, please give a warm welcome to the finest contralto alive, Clara Butt."

There was an explosion of cheering and clapping from everyone on the first and second floors.

Mister Rumford began to play a tune on the piano just inside the drawing room. The singer's eyes closed. Her lips trembled. She took a breath. Then she started to sing.

Hers was the richest of contralto voices, with a range as unique as the variation in her volume. Every note was struck with perfection. Some of the audience lifted their hands to their mouths. When she finished, there was a hush as if everyone within the sound of her melody had been overcome by a strong and sacred presence.

Then the audience clapped. The children cheered. The light of the oil lamps seemed to grow stronger and brighter with the roar that greeted the end of each song.

After the final ballad, everybody cheered again. The singer ushered her husband into the hall. He bowed to the left, right, and front. Then he turned around and bowed to the front door, much to the amusement of everyone who could see him.

The rector then reappeared with his wife. Their faces had a different expression - grave, forlorn even.

Everyone fell quiet.

The church clock struck nine times. The rector waited until the bells had stopped.

Then he spoke. "As we all know, Britain is at war with Germany. I have therefore asked our guest if she will sing a song to rouse our spirits. She will introduce it first."

Clara spoke. "The song came about thirteen years ago when I was sitting next to Edward Elgar during a concert of his own music. When one of his marches was being played, I whispered to him, asking him to write something similar for me. He replied, 'You shall have that one day, my dear.' That song is *Land of Hope and Glory*."

There was more murmuring.

And nodding.

She said, "I regard it as a sacred mission from Almighty God to bring hope to those whose hope is languishing. I will sing this great song now, because its melody and words are for such a time as this. You may join in with me if you wish."

When Clara sang, it was like a bugle sounding the charge. Everyone sang and the house shook with it. Even the tiniest children were humming the tune.

When it ended, the rector asked every head to bow as he uttered the Soldier's Prayer. "Almighty and Everlasting God, by Whose grace Thy servants are enable to fight the good fight of faith and ever prove victorious..."

And so on.

When he finished praying, there was a loud Amen.

The rector gave the blessing before thanking his honoured guests and bidding everyone goodnight. The woman in the shimmering green gown disappeared, along with the man in tails.

When the house was empty and all was quiet, the rector sat at his desk. He threw away the notes for the next Sunday sermon and started to scribble a new theme. He gave it the title, 'Mightier Yet.' As he wrote, he sang in a muted voice.

Wider still and wider
Shall thy bounds be set.
God who made thee mighty
Make thee mightier.
God who made thee mighty,
Make thee mightier yet!

26

THE ESCAPE

Back in Chelsea two days later, Tony received a call from Nadiya. "I need to let you know that Maul's legal team have sent over a photocopy of a handwritten document. It's Maul's handwriting. The ideas are the same as in *Dreamers*. The date on the document predates the publication of your book."

"It's a forgery," Tony said, shaking his head.

"We'll get a handwriting expert onto it."

"How long before we know their findings?"

"Several months to be honest. In the meantime, could you get the paper trail from your ex?"

"I'll speak to her now."

Tony dialled Renée.

Voicemail.

He left a message.

"Maul has now forged an incriminating document. I need the paper trail. Have you found it?"

Tony carried his travel bags outside and entered a limo.

Once inside, he waited for his ex to reply.

When she did, she sounded breathless. "I'm sorry," she said. "I haven't started my work on the laptop. There are so many documents to trawl. Just give me some time."

"Time is what we don't have."

"Okay. Okay."

She left the call without saying goodbye.

Tony could see the driver looking at him in his rear-view mirror. He was gearing up to talk, so Tony slipped on his wireless earphones and started playing Clara Butt's rendition of *Eternal Father*. It had always been his favourite hymn at prep school. As he listened to the opening bars, he glimpsed the driver's lips beginning to move. He was just in time. Tony closed his eyes, blanking the rest of the world. He imagined himself in peril on the sea, floundering in the angry tumult of restless waves. Then he heard the prayer. 'O Trinity of love and power, thy children shield in danger's hour." Peace filled his mind. The peace that he had known at school when the waves threatened.

When he arrived at the airport, Tony headed into a private section of the VIP lounge.

He texted Wendy. "I've reached my limit, Wendy. Please put my Chelsea house on the market."

She rang straightaway.

"Are you okay, Tony?"

"I may need the money for legal costs ...."

"I'm sorry."

There was a pause.

"I'm not sure how fast it will sell. The market's slow."

"I know you'll do your best, Wendy."

"What are you going to do with all your furniture?"

"I don't want any of it."

"You want me to sell it all?"

"Everything except my dad's old desk. I've labelled that and a few other items for the Old Rectory."

"Are you at the airport yet?"

"I am. My plane leaves in two hours. Landing at JFK tonight - early evening, Eastern Seaboard Time."

"Good. I'll get onto the house sale right away. I'll give you updates by email. Safe trip!"

Tony was about to read an online article he had found about Catherine Parr when he received notification of an incoming video call from Ella at the Old Rectory.

"Hi Tony. You got a minute?"

She panned around her surroundings. There was old plaster and broken timber everywhere.

"Is that the drawing room?" Tony asked.

"Yes. Mister Musgrave has taken down the wall."

"You've started already!"

She nodded.

"What's the estimated end date?"

"Nine months, all going well."

Tony said, "I'm going to be away for at least six months States side. I've got to do a lot of TV work. I may be able to nip back at Spring break, but I can't promise."

"I can always give you video updates," Ella said as she climbed the stairs, filming as she went.

"How many people have you got there?"

"There's twenty in the house. Six in the gardens."

Ella headed into the room with the old Tudor window.

"Wait there!" Tony exclaimed.

She paused.

"You'll be receiving a desk from my place in Chelsea. Belonged to my dad. Please look after it. And when that room's finished, could you position it under the windowsill?"

"Of course! Is it Victorian?"

"It is! Don't worry about everything being original, Ella. Especially with the kitchen."

"Oh, that's a relief. I've been having difficulties acquiring a few original items. It's easy enough to find them. Not so easy to persuade the owners to sell them at a decent price."

Ella headed downstairs into the hallway, then out the front door and onto the drive. Tony drank it all in, aware that this was the last time for a while. The trees. The lawn. The old cob wall.

Ella pointed to some green saplings. "They're the new yew trees for the Queen's Walk. My team are just finishing putting gravel down for the path around the garden."

Ella returned to the house and reversed the camera. She removed her hat. "Notice anything?"

Tony gasped.

There were tufts beginning to sprout like thickets from her bald scalp. "My hair's growing back!"

Tony smiled.

"That's wonderful, Ella!"

"Is that a tear I see, Tony?"

"I'm thrilled for you, Ella. Just thrilled."

Ella turned away. "Got to go. I'll keep you posted, Tony. I hope the trip goes well."

Tony said goodbye and then ordered a bourbon from a hovering waiter. He was still seething from Nadiya's call and needed to climb down from his sense of frustration.

How could Maul descend to such tactics?

And Renée, what was taking her so long?

Then he had an idea. He could not believe he hadn't thought of it before. His amnesia had so messed with his brain that even the most obvious courses of action seemed opaque.

He texted his literary agent.

Hi Sarah. I'm heading to New York for a long stint of filming. Are you there? I'd love to catch up with you. I'm being put up in an apartment just off Central Park West.

Seconds later, her reply arrived.

Yes, Tony! I'm here at our NY offices for another week. Let's meet up. Let me cook dinner for you at your place. Just name the day and time and I'll be there.

Tony smiled. Sarah was an exceptional cook. And even more exceptional company.

He closed his eyes.

"Would you like a massage, sir?"

The voice came from a young woman in a white uniform standing to his right. At first, Tony thought she was a nurse. Then he remembered; this was all part of the service.

"Just my head, neck, and shoulders, please. I'll listen to some music while you work your magic."

Tony moved to a side room of the lounge and straddled the special massage chair. He selected a song and fixed his earphones before draping his shoulders over the leather armrests.

He leaned forward. Dame Clara's soothing voice started to flow into his ears.

O for the wings, for the wings of a dove!
Far away, far away would I rove!
In the wilderness build me a nest,

and remain there for ever at rest.

As the therapist began to knead his neck, Tony thought of the plane he was about to board and the first-class service that awaited. Not long now and he would be out of the country, 35000 feet away from Maul's prying eyes and acquisitive hands.

27

THE AGENT

Sarah Bernstein showed up on Tony's sixth evening in New York, just as the snow became heavy underfoot. She parked in one of his two reserved spaces in the communal garage at the base of the building and was escorted up to the eighth floor. When she arrived, her rosy face looked even redder from her exposure to the icy wind.

Tony took her thick woollen coat and scarf while she marched right into the bright and gleaming kitchen and put a large brown paper bag of groceries on the island.

"This is posh," she said.

"Five bedrooms and five bathrooms," Tony said. "I'm still working out where to sleep. I've tried all five. I'm still not sure. The rooms are all so luxurious and comfortable."

"It's a very lavish pad," she said. "There was some chatter when this place was built almost twenty years ago. It was described as the most powerful address in the city. But..." Sarah walked over to a wall and knocked on it. "These are made of common plaster board like in any other place. It's all ultimately an illusion."

"Bloody expensive illusion," Tony said.

"I know. I don't think I'd complain for a moment if I had to live here for free."

"You're welcome to choose one of the rooms and crash out whenever you're visiting."

"I could be your live-in chef!" Sarah said.

"You'd get no complaints from me."

Sarah headed to cupboards and drawers, inspecting the contents. She was about to start cooking when Tony invited her to come to the window of one of the two sitting rooms. He pressed a button on the remote lying on a glass coffee table. The window slid open, and Tony invited her to step onto the balcony outside.

"Wow!" She exclaimed. "Central Park is just breath-taking at night. I love the snow on the paths and the old-fashioned streetlamps. It's magical. Like Narnia."

"And look at the skyline," Tony said.

They both stared at the millions of lights shining from the tiny windows of the high-rise buildings surrounding the park. Every tower seemed to be alive. Even in the darkness, they could see blues, pinks, yellows, greens. Vibrant, Glowing.

And then, at ground level, the roads of the city, filled with the flickering, shimmering lights of an uncountable assortment of vehicles, all making their way over the snowy asphalt in a stop-start rush of intimidating flashes and grumpy horns.

They headed back inside.

"That is quite some view," Sarah said. "I guess whoever owns this place has to pay through the nose for it."

Tony gestured for her to stand still.

"You're standing in roughly one square foot of this piece of real estate," he said. "Like to guess how much this small space under your feet is worth in the current market?"

"No idea."

"$10,000!"

"You're kidding!"

"I'm not. This unit is currently worth about 35 million."

"That's insane!"

"I know!"

"Why would anyone pay so much money for a place that has absolutely no history."

"Precisely. They pride themselves on the English oak panelling and the Italian marble downstairs, but frankly it all feels a bit out-of-place in an almost brand-new building like this."

"Well, I guess we shouldn't complain," Sarah said. "There will be plenty of people sleeping rough on the streets tonight. I'm sure they'd love to trade places with us."

Tony nodded.

They walked back into the kitchen.

Tony poured them both a glass of wine.

"This place has got an amazing cellar," he said. "I've been told to help myself!"

"Sababa!" she cried.

"Come again?"

"Cool!"

As they sipped the claret, Tony watched Sarah preparing dinner. "It's really good to see you," he said.

He raised his glass.

"Cheers!"

"La Haim!" she replied.

"What's been going on in your world?" she asked.

"The divorce has gone through. Renée and I agreed a financial settlement in the end."

"Did she play hardball?"

"What do you think?"

"She played hardball." Sarah sautéed some sliced shallots and then added cream.

"In a way, she still is."

"How do you mean?"

"It's to do with that writer, Matt Maul..."

"Oh him. He's got a very bad reputation."

Tony nodded. "He is trouble. He's launching a claim, saying that I stole the idea for *Dreamers* from him."

Sarah dropped her spoon in the frying pan. "He said what?" She retrieved the dripping implement.

"He's got a team of lawyers and he's claiming copyright infringement. It's a complete lie. But it's likely to cost me a lot of time and, potentially, a lot of money."

"You could do without that," she said, pausing from her cooking and looking at him.

"I really could."

"What's your plan?"

"I've asked Renée if she'd find the paper trail for the book. It's been a long time. I'm a bit forgetful."

Sarah turned the heat right down. "Are you alright?"

"I have dissociative amnesia. One of the side effects is forgetting how to do tasks that were once simple, like finding documents on my computer with a digital footprint. I know they're there, but it's like I've forgotten how to find them."

"I'm sorry. Has Renée come good yet?"

"I gave her my laptop before Christmas, but she'd not even started when I phoned her a week ago."

"Has Maul given a specific timeframe when he alleges you stole the idea for your book?"

"He has."

"And had you sent me emails and drafts before that?"

"I had."

"Then let me look at my records."

"I would appreciate that."

"I may not have everything you need. But I'll have at least something that shows you didn't even know the man when you were developing your synopsis and pitch."

She turned back to her cooking. A minute later, the food was on two plates, and Tony was making a toast.

When they finished, Sarah put her fork down.

"This Maul nonsense, it must be affecting your writing."

"It is. I won't lie to you."

"Have you written anything recently?"

"It's been a long time."

"I'm sorry about that. You have a great gift, Tony. People miss your books. Is there not even a spark?"

"Funny you should ask that..."

He took another sip of claret.

"Let me tell you about my dream house."

"Dream house?"

"Yep."

And he was away. For the next ten minutes, the words poured out of him like water from a freshly dug well. He told her about his first visit, the ghost in the garden, the dreams, remembering them so vividly, and writing them down in detail in his journal.

Sarah looked shocked.

"So, you *are* writing, Tony!"

"In a way, yes."

He pierced some remaining chickpeas and a stray piece of pan-fried chicken. "This is so good," he muttered.

"It's a pleasure, Tony."

He laid his fork to rest and said, "It's like there are two powerful energies at work in me. There's a gravitational force, pulling me down, stopping me writing."

"Matt Maul?"

"And Renée."

"And the other?"

"I would describe that as an aerodynamic energy, creating a sense of uplift, making it feel like writing is flying, being carried upwards on eagles' wings into a whole new realm."

"And it's your house that's causing that?"

"It's making me dream again, yes."

"So, there might be another book."

"Yes. Something's shifting."

"Have you dreamed since being in New York?"

"No. I seem to dream when I am in the house, or the grounds of the house. Then, that night, I'm away..."

"Sounds like you need to get back there."

"That's easier said than done. I'm booked to interpret and talk about dreams on the late-night show. Live Q-and-A segment each night. People are going crazy for this dream stuff. The gig's a long one. I'm going to be here six months."

"Where's the studio?"

"In a theatre in Manhattan."

"Every night?"

"Mondays to Thursdays, yes. Twice on a Thursday. Then

we're off for the weekends, although those are now filling up too."

"You need to leave some time to write."

"I know."

They cleared the dishes together and Sarah made for the door. Retrieving her coat and scarf, Tony thanked her for the dinner, telling her she was welcome to stay anytime.

"I'd like to," she said. "Although my agency does have a deal with the Marriott, so we'll see. In the meantime, I'll start looking into that paper trail. I'll get back to you soon."

They hugged.

Sarah departed for the city that never slept.

Tony for a room where he did not dream.

28

THE DOCUMENT

After conquering his jetlag, Tony slipped into a routine. Each day, he would wake up midmorning, have breakfast, answer emails, then head to the communal fitness room. After a workout, he would shower in his apartment and then head out into Central Park for a walk, wrapping up not only to protect himself from the wintery weather but also from being recognised. He would use this time to prepare his head and heart for the questions that night on TV. On returning to his rooms, Tony would conduct research into the theme of the show that night while nibbling on a salad brought up from the kitchens. His chauffeur Angelo would drive him to the theatre late afternoon for rehearsals before the audience arrived. After the show, Tony would head out for a very late dinner with the other V.I.P guests. Angelo would drive him back to his Central Park apartment at about 0100.

On Fridays, there would be no filming, so Tony would spend time catching up with work. It was on one of those

Fridays, six weeks into his stay in New York, that Sarah sent him everything she had discovered on her computer. It arrived midmorning in one large zip file. Tony was dredging through it all and marking significant documents and dates when he received a text from Nadiya asking if he was free for a video call. "I know Friday is your day off filming, so I'm hoping you're available." He texted right back to say yes.

"Hi Tony," she said. "How's the Big Apple?"

"They're working me hard. How's the Big Smoke?"

"Cold," she said, faking a shudder.

"It's the same here. Any news?"

Nadiya produced some papers from an old orange file. She said, "I take it you've now had a chance to read the document that Maul's lawyers sent us before you left for the States."

"It's a complete fabrication," he said.

"That may well be, but the challenge we have is that this is a distillation of ideas in a physical form. While ideas are not recorded, say in writing, then they cannot be copied, as Mister Justice Whitford argued in 1977. But these are written."

"He's written this recently," Tony said. "And then backdated it to the time of our friendship. He's used writing paper he had at the time. I also see he says I read it at one of our dinners."

Nadiya put the papers down. "Our handwriting expert has spent the last six weeks subjecting it to examination. The problem is that he is working with a photocopy rather than the original, so it's impossible for him to date the original. But the handwriting, he says, is like other examples he's found of Maul's from the same date. It's going to be hard for us to dismiss it yet."

"You mean, it could hold up in court."

Nadiya nodded. "The document isn't digital, and therefore doesn't have a footprint."

Tony took a gulp of coffee.

"And there's something else...."

"Oh good."

"His lawyer is claiming that it was lodged in his safe at the time Maul says it was written."

Tony slammed his mug on the table, spilling coffee on the glass. "What the ....! Maul stops at nothing. Now he's even managed to get a dodgy lawyer to support his lies."

Nadiya lifted the document. Tony could see various phrases highlighted in yellow. "The wording in these passages is identical to what Hamish has found in *Dreamers*."

"Yes, of course they are. That's because he copied them from me, not me from him."

"That's what we are arguing," Nadiya said. "At the moment, we're simply stalling his legal team, ratcheting up the levels of frustration their end, and the expense, while we assemble our counter evidence. Do you have anything from your ex?"

"No, but I do have a file from my agent. She's just sent it this morning. I was studying the contents before you called. It looks like we have emails that prove I was sharing the ideas with her five years before I ever met Maul. And there are also early drafts of the book that predate my first encounter with him."

Nadiya pointed to her highlighted copy. "We'll need to make sure that the parts I've highlighted in Maul's document were written by you before you met him, and in the same words. Could you email me Sarah's file, so Hamish and I can examine them?"

"Yes, of course."

"There's something else I need to ask you," she said. "We are going to need to find a witness who can corroborate the first date you met Maul. Ideally, someone present at the dinners where you shared ideas together about your books."

"You mean my ex?"

She nodded.

"Good luck with that."

"Actually, Tony, I need you to ask her."

Tony sighed. "This just gets better and better."

"I'm afraid I've got something else. And this one is also sensitive, so forgive me for asking it."

Tony braced himself.

"Yinka told me that you're receiving treatment for dissociative amnesia disorder. Is this true?"

"It is."

"Does Maul know?"

"I hope not."

"Good. Let's keep it that way."

"Why?"

"If Maul's lawyers find out you have been suffering from any form of amnesia, they will have a case for arguing that you are an unreliable witness. They'll conclude that if you're being treated for amnesia, you cannot be trusted to remember what happened in relation to your conversations and interactions."

"That's easy to answer."

"Is it?"

"Yes, it is. My amnesia is localised, not generalised."

"Meaning?"

"Meaning, I don't remember details around a particular trauma I suffered as a boy, as opposed to not remembering anything from my past. There's a huge difference."

"And this is psychologically verifiable?"

"It's 101-stuff when it comes to my condition. My therapist discussed it with me several months ago - as soon as she saw what was really going on."

Nadiya smiled for the first time during the call. She said, "I'll have Hamish study the standard psychology textbook, DSM-5 I think it's called, and provide some wording around that."

Tony snatched a tissue out of a box nearby and mopped up his spilled coffee. As he removed the last drops, he asked, "What's the next step in the legal process?"

"If things go like they usually do, Maul will get fed up with our refusals to come to a resolution and instruct his lawyer to issue a claim in the court. This will effectively mark the beginning of the case and we will have one month to agree our defence."

"And after that?"

"After that, we will either have to settle out of court, which happens in the majority of cases, or take it to trial."

"If it goes to trial, when will that be?"

"Probably a year from now."

Tony shook his head. "That's a big chunk of my time and finances wasted on all this."

"Try not to let it worry you, Tony."

"But I *am* worried. It feels like his word against mine. I don't see any other solution but to settle. But that's the last thing I want to do. If I do that, he's won."

"Tony, I've been doing this a long time."

"I know. I'm sorry."

Nadiya continued. "There'll be a stage quite soon in which both parties will need to disclose everything they have to each other. When they see that we have a paper trail that undermines Maul's document, that may change the goalposts."

"Will they have to hand over the original document?"

"Yes."

"Do you have faith in your handwriting person?"

"I do have faith in him, yes. However, the difficulty is that lawyers have recently been advocating caution when it comes to the testimony of handwriting experts."

"Then why are we bothering with him?"

"When he gets the original, he'll subject the ink and paper to forensic analysis for purposes of dating. So, it won't be a waste of time and money, Tony. Not at all."

"Sorry, Nadiya."

"That's okay. You're under a lot of pressure. You just get on with what you're good at and I'll do the same. Hopefully, we'll have good news at some point soon."

They ended the call.

Tony opened his laptop and began to type an email.

Sorry about this, Renée, but I have another favour to ask of you, on top of locating the paper trail, my legal team are asking you to be a witness concerning our dinners with Maul...

Even as he typed, he knew what she would say.

29

THE EMAIL

And, as it happened, Tony was right. It took a full week before she replied, but the following Friday Renée's answer dropped into his inbox like a grenade. The tagline said it all. "NO CHANCE." Tony emailed Nadiya and shared the bad news.

I've received Renee's answer. Something along the lines that it would be over her dead body... And she still hasn't sent the paper trail. It's lucky my agent came good.

Tony was about to close the laptop and go for a swim downstairs, when he noticed another email had just arrived in his inbox. It was titled, "The Queen who Survived."

The email address was from a university department.

The sender was a professor.

He clicked on the message.

Hi Tony (if I may).

My name is Tita Nakamuru. I received your email address from your host on the late show. She and I are old friends from High School days. She said you wouldn't mind her giving it to me, given our shared passion for the history of Queen Catherine Parr.

I'm a professor of history on the West Coast and I'm writing a book about Catherine Parr. I heard you on TV talking about your new house and its history. I was hooked. I knew about Catherine Parr's other residences. These, as you will know, are:

The royal palaces (of course).

Chelsea.

Hanworth.

Sudeley castle.

But I had no knowledge of the Royal Manor House on the site of your property. This is a vital new story arc. From what I can piece together, it's quite possible that Sir Thomas Seymour and Queen Catherine met there. Although the distance from London must have meant some discomfort with the travelling, I think it also would have allowed them to meet without fear of being seen. I'm proposing that Mary Seymour was probably conceived at one of these trysts. I'm planning to write a book about her too.

If you're willing and free, I'd love to meet you and discuss these things. Maybe over dinner? On me?

I could fly to New York and meet you when you're not filming. I really think we'd both find it interesting.

Please let me know your thoughts.

Kind regards,

Tita.

PS. I hope you like oysters!

Tony sighed.

He texted his TV host.

Briony. What the heck do you think you're doing sharing

my email address with Tita?

(Angry face)

Who is she? What's she like? Can I trust her? And what's this about me liking oysters? Is that flirtatious?

(Smiley face)

Tony only had to wait a minute before the reply came. It was a link to Tita's university profile.

When Tony saw her photo, all the indignation left. Tita was stunning. She had slicked-back black hair with a sharp centre parting and an edgy topknot. She was ten years younger than Tony but looked younger still. Her dark eyes, brown skin, and finely defined eyebrows suggested her family might have been Latin American. But there was something else: the way her top knot was held in place by what looked like ornate chopsticks, that suggested a Far Eastern vibe. The cool clothes she was wearing, along with the bangles and beads, just added to her uniqueness. She was beautiful.

As Tony read about her research interests and publications, he became more and more open to her invitation. Normally, he would have dismissed such overtures. He received so many that he had Wendy provide a standard refusal. But this all felt very different. His host on the late show had confidence in Tita and, if he was honest, he thought she was attractive. Most of all, they had a shared passion, an obsession with Catherine Parr. Even the mention of the Queen's name had resurrected a sense of homesickness for the Old Rectory. During his first months in New York, he had suppressed it. Now, with Tita's email, it surfaced with such force that he wanted to talk to her about the house.

He typed his answer.

Hi Tita.

Great to hear from you. I'd love to meet and discuss what I know about the history of my new home. I'd also love to hear what you have learned. I'm sure you know a lot more than I do.

I am filming for the next four months. How about a Saturday evening after my stint ends late April - before I'm scheduled to return to the UK in the summer?

Tita's reply came just as Tony was preparing to close his laptop.

She had written a smiley face.

This was followed by some suggestions for their meetup.

A Saturday evening in early May.

One of her favourite restaurants, on board an old, converted steamboat on the Hudson River.

A private room.

The chef's speciality ... oysters.

(Smiley face).

And that was that.

Tony had a dinner date.

30

THE RESTORATION

Ella contacted Tony mid-April, just as Central Park was beginning to show off its palette of magnolia, cherry, violet, yellow, and green. She suggested a videocall. They arranged a time. When Ella's face appeared, Tony could see that she had a full head of hair. Cropped and styled, yes. But thickening everywhere.

"You like it?" she asked, placing one hand beneath her chin while sweeping back her head.

"I love it, Ella. You're looking so well."

"Thanks in part to you."

She saw the questioning look on his face.

"This project... it's giving me such a lift. Something to get up for. I really think it's helping me get better."

"I'm so pleased," Tony said.

Ella shook her head and said, "Sorry! This call isn't about me. Let me show you the gardens first."

She took her phone outside and showed him the grounds. Tony could not believe the transformation. Lawns cut.

Edges trimmed. Fruit trees pruned. Yew trees planted and clipped. Even the old beach tree seemed to be coming back to life.

"We've finished the Queen's Walk," Ella said. "I recall you saying that its four corners were marked by boxed yews. So that's what we've done, recapturing how it must have looked."

"You've done a brilliant job," he said.

"The walk ends at the large yew tree to the left of the apple tree over there. That's the oldest yew in the garden. It's a Tudor yew, over five hundred years old. It's been growing all this time in the shade of the taller trees. It's magnificent."

Tony imagined Queen Catherine Parr walking with her ladies-in-waiting around the garden, pausing at the end of the walk and admiring the evergreen foliage of the tree. Today, its broad crown was bowed with age. But then its needles must have been a fresh and vibrant green, and its bark smooth, fluted, and reddish brown. Brown with a tinge of purple. The colour of royalty.

"Then there's the interior," she said.

She was in the hallway of the house now.

A long oak chest stood to the left, next to the freshly painted wall. The front of it was covered in ornate, floral carvings. It was about four-feet high and stood on a new carpet that ran along the length of the stone floor towards the first steps of the staircase.

"The drawing room," Ella said as she crossed the threshold of the first door to the left.

Tony gasped.

"We knocked the wall down. We were lucky. The walls on the other side of the hallway are made of stone and from the original Manor House. You wouldn't know from the plaster and paint. But they are. This side, however, they were made of wood."

"It looks so much better," Tony said. "I love the shelves, the lights, chairs, tables, curtains, everything."

"It's all Victorian," she said.

"You've put in a new fireplace."

"Old, actually."

Ella continued her tour, taking him into the dining room. She had found a long mahogany dining table and chairs. The room, with its working fireplace, looked fit for a royal.

"I love it!"

"I'm so pleased."

"You've made the place look uncluttered, yet you've also made it look grand, but not too grand. I don't know how you've done it, but it's magical. I absolutely adore it!"

"Thank you."

Ella walked out into the hallway and on to the second door to the right, covered by the green baize that signalled the separation of the servant's quarters from the private rooms.

"I thought we could keep the door," she said.

She walked into a small reception room with a row of small handbells hanging just beneath the ceiling on the far wall. Each bell had a stone weight suspended beneath it.

"Thought I'd keep those too," she said, pointing at the bells. "They're original. The weights kept them ringing so that the servants would get to them in time."

"I'm guessing each bell was for a particular room," Tony said.

"That's right. It must have been a large household in the

Victorian era. Lots of servants."

She passed through another door into the kitchen.

"I've kept the aga, but everything else is new. It wasn't possible in the end to have a Victorian kitchen. All my design attempts failed. So, I've gone for something that looks old-fashioned but has state-of-the-art accessories without parading their modernity."

"It's excellent, Ella. I love the cupboards and worksurfaces, and the paintwork and flooring."

"You sure? We still have time ..."

"It's all good."

Ella showed the redecorated snug beyond the kitchen before taking him back through the old servant's quarters to a cloakroom area – an outer room with a toilet beyond.

"Victorian toilet?" he enquired.

"Armitage Shanks," she replied with a giggle.

"Just like school," Tony said.

"I can replace it if you like."

"No need, Ella. In any case, the toilet I used most at school was private even if it was cold. It was the only room at school where I could lock out the world."

She passed through a back door into a stone-paved courtyard. A few steps to the right and she bowed, taking the camera closer to what looked like a hole in the ground.

"This is a Tudor well," she said. "You may not have noticed it before. It was covered by a lot of rubbish. Anyway, I've taken the liberty of testing the water. Mister Musgrave says its source is in the hills. He says you've got your own supply of fresh water."

"Is it usable?"

"It's as good as Harrogate," she said.

"Harrogate?"

"Harrogate has the best water in England."

She stood and directed the camera at some outhouses across the courtyard. "Those are the Victorian laundry rooms," she said. "They were filled with all sorts of clutter and debris. We have cleared them out and cleaned them up. Fresh lick of paint. Everything. You can use them for whatever you like in the future."

"I won't have any clutter," Tony said.

"And that's really all I need to show you for now. Mister Musgrave and his team are working their way through the upstairs rooms, including the attic. It'll be another three to four months before I can show you what that looks like."

She headed through the baize-covered door into the hallway, then to the drawing room. Standing in front of the windows, she revealed the lawn where the ghost had appeared. A sadness swept over him as Tony sat at the table in at his kitchen nook in New York. He longed for the Old Rectory. Longed with an intensity he had not felt since he was a child. A child sent away to boarding school, missing his home, bedroom, books, and toys. Clinging to his teddy underneath the bedsheets at night. Stifling the sobs. Trying to process the sense of being in exile. Far away from the familiar, the safe.

It took Tony a few moments before he pulled himself together, castigating himself for being so lucky and yet so ungrateful. When he composed himself to speak, the camera was still trained on the lawn, with the apple tree in the centre of the frame.

"Thank you, Ella."

His voice was soft.

"You okay, Tony?"

"I miss it," he said. "Don't get me wrong, I'm very aware how lucky I am to be doing what I'm doing, staying where I'm staying. But I miss it. The Old Rectory. You're making an incredible home, Ella. I will never be able to thank you enough."

Ella reversed the camera again.

There was the hint of a tear in each eye, a reddening of the face. "It's a real pleasure, Tony. I can't tell you how much I'm enjoying it. This house has an amazing atmosphere."

"I think that's why I miss it," Tony said. Then he asked, "Are you on schedule?"

"We're exactly halfway, and yes, we are. The second phase has its own challenges. There's a lot of work to make the attic into a functioning living space. Then there's the work on the exterior."

Tony nodded.

"When do you think you'll be home?" she asked.

"I was hoping sometime soon, but that's not going to be possible. I'm going to have to fly to the West coast and do a cameo for a new feature film after I'm done with the late-night TV show in Manhattan. So, it may be late July before I get back."

"You must be exhausted."

"I am beginning to feel tired."

"What's the place like where you're staying?"

"Empty."

"What do you mean?"

"It's Central Park West. The view is fantastic, and there's a fitness room, but the place ... Put it like this, there are five bedrooms and bathrooms for just me. It's all very ... soulless.

Like my lawyer's offices in London, only limestone instead of steel."

Ella frowned.

"I know I'm very privileged, but I just can't wait to get back now. I miss the garden. And I just wish I was with you watching the restoration of the house. I feel like I'm missing out..."

Ella's frown deepened. "I'm sure the time will fly, what with all the work you're doing. And don't forget, absence makes the heart grow fonder. Isn't that what people say?"

Tony nodded.

"Please take care of yourself," she said.

"Same."

Ella left.

But the ache remained.

31

A DREAM

That night, Tony was surprised to have a dream. He saw the house just after it had been rebuilt in the Queen Anne style. There was a commotion in the hallway. A young man was assembling the servants, preparing them for someone who had just arrived in a carriage.

"Have the blanket ready, Mrs Seaton," he said. "My father must be protected against the cold. Lead him straight into the drawing room and let him sit beside the fire."

Mrs Seaton drew aside the frayed edge of the rug she was holding, as if folding the corner of a page.

The bell rang and a servant opened the door.

A clergyman about twice the young master's age, and dressed in a black cape, shuffled over the threshold. His limbs were almost unable to bear what little weight he had.

When the servants saw him, they gasped. One of the younger maids began to cry.

"Hush now, Lizzy," Mrs Seaton said. "Can't you see the rector has enough on his plate without you adding to his woes."

The rector crossed over into the vestibule and the front door was closed behind him. As the carriage left the grounds, the younger man stepped forward to offer a greetings

"It is good to have you home, Father."

The older man squinted. His face was pale. There was grey-flecked stubble on his chin and throat.

"Is that you, my son?"

The lenses of his spectacles were grimy, and he seemed to find it hard to focus on his surroundings.

"It is Peregrine."

"Where is John?" the rector asked.

Lizzy put her hand to her mouth to mute her cry.

"He is not here, Father."

"Not here? Then, where is he? He should be here, as you are, to welcome his father home."

"Come this way, Father," the son said, taking the rector's hat and scarf, passing them to Lizzy.

There was more shuffling.

As one of the servants stoked the fire, the rector headed to a chair near the hearth. Mrs Seaton draped the cloak around his emaciated and fragile frame. Then he began the task of sitting, taking care in his descent, aided all the way down to the cushion by his son.

When the servants departed, the rector stared at the logs crackling in the grate. He whispered, "I do not understand why John is not here to see me. It is so unlike him..."

"Father," Peregrine said.

"What is it, boy?"

"Do you not remember?"

"Remember what?"

"What happened to John?"

The lines on the rector's forehead protruded as he strained to understand what his son was saying.

"Oh..." the rector cried as one of the burning logs cracked in the hearth. He shuddered as if he had been wounded by a fiery splinter shot from the spitting wood.

He remembered.

He uttered a deep groan, like the low moan of the wind in the garret of the house.

"He is..."

He could not bring himself to say it.

Peregrine helped him. "He is in heaven."

The rector's shoulders drooped. "Remind me."

"It was when we were at Winchester College... the great swim in the Itchen. There were over a hundred swimmers. John was struck with cramp, just yards from the shore. No one saw him.... He drowned. His body was discovered in shallow water..." Peregrine was whispering now. "But by then, all was lost."

The older man emitted a faint cry.

"How ... how old was he?"

"Sixteen..."

The two men sat in silence.

Then, after a while, the younger of the two began to utter some words. He seemed to be almost in a trance, as if he was not quite there. The older man stirred.

He cupped an ear. "What did you say?"

Peregrine spoke again. His voice stronger now.

"I'll make me pinions light
I'll fly a secret flight
And mount on the wings of the storm

And if my love be cold
My arms shall soon enfold
And bid his breast with love again be warm ..."

"Where is that from?" the father asked.

"I wrote it."

"Speak up!"

"I wrote it," he repeated, louder this time. "It's part of a collection I'm composing called *The Pain of Memory*."

The father looked surprised. "I'm glad you're writing. It's beautiful, my son. Truly beautiful."

"Thank you, Papa."

The old man removed his glasses. He tried to give them a wipe with his rug, but he could not seem to align the movement of his hands with the desires of his heart.

"Here," the son said, taking the spectacles.

He sat back down and took a handkerchief from his pocket. In slow motions, he applied pressure to the lenses, wiping away the dirt, staining the white cotton.

He returned them.

"Thank you."

The old man saw clearly now.

"How long have I been gone?"

"Two years, Father."

"Is it really that long?"

The son nodded.

"What was I thinking?"

"Father, it is understandable. You were trying to get away from the pain. Everything in this house reminded you of..."

"Of John's absence," the rector interrupted.

"Not just John's..."

"Then who else?"

The son was the one to utter a groan this time.

He said one word.

"Mama..."

The rector whimpered.

"How long ago?"

"Twenty-four years."

"What happened?"

"It was after John was born... several days later... dropsy..."

The rector strained his eyes and face, as if he had been dazzled by a great light.

"The chancel of the church!" He cried.

"Yes, Father. Mother is buried there."

The rector shook his head. "1756... terrible winter. It was so cold and dark..." There were tears running down his face. "Sarah. My beloved Sarah," he said, his body trembling.

When he was calm again, his son said, "That is why you left us all here. You couldn't bear it any longer."

"What?"

"This house. Every chamber, every piece of furniture, every nook and cranny provoked your suffering."

A cold wind blasted against the windows of the drawing room. The flames in the grate trembled.

The son continued. "You decided to go and live at the Rectory in More Critchil."

"Then why have I come back?"

"You asked to."

The rector strained his mind again. "Was I sick?"

"You were homesick."

"What do you mean?"

"You told me that you longed to be back in this house."

The lights were coming on now. "Ah yes, and I kept

getting a fever, did I not?"

"Yes, Father. The Rectory at More Critchil is built on low, damp soil. Some of your predecessors there have succumbed to a fatal ague. It was not the respite you had imagined."

The rector nodded.

The son said, "I am glad you are home. The servants are too. The whole village is pleased."

The flicker of a smile appeared on the son's face.

"You know what they say about you in the village?"

The rector shook his head.

"That you are a kind and caring man. Learned, but not aloof. No one will speak ill of you."

The rector ignored the compliment. He asked, "Who has been looking after the church while I have been sick?"

"The curate."

The old man looked doubtful.

"The one you say preaches like a Methodist," his son said.

"Ah, yes. He is full of enthusiasm. I am less fanatical. More reserved. More tedious."

They both smiled.

"In the pulpit," the son said. "He works himself up into such a great frenzy of intemperate passions that I do not think it will be long before he finds himself in an asylum."

"Now, now, my son."

"I'm not the only one who says so."

The rector pretended to show a measure of disapproval. Then he shook his head again and smiled. He opened his hands, beckoning with his thin fingers to the boy.

The son hurried to his father and knelt. He leaned into his father's chest, moving with care, nestling into the brittle and skeletal frame, his hands resting on his father's back.

The older man sighed.
The younger cried.
His father whispered in his ear, "Home at last."

32

THE LONGING

Before he had left for the States in January, Tony had agreed with Shree that they would conduct virtual counselling sessions when needed. After four months in New York, with a punishing schedule of daytime interviews and late-night shows, he could sense the tell-tale symptoms of unrest. He needed to see Shree's face and hear her voice.

One morning in late April, as a thick mist enveloped the tops of the trees in Central Park, Tony sat at the window with his laptop. He took a gulp of coffee and then clicked the link Shree had sent. Seconds later, Shree admitted him to the session.

"Tony! How's the TV work?"

"It's good. Challenging sometimes, especially when I'm performing my Agony Aunt role."

"I've been following some of the shows," she said. "That section about dreams you do each night... your interpretations have been brilliant. You've been getting rave reviews."

"Thank you."

"Speaking of which, have you been dreaming?"

"Once."

"About the house?"

"Yes."

"I thought you only dreamed when you visited?"

"That's true. But Ella, who's the site manager for the work on the house, she took me on a virtual tour. I dreamed that night. It really took me by surprise."

"Did you write it down?"

"I did. And I had the same experience. The house seemed to be telling its story through me."

"Were you back in Tudor times?"

"No. Later."

"When?"

"Eighteenth century. George Bingham, the longest serving rector. He died in the year 1800." Tony took another sip of coffee before continuing. "It was all pretty sad."

Shree waited.

"He seems to have left the Rectory to recuperate, due to the death of both his wife after childbirth and his son in a drowning accident at Winchester College."

Shree shook her head. "That's awful."

"He kept catching a fever in the Rectory he went to stay in, due to a problem there with damp. He came back after several years to be reunited with his son and his house."

Shree waited until he finished, then said, "Sounds like your dream was about loss and memory."

Tony nodded. "And writing..."

Shree let him to explain.

"I knew the father was a writer, but it seems the son,

Peregrine Bingham, was a poet. He published a book of poems called *The Pain of Memory* not long after his dad died."

"How has your dream made you feel?"

"It's strange. You know that sensation of having something on the tip of your tongue all the time?"

She nodded.

"It's like that. It's like I'm almost about to see something. Flashes of memory. To do with my mother and father. The accident. And the trauma of hearing about it."

"The pain of memory," she said.

"The pain of memory," Tony repeated.

She waited again until she knew he was done, then she asked, "How's the restoration going?"

"Ella and her teams are working their way through each room, and each section of the garden. From what she's shown me, it's beginning to look amazing."

Shree said, "I was very struck by the house in the last session we had in the driveway. You must miss it."

Tony nodded.

"What's up, Tony?"

"I've never felt this way before... It's a house for heaven's sake!"

He paused.

"I feel homesick."

"Take your time."

"I have forged such a strong connection with it. I've been trying to work out why. I think some of it may have to do with so many of the owners and occupants being writers."

Tony watched the mist begin to clear outside and the tops of the trees emerge from a soupy fog.

"Actually Shree, I should tell you about another dream. I had it the last time I visited the house, just before flying out here. Con came round and was surprised to hear me listening to some old recordings of Dame Clara Butt..."

"Clara who?"

"Butt."

"Never heard of her."

"She was the most remarkable female singer of the early twentieth century. The Barbara Streisand of her day. A contralto with a unique range. The best contraltos have a range of two octaves. Clara could cover three. She was a vocal magician."

"And you know of her how?"

"My father had his father's gramophone records of her songs. He used to play them all the time when I was a boy. Before I was sent away to school, her songs filled the house. When Con heard me listening to them, he said that Clara had done a house concert in the Old Rectory. That night, the house shared its memory of it. It was stunning. I've been listening to those songs again ever since,"

Tony took another sip of coffee and watched the sun breaking through the clouds, dismissing the last wisps clinging like gossamer to the trees in the park below.

"It's like you said before, the house is helping me to remember. It's reconnecting me to my buried past. To the happy times before I was sent away to school."

The great park was bathed in sunlight now.

Shree said, "There are houses that haunt and there are houses that heal. Yours is a house that heals."

"Which is probably why I'm experiencing this intense feeling of homesickness out here."

Shree looked at him, concern in her eyes. "Are you managing your stress levels?"

"I'm worried about Maul. He's issued a claim in court. My lawyers are preparing a defence. I feel tired to be honest. It's hard work out here. I'm lonely. And I'm angry with Maul."

"Do you have anything to distract you?"

"Maybe."

"Who is she?"

He laughed. "A rather beautiful academic called Tita has invited me to dinner. She's a professor of history, writing a book about Catherine Parr. Wants to talk about the house."

A smile broke out on Shree's face.

"My host is a friend of hers. She says Tita's single. Charming. Charismatic. And very clever. When I asked why she wasn't married, she said it was because she had never found anyone who shared the same passion for history, especially Tudor history."

"A lovely distraction!" Shree exclaimed.

"She's very different from Renée. From Tita's emails, and from what Briony's told me, she seems lovely. Warm too. I saw an interview she did on YouTube. When she smiles, it's like someone's just switched on the Christmas lights."

Shree laughed.

Then she checked the time on the call and looked at Tony, her dark eyes shining.

"Tony, I believe you are close to a therapeutic breakthrough, so take special care of yourself. When you start to feel the pain of memory, you may feel fragile. If you need me, text me and I'll get to you at the earliest opportunity."

Tony could already sense the floodwalls he had built over

many years beginning to shake. He knew she was right. It would not be long before bricks began to crumble, and holes appear.

"If you have time after your dinner date, send me a brief message telling me how it goes with...."

"Tita," he said.

"Yes, with Tita."

"I will."

Shree waved.

Then left the meeting.

Pouring himself another coffee, Tony chose a track from the playlist on his phone.

Music began to play through the kitchen speakers.

Dame Clara's rich and velvety voice filled the apartment.

"There's no place like home."

33

THE DINNER

Early in May, Tita came for dinner. She looked even more stunning than Tony remembered from her photograph.

"This place is gigantic... and luxurious!" she cried, wandering around Tony's rooms, opening every door, admiring every chamber. "When I was a child, I never imagined being somewhere like this. There's so much space."

"And don't forget the view," Tony said.

Tony escorted her to the balcony. They leaned out over a steel railing and watched a young couple having a picnic in the park. Their Yellow Labrador had her nose in their picnic hamper. She was tossing out the contents, searching for biscuits.

"You were talking about your childhood," Tony said. "If you don't mind me asking, where was that?"

"Mexico City, in a barrio called Tepito. Our house was very simple. We had nothing materially."

"Does your family still live there?"

"Not in the same place. From my first teaching job, I've lived in college digs, saving as much of my salary as possible. A few years ago, I bought my family a home in a safer barrio."

"That was kind," Tony said.

An ambulance flew past on the road below, its sirens bawling at cars and walkers.

"It was just in time. My father lost his job just afterwards. He felt ashamed. I was scared the new home would make that worse, but he said he felt very proud..." Tita's eyes watered. "Look at me, sharing all my family's secrets and we've only just met."

"I take that as a compliment," Tony said as he led her back inside his suite of rooms.

Tony phoned his chauffeur and ten minutes later, after Tita had freshened up, Angelo drove them from Central Park to the banks of the Hudson. Tita talked with Angelo all the way, finding out about his family, where he lived, where he had come from before they moved to New York. By the time they arrived at the river, she knew more about him after one journey than Tony had from hundreds.

"I don't know how he gets by," Tita said as they climbed the gangplank of a refurbished steamboat. "He and his family haven't had a proper holiday since they moved here."

"I can do something about that," Tony said as they walked through the bar. "I'll invite him and his extended family to have my Central Park rooms for a week, with all the amenities, and all expenses paid. As a thank you for all he's done."

"I love it!"

The manager escorted them to their seats in a room with a single table, its window overlooking the Hudson.

"This is nice and private," Tony said.

A waiter arrived with a low-rimmed silver platter covered in ice, with oysters lining the circumference. As Tita smiled, Tony noticed the dark, crisp, and distinct outline of her lipstick.

"Tip the oyster to your lips and suck the juice," she said. "Then take your time to taste and relish the meat. Don't hurry it. Too many people are too quick to swallow."

Tita demonstrated the manoeuvre. When she had finished the last drop of liqueur, she said, "Did you know that New York City used to be called the Big Oyster?"

"I thought it was called the Big Apple."

"Not always. Between the 1600s and 1800s, New Yorkers harvested oysters around the coast. Some of them were the size of dinner plates. They used to sell them from carts, in much the same way street vendors sell hot dogs today."

"You make history interesting," Tony said.

"Speaking of history," she said, "tell me about your house."

"Do you believe in ghosts?" Tony asked.

"I'm from Mexico City!"

"Then you'll understand when I say that I believe a ghost drew me to the house."

Tony told her the story and she listened without either eating or interrupting. "Every time I visit, I have a dream in which the house relates a part of its history."

He began to share what he knew of the house's past as the next course arrived. More oysters. This time roasted with cheese and in eggplant broth.

"I'm slightly surprised that you're such a fan of Queen Catherine Parr," Tony said, after finishing his story.

"Why?"

"Well, you're from a Catholic country."

"I'm also half Japanese. My father taught me that one kind word can warm three winter months. So, my faith is defined by kindness, not by quarrelling."

"I like that," Tony said.

In fact, he loved it.

She took a sip of rosé, then asked, "When are you thinking of returning to your house in England?"

"It's looking like late July, after my filming."

"Will the restoration be finished?"

"Indoors, yes. The exterior will take a few more months. We're looking to complete in September."

Tita clapped her hands.

"What's up?"

"My sabbatical begins in September."

"I'm very happy to hear that."

"No, I mean, I could come and visit!"

Tita paused.

"If you're okay with that..."

"I'm not okay with that," Tony said.

Tita looked crestfallen.

"I'm more than okay."

She smiled.

"In fact, I'm delighted."

She laughed.

And so did Tony.

What seemed like minutes later, but which was in fact several hours, Tita asked for the check.

Tony shook his head. "I know I may be old-fashioned, but I'd like to pay for this. Besides, it would comfort me to think that you'd be saving money for your family."

"That's very kind, Tony."

Tony attended to the card machine.

"What about your family, Tony?"

"My parents died when I was little. I'm an only child."

"I'm very sorry to hear that."

"Thanks."

He pocketed the receipt and texted Angelo.

They rose and walked out into the bar towards the exit. The manager met them at the door.

"I see you're donating all your oyster shells to the reef project," Tita said to her.

"We are madame."

"I'm very glad."

They walked down the gang plank.

"What was that about the oyster shells?" Tony asked.

"They're one of nature's most effective defences against erosion and storm damage. There's a huge drive to get them put all around the city's shores here."

"I had no idea."

Angelo pulled up and they climbed into the back of the limo. Tita sat close to Tony for the first two minutes, then leaned forward to talk to her new friend. "Angelo, I have some news for you. Tony is going to lend you and your family his suite of rooms so that you and your loved ones can have a week's holiday at his expense!"

"Is it true, boss?"

"It's true."

"No, really... it's too much. And anyway, I won't be allowed... not someone like me..."

"They will allow it," Tita exclaimed, "Or your boss

will kick up a big fuss. And if that fuss is too English and restrained, then I will add some hot Mexican sauce to it!"

"She's right," Tony said. "I will cause a stink!"

"You see!" Tita cried. "Mister Tony will make a big smell!"

When they arrived at the entrance of Tony's building, he indicated to Angelo to stop. He was about to ask Tita if she wanted Angelo to take her back to her hotel when he saw something. A man standing beneath an illuminated lamppost just down the street.

Tony rubbed his eyes.

"Where to, boss?" Angelo asked.

Tony did not respond.

His heart was racing.

His chest tightening.

"Tony!" Tita said.

"You okay, boss?" Angelo asked.

Tony stared at the man under the streetlight. He was leaning against the park fence with a cigarette hanging from his lip, like something from an old movie. He was wearing a long coat. And on his head, a familiar beret.

34

THE SPOON

When he came to his senses, Tony had no idea how he had traversed the distance between Angelo's car and his rooms, nor how he had managed to get onto one of his five beds. When he wiped his eyes, he saw Angelo standing by the bedside with a glass of water in his hand. Tita was perched next to his torso, holding his hand, rubbing his fingers with hers, a concerned look on her face.

"Do you need a doctor, boss?" Angelo asked.

"I don't think so."

"What happened, Tony?" Tita asked.

"I saw someone and panicked."

"Who?"

"A guy who's been giving me some grief."

"What kind of grief?"

"He fabricated a story about me stealing his ideas for my first book. He's filed a claim in the courts."

Tony sat up and rested his back against the pillows.

"I thought that coming here to New York... that I'd get

some respite from him. But he's started doing what he did outside my London home... stalking and intimidating me..."

"Qué cabrón!"

"Come again?" Angelo said.

"Bastard!"

Angelo nodded. He thought for a moment before asking, "Do you have a photo of this man?"

"Why?"

"So, we can recognise him," Tita said.

"I can find one."

Tony reached for his phone.

"That's him," he said, pointing to a stock picture.

Tita took Tony's phone. "Matt Maul," she muttered. "Never heard of him. That beret makes him look stupid..."

"It's part of the act," Tony said.

Angelo conducted a search on his phone. "That him, boss?"

Tony nodded.

"I am going to alert security downstairs," Angelo said. "And at the theatre too. Everyone will have a copy of this picture. We will all look out for you, boss. We've got your back."

"That's very kind of you, Angelo. But please... don't land me in any more trouble. I've got enough on my plate..."

"I won't, boss."

"And one more thing..."

Angelo nodded.

"How soon can you spend that week here?"

"As soon as you need me to, boss."

"How about Monday?"

"That only gives him tomorrow to get ready," Tita said.

"I can do it," Angelo said.

"Are you sure?"

"Yes, Miss Tita."

Angelo looked at Tony. "Where will you stay, boss?"

"The Plaza. I love it."

"Will you be safe?"

"Don't worry about me, Angelo. I'm resourceful."

"Like Kevin in *Home Alone 2*!" Tita exclaimed.

After Angelo left, Tita gripped Tony's hand. "So, you saw Maul outside when we returned?"

Tony nodded.

"And you're sure it was him?"

"Certain."

"What's he doing here?"

"It's the lawsuit. He's trying to unsettle me. Both sets of lawyers have been going at it since January, but Maul is resorting to some dirty and underhand tricks now."

"I don't understand," Tita said.

"What?"

"What's his problem?"

"I'm not a psychologist," Tony said. "But analysis aside, I'd say he's a very angry, greedy, and lazy human being. He thinks he's entitled to wealth when he's done nothing to deserve it. He sees me as his passport to the riches he lost."

"He was once wealthy?"

"Yes, he was. Then he started getting flashy with his money and frittered it all away."

"Why didn't he just write another bestseller?"

"It's a long story."

"You've been through so much," Tita said. "I'm surprised you're functioning at all."

"I have a great therapist in London. Shree's been helping me deal with my stuff."

"Is she good?"

"I don't think I'd be here if it wasn't her."

"Shree is a lovely name."

"She's a lovely person too," Tony said.

"Are you two ..."

"Dating?"

Tita blushed.

"No. Shree is in a relationship with a woman called Ana."

"That name sounds Japanese!"

"It is..."

"Is what?"

"Japanese."

"Maybe I'll meet her someday."

"You probably will if you come and stay during your sabbatical." Tony grinned as he reminded her.

Tita blushed again.

"I did kind of invite myself," she said.

"I don't mind at all."

Tita manoeuvred the pillows to make Tony more comfortable. "Would you like me to stay with you tonight?"

Tony nodded.

He was about to speak again when there was a knock on the door.

It was Angelo.

"He's gone, boss."

"What did you do, Angelo?"

"I phoned my cousin Marco."

"Who's Marco?"

"My cousin, boss."

"You already said that."

Angelo tapped his nose.

"Okay, okay. Just so long as he didn't do anything that's going to come back and bite me in the six o'clock."

"Six o'clock?"

"His ass!" Tita said.

Angelo smiled.

"Could you get Miss Tita's things from her hotel?" Tony asked. "She's staying here tonight."

"Of course, boss."

Tita gave Angelo the directions and her room key.

"And Angelo, you and your family can move in here Monday morning. I'll make sure it's all okay."

Angelo said thank you and left.

Half an hour later, Tony was beginning to feel drowsy when Angelo returned and handed over Tita's case. While she changed in the bathroom, Tony pulled the sheets over his head and buried his face into the pillow. As he drifted towards sleep, he remembered lonely nights away at school when he was a boy, holding his teddy beneath the rough, over-washed sheets in his dormitory.

Tita climbed into the bed.

She turned the lights down.

"Thank you," Tony said.

"You're welcome," she whispered, wrapping her arms around his back.

"When will I see you again?" he asked.

"In England, September, when my sabbatical starts. If you'll have me to stay..."

"I would love that," he whispered.

"I may be gone when you wake up," Tita said. "Angelo

wants to take me to JFK early."

Tony managed to nod as he slipped to the edge of sleep.

Tita kissed him on the back.

One, light, lingering kiss.

"I've got your back, Tony."

Then he was gone.

And when he woke the next morning, so was Tita.

35

THE BATTLEPLAN

After hearing about the incident with Maul, Nadiya and Hamish flew out to New York. Tony gave them two of the empty rooms overlooking Central Park. On their last morning, they held a conference together in the dining room. It was a cloudless June day and the trees of Central Park seemed to be greener than ever.

"Good day for flying," he muttered.

"Thank goodness," Hamish said.

"You don't like planes?"

"Hate them."

"What's on the agenda?" Tony asked.

"Some bad news," Nadiya replied.

Tony braced himself.

"After the disclosure from both legal teams, we received the original copy of Maul's document, the one we've been waiting for." She drew it from her folder.

Tony studied it.

"If you observe, it's a page of lined A4 paper with Maul's

handwriting on it. You know the content. It purports to be a summary of ideas that he claims he presented to you, using this very document, at one of your dinners fifteen years ago."

Tony shook his head.

"I know, Tony. We realise it's fake but proving that is another matter. We've had our handwriting expert on it since we received this version. We've just read his final report."

"And?"

"It's inconclusive."

"Damn!"

"I know, although I warned you that this might happen. I told you there's too great a margin for error here. Assessing handwritten evidence is not a perfect science."

"What's the good news?"

"Do you remember I asked if Renée would give testimony about the dinners you had with the plaintiff?"

Tony did not need reminding.

"She refused point blank," he said.

"That was a setback. But then I got Hamish onto the one other person who was at those meals."

"You mean Maul's girlfriend."

"Hamish found her online addresses and then trawled through her social media. Turns out that Maul dumped Miss Naomi Marsh two weeks ago and she's angry."

"Livid!" Hamish added in his broad Scottish accent, nodding his head, affirming his senior.

"Tell us what happened," Nadiya said.

"I messaged her. I didn't hide who I was. No deception. Came straight out with it. Told her I was part of Mister Lawson's legal team. Invited her to have coffee."

"What did she say?" Tony asked.

"Said yes. We met the next day."

"And?"

"And she's mad about the way Maul treated her."

"Will she help?"

"She's thinking about it."

"We need more than that."

"I know we do," Nadiya said. "But we can't *force* her to cooperate. She needs to make up her mind in her own time. We can't be seen to be exercising any hint of control."

"Did she say anything about this document?"

The two lawyers looked at each other.

"She did," Hamish replied. "She confirmed off the record what we know - that Maul had not written it before or during the time of the dinners you all shared."

"Damn right!"

"Naomi also testified that Maul created this document after Christmas last year. She said he found some old paper and ink in a cupboard and forged it while she was with him. Said he's jealous that your stock is rising while his is falling."

"Then we've got him," Tony said.

"She hasn't agreed to testify yet."

"Will she?"

"Hamish is on her case."

Nadiya looked at her junior.

"I am indeed," he said.

Nadiya continued. "That brings us to our tactics."

"What are our options?"

"Option 1 is to let this go to the High Court, to contest Maul's claim there, and hope we win."

"What chance do we have of losing?"

"Even in a case like this," Nadiya replied, "we cannot

guarantee a favourable outcome."

"So, once again, it's not a perfect science."

"Exactly, and it's not a quick journey either. The trial's set for a year from now. The whole process will be very costly in terms of time, energy, and money. Seven figures, most likely."

"What's option 2?"

"You agree to come to the table to settle."

"That's absurd! I don't owe him anything."

"Tony, coming to the table doesn't mean you're admitting guilt or agreeing to give compensation to Maul. It means that we meet to discuss the possibility of an agreement."

"You mean we could get him to stop?"

"Sometimes that happens, yes."

Tony shook his head and said, "Maul will never back down. He'll come to the meeting in a highly combative mood. He'll not leave until he's got what he wants."

Tony drained his cup of coffee.

"And that's why I think we should lay down a condition," Nadiya said. "We don't meet unless we have an independent mediator, otherwise things could get very heated."

"And protracted," Hamish said.

"How protracted?"

"I've known them go on for 36 hours," Nadiya said.

"36 hours!"

"I'm afraid so. People often want to take a break to sleep, but you can lose momentum if you do that."

"Good grief!"

Nadiya looked at her watch.

"What are your instructions, Tony?"

"Option 2. Agree to a settlement meeting. I just want this

over with now. I'm sick and tired of him occupying my head and consuming space that could be given over to writing."

"And do you want a mediator?"

"I do."

"When do you want this meeting?"

"The day I fly back."

"The same day?"

"Yes."

"Are you sure?"

"Absolutely. Let's not waste a second."

"You have a date for your return?"

"It'll be the end of next month."

Tony gathered up their coffee cups.

Nadiya stood.

She was collecting her dispersed papers when she paused and said, "Everything hangs on us proving that this is fraudulent. Then it's a *loser pays* for him, not only his own costs but most of yours as well, Tony. The aim is to get Maul - and here I'm going to use the technical and legal term - *to drop hands.*"

"That would be a big slap in the face," Tony admitted.

"Speaking of a slap..." Hamish began. Nadiya shot him a glance. Either he did not see it, or he ignored it. "Have you heard of SLAPP litigation, Mister Lawson?"

"That's libel, not copyright law!" Nadiya interjected.

"What's slap?" Tony asked.

"It stands for Strategic Litigation Against Public Participation," Hamish said, keeping his eyes away from his senior. "It's used by very rich people to exert extreme pressure financially against individuals, usually with the threat of ruining them. So, you could give the plaintiff a

SLAPP, if you feel he was guilty of libel in the question he asked at the end of your TV interview with Fiona."

Tony said, "I'm afraid Maul was very careful not to accuse me directly of having stolen his ideas."

"He was," Hamish agreed. "At the same time, if that question was deemed to have damaged your reputation, if even a few people understood it as directed against you personally rather than as a general statement, then you could issue a SLAPP."

Tony said, "Giving my stalker a SLAPP sounds like bullying to me, and I vowed a long time ago that standing up to bullies would not involve me becoming a bully. So, no thanks."

Nadiya breathed a sigh of relief. She looked at her watch, put her papers in her briefcase, and stood. Hamish, blushing, mouthed the word "sorry" to his senior and followed suit.

"Thank you for your hospitality, Tony," she said. "It's been really kind of you to let us invade your private space." Turning to Hamish she said, "And don't get any ideas that this kind of luxury is normal." Seeing Hamish looking penitent, she smiled at him.

"You've both been very good company," Tony said.

The two lawyers headed into the hall, took their bags, and rode the elevator down to the exit. There a yellow cab carried them and their luggage to JFK for the flight home – Nadiya at the front of the plane, Hamish at the back.

36

THE MEDIATION

On July 29th, Tony flew back to the UK on the red eye from JFK, arriving on a cloudy, drizzly dawn at Heathrow Airport. After a quick shower and a change of clothes at the airport lounge, he drove to Yinka's offices for the meeting with Maul and his lawyers. On arrival, Yinka took him into his office and poured him a double espresso.

"You must be exhausted," he said, handing him the coffee.

"I'm just fine. Slept all the way."

"And you're sure you want to do this now? We can move for a delay if you want us to."

"No, Yinka. This boil needs to be lanced."

Just as heavy rain was starting to lash the window, Nadiya stepped into the office. She was accompanied by a man in his fifties whose pitted face seemed familiar to Tony.

"Our mediator," she said.

Offering his hand, the man said, "Pete Riley."

The penny dropped.

"You used to be a premier league referee!"

"That's right, Mister Lawson."

"Please, call me Tony."

"All right, Tony. Let me tell you how we intend to proceed. There are three rooms. The main room - the boardroom - is where we will begin. Both sides will have an opportunity to speak. Then, if there's no immediate agreement, we will split into groups, one for the plaintiff and the other for you, the defendant, to discuss adjustments to your position, in the hope you'll reach a compromise."

"I'm very doubtful that the plaintiff will let us resolve anything quickly," Tony said.

"In that case, we will continue until we reach an agreement that both parties are happy to sign."

"What happens if he's disruptive?"

"There are some ground rules. I'll set them out right at the start so that no one's in any doubt."

"I hope you've brought your whistle," Tony said. "And you may need a red not just a yellow card."

Pete smiled.

Yinka wished Tony luck.

Tony walked with Nadiya and Hamish to the boardroom where Maul was sitting with his two lawyers, shifting in his seat. He looked pale, angry, and impatient. When Tony sat down, the left side of Maul's mouth extended into a sneer.

Pete entered. He told everyone present that both sides would have a chance to speak, the plaintiff's side first.

"I want to say right at the outset that if any of you feels like walking out, I would like you to tell me. We will have a five-minute cooling process while I listen to your concerns. But no one is allowed to leave without permission until we are done. We are here until an agreement is reached. While the meetings are in play, all phones are to be switched off until the comfort and food breaks."

Maul clenched his fists.

Pete handed the floor to the two teams.

Maul's senior went first, speaking in a monotone about the claim, restating that his client was not going to settle for less than a million, and that Mister Matthew Maul had been subject to a great injustice. He then presented the handwritten document, quoted text from Tony's first book, and summarised Maul's case.

Nadiya went second. She dismissed the claim, stating that her team was prepared to pay no more than 50k, and this not as an admission of guilt, but contingent on the plaintiff going away and never making the claim again. She added that both parties would sign an agreement with a commitment to complete confidentiality.

Maul did not wait until Nadiya had finished.

"This is bollocks!" he shouted. "What more evidence do you need that he stole my ideas?"

Tony shook his head.

The mediator urged everyone to express themselves in a calm and dignified manner.

When he had the room back, the mediator gestured to Nadiya, whose hand was raised.

"Let's just think about this alleged evidence," she said, picking up the handwritten page. "We had our handwriting expert examine it, both in its photocopied and original form."

"Yes!" Maul shouted. "And they said they couldn't prove it was a forgery, as you keep claiming!"

"That's true," Nadiya said, her tone calm, her voice

measured. "The expert's report was inconclusive, as you rightly state. But that cuts both ways. It cannot be said to be a forgery. But it also cannot be said to be authentic. So, the evidence should be dismissed!"

Maul's senior started to chuckle. "I doubt that argument would stand up in court."

The mediator intervened. "I think it's time to disperse," he said. "Let's form into our two groups and head to our breakout rooms. Try not to be stubborn. Both parties may need to consider yielding some ground here, especially if you both want to avoid the expense of a trial. See if you can be flexible."

He handed both seniors a card as the two groups left the room. When Tony's team arrived at Nadiya's office, she leaned the card next to a pot plant in the middle of the glass table. It read,

Blessed are the hearts that can bend; they shall never be broken.

Albert Camus.

"This guy's good," Tony muttered.

They discussed various compromises for an hour. Then they went back to the boardroom where they were dismissed in less time that it took to mention them. As it turned out, Albert Camus's blessed thought failed to have any effect.

After another hour, off they went again into their smaller spaces. This time, Pete tried a different card.

A man is born gentle and weak. At death, he is hard and stiff. Therefore, the stiff and unbending is the disciple of death, and the gentle and yielding is the disciple of life.

Lao Tzu's thoughts had no effect either.

Once again, Nadiya suggested compromises. They would

offer £150k for Maul to go away.

Once again, their attempts at flexibility were refused. It seemed Maul was quite content to be a disciple of death.

After lunch, there were more inspirational cards.

The measure of intelligence is the ability to change.

Albert Einstein.

"He's going to run out of cards soon," Tony said as Nadiya closed the door to the breakout room.

On and on they went.

Beyond pizzas at 7pm.

Right up until midnight, whereupon Hamish excused himself, asked the mediator permission to leave for an hour, and disappeared from the building.

At 0100, there had been no movement at all. Nadiya's final offer, £250k, had been turned down. "Nothing less than a million!" Maul shouted, slamming his fist on the glass table.

Maul was getting fatigued now. Tony, on the other hand, was still operating with his New York body clock. It was early evening for him; he was just beginning to get a second wind.

The mediator, looking frayed at the edges himself, told them to go into their breakout rooms, saying they could have two hours together, adding that this was the last time if there was no yielding on both sides. Trying to lighten the mood, he said, "Once more unto the breach, dear friends. Once more..." But Maul dampened it with the muttered words, "Not if I can help it."

We are stubborn on vision, flexible on details.

Jeff Bezos.

As it turned out, Maul's team were stubborn on both.

At 0245, Hamish entered the office and whispered in Nadiya's ear. Her whole demeanour became re-energised. Hamish, it seemed, had brought some hope into the room.

When Tony's team returned to the boardroom, Nadiya started playing hardball. She returned to the original offer from the previous morning. "50k, nothing more." This time she added that they would not be paying Maul's costs either.

All hell broke loose.

Maul walked out, followed by the mediator, who was trying his level best to persuade him to stay. But he would not. He was out into the night and off to a bar. He returned at 0700, his worn black beret freckled with shiny raindrops.

When he sat, he stumbled while negotiating the curved metal legs of his boardroom chair.

"He's been on the sauce," Tony whispered to Nadiya.

When Pete had bid them all good morning, and Hamish had brought everyone fresh coffee and croissants, Nadiya whispered something to Hamish, who then left the room.

"Before we begin again," Nadiya said. "I would like to alert everyone to a new development."

Maul lurched forward, staring at her. "What new development?" he said, his voiced slurred.

"One that's come to our attention while we have been discussing your claim overnight."

He looked puzzled.

The door opened.

Hamish entered first.

Then Naomi Marsh.

Maul shouted, "What the hell!"

"Calm down, please!" the mediator said.

Hamish pulled out a chair and Naomi sat.

"Would you like to say anything, Naomi?" Nadiya asked.

She shared the whole sorry and sordid tale.

Maul's plan to forge a document.

His fraudulent story.

His lies.

His penning of the document in her presence.

His lawyer's complicity.

When she mentioned the last point, both members of Maul's legal team looked set to run.

After she had finished, Maul's senior tried to object on the grounds that the witness's statement had not been included in the disclosures from both parties. Nadiya pushed back, saying that Naomi had only texted her junior at midnight to tell him she was willing to share what she knew. The mediator confirmed the story.

Maul removed his beret and put his head in his hands. It was only then that Tony saw how much his hair had receded and greyed since the days of their friendship. He was tempted, for the length of a single tick of a clock, to feel sorry for him. He stood to speak.

"This is the first time I have spoken in this boardroom since these discussions began. And I have only one thing to say. If I ever even catch a whiff of you causing me any more trouble, I will sue you two for malpractice and you ..." pointing at Maul... "I will sue you for libelling me on live TV on Fiona's show."

He sat.

"Do you agree to drop hands?" The mediator asked.

Maul's senior conceded before he and his comrades in crime left the building.

As the rain stopped and the sun shone through the

enormous windows, Tony shook hands with Pete, the weary referee, who left for another mediation.

Tony headed to Naomi and gave her a hug.

"Thank you," he said.

"You were always good to me, Tony."

"I always thought Maul was punching," Tony said.

"That's kind. I'm glad I saw through him in time. And I'm glad I could help stop him."

Tony asked, "What are you doing with yourself these days?"

"I'm between jobs."

"Still living in that flat?"

She looked down at her feet and nodded.

Tony called Nadiya over.

"That 50k that we earmarked for Maul," he said.

"Yes. What about it?"

"I want Naomi to have it."

Nadiya smiled.

Naomi started to cry.

Tony said, "It's small compensation for all you've been through, and for what you've done here."

"It's not small to me," she said.

"Thank you again," Tony said.

"You still living in Chelsea?" she asked him.

"I had to sell it. Too many memories."

Naomi sighed. "I get that. Where are you living now?"

"I bought an old house far away, partly to get away from Maul. It's just perfect for writing."

Tony took out his phone and showed her a photo.

"It's being completely done up and will be finished in the autumn. I'll very likely have a house-warming party before

Christmas. I'd like you to be there. With your plus one, of course."

"If I have one by then..."

"I'm sure you will. Just avoid getting mauled again... if you know what I mean."

Tony turned to Nadiya and Hamish who looked exhausted. "And you two," he said. "You'll be invited."

Tony shook hands with them. "Thank you both," he said. "Bringing Naomi in was a masterstroke."

Nadiya smiled at Hamish and said, "My junior did a good job in the end, didn't he?"

"You both did."

"Do you need somewhere to sleep for a while?" Nadiya asked.

"I'm good. What about you? Are you going to have a rest?"

"Don't worry about me," Nadiya said. "I'm going home."

"So am I," Tony replied.

37

THE RETURN

Tony's excitement at seeing the Old Rectory was the only thing that kept him awake as he drove from Yinka's offices to the West Country. He had texted ahead to Ella who opened the gates in preparation for his arrival. When he parked on the gravel drive, he gazed in awe at what she and her team had done to the garden. The Queen's Walk was now visible, running from the far wall of the house, up the right-hand side of the garden as he looked at it, and then along the perimeter at the top, back down on his left to the Tudor yew tree. The lawn where the ghost had appeared was freshly cut and surrounded by beds with well-fertilised soil and blossoming flowers.

"To paradise well comparable!" he said as he hugged Ella on the drive, casting a glance back towards the lawn.

"Welcome home," she said.

"How are you?" he asked.

Ella removed her cap. Her head was covered in thick wavy ginger hair which fell in lush folds to her shoulders.

"You look amazing!"

She blushed.

"You must be exhausted," she said.

"I'm fuelled by the excitement of seeing what you've done," he replied. "We had an all-nighter at Yinka's offices. I'm happy to say we won. That's energised me too."

"I'm so pleased. Does this mean that dreadful man's not going to hassle you anymore?"

"We live in hope."

They walked to the front door.

"We'll start on the façade in a few weeks," she said. "And that'll include the roof. It needs a lot of work."

"How's it going upstairs?"

"Well, if you'd stayed in the States a week longer, I would have sent you another video. The team's finished the second floor. There's about ten people working on the roof space now."

"Roof space?"

"Sorry. Attic!"

"How long will that take?"

"Half the team will work on the façade, the other on the attic. It'll take them both until September."

"You're on schedule, then?"

"We are."

As Ella showed him around every room on the ground floor, Tony could not stop gasping.

"You've done a phenomenal job."

"You haven't seen the upstairs yet."

She led him up to the next floor. "We'll recarpet the stairs when everyone's finished."

"This is just what I wanted," Tony said as he went through

every room, including his new study, with his father's old desk standing underneath the Tudor window.

"It fits perfectly," she said.

After the study, she opened the door to the master bedroom. "I've gone for a more Gothic style in here," she said. "Your eyes should be drawn first to the fourposter bed."

"They are. I love the carved headboard and footboard," he said. "And the twisty columns."

"I hoped you would."

"The bedside tables are also perfect," he said. "They're ornate without being over the top, and the dressing table is great too, although of course I'm not sure I'll ever use it myself."

"Maybe not, but one day a guest of yours might appreciate it." Ella winked at him.

"Is everything the same wood?"

"Mahogany. All of it."

"Victorian?"

"Yes, everything." Then she pointed to items in the room. "Those two chests of drawers, the triple wardrobe, the occasional table, the dressing table, the upholstered chairs, the bedside tables, the over-mantle mirror above the fireplace, everything... it's all mahogany, all Victorian, all good condition. And it's the wood that's creating that dark, rich vibe you're feeling..."

Tony chuckled.

"I am definitely feeling it."

She led him to the windows. "The under curtains are white cotton. Very intricately patterned, as you can see. And the main curtain... that's green velvet. A very Victorian combination. Together, they'll keep the sunlight out during these summer months."

Tony stepped forward to close them. Ella intervened. "Here, let me show you." She pointed to some tasselled ropes. "Pull them this way, and in this order."

She switched on a bedside lamp before pulling the final curtains shut. It provided enough light for them to proceed to the adjoining chamber – a private bathroom.

"The Kingsley bath!" Tony exclaimed.

"I had to bite my tongue the first time you used his name," Ella said, her face serious.

"What, Kingsley?"

"Yes. We Irish don't like him. He called us white chimpanzees and described our homeland as a horrible country."

"That's terrible. I honestly didn't know that! I had always assumed he was a kindly clergyman, a reformer with a compassion for the poor, especially chimney sweeps."

"He was, but this compassion only stretched to his own kind. I'm afraid he had a bit of a dark side."

"I didn't know."

"It's all right," Ella said with a laugh. "I'm still a fan of *The Water Babies*, but it just shows that even the greats get it wrong sometimes, and he was no exception."

As Ella headed back to the door of the bedroom, she said, "I've told the guys upstairs in the loft to be quiet. I've explained that you've had no sleep for two nights."

"Thanks," Tony said. "Let me just say hello."

She took Tony up a smaller, wooden staircase to where eight men and two women were standing on bare floorboards that stretched the full length of the attic. The oldest, a man in his mid-seventies, stretched out a hand flecked with magnolia.

"Mister Musgrave," Ella said.

"I've heard a lot about your work," Tony said, shaking his hand. "You and your team have done a brilliant job."

"I'm glad you like it," he said. Then, "We'll keep it down today, Mister Lawson, so as you can sleep..."

"I appreciate that."

Mister Musgrave turned back to his sanding.

Ella led Tony downstairs to the door to his bedroom. "What do you think of it all?" she asked.

"Feels like home already."

"Get some beauty sleep, Tony."

"Will you be here tomorrow?"

"We'll all be here."

Tony nodded, murmured something about that being good, and headed into his bedroom. Only then did he notice that one of the top corners of the bed had been turned back. His old teddy was sitting between the two sets of plumped up pillows. "Ella," he muttered with a smile. "You think of everything."

Tony headed to the bathroom and had a shower. He returned to the bedroom, searched through some drawers, found his nightclothes, uttered a whispered thanks to Wendy for transferring his wardrobe, and then climbed into bed. He sank into the new mattress and pulled the duvet over his chest. He looked up at the freshly varnished panelling of the hood of the four-poster. He could not believe how cosy the mattress was nor how safe and content he felt.

Taking his phone, he sent a text to Shree, telling her he was back home. *Home, as in the Old Rectory*. She wrote back and wished him a happy homecoming, adding that she would be in touch in a few days, when he had recovered from the jetlag.

Then Tony messaged Tita.

I'm in my new bed in my new house just about to go to sleep. I just want you to know that I miss you very much. I can't wait for you to visit in September. I really wish you were here.

His phone vibrated. A large, red love-heart emoji appeared. Followed by a new text with four kisses.

Tony sent four kisses back.

As his phone fell out of his hand, he pressed his nose against the fur in the nape of his old bear's neck. He thought of the night with Tita in the Big Oyster. He remembered the scent of her dark hair. The softness of her perfect skin. Her fingers stroking his forearm.

And then he was away.

38

A DREAM

In his dream that night, Tony saw Sir Thomas Seymour, the Queen's lover, approaching the lodge. The Lord Admiral could have leapt over the walls if he had wanted, but he was discrete, designing his approach to avoid suspicion. He had arrived just after midnight when the gardens were quiet and the household asleep. Tall, strong, and nimble, he entered the house through a back window. He ascended the stairs and tiptoed across the landing to the Queen's chamber.

He tapped on her door.

The sound muted by his gloves.

Three slow knocks.

The Queen pressed her hands to her mouth.

She turned the key and handle.

Her chest heaving.

The Lord Admiral entered.

She gazed at his handsome face, his long auburn beard.

Then he knelt at her feet and kissed her hand.

She pulled him back to his feet.

Wrapped her pale arms around his neck.

"Thomas," she said with a sigh.

He bowed to take her chin.

They kissed.

When they had satisfied their passions, they lay together on the Queen's bed. They whispered to each other, taking care not to awaken the ladies in waiting.

"We must wed at the end of May," he said.

She replied, "We will need to have a quiet ceremony, away from prying eyes and censorious hearts."

"Why does it matter what others think?"

"It does matter, Thomas. The King only died four months ago. The widow's period of mourning is two years..."

"You said you would wait two months, not two years."

"You paraphrase me, darling."

"You are the expert in paraphrasing."

He sighed.

She made to kiss him.

But he was not done. "We have waited too long already. If the late king had not postponed our love by five years, we would have the beginnings of a royal litter by now."

"How many children have you been expecting?" she asked, pushing him away with playful indignation.

He laughed under his breath, then enfolded her, his firm white arms around her back. She, resting in his embrace, stroked his beard. Soon, the two were sleeping.

But not for long.

The Queen was awakened by shafts of light penetrating the cracks in the curtains.

She shook him.

"You must get dressed."

He kissed her again.

He looked at her and said, "Next month. After Whitsun. Let us wed then, my love."

"It is not as simple as that."

"What do you mean?"

"I will need to play a clever game with your brother, with your Privy Council, and with Edward."

"Edward is but a boy. He loves you. He will say yes."

"He is a boy, yes. But he is also a king, and he will be advised to do his duty, not defer to his sentiments."

Thomas frowned.

"And your brother," she said. "He will not be straightforward. I will need to be as cunning in persuading him to let us wed as I was with my late husband to let me live."

The Queen clasped her lover's hands in hers.

"Your brother is playing the part of Lord Protector with a clenched not an open hand. It has not been easy to get him to acknowledge my title-for-life for this house, even though the king gave it to me. But I will hold the lease, and the grazing rights."

The Lord Admiral said, "I am more concerned about him agreeing to our marriage than this house."

"I am concerned for both."

He looked unconvinced.

"Do not lose heart, my lord. I can understand the Lord Protector's hesitation over our marriage. He wants to be sure that I do not bear King Henry's child."

"You are more likely to be bearing mine," he said.

He stepped out of bed.

She stood and took his chin in her hand. "We will marry

at the end of May. In fact, I will be married to you even while I am petitioning to your brother on our behalf for his blessing."

"Who will officiate at such a union?"

"My chaplain, John Parkhurst will do it. It will be without pomp or ceremony, but it will be lawful in the sight of God, even whilst it is hidden from the eyes of those at court."

He seemed placated.

She said, "I would that the world was as well pleased with our love as I know the goodness of God is. But the world is wicked and not contented with good things."

"They will have no choice but to accept our union," he said. "Even if they balk at the timing of it."

The Queen frowned.

"My lord, once it is done, it is done. Your brother can utter to me all the choler he wants."

He turned to the open window. "Write one of your letters to me soon, your highness."

"I will, my lord."

"And send me one of your small pictures so that I may gaze upon you while we are apart."

"I will summon Mistress Terrlinc this morning."

"The paintrix?"

The Queen nodded. "She has travelled here with me. She will furnish me with a portrait in miniature. I will send it with my letter in five days. My groom, Walter Erle, will bring them."

"I am in your debt, your highness."

He opened the latch on the window, taking care not to allow the mechanism to rouse the house. He pulled himself onto the ledge and was about to leap when she grabbed his arm.

"Promise me one thing."

He paused.

"My stepdaughter."

"Mary?"

"No, Elizabeth."

The Lord Admiral squeezed the tip of his nose, as if he had been afflicted by a sudden itch.

"Are the rumours true?"

"What rumours, my love?"

"That you proposed to her two months after the King's death."

He sniffed and said, "By God's precious soul! She is thirteen years of age."

"That is not an answer."

"You are the only one," he said.

"Promise me, Thomas."

"Promise what?"

"That you will make only me the white hart of your affections. That you will hunt only for my love and my love alone. That you will let young Elizabeth find love in the arms of another man."

"Your highness!" he protested.

"Promise me, Thomas."

"I have just this night proved my love for you. What more can I do to pledge my troth?"

The Queen looked unconvinced.

She looked into his eyes and into his soul.

"I love you, Thomas. My desire is for you. Only for you. For five years, even while I was with the King, I longed only for you, and nothing has changed in that regard."

He shook his head as if he was the one wounded. He reached out to her, pulled her to his side, kissed her, then slipped out of the window saying, "I will come again at Hanworth."

She watched him scale down the wall and tracked him running low to the ground across her orchards. When he reached the outer wall, he waved, and she waved back.

Then, with one leap, he was gone.

The Queen sighed.

She turned back into her chamber.

Her eyes bloodshot and sad.

She knelt for a moment to pray, asking for forgiveness for what she had just done, consummating her marriage before her union had even been consecrated.

Then the Queen rose, tidied her bedclothes, straightened her hair, and opened the other windowpanes to let the cool breeze drive out the odour of their coupling.

Checking her posture, she summoned her ladies in waiting to help her prepare for the day.

"Call Walter Erle," the Queen said to Lady Jane Grey. "And have him bring his lute. His melodies will soothe me."

39

THE SEDUCER

Tony set his laptop down on his father's desk in the study. It was midday two days after his return from the States and the sun was shining. He glanced through the Tudor window at the lawn below. It was deserted. He turned to the screen and connected his computer to the internet. Ella had set up the best speed available.

Seconds later, Tony's heart missed a beat.

"I've missed you so much," Tita said, her eyes watering.

"I've missed you too," he said, his voice soft.

"How is the house?"

"Amazing. I think you'll love what they've done."

"Are you in the upstairs room at your father's desk?"

Tony nodded.

"Seen your ghost yet?"

"Not yet."

"What about dreams?"

"That's one of the reasons I wanted to talk to you, besides seeing your face and hearing your voice."

"Right back at you," she said.

They laughed.

"I had a dream about Thomas Seymour and Catherine Parr. It was extremely vivid. Passionate too."

Tita's eyes widened.

"Thomas came here," he said. "To the house, in the middle of the night, so as not to waken the Queen's household. They made love in the light of the moon."

"How very romantic."

"It was and it wasn't. Something didn't feel quite right."

"You mean because they weren't married?"

"No, that isn't it."

"Because it was too soon, then."

"That issue was raised, yes, but that still wasn't the thing that troubled me while I was dreaming... troubled me even more when I journaled it a little while ago."

"What then?"

"This is one reason why I wanted to chat. You have done so much more research than I have into these two. I was troubled because the Queen seemed to be troubled. Something to do with rumours about Thomas's feelings for Elizabeth..."

"Oh, that."

"Can you help?"

"I can, but it will involve destroying the romantic ideal you may have constructed around Seymour."

"I think I can deal with that."

"From my research, this is how I see it," Tita began. "The thing you've got to realise about Thomas Seymour is that the love of power was greater than the power of love. In other words, he did love Catherine, yes, but he also loved her because he thought she gave him the chance to become more powerful than his older brother Edward. That seems to have been a huge ambition in his life."

"So, you're saying he had mixed motives."

"Let's just say he was complex. He had feelings for Catherine, but the greater passion in his life was to be the most powerful man in England. That's why he tried to seduce Elizabeth..."

"The future Elizabeth I?"

"That's right. After the death of Henry VIII, Thomas proposed to Elizabeth before he returned to Catherine. Elizabeth was Catherine's stepdaughter. She was only thirteen at the time."

"Was that acceptable in those days?"

"Technically, yes, but Elizabeth turned him down on the grounds that she was too young."

"Okay," Tony said. "Then this means Elizabeth was Thomas's first choice, and Catherine his second."

"That's very possible, yes."

"And the reason for that," Tony said, "is because Thomas knew that Elizabeth would one day take the throne and he would become the prince consort, like Albert to Queen Victoria."

Tita nodded again.

"So how did Catherine take this? I ask because in my dream she had heard the rumours about him proposing to Elizabeth and she was trying to get him to admit they were true."

"Did he confess?"

"No, he avoided answering the question directly."

"That means he was lying."

"Elizabeth was right to suspect him, then?"

"She had good reason to be suspicious."

"Why?"

"Catherine and Elizabeth were close. Remember that Elizabeth's mother, Anne Boleyn, was dead. Elizabeth treated Catherine as a substitute mother. She often stayed at Catherine's houses in London, including when Seymour was there."

"What happened?"

"Thomas tried to seduce the princess."

"What? Even when Catherine was in the house?"

"He would go to her bedchamber first thing in the morning and get into bed with her."

"Wait a minute! I thought Elizabeth was a virgin."

"She was. She was frightened of Thomas. Hid from him when she could. She did not yield to him."

"Did Catherine find out?"

"She did. At first, she didn't believe there was anything more to it than her husband being playful. But then she caught him kissing Elizabeth, and that was that. She sent Elizabeth away and was furious, quite understandably, with Thomas."

Tony said, "He'd have been arrested today."

"How did your dream conclude?" she asked.

"With Thomas leaving, making out that he was offended that Catherine had even suspected him."

"And Catherine, how was she?"

"She sent for a lutist to console her."

"That's sad. Very sad."

Tony thought for a moment, then said, "I'm guessing it was the night's passion that I saw in my dream that caused

Catherine to become pregnant. Was the resulting baby the daughter you want to write about in your second book?"

"Very possibly. Catherine gave birth at Sudeley Castle in September that year, so that all adds up. She died several days later. The infant was looked after by friends of Catherine for a while, but then she disappeared from the records."

"Thomas didn't look after her?"

"He did not. He turned his attention to getting close to the new king, young Edward. Thomas was eventually arrested and executed for breaking into the king's bedchamber."

Tony cried, "He seems to have been obsessed with breaking into people's bedrooms!"

"He was caught carrying a pistol. When Edward's dog started barking, Thomas shot it dead."

"What a horrible man!"

"He was very foolish."

"How did he think shooting the poor dog was going to endear him to the young king?"

"I know! Historians believe from the trial records that he was in fact trying to kidnap Edward."

"What on earth was he going to do with him?"

"Nobody knows."

"He sounds desperate to me."

"And deluded," Tita added.

As Tita said this, something caught Tony's eye.

Something on the grass below.

He stood.

"You okay, Tony?"

The ghost was back.

Smiling.

Curtseying.

Drawing her hands across the grass.
Taking her keys in her hand.
Disappearing.
"Tony? Talk to me!"
Tony fell back into his chair.
"Are you alright, Tony?"
Tony could not speak.
"Did you see her again?"
He nodded.
"The same as before?"
He nodded again.
"I'm sure she's trying to tell us something," he said.

40

A DREAM

In his dream that night, Tony saw the Queen, heavily pregnant with Seymour's child, saying prayers in her chamber. When she finished, she opened her eyes. Her ladies in waiting, who had also been kneeling, rose and helped her to her feet. The Queen's pale face was redder than usual. She grimaced as she stood on her swollen ankles.

She turned to Lady Jane Grey, a girl of no more than eleven. "This summer is far too hot to be bearing such a load," she said, patting her large belly with her pale fingers.

Lady Jane smiled as did the three other women. Even with a burden that was far from light, the Queen's fair face looked luminous, her poise unblemished. She was wearing a French dress, crimson and black, with stiff Medici collars.

"Please call my chaplain," she said.

The oak-panelled door opened as John Parkhurst walked into the room. He smiled and took two steps towards the Queen. His hands were clasped together. When he lifted his head from his low bow, he stroked the end of his beard.

"How fares your Majesty this morning?"

The Queen dismissed the ladies in waiting with her hand and then bade her chaplain sit with her. She sat on an ornately carved oakwood chair, with a silk cushion as soft as a pillow and armrests to help her maintain her posture.

"I have felt better, John."

The chaplain looked concerned. He waited for her to elaborate. He knew that there was a time to speak and a time to keep silent, especially in the presence of his Queen.

"I am weighed down. Burdens of mind as well as body. And no amount of praying seems to relieve it."

She looked down, examining one of her many pairs of shoes with a look of affection.

"I am anxious for my marriage, John." She sighed and looked away towards a tapestry on the wall. She stared at the picture woven into its fabric. Henry, her late husband, on horseback, a crossbow in his hands. He had just released the bolt which had struck a white hart, the one he never managed to kill.

"My husband has been flirting with young Elizabeth again. I have sent her away to live at Sir Antony Denny's house. Elizabeth has sent me a letter blotted with tears, but my husband is unremorseful. If anything happened to me, he would propose to her more quickly than he did to me after the king's death. I cannot trust him, John."

The chaplain sighed.

He still did not speak.

"And that brings me to ..." she caressed her belly before she continued. "To the little one."

The chaplain's expression was unchanging. He was focused on his Queen. His thin frame was still.

"I have been having grim forebodings about the birth." Her eyes were looking into the distance, disconnected from the chamber and the chaplain. "In the ordinary course of things, there would be dangers. But at my age..." she did not finish her sentence.

"Your Majesty," he said, his voice soft. "Margaret and I are praying for you and for the child. My beloved wife keeps a holy vigil for you in the watches of the night."

The Queen stirred from her trance. "I love the way you speak of her. Never was a husband so honouring of his wife. And that reminds me ... May I ask you a personal question?"

"Always," he said.

"Why do you not have children? Forgive me if it is inappropriate. You can say so if it is."

"We ... cannot," the chaplain said. His voice wavered.

The Queen frowned. "I am sorry."

"It is our heavenly Father's good and perfect will."

"Hard, no doubt, nonetheless."

"Very."

"It is in the light of that," the Queen said, "I would like to make a request, one that you are entirely free to reject."

The chaplain nodded.

"If anything happens to me after my child is born, I cannot be sure that my husband will act responsibly as a father. In fact, in my dreams I see him in a prison cell. He is an unruly stallion. He will not take good care of my beloved child."

A cloud passed over the sun.

"Will you be there for me then, as you are now, John?"

"Your Majesty, *you* will be there for the child, and I will be there for you both, as will Margaret."

The Queen smiled. She withdrew a small volume from a

concealed pocket in her long dress. It was bound in leather, with golden lettering on its spine.

"Are you familiar with the Roman virtue of *prudentia*. It is often translated as wisdom."

The chaplain replied, "*Prudentia* is the ability of a leader to look ahead and plan, like a player of chess."

"Thomas More is not a Reformer," the Queen said, "but he uses the term in this book. For him, an ideal world is unimaginable without leaders who govern with foresight."

The chaplain nodded.

"In truth, I wouldn't be alive today if I hadn't anticipated what the Bishop of Winchester planned for me."

"True, Majesty."

"If what I fear is not a portent of misfortune," the Queen said, "then take it as an act of prudence, one befitting a person in my position, a mother focused on the future of her child, a Queen anticipating troubling and uncertain times."

She put her book away.

"King Edward is a friend of the Reformers," she said. "But if Mary should ascend the throne, then she will reinstate the Catholic religion in England. She may forget her affections for me and see my child as a threat to the crown."

The Queen turned towards an oak chest. "Fetch me the letter from the drawer over there."

The chaplain walked to the chest.

"The left one, at the top," the Queen said.

The chaplain withdrew a letter bound together by the Queen's bloodred seal.

"Do not open it until I die," she said.

The chaplain frowned, then asked, "What is this, your

Majesty? Am I allowed to know anything of its contents in advance, so that I too can exercise *prudentia*?"

The Queen bade him bring the letter and return to his seat. She said, "When my second husband, Lord Latimer died, he stipulated in his will that I was to be Margaret's guardian, leaving £30 a year so that I could support my stepdaughter. This is a duty that I have faithfully and joyfully discharged to the letter."

"I have witnessed this," the chaplain said, adding, "as well as your love for the king's daughters. I know of no other woman who would have been as virtuous as you have been to Mary, Elizabeth, and Edward. Your compassion commends you."

The Queen seemed not to hear the compliment.

"If I should not survive, then provision must be made for my child if she outlives me, especially in the event of her wandering father being disinterested, distracted, or deceased. I would like to entrust you and Margaret with that duty."

"But, your highness, why not stipulate this in your will?"

"You and I, as well as my physician, will draw up my will when we arrive at Sudeley Castle," she said. "But I cannot include my wishes for the child. Others will learn of them."

The chaplain frowned. Then he took a step towards the Queen and knelt. He stretched out his hands which the Queen took in hers. "Whatever you wish is my desire."

She leaned towards him, her eyes filling with tears. "Thank you, my dear, dear friend."

They loosened their hands.

The chaplain rose.

"If I die," the Queen said. "I have two wishes. The first is that my child should not be an orphan."

"And the second?"

"That you and Margaret should not remain childless."

The chaplain nodded.

"Hide the letter," the Queen said. "You cannot destroy it because you may one day need it. But you must also conceal it well. It must never fall into the wrong hands."

With that, the conversation was over and the chaplain, secreting the sealed letter within his black robe, made to leave. Before he crossed the threshold, he turned to the queen and bowed.

"Your plans, Majesty. To quote More, they are *prudentissima atque sanctissima*."

The Queen smiled.

After he had left, she placed her right hand on her stomach. "Steady, little one," she said. "Not long now."

41

THE ANGEL

After this, the dreams dried up until late September, when the soil had been softened by rain and the leaves were beginning to fall. Two weeks into that month, Ella was walking with Tony across the lawn. She became rooted to a spot a few metres beneath the apple tree.

"Are you alright?" Tony asked.

"Can't move...."

He took her by the arm.

She shook her head.

He let go.

"Something's here," she muttered.

"What do you mean?"

"Under the ground."

"How do you know?"

"I can just ... well... feel it."

"I didn't know you were into this kind of thing."

"There's a lot you still don't know about me, Tony."

"Do you have some kind of gift?"

"My mother back in Ireland had the charm."

"What on earth is that?"

"It's a special insight."

"Paranormal?"

"You could call it that."

"What would you call it?"

"More spiritual than paranormal."

"So, what's going on?"

"I'm sensing something."

"Under the lawn?"

"Yes."

"Well, we need to investigate."

"I'll get my metal detector from the van," Ella said.

"I didn't know you had one of those."

"Like I said Tony, there's a lot you still don't know about me!"

Tony made to follow her.

"No! You stay right there. Mark the spot."

Two minutes later, she was back with a spade and a long black robotic arm. Using the mechanical arm, she began to scan the ground around Tony's feet.

He heard a sequence of loud beeps.

These increased in speed until there was one long and uninterrupted sound.

"Something metal," she said. "Could be a lot more interesting than just a hairpin or a thruppenny piece."

She took a pair of what looked like surgical gloves from her pocket and slipped them on. She grabbed the spade and began to dig into the ground. She formed the shape of a square with each thrust, then forced her hands into the tiny spaces she had made and began to lift the block of earth.

When she had set it down beside the cavity, she took the metal detector again and lowered it into the hole. The beep was louder now. Constant. Uninterrupted. Insistent.

As Tony looked over her shoulder, Ella started to stroke the top of the soil. She worked in gentle movements, sifting the earth, as if panning for gold. He bent down and helped her.

"What have we here?"

She raised what looked like a small clump of mud. But as she removed the grimy accretions, Tony began to see what she had unearthed. It was golden. Engraved.

"Is it a coin?" he asked.

She nodded.

Ella continued to clean the object.

"My goodness! It's an Angel. I've been looking for one of these since I was a girl."

"What's an Angel?"

"It's a coin dating from the time of the Tudors," she said, rubbing away the final blemishes. "See here." She pointed at the engravings on both sides of the coin. "This side a ship." She turned it over. "This side is St Michael slaying the dragon." Then she pointed to a small hole at the top of the coin. "This was bored by a blacksmith."

"Why?"

"So that the coin could be a touch piece, worn around the neck of someone who was ill."

"Come again?"

"As I recall, this coin was known as an Angel because the kings and queens of England would give it to a sick person as part of a service of healing known as the Royal Touch. It's very rare. They went out of circulation in the seventeenth century."

She handed Tony the coin before replacing the square block of earth and restoring the soil.

Turning the coin in his palm, Tony said, "What do you know about this Royal Touch?"

"Only that the first of the Tudor Kings, Henry VII, was a fan of the practice and began using a religious ritual in which he would pray for very sick people."

"Did he touch them?"

"He laid hands on them."

Tony frowned. "Sounds like the charm to me."

"Not exactly," Ella said.

"Was Henry VIII into this?" he asked.

"Very much so. At the start of the 1530s, he touched about 60 sick people in two years. Then he became paranoid about catching diseases, so he stopped the ritual."

Tony shuddered.

"I think I know why it's here," he said.

"Why?"

"I'm told the kitchens and cellars of the old Tudor house are buried under this lawn. It must have something to do with that. Perhaps it belonged to someone who worked there. If it is, that could be a key to the house's story."

Ella nodded. "Do you want me to get a team in to excavate this part of the garden?"

"Yes please. As soon as possible."

As Ella headed back inside to make some calls, Tony stayed on the grass, recalling the graceful, balletic movements of the ghost. He shuddered again. What if she had been sweeping the surface of the lawn as Ella had just done? What if she had been gesturing, pointing to the very spot where the Angel was buried?

The more Tony thought about it, the more he began to speculate that the Tudor maid had been performing something more than just the requirements of social etiquette.

As the day wore on, he could not wait until the builders had gone and the house was empty. He could not wait for darkness to fall. For his bed to beckon. He knew that that even though the dreams had been infrequent, he would dream that night.

He longed to know more about the Angel that Ella had unearthed beneath the surface of the lawn.

He ached to know what lay beneath.

42

A DREAM

Tony's dream that night disturbed him. There was an outbreak of what Con would later identify as "the sweating sickness." Its groping unseen hands had reached over the walls of the gardens and intruded, uninvited, into the household. It was not a winter disease, like influenza, nor was it the plague. It had last appeared before the three built the house, just over twenty years before. But now it had manifested from nowhere, in the summer months when the skies were blue. It had not claimed the very old or the very young. It seemed to have no interest in them at all. Its victims had been mostly men, between eighteen and thirty years of age, and these it had seized with deadly speed. In many cases, the men died within an hour of the sickness striking them. The physicians said, "If you can survive the first twenty-four hours, you have a fighting chance of living."

When the sweating sickness came to the house, it was in August, and the men who worked there were felled first. One dropped stone dead while gathering fallen apples. Another, tilling the soil in the gardens, was taken ill and expired an hour later. Four other men, and two women, were taken to beds provided by John and Margaret Parkhurst. These two kind souls had been tending to them, covering them in blankets according to the advice of doctors such as John Caius, who had counselled those infected to lie still under their bedclothes and sweat out the disease for as long as they could.

Every bed was now occupied.

The house resembled a hospital more than a hunting lodge.

"This is how you do it," Parkhurst said. He was leading a child, a girl under four-years-old, to a bed where a man who had fallen sick no more than twenty minutes before was lying.

"Should she be here, John?"

The question came from his wife, Margaret.

"The sickness does not affect our children," he said. "She is safe. She needs to know what to do."

The sick man's body, up to his throat, was hidden by a blanket. The rector took out a golden coin with a small hole, a leather necklace threaded through it. He placed it over the man's head. He was about to pray when Margaret scolded him.

"John! You should not be using that."

"But sweetheart," he replied. "Did not the first followers of our Lord ask the apostles to bless their handkerchiefs? And did they not then use these to place upon the sick, with great miracles resulting from their touch? Why not this royal coin?"

Margaret sighed. "You have a wise answer to every

question."

He continued with the ritual.

The freckle-faced girl was standing next to the bed, watching her master with wide eyes, mouthing his words. Tony could tell this was not the first time he had performed the service with her. There had been so many afflicted with the sweating that she knew the words by heart, as well as the actions he performed.

When he finished, he took her by the hand and led her from the chamber. He had taken only two steps into the hallway when he stumbled and fell to the floor.

"John!"

Margaret heard the thud.

She herded the nearest maids to the scene. "Hurry!" she shouted, stifling her sobs.

Within two minutes, the rector was on a makeshift bed upon the floor, insisting in his last moments of consciousness, "No one is to yield their bed for me."

Margaret and the maids covered him until even his head and beard were invisible. There he remained until the sun had set. The young girl stayed at his side the entire time.

All through the night she watched and waited there, her hand resting on his aching body. She pulled the sheet down from his head and wiped his brow and face with a wet cloth that Margaret brought on the hour every hour.

When Margaret arrived again just before sunrise, there were tears in her eyes. She could not hear her husband breathing. There was no sign of movement in his body. She reached into a pocket in her dress and handed the golden coin to the child.

"It belonged to the Queen," she said. "I should not have

questioned my husband."

Desperation had dispelled her doubts.

The child took the leather necklace and lowered it over the rector's head until the Angel was resting over his heart. As the metal touched his chest, his lips twitched.

The child closed her hands and eyes. She began to speak. "They shall lay hands on the sick and they shall recover," she said, her voice gentle, her tone confident.

She opened her eyes and prayed.

"O merciful God, the eternal health of all who put their trust in Thee, we humbly beseech Thee on behalf of this Thy servant, for whom we call for Thy merciful help, that he may recover health and give thanks to you through Christ our Lord."

She placed her soft hands upon the Rector's cold, wet head. There they rested.

Meanwhile, her lips kept moving.

Her fingers trembled as if some unseen power was at work, making its way through her hands.

In his dream, Tony saw the orange light of the emerging sun catching the golden coin around Parkhurst's neck. He sensed the power, like a warm wind, passing from the Angel through the rector's body and throughout the house.

The child's eyes stared in wonder as the light of a new day broke and the slumbering inhabitants began to stir. The sick men and women in the bedrooms were roused first, a look of surprise and confusion etched upon their faces. They could not believe they were still alive, nor that they had been raised from what they considered to be their deathbeds. They were stretching. Yawning. Reaching with their feet to the floor. Emerging from their sheets like Christ from his graveclothes. Bathed in the light from outside, they were warmed by the new life and strength coursing through their bodies.

And then it was the rector's turn.

He opened one eye. Then the other. Seeing the child, he looked with such love at her that it looked as if he was going to be transfigured. She, seeing the radiance in his eyes and the smile on his face, was so overjoyed she was weeping.

"Mary!" the rector whispered.

"My Master!" the child cried.

43

THE DIG

Two weeks before the archaeologists arrived, Tony tore himself away from his beloved house and headed to Harley Street for a long overdue appointment with Shree. As soon as he sat, Tony started to speak about the Angel. He narrated the dream of the rector's miraculous recovery at the hands of a fair-haired girl called Mary.

Shree frowned. "You're getting close."

"Another one of your hunches?"

"I can sense it."

"Close to what?"

"You made reference to Jung in your Hugh Ellman podcast," Shree said. "Jung said the house of the soul has two storeys, the upper – which signifies the conscious – and the lower..."

"The unconscious," Tony interrupted.

"Yes. But don't forget that beneath the ground floor, there are two further levels..."

"The cellar and the cave," he said.

Shree nodded. She leaned forward, her dark eyes gazing into his. "There's a cellar in your mind, and a cave beneath the cellar. Perhaps everything is lining up now for you to unearth what's in your soul, as well as what's in your garden."

Tony sighed.

"Just relax, Tony. In this session, I want you to dig deep. Hold a cushion if you want to."

"I think I'd prefer to hold something else."

Tony reached down to his father's old briefcase, opened it, and withdrew a raggedy teddy bear. His brown eyes were scratched but still shiny. His hair, what was left of it, stood out in tiny tufts. He was a shadow of his former self.

"I hugged this bear at school," he said. "After lights out. When I missed my parents. He's been with me through thick and thin ever since. He sits on my bed at home."

"You should send him to the repair shop," she said.

"This is the repair shop," Tony replied. "Right here. Once I'm restored, then Andy can be too."

"Is that your bear's name?"

"It's a long story. Maybe for another time."

"No problem. Hold Andy tightly. Close your eyes. Breathe slowly. Imagine it's lights out. You're under the bedclothes. All the other boys are falling asleep. But you're still awake. It's your first night at prep school. How are you feeling?"

Tony's heart began racing.

"Lonely."

Shree waited.

"Confused."

She waited some more.

"Afraid."

Tony was less aware of her presence now. He was back

there. In the dormitory. He could hear muffled crying from some of the other twelve beds. Raw emotions started to surface, ones he had not felt for over four decades. The sadness. Deep-down sadness. Deeper than sadness. Visceral. Grief. As if his parents had died. As if orphaned. Exiled from home. Not worthy of belonging in their house, in his old, safe, familiar bedroom, with his toys and books.

"Ashamed," he said.

"Anything else?"

Something began to shift. Lava was bubbling in the magma chamber of his heart. Something he had buried for so long. Something he had forgotten was even there. A now-active force, waiting for its moment. A seething, rising mass of fire.

"Angry," he said, gritting his teeth, trying to force down the rising tide of wrath.

The surge triggered another memory.

He was sitting in a darkened hall at his prep school on film night. He could hear the reels and the spool mechanism of the projector, the huge screen at the front of the hall, suspended from the ceiling in front of a racing-green curtain, beyond which lay the stage where the headmaster would sit in an old bishop's chair with a cane in his hand, administering public beatings to errant children.

Tony recognised the movie.

James Mason, *Journey to the Centre of the Earth*.

It was near the end, in the lost, buried city of Atlantis. Four brave explorers were sitting on a huge altar bowl being propelled at increasing speed up the flue of a mountain, pushed by the rising lava beneath them. Led by James Mason, they were heading up towards an ever-growing hole in the summit. They could see blue sky. Then they were through. Out. Into the blue expanse. Free.

The volcano erupted.

Tony started to shout.

To rage.

To scream.

All the pent-up wrath at being left behind and left alone poured from his intestines, up through his oesophagus, out of his mouth, into the open, for the first time.

How long he continued like this, he had no idea. But when he emerged exhausted from this overflow, Shree was there, leaning forward, looking at him, the glint of a tear in her eyes.

"How are you doing?"

Tony was going to say okay, but then he realised that such an evasion would not work anymore. He wanted to be transparent now. He wanted that eight-year-old boy to be free. He longed to make peace with his past. He decided to tell the truth because, as Shree so often said, getting real was the key to getting healed.

"Eviscerated," he said.

"That's good."

"Is it?"

"Good that you're owning what's going on inside and what's just happened to you. Internalising your pain has done you no favours over the decades. But venting your anger, as you did just now, is critical if you're going to be free."

Tony nodded.

That made sense.

"What do I do with all this pain?" he asked.

"Name it."

"What do you mean?"

"When we name our pain in the presence of a trusted other, we begin to defuse its power. So, name it."

He thought for a moment. "I'd call it trauma."

"Remember, Tony, there are two types of trauma - sudden and gradual. Which kind is it?"

"Bit of both."

"Talk to me about that."

He took a deep breath. "I knew I'd be sent away to school about a year before I went. The sense of dread grew over time. But the actual day… that felt more like a sudden blow."

"And what would you call this blow?"

He wracked his mind. Then a word began to emerge from the depths. A word he had avoided for so many years. A word he had never dared to speak with reference to his own life, lest he surrender to the fear that came with it.

"Abandonment."

Shree nodded.

"And how did you deal with that feeling? How did you learn to survive having felt that all those years ago, when you were far away from home, an eight-year-old boy?"

"I stopped feeling."

"You disengaged."

"Yes."

"And that was your survival strategy?"

"Yes."

"And is that switch still in the off position?"

"Not anymore."

"That's good, Tony."

Shree passed a fistful of tissues.

Wiping his eyes, Tony thought of his ten years away at school. He could not remember a moment when he had been emotionally intelligent or healthy. He had learned to push everything down. Putting on a brave face. Cultivating a stiff upper lip. Believing the lie that "big boys don't cry," soldiering on regardless.

Then came the killer question.

"And how did all this affect your marriage?"

Tony put his head in his hands.

He began to moan.

Groan.

The visceral made vocal.

Again.

When he had finished, Tony realised just how much he needed to apologise to Renée.

"It affected everything."

"How?"

"I can see it now. I was detached from the beginning. Leaving boarding school, I didn't reengage my emotions. I didn't know how. I just carried on living from my head, not my heart. She complained that I never expressed my feelings. It enraged her, my coldness. But the coldness was my protection."

"So, you began your marriage with frozen feelings."

"Yes, and I continued in that vein until the day of my divorce. I guess I was always afraid."

"Afraid of what, Tony?"

"Of history repeating itself."

"Of Renée abandoning you?"

Shree was silent for a good minute before she spoke again. She was waiting to see if Tony was ready for her question.

He could tell what it was even before she asked it.

"Is that why you left her?"

Tony nodded.

"You left Renée because you were frightened that she would leave you. And you decided that it was better for you to take the initiative and get in there first. Less painful, even though the whole process has been excruciating anyway."

"Yes."

"How do you feel about that now?"

"Like I should one day, when it's appropriate, explain all this to her and say that I am truly, deeply sorry."

"I suspect she already knows, Tony."

"I still need to say it."

Tony could see from the wall clock behind Shree's head that their hour was five minutes from being done. He placed Andy back into the briefcase and thrust the wet tissues into his pocket. He looked at Shree and shook his head.

"That was invasive," he said.

His voice was softer.

Less aloof.

Less arrogant.

More real.

More vulnerable.

More him.

Shree walked to her desk and checked her calendar. "We're meeting the same time next week."

Tony checked his phone and said, "I'm free."

"You will be," she replied with a smile.

"Isn't it all over yet?"

"Not yet."

"What's next?"

"Tony, what we've done in this session is brilliant. But there's something even more important."

She could see his confusion.

"Look, we've done some vital excavating today. We've dug deep into the cellar beneath the ground floor of your soul. But there's more to come. There's a cave beneath the cellar, and there are some old skeletons we need to confront there."

He sighed.

"Don't worry," she said. "You're going to be all right. In fact, when you've put the worst behind you, you'll find that the best lies ahead of you. I'll help you with that too."

As Tony looked at her, a ray of sun pierced the room and flooded the smooth dark skin of her face.

"You're an angel," he said.

44

THE TOUR

That night, having returned to the West Country, Tony invited Con to come and look around the restored house. Con had not visited for several months, and Tony was keen for him to see the transformation. When he arrived, he was in the familiar black suit with the long tails. His black shoes and golden buckles glinted in the hallway light. Tony could also make out part of the chain attached to his timepiece. It was peeping out of the top of his waistcoat pocket.

He took Con's brimmed cap and hung it on a hook.

Con looked around the hall and glanced to the right and the left into the dining room and drawing room. He smiled. "You have nearly finished, no?"

"They are done," Tony replied.

Tony led him into the drawing room.

"You have decorated in the Victorian style," he remarked.

"That was my plan. Most of the furnishings are original, but there are a few imitation pieces. Ella and I had no choice, I'm afraid. There is a limit to the availability of original items. I expect you can tell which ones are genuine."

Con nodded.

"It is very impressive," he said. "It almost has the resonance and likeness of the house as it was originally."

Tony showed him the dining room.

Con stood still.

"Although not this wall," he said.

He was looking at the Victorian paintings.

"What do you mean?"

"This wall is stone, and Tudor. It had large tapestries extending the full length of the room. There were three - a triptych. A story told in three acts, you might say."

"What story?"

"Of the encounter between Mary Magdalene and the Risen Lord in the garden. It is recorded in the twentieth chapter of John's Gospel. It is a most touching reunion. Although, I should add, that touching may not be the best word to use."

Tony looked confused.

"Mary goes to the garden tomb to embalm the body of her Saviour. But he has risen. She weeps. Christ appears, but she mistakes him for the gardener. Then he speaks to her. She recognises him. She tries to hold him, but he tells her not to touch him."

"That sounds a bit cold."

"No, my friend. He was trying to tell her something."

"What?"

"That the time for relating to him as a physical being was about to end and the time for knowing him in a spiritual way was about to begin. He was trying to help her to adjust."

They wandered into the kitchens and the rest of the

downstairs rooms before ascending the main staircase to the landing and looking through all the second-floor rooms. The bedrooms. The bathrooms. And, of course, Tony's study.

"This desk," Con said.

"This piece is an original," Tony said. "It's Victorian. Belonged to my father and his father. It's the only connection I have with my parents. They died a long time ago when I was eight."

"I am sorry. It fits well there, beneath the splendid window from the Tudor house."

"I agree."

Con gazed at the stone surrounds and the mullioned panes. He seemed to have gone somewhere faraway in his head. Tony was about to nudge him back when he spoke.

"It is amazing to think that she peered out of this very window, looking out for the coming of her lover, when he was home from crossing the sea and fighting for his country."

"Do you mean Catherine Parr?"

"Queen Catherine, yes," he said. "It is surely an honour to imagine that our lowly eyes look through the same windows as her more noble, royal eyes once did."

"It is."

They headed back downstairs and stood at the windows looking out onto the lawn.

"I have a digger coming."

"Digger?"

"To excavate the lawn."

"Ah, I see."

"I want to know what lies beneath it."

"Why now?"

"We found something last week, just over there, about one foot beneath the top of the lawn."

"What was it?"

"An Angel."

He frowned. "I don't understand."

"A golden coin."

"Ah, I thought for a moment ..." He chuckled.

"I had a dream that night about it," Tony said.

"Please to tell me."

Tony shared about the sweating sickness.

"That was 1551," Con said. "The last time it was seen in England. It left as mysteriously as it had arrived. Like the Holy Spirit, no one knew where it came from or where it had gone. Except that of course the Holy Spirit brings life."

Tony went on to describe his dream about the girl.

"You saw her?" he asked.

"I did, yes."

"What did she say?"

He told Con about the little girl raising the sick man from his deathbed. Con insisted he share the exact words that Mary had spoken. Tony fetched his journal and read the entry to him.

"That little girl was employing the ritual of the Royal Touch," Con said. "All four parts of it. She recited a Scripture. Prayed the same simple prayer that was prayed by kings and queens. She laid hands on him. And she placed the Angel around his neck."

"Perhaps you can help me to understand where the coin came from," Tony said. "It was obviously something handed out by monarchs. So, what was it doing in the house? Had someone living here received an Angel when the king prayed for their healing?"

"Possibly," Con said. "But I think it far more probable that it came from Queen Catherine."

"But if it was the sole privilege of a king or queen to bestow it, why do you think this humble child was using the Royal Touch and putting an Angel around John Parkhurst's neck?"

At the first mention of John Parkhurst, Con bowed his head. He seemed caught up in such an attitude of profound sadness that Tony thought he was going to cry.

Pulling himself together, he said, "You'll have to forgive me. I admire Mister Parkhurst. Not only was he a fine poet. He was also a very faithful chaplain to the Queen and an equally faithful servant to the King of kings. He was committed, as she had been, to the Reformation of this nation, at great cost to himself and his wife."

"Cost?"

"While the young King Edward was on the throne, Mister Parkhurst was able to share his views freely. The king was a champion of Reformation doctrine. John felt free to use the pulpit of his church here to spread the same emancipating truth."

There was a *but* coming.

"But then the king died young, and another Mary, daughter of King Henry, took the throne and sought to reinstate the Catholic ways, leading to many English Reformers fleeing from England to the Continent. They were known as the Marian Exiles."

"Were John and Margaret among them?"

"They were."

"Where did they go?"

"Switzerland."

"What happened to their household?"

"A new rector arrived, one more Catholic in his faith. His name was Mister Elmer. Although he regarded his predecessor as an enemy, he did not take revenge upon those who had lived and worked here. He was kind to them and kept them on."

"Including the little girl?"

"Yes."

"And Parkhurst ... What happened to him?"

"He remained in Switzerland until Queen Mary was succeeded by Elizabeth, a friend of the Reformers."

"Did Parkhurst return here?"

"Only briefly, in 1560, to visit his servants and friends, who were now nearly ten years older."

Tony poured Con a drink. They talked until he withdrew his timepiece. "My goodness! Is that the time?"

They walked into the hallway.

As Tony opened the front door, he said, "The little girl called Mary I saw in my dream. The one with the Angel..."

"Yes?"

"Who was she?"

"I think you already know."

With that, he was away.

45

A DREAM

Tony was back again inside the Tudor House. Every member of the household, including the gardeners, had assembled in the great hall. About twenty adults were present, along with their children. Everyone was standing in neat rows - everyone except the cook's young daughter whose face looked flushed with toothache. She wanted to whine but her mother was telling her to chew harder on a cotton handkerchief now soaked with the girl's saliva.

The little girl was not the only one endeavouring to bury their pain. Several of the younger maids were crying. They were being as discrete as they could, but the tears would not be cauterized, even after the muted reprimands of the men nearest to them. The cook's daughter would not be consoled nor cajoled, nor would she stand still. She broke ranks and wandered towards the fire.

Just then, John and Margaret Parkhurst walked into the hall. The little girl turned her head from the flames. Seeing them, she offered the sweetest, deepest curtsy. Her elegance was quite remarkable for one so young. The rector and his wife applauded, as did the assembled staff, prompting the girl to rise and start back to her family. She was too late, however, and Parkhurst caught her. For a moment, everyone stared in silence, wondering if the master would be cross. He was not. He picked her up, held her in his arms, and smiled.

"Oh Mary, how you are so grown up! And your curtsying is a tribute to your mother."

Sensing her beginning to wriggle in his strong arms, he let the child down. She rushed across the wooden floor to the anxious cook, seized her apron, and stood with reddened cheeks staring at the rector, whose expression had turned from undisguised happiness to a frowning, grey-faced agitation.

"The news is grave," he began. "Two days ago, our beloved Queen Jane, whose gentle feet trod these floors many times, was deposed and Mary seized the throne."

There was a gasp.

"This has placed your mistress and me in danger. We are known to Mary as loyal friends of Queen Catherine."

Several older men bowed at the mention of her name.

"Queen Catherine left this, her house, to your mistress and me, and it has been our honour not only to live here with you, but to worship with you in a simple manner faithful to the Reformers. And therein lies the problem. Queen Mary is an ardent disciple of the Catholic faith. She has the same devotion that her mother had, and she will not rest until her religion, the religion against which Queen Catherine protested, is imposed once again in this land."

The members of the household looked at each other, worry clouding their faces. The two young women who had been crying were finding it hard to stifle their sobbing.

"And so," the rector said, "your mistress and I now find ourselves, within a matter of days, no longer free to follow our faith but in danger of a persecution that we do not want to touch these doors and, more important still, to harm your lives."

Parkhurst gazed at the people who had served him, and whom he had served. There was already dread in their eyes, mixed with a grim, anticipated mourning.

"I am afraid that your mistress and I must leave."

There was a groan.

"We are travelling to Zurich this very night," Margaret continued as her husband struggled to compose himself. "There we will join our friend, a teacher of theology and philosophy at the Carolinum. He has been here several times. You have all met him. He is a kind as well as a learned man. We will both be in safer hands with him, and you will be in safer hands without us."

"Will you ever return?" the cook asked.

"Our hope," the rector replied, "lies in Princess Elizabeth. If she becomes queen, she will undoubtedly reinstate the principles and practices of the Reformers."

"Until then," Margaret continued, "you will serve the rectors who are appointed here, whether they are of Queen Mary's persuasion, or Queen Catherine's."

John Parkhurst concluded, "It was always Queen Catherine's wish that this great house should be a home for the rectors of this fair village. Whoever comes here next, serve them as well as you have served us, and they will, I am sure, treat you well."

As John and Margaret Parkhurst left the house, the sound

of weeping grew. Once outside, they called for the cook and her husband. When both parents and their little daughter were at the window of the carriage, the girl in her mother's arms, Margaret passed a wooden chest to the sad-faced father.

"This is for your daughter. Not to be opened until she is of age. It must be kept carefully hidden from all others. It contains items that are precious to us. Guard them well."

John Parkhurst reached through the window to hold the little girl's face in his gloved hands. She clasped them in hers as tears began to form in her eyes, and his.

"Oh Mary!" he cried.

"Come now, John," Margaret said.

The rector pulled himself together and sat back in the carriage. The three waved to them as they left, the little girl swishing her white handkerchief above her auburn hair.

As the wheels turned and the carriage left the gates, the rector and his wife waited until they were out of sight. Then they fell into each other's arms and wept.

46

THE DESCENT

Sitting in Shree's chair in London, clutching his bear again, Tony was nervous. He had already visited the dusty and unvisited cave beneath the cellar of his soul. Now it was time to go further.

Shree settled him.

Tony closed his eyes.

Imagined his descent.

Imagined it until the border between the imagined and the real became blurred.

Shree said, "Tell me what you see."

He gazed at the hard, unyielding walls of the cave.

Nothing.

Then he looked at the damp, stone ceiling.

Nothing.

He stepped forward.

His right foot tripped on something.

He took out his phone and pressed the torch icon. Later, Shree would say he had done this while sitting in the chair.

The light had been so dazzling that she had to look away.

"Bones," he said.

He knelt and examined the remains.

Two skeletons.

One female.

The other male.

Both charred.

He shuddered.

"They were burned."

Then came the shock.

"It's Mum and Dad."

Tears began to form.

"I remember..."

Teardrops fell onto his lap.

"I remember what happened."

If Shree asked him to share, he did not hear it.

"The headmaster summoned me to his study. He told me there had been a terrible accident. That my home had burned down. Mum and Dad had been asphyxiated by the smoke. I remember not understanding what that word meant. *Asphyxiated*. I looked it up in a dictionary in the school library after he'd finished."

More tears now.

"They were dead. And my house was gone. I couldn't process it. In the space of a few seconds, my whole world imploded. I was an orphan. I was homeless."

His face was wet now.

"I waited for them at the window upstairs at my prep school. Day after day. Month after month. Always watching. Longing for them to come back. To take me home. Tuck me in. Hug me. Say goodnight. For everything to be the way it had been."

Tony sighed.

A sigh that came from the centre of his earth.

"This is my trauma," he said. "Being left alone at my prep school. Then being told that my parents would never come back because they had burned to death in a terrible fire."

He stared down at the bones.

He fell on his face between them, holding out his arms to embrace what was left of them both.

"Mum! Dad!" he sobbed. "I miss you so much. I can't even… I can't even begin… you left me. I know you didn't mean to. But you hurt me so bad. You abandoned me."

The sob was almost a retch.

When it subsided, Tony said, "I need to make my peace with you. With yesterday's child. I can't go on like I have. It's destroyed everything. My marriage. My creativity. My life."

His whole body was trembling.

"I forgive you for leaving me behind," he said.

There was a breeze in the cave.

"And I forgive myself."

A strong wind now.

The dust on the ground began to dance around the bones. As the gusts grew stronger, the dust swirled across the floor, like sand in the first stages of a desert storm.

The skeletons began to disappear.

One by one the bones disintegrated, their brittle form turning into the tiniest motes and particles, before hurrying away, dissipating like the drawings Tony used to do on his old, red-framed Etch-a Sketch when he was a boy, whenever he shook it to wipe the slate clean. It had always seemed so magical. Just as this did now.

His trembling turned to shaking.

At first, Tony thought it was because he was sobbing. Then he realised it was Shree, pulling on his arm.

"Tony," she cried.

"Yes?"

"You've been under for over an hour."

"Sorry."

"Stop apologising for things you don't need to," she said. "It's so, so... boarding school."

He nodded. She was right.

"Do you realise how big this is?" she asked.

Tony shook his head.

"We know you've been suffering from DAD - Dissociative Amnesia Disorder. For decades, you've had these two traumas buried in the cave of your subconscious. And that's understandable. You were eight. How could you do anything else? If you were to survive, you had to forget. But surviving is one thing. Thriving is another."

"What do you mean?"

"Forgetting allowed you to go on existing. But it's remembering that enables you to start living. Really living. You've been half awake for years, Tony. Today, you've attained a new level of consciousness. You've started to remember."

"Do you think so?"

"I know so."

Tony sat back in his chair, holding Andy close to his heart.

"You know what you've been feeling all these years?"

"Abandoned?"

"That, and ashamed."

The tears began again.

"Remember, shame is feeling unworthy, not deserving your parent's love, not being good enough to simply enjoy their affection, as well as a sense of belonging."

More tears.

"But I want to say something to you, Tony. I want to say something that I hope, no I *pray*, will change the way you think about yourself and about your life for the rest of your days."

He wiped away another tear and looked at her. Staring. Waiting. Yearning for all this to end.

"Tony Lawson, you are worthy of being loved, including being loved by another woman, or man, whatever. And you are worthy of belonging, of finding your way home, of enjoying your new house, and feeling settled there, not feeling like you're passing through as a visitor, but staying as the rightful resident."

The floodgates opened.

There were now blotches on poor Andy's face. But then again, his bear's scarred eyes had seen it all before. The departure of Tony's parents at the prep school drive. The look of abject loneliness on Tony's face. The crying under the bedsheets.

Andy's half-furry face was covered in his master's tears then, after matron turned the lights out.

Just as it was now.

Except the lights were no longer out.

In Tony's mind, sunlight was piercing through the cracks between the jaded dormitory curtains.

He uttered a yawn.

Stretched his arms.

Leaped out of bed.

Dressed.

Brushed his teeth.

Ran down the heavy oak staircase.

Out of the great front doors.

Over the gravel.

Out of the gates.

Running.

Running and laughing.

Throwing his blue school cap, with the school crest, into the air and not bothering to retrieve it.

Heading away from the old country house.

From his Mossman trunk and his drab school clothes.

He was free.

His eight-year-old self was free.

Free to come home.

47

THE REUNION

After his session with Shree, Tony headed for the airport and waited for Tita. She waved when she saw him. She was as stunning as ever, even after her overnight flight from the States. When she reached him, she threw her arms around his neck.

"Tony!" she said. "I swear I have never seen your eyes so blue. What's happened to you?"

"I've just been with Shree. I'll explain in a bit."

When they were on their way to the restored house, Tita asked him about his session.

Tony told her about the cave, the bones, the wind, and the tears. About the fire that had killed his parents and destroyed his home. About burying these traumas for decades.

"Are you okay?"

"A bit tired."

"Do you want me to be quiet?"

"No. Please no."

"How are things going at the house?"

"By the time we get home, the archaeologists will have spent their first half day excavating the lawn."

"What do you think they'll find?"

"I really don't know."

Tita sighed. "I really hope they find some evidence related to little princess Mary."

"Do you think she grew up there?"

"My academic colleagues would say no."

"Why?"

"Because of a poem."

"What poem?"

"A Latin epitaph by John Parkhurst, the man whose life was saved from the sweating sickness by the prayers of a child, at least according to the dream you shared."

"Not John Parkhurst again!" he cried. "His name keeps cropping up. What did the epitaph say?"

Tita took out her phone.

"Shall I read it out to you?"

"Yes, please."

"A year before he died in the early 1570s, aged 63, John Parkhurst published a book of Latin poems that he had been preparing since his time in Zurich in the 1550s."

"I know of this book," Tony said. "Con, the man you think is a bit strange, told me a little about it."

"But did he tell you that among them there was this epitaph that some historians say was written by Parkhurst for the infant child of Queen Catherine Parr?"

"He did not."

"It's written from the child's perspective."

"I'd like to hear it."

Tita began to recite.

I, who at the cost of her own life,
My queenly mother bore
With the pangs of labour,
Sleep under this marble,
An unfit traveller.
If death had given me to live longer
That virtue, that modesty, that obedience
Of my excellent mother,
That courageously heavenly nature
Would have lived again in me.
Now, whoever you are, fare thee well,
Because I cannot speak any more.
This stone is a memorial to my brief life.

Tita added, "There is a wordplay at the end. In Latin, *infans*, from which we get infant, means literally one who cannot speak. Hence, 'I cannot speak any more'."

"Do you think Parkhurst was referring to this child?"

"Yes," she said.

"Does that mean you agree with other historians that little Mary died aged two?"

"It does not."

"I'm really confused now."

"I believe John Parkhurst wrote these words to make it look as if the daughter had died."

"You mean he was trying to deceive people."

"I do."

"Why?"

"To protect her."

She turned and looked at Tony. "I think your dreams have been telling us what happened. That John Parkhurst promised Catherine Parr that he would look after her daughter. He did that by bringing her to your house after the Queen died and the money ran out for little Mary's upkeep. He handed her to a man who worked there who was prepared to adopt her as his own. She then grew up as a humble kitchen maid, not knowing who she was until one day she opened the treasure chest you saw in your dream."

"Or maybe she didn't ever find and open it," Tony said.

"Exactly."

"So, the Angel may have been part of that treasure?"

"It may well have been."

After a few more miles, Tony asked, "Do you think the archaeologists will find it?"

"I hope so. If I write this story, my colleagues will rightly ask for physical evidence. Dreams are not going to be enough to convince sceptical historians, however moving."

"Then, let's hope they unearth something."

When they arrived at the Old Rectory, there was a mini digger on the drive. It had produced several shallow trenches on the lawn, now cordoned off with posts and string. A man was scanning what lay beneath the furrowed lines of open soil. He was carrying a metal object the shape of a large H in front of him.

Ella appeared from the dig and ran to the car.

"Have they found anything?" Tony asked.

"Yes," she answered.

She called the site manager, a woman called Rose with greying mousy hair and oval spectacles.

"We've conducted two tests so far, Mister Lawson," Rose said. "The first by our geophysicist has shown signs of walls. We will dig carefully tomorrow to see if we can find some of the brickwork. We think we have discovered the remains of a floor tile dating to the early 16th century. So, it feels like we're on the right track."

"And the second?"

"Our magnetometry tests indicate that whatever is buried here has been subject to a great deal of burning."

"How do you know?"

"With our equipment, we can detect levels of magnetism, especially where there has been burning. Burning can indicate the presence of a sub-surface object or building."

"I don't understand."

"We have been scanning for variations in the magnetism of the soil and then comparing the results against the bigger background of the earth's magnetic field. We are getting higher readings for some areas of the site, which suggests deposits of burned material. Others are giving us lower readings, which suggests walls and floors."

"And you know this for sure?"

"We're using a fluxgate gradiometer. It's our new toy."

Tita leaned over and asked, "How far down can you go with these readings?"

"Between one and two metres. We are picking up measurable patterns of contrast at the limit of our range."

"Do you think it's a building that burned down?" Tita continued. "Or is it possible the area was used as a kitchen, with a lot of burning stoves, spits, and cauldrons?"

"I can't say yet, but it looks more likely that the area was, at some time or other, engulfed by fire."

"We'll have to wait, then," Tita said.

Tony could see Tita was tired from her flight, as was he from his session with Shree. "That's enough for now," he said. "We'll reconvene in the morning."

"Please, if you go anywhere near the site," Rose said, "remove all magnetic objects such as watches, credit cards, jewellery. You cannot wear clothes with metallic zips or studs."

Rose and Ella returned to the dig.

Tita held Tony's arm.

"Are you okay?"

"Why do you ask?"

"All this talk of fire."

They unpacked the car and headed into the house. As Tita started hurrying through each renovated room, her fatigue evaporated. "This beautiful house...." She cried, her eyes blazing. "It's ... it's... what's the word I'm looking for, Tony?"

"Restored?"

"Yes! That's it! Restored!"

48

A DREAM

That night, Tony dreamed about the destruction of the Tudor house. The rector, Mister Thomas Stephens, had gone to bed, but he had not been careful. He had not blown out his candle which was still burning when he fell asleep. The wax melted and the shaft of the candle started to lean away from its brass dish on the bedside table. Tony watched, powerless, as it tilted towards the old dry drapes that surrounded the bed. The flame ignited the material. The fire spread up towards the ceiling and across the plaster to the walls.

So much of the house was made of wood that when the conflagration started, Tony knew it would be catastrophic. The rector woke up, a look of terror on his face, but he was too late to do anything. He ran out into the hall and shouted to everyone in the household to fetch water. His wife, who had fallen asleep in a rocking chair downstairs, seized her throe and raced upstairs, covering the flames with her garment, trying to suffocate the fire.

As the timbers cracked, hissed, and spat, the house was overwhelmed by the raging and roaring that followed. Every chamber was being consumed.

"Everyone out!" the rector shouted.

The servants hurried onto the lawns and looked back at the burning house with gaping mouths.

The rector's young daughter was still in the study, gathering up her father's papers, stuffing them into her nightclothes, wedging them beneath her arms. She dashed out of the front door just as the upper floor tumbled with a loud crash into the floor below, and then that floor cascaded into the kitchen in the cellars.

The girl's mother looked at her. "What did you think you were doing, Anne? You could have been killed!"

"I had to rescue Papa's book," she cried, kneeling to press down some stray leaves about to scud away in the gusts of wind coming from the fire destroying her home.

As the cinders rose into the night sky, the household looked with horror upon the shattered façade, the eyeless sockets, the groaning limbs of the house.

But they did not see what Tony saw.

The three.

The architect who designed it.

The carpenter who built it.

The gardener who adorned it.

They stood in the furious disintegration. They bowed their heads, their form surrounded by an orange glow.

There were tears in their eyes.

They knew all about fire.

They had been consumed by it too.

When the walls and halls were no more than rubble, all

that remained was the stone archway and the windows above. They, by some miracle, remained intact. Even the windowpanes that the three had so carefully installed. The blackened stonework had survived too, and everyone could now see it as the dawn broke, still rooted and upright in the charred detritus.

The rector spoke. “We will rebuild this house. It may take years, but we will rebuild it.”

“But Mister Stephens,” a nearby servant cried. “We can never recreate it. It is nearly two hundred years old. We cannot build a faithful copy of such a mansion.”

“I must take the blame for what has happened,” the rector said, his face downcast. “But I promise this. The glory of the latter house will surpass the glory of the former house.”

There was a murmur of approval.

The rector turned to his daughter. “Sweet Anne. You have been so very brave. How can I ever thank you?”

He leaned forward and kissed the top of her head. She, in turn, started lifting the leaves of his book. Some of them had burned edges, but all still showed the lines and lines of ink-formed words that he had spent years writing. He received them with teary eyes and formed them into a single manuscript.

“You are such a good girl,” he said. Over-and-over he repeated it. “You are such a good girl.”

As many others from the village arrived, the members of the rector’s household were draped with blankets and led away to other homes and beds.

All the while, the three stood in the ruins.

Until all the people had left.

Then they started to fade.

The three were gone now as well.

Tony, who felt he was there, was left alone, watching the grim smouldering in the ruins.

But he was not alone for long.

Two figures approached the debris.

A man and a woman.

In their late thirties.

They were also covered in a shimmering, orange film.

Holding hands.

Standing in the smoke.

They were looking at Tony.

Such compassion in their faces.

She had olive skin.

And he had the bluest eyes.

49

THE COMFORTER

When Tony wakened from his dream, it was the middle of the night. The thick curtains were closed. The bedside light was off. His bedroom was pitch black. And he was shaking.

"Are you all right, sweetheart?"

"Bad dream," he said.

His teeth were chattering.

Tita held his back.

He clutched her forearms.

"Tony! You're shaking!"

Tita pulled herself closer to his back and held him even more tightly. "Everything's going to be okay now," she whispered. "Was this to do with what you talked about with Shree?"

"Partly."

"Do you want to tell me about it?"

"I dreamed about the Tudor house.... When it burned down... I think in 1703... I was there ... It was terrifying..."

"Oh, Tony. I'm so sorry."

She squeezed his hand.

"I felt as if I was burning too..."

"You do feel hot."

"I saw the three ghosts again..."

"The ones you told me about?"

"Yes..."

He paused.

Inhaled.

"And I saw my parents."

Tita squeezed him.

"They were in the rubble. Hand in hand. Just looking. Just standing there..."

"Did they seem sad?"

Tony couldn't answer.

After all these years, so many tears.

Tony had no idea how long he was in this state, but the tremors only subsided when the first intrusions of the dawn began to bring a welcome respite from the darkness. As the room grew brighter, Tony sensed a strange warmth in Tita's hands.

She said, "This is all part of the healing."

He sighed. A long, drawn-out exhalation, more like an expulsion than a breath. And at the end of it, peace. Relief. Like the time when he was a little boy. The time when his ears became blocked. The doctor used a big syringe to remove all the earwax with a jet of water so warm and clean it made him smile.

Tony turned over to look at his comforter.

"Thank you. Thank you so much."

Tita cupped his face in her hands and kissed him on both cheeks. Once. Twice. Gentle. Careful. Removing the stains with her lips. Softer than he ever remembered. Causing him to close his eyes and open his mouth in wonder.

"Sleep now, baby," she said. "Sleep deeply."

"Don't leave me," he whispered.

"I will never leave you."

"All my life I've been looking ...," he said, his voice drifting away. "For someone who will stay ..."

"You've found her," she said, as Tony at last gave way to sleep.

50

THE GREYHOUND

Later, Tony and Tita sat at the kitchen table eating brunch and drinking rich coffee. Tita had brought some beans with her from Mexico City and had created a strong and aromatic brew.

"Ah, that's better," Tony said.

"Good, isn't it?"

"Very soothing," he replied.

"How are you feeling this morning?"

"Much calmer, thanks to you."

"I'm so pleased."

Tony's phone pinged.

"Mind if I look at this?"

"Not at all."

He accessed his emails.

"Damn it!"

"What is it?"

"Maul."

"I thought he was history."

"Me too."

"What does he want now?"

"It's from Yinka, my lawyer. He says Maul's lawyer has contacted him in confidence. Maul's livid about having to drop hands and about losing his money. He's hellbent on revenge. His lawyer decided to do something decent at last and warn us."

Tita raised her dark and perfectly groomed eyebrows. She said, "*Como agua para chocolate.*"

"What does that mean?"

"Literally, it means 'like water for chocolate.' When emotions are about to boil over."

"That seems to be Maul's permanent state," I muttered.

"What are you going to do?"

I read to the bottom of the email. "Yinka says that Maul has found out about this house and knows where I now live. He's realised that I've sold my place in Chelsea."

"He such a mosquito," Tita said.

"Let's find some distractions," Tony said. "There's a couple of important jobs. Do you want to help?"

"Love to."

"Good."

"What's the first?"

"To ring the local dog sanctuary and see if they have a greyhound in need of a new home."

"To use as a guard dog?"

"Partly. It's common knowledge burglars avoid houses that have large dogs. Maybe a greyhound will act as a deterrent for Maul. But more importantly, I've always wanted one."

"Why a greyhound?"

"There's a long history of greyhounds living in these

grounds, right back to the time of King Henry VIII who bred them here. Plus, we had one when I was very little. After the fire, he was given a new home. I think I've missed him all my life."

"What was he called?"

"Rocky."

"Cute! What's the second job?"

"Security cameras and lights. I need to get them installed. We need to get some experts to buy and set them up without them being visible or impairing the façade of the house."

He took another sip of the coffee.

"This is bloody decent," he said.

She laughed. "Bloody decent!"

"I tell you what," Tony said, placing the mug down on the rush mat coaster. "Could you phone around the dog shelters while I deal with the lights and cameras?"

"Of course!"

Tita placed her phone on the table and started pressing away with her ringed thumb.

As she began her first conversation, Tony went upstairs to his study. He found a local firm specialising in security cameras and called them. As he watched the archaeologists dig deeper into the lawn outside, he explained that he wanted an urgent installation. If they couldn't send someone out today, he would find someone else.

"Can I have your details and I'll ring you back."

He shared his address and name.

"*The* Tony Lawson?"

"Yes," he said. For once he didn't evade the issue. If it could help accelerate his request, he didn't mind.

Within two minutes, his phone rang.

"Hi Tony. This is Peter Frampton. I own the company. I can come out right now if you're in."

"Fantastic!"

Half an hour later, a large van with a folded ladder on its roof drove through the gates.

"Hi, Tony," the man said, proffering his hand.

"Peter Frampton, I presume." Tony recognised his voice from the phone call.

"The same."

"Thanks for coming. I need you to set up security cameras and lights. I've drawn a map where I'd like them. If you think these are optimum locations, then crack on."

Peter studied the map. "With minor variations, looks good. I'll get started. When do you need this done?"

"It's urgent."

"Are you expecting visitors?"

"We've had a warning."

"In that case, I'll need to get some of my boys in to help. It'll cost more, I'm afraid, because I'll have to pull them off other jobs, but it'll be a lot quicker than just me."

"That's perfectly okay."

Peter walked to the back of his van. He looked over to the lawn. "What's going on there?"

"They're digging down to the old kitchens from the original Tudor House."

"You expecting to find treasure?"

"You never know."

Peter chuckled.

Tony, meanwhile, headed back inside and found Tita, who was wearing a broad smile.

"I struck gold," she said.

"You've found a Rocky?"

"Yes, in a shelter not far from here. He's seven years old. A retired racer. Want to see a photograph?"

She passed her phone.

"Bloody hell!"

"What?"

"He looks just like Rocky. Same brindle coat. Lemur-like tail."

She laughed. "Maybe it is Rocky's spirit!"

"When can we get him?"

"They said straight away."

When they arrived at the shelter, they caused quite a stir. The silver R8 was enough to bring people outside. But then, when they saw Tony and Tita, others began to assemble.

They walked inside the office, met the manager, and had their first encounter with the greyhound.

"He's got blue eyes, just like you, Tony!" She held the dog's head and kissed his long snout.

Tony laughed.

"What's his name?" Tita asked.

"His previous owners called him Tiger."

"Then Tiger it is," Tita said.

On the way back to the house, Tita insisted that Tiger sit on her lap. In the end, he somehow managed to curl himself up into a ball and tuck his front feet under his chest. His body covered the entirety of Tita's lower torso and legs. The sight of such a large hound being treated like a lapdog was too much for Tony. He shook his head and muttered all the way home. Tita, in return, just laughed.

When they returned, Tiger exited the vehicle in slow and ponderous movements. Once his paws were on the gravel, he uttered a loud yawn then strode towards the archaeologists. He introduced himself to Ella first, swishing his tail in slow movements like a horse swatting flies from its backside. Then he nudged Rose, the bespectacled site manager, before descending into what was now a very large cavity in the ground and making himself known to the other diggers. By the time he emerged again, Tiger was a hit with the entire team.

"Anything to report?" Tony asked.

"It's definitely the Tudor kitchens," Rose said. "They've managed to get down to the level of the original ceiling. They're now digging their way into the cellar itself."

"Please keep me posted."

"I will."

Tony called to Tiger who followed him as he walked around the grounds inspecting the work Peter and his team were doing, installing hidden cameras and lights overlooking the front gate, the drive, the gardens front and back, and the front door.

Once inside the house, Tony sat at the kitchen table while Tiger lay on a mat warming himself next to the aga.

"He's made himself at home," Tita said.

"I'm not sure how effective he is as a guard dog," Tony said.

"Well, we'll still love him even if he's not."

"If his royal walkabout outside is anything to go by," Tony muttered, "he's more likely to welcome intruders."

"Look! He's smiling!" Tita cried.

She snuck over to the aga and wrapped her arms around the dog's neck. "He's got lovely black lips! And look at his big paws, and his baggy and furry britches ..."

Tiger looked at Tony from the corner of one eye as if he was suffering an onerous ordeal. The feeling was confirmed when the dog uttered a long and indignant groan.

"I don't think he's used to being loved," she said, looking back at Tony with sad eyes.

"I don't think anyone's used to being loved in the way you love them," Tony said. "Give him time."

"I'll give you time too," she said with a wink.

"Speaking of time," he said. "Everything's on course for tonight. The lights and cameras will be installed. We'll put Tiger's bed in the hallway so he can..."

"No!" Tita cried. "He can sleep with us!"

"There's two assumptions in that statement," Tony said. "First, that you're sleeping with me."

"Well, aren't I?"

"You are."

"Good."

"And the second is that Tiger's sleeping upstairs."

"Well, isn't he?"

"He is not. He won't hear people outside unless he's on the ground floor and the hallway is the best place."

Tita threw her arms around the poor dog's neck again. "Your new master is so cruel. I'll protect you."

Tony sighed.

Tita, meanwhile, gave him the side eye and said, "You're a meanie, Tony! Tony the Meanie. That's your new name. The two men in this house are called Tiger and Meanie."

Tony shook his head.

"You're not going to have a fit, are you?" Tita asked.

"Like water for chocolate," Tony said.

And Tita laughed.

51

THE CASKET

On the third day of the dig, Ella rang the doorbell. It was midday and Tita was preparing lunch for all the team in the kitchen. As soon as the couple walked out of the front door, they could tell from the commotion in the cordoned area that something was afoot. Even Tiger seemed excited. He bounded towards the yellow mini-digger as if he was trying to chase it away from the grounds.

Rose met them on the edge of the lawn. "Please follow me," she said. They both detected restrained excitement.

Tony could see that the archaeologists had dug deeper and discovered a chamber. Several of the team were dusting the floor tiles. Others were cleaning objects they had found buried there. These were mainly kitchen utensils of a very great age. Tony noticed seven iron pots of different sizes and one large cauldron.

They climbed down into the chamber while Tiger stayed above, watching every move they made. Ella patted him on the head before descending the ten-foot slope and joining

Tony and Tita in the freshly excavated pit. When she reached them, she smiled and said, “It’s just as you thought, Tony. A fine Tudor kitchen. The utensils and tiles date from the early to mid-1500s.”

“Did you find anything unusual?”

“We did indeed. We’ve found a great deal of cutlery and coins. In fact, we think we’ve cleared pretty well the whole of this upper floor of every metal object.”

“You said *upper* floor?”

“There’s more to this than we thought,” Rose said as she joined them. “There’s another floor below.”

Tony’s heart began to race.

Rose led them to the far end and pointed to an iron handle attached to a flagstone at her feet.

She lifted what looked like a door and headed down some stone steps into an underground chamber much cooler than the one above. They could barely hear Tiger barking.

“A storeroom?” Tita asked.

“Yes,” Rose answered.

She walked towards the wall furthest from the steps and shone a torch onto the wall. Tony could make out the outline of a large square. She said, “This room was also used to hide things.”

She pressed one side of the square. It disappeared into the wall while the other half opened towards them.

“It took us a while to open,” Rose said.

“When I used the detector in here,” Ella said, “it picked up something behind the wall.”

She trained her beam on the space beyond. She nudged Tony, nodding her head towards the hole.

Tony thrust his hands into the space behind it. He

touched what felt like a box. Inch by inch, he manoeuvred it towards the opening until it was out of its hiding place and in his hands.

"Could it be?" Tita asked.

Ella shone her light on the object. It was a square coffer covered in a cotton velvet material. She studied it, then said, "The material covering this thing is expensive, and very old."

"Have you looked inside it?"

"No. We don't have the key, and in any case, it's your land so it's your privilege."

"How are we going to get it open?"

"I can pick it," Tita said.

"Really?"

"Yes!"

She removed a hairclip from a tiny wallet in her pocket and began twisting and turning the mechanism. At first, all she could do was remove the dirt and sediment within the clogged opening of the lock. But after she had cleared the tiny pieces of debris, she manipulated the mechanism until they all heard a click. "My misspent youth," she said, lifting the lid and smiling at Tony.

As Ella illuminated the box, they all gasped. The casket was constructed like the interior of a house. It had three levels, with each part of each level divided into the equivalent of rooms, some small, others large. The whole design was clever and intricate. When you moved one drawer, you had to make sure it returned to the same place, or the entire architecture would be thrown out of kilter.

Looking at Tita, Tony said, "You do the honours."

Tita sat down and laid the chest to rest on the ground. Rose passed her some gloves. As Tita opened the drawers,

Ella recorded the findings using the video camera on her phone.

Tita began with the uppermost level.

"Two rings of gold set with nine diamonds in each, the diamonds of different sizes. One ring set with a long diamond. Two rings of gold set with an emerald. Three hoops of gold. Two turquoises set in gold. A gold broch. A purse of green silk with ten buttons of gold, enamelled black. A whetstone tipped with silver. A collar for a dog, crimson velvet, embroidered with gold and silver."

"Tiger would look good in that," Ella said.

Tita opened the second till of the coffer. "A book of prayers, with a purple velvet cover garnished with gold." She opened the cover. "A prayer book belonging to..." She gasped.

"What is it?" Tony asked.

She recovered her poise and continued. "A prayer book belonging to Queen Catherine Parr."

A shiver went down every spine.

"A Book of Psalms, also belonging to Queen Catherine Parr. A New Testament in French, covered with black velvet, also belonging to the Queen. And a purple velvet New Testament in English, garnished with silver. This says that it is a gift from the Queen to..." She struggled to stay calm and put the book down on her lap. Then she took a deep breath, lifted it, and read, "A gift given from the Queen to her beloved daughter Mary, on the occasion of her birth."

Tita could barely contain her excitement.

"There's more in here," she gasped. "A primer in English, covered in crimson velvet, with no inscription. A little book of prayers in purple velvet. And that's it for the second level."

Tita gently pushed the drawers back into place and withdrew the third level of the casket. "A bundle of what look like letters tied together in a purple ribbon with a bow. I'm going to have to wait until we're inside to inspect these."

Rose now spoke. "These are all very significant and valuable treasures. You'll need to report them to the local coroner within the next fourteen days. An officer will come and inspect the items. Most likely, a museum will want them. They'll only be in your hands for a short while. Make the most of the time."

"Thanks," Tony said, adding, "Please don't say anything to anyone about the contents of this box. I don't want this getting into the press yet. Ella, Rose... you promise?"

They nodded.

They ascended to the upper floor of the kitchens and then up to the lawn. When the team members saw the casket in Tita's arms, they clapped and cheered.

Tony headed back to the house. As he walked into the kitchen, Tita placed the box on the table and patted Tiger on the head.

Tony took Tita in his arms. "I think we may have the material you want for your next book," he whispered.

"And for yours," she replied.

52

THE LOCK

That night, while Tita sat in the study upstairs examining the letters from the casket, Tony texted Shree and told her that they had found something. He added the word treasure.

She texted one word back.

Zoom?

The next minute, she was staring wide-eyed at him.

"Tell me more!"

"The excavation has gone better than I could ever have dreamed. We found the original cellars, used as the kitchens for the Tudor mansion. There were pots and pans and all sorts of other things buried there, dating back to that period. But then the archaeologists found something else. An iron ring-shaped handle attached to a flagstone. A door. Some steps down into ..."

"Don't tell me. A cave?"

"Well, yes, you could call it a cave. Rose thinks it was used as a storeroom, mainly for keeping food cool. But she and Ella also found a door in the wall and behind it a casket."

Shree clapped her hands.

"When we looked inside, it was designed like a little house. There were three floors to it. In the upper floor, the drawers – which were like rooms – were full of priceless Tudor jewels."

More clapping.

"However, that's not all. The second floor was even more valuable, although not in monetary terms necessarily. There were books. Beautifully bound and covered. Some belonged to Queen Catherine Parr who once lived in the house. One was a gift to her daughter Mary, on the occasion of her birth."

"Which Mary is this?" Shree asked.

"It's a bit confusing, so bear with me. There are three Marys in this story. There's a Mary who was one of the three who built the Tudor House in 1530. There's a Mary who was the only child of Queen Catherine and Sir Thomas Seymour. And there's the Mary who reigned after the death of young King Edward."

Shree said, "I presume the Mary you're talking about is the child of Queen Catherine."

"That's right. Catherine Parr became sick after giving birth. She had been married four times and never had children, until now. A fever took her, and little Mary was motherless."

"What about her father, Thomas Seymour?"

"He was not a good man. Tita believes he married Catherine Parr to get as close as he could to the throne. When he became bored with her, he recommenced his flirtation with her stepdaughter, young Elizabeth, the daughter of Anne Boleyn."

"Was she the one who became Elizabeth I?"

"Yes, the Virgin Queen."

"What on earth was Thomas Seymour doing? She must have been much younger than him."

"She was nearly fourteen. He was nearly forty."

Shree frowned. "I know I'm supposed to show unconditional positive regard, but this time I'm not going to. What a horrible man. Why did he behave in such a way?"

"Many reasons, some of them very basic. But I also think he saw Elizabeth as a likely future monarch and shifted his affections from a queen who was on the way down to a queen who was on the way up. In short, I think his motives were political."

"What happened to him?"

"He was arrested for trying to break into King Edward's bedroom. Tried, then executed."

"So, Mary became an orphan."

"Sadly, she did."

"Who looked after her?"

"It's a long story, but my dreams have been telling me that Queen Catherine's chaplain, John Parkhurst, looked after her here at the Old Rectory. In my dreams, the house seems to be telling me that Mary was adopted by one of the servants and that she lived incognito here away from the eyes of those who would harm her."

"Who would want to hurt the girl?"

"That's where Queen Mary comes in. She was a Catholic and wanted to return the country to her faith. Catherine had been a great champion of the Reformation and wanted the complete opposite. To Queen Mary, Catherine's child would have been a threat. John Parkhurst decided to hide her here, at the Old Rectory."

"How is the treasure relevant?"

"It's vital. Up until now, I've just had my dreams, but dreams aren't enough to prove a theory. The books and letters change everything. They are physical evidence."

"Letters? You didn't mention letters."

"Oh, yes, we got distracted."

"Sorry!"

"That's okay. The third level of the casket contained letters. It's probably going to take a few days because many are in Latin, but Tita started examining them this evening."

"Oh yes, tell me about Tita."

"Tita and I are now friends."

Shree smiled. "Friends?"

"Well, maybe a little more."

"Don't be coy, Tony. I'm your therapist, remember? You can share anything with me."

"Okay, I'm in love with her."

More claps.

Shree fetched her iPad. "I'm just going to share something with you." She found a page and looked at me. "You remember I sent you that book, *The Poetics of Space*?"

"How can I forget?"

"He talks quite a bit about caskets."

"I do recall something about that."

"Then you'll know he spoke, as you just did, about the casket as a kind of dwelling place, that 'a house is hidden in it.' Your casket, the one you've just found, is like a house within a house."

"That's right," Tony said.

She continued, "Caskets hide secrets."

Tony nodded.

Shree continued reading from her notes. "He quotes a French writer who said that we can never reach the bottom of a casket because its secrets are endless, almost timeless."

She scrolled down the page. "Here, listen to this purple passage. You may remember it, Tony."

As it happened, he did.

"The casket," Monsieur Blanchard writes, "contains things that are *unforgettable*, unforgettable for us, but also unforgettable for those to whom we are going to give our treasures. Here, the past, the present, and the future are condensed. Thus, the casket is the memory of what is immemorial."

Tony shook his head and said, "If ever a philosopher was a poet, it was Blanchard."

"He was more than that."

"In what way?"

"For all his scepticism about psychology, he was also psychologically astute, especially in his understanding of how caskets and houses affect us emotionally, intellectually, and even spiritually. No one else gets close to his level of insight."

She found another page.

"Look at what he says about locks. I presume you had to work quite hard at unlocking the box?"

"Tita cracked it using a hairpin."

Shree laughed

"I bet when you unlocked the chest and opened it, a whole new world opened to you. That's why Blanchard says, 'A lock is a psychological threshold'."

"I don't follow."

"He means that unlocking that box is going to change everything for you, Tony. It's going to change the way you think about yourself and about life. It's going to stop you from ever again feeling ordinary, and it's going to help you feel special."

"Stop that," Tony said, his eyes watering.

"No, I won't. We've always known that the house of your soul needed therapy as much as the soul of your house. That's happening. Both you and the house are being restored. There's a perfect synchronicity and synergy here."

Tony sighed.

"I don't think you're done yet," Shree said. "There's more to come. Be open to that. And, in the meantime, go and find Tita and let her hug and hold you until the scars heal."

Tony nodded and headed to his study.

Tita turned as he entered. She took one look at him and stood. She put her arms around his neck, nestled his head on her shoulder, and stroked his aching back until the tears stopped.

53
THE QUESTION

The next day, after the team of archaeologists had conducted their final scan of the excavated area, they made to leave just as the sun was setting. Rose knocked on the front door before she drove with the others to the nearby Farquharson Arms.

"Tomorrow will be our last day, Mister Lawson. We'll fill in the site and put the lawn back as it was. Not a moment too soon. The leaves are becoming a bit of a nuisance."

Tony thanked her and gave her enough money to buy the team a couple of rounds and some pub grub. He then walked into the hallway just as Tita came downstairs from the study.

"I've done enough for today," she said.

"You've been at it since dawn," Tony said. "You deserve a break. I can't thank you enough."

They sat in the kitchen and ate some warmed-up leftovers from the dinner Tita had made the previous evening. "You're a brilliant cook," Tony said. "Every meal's a masterpiece, even the leftovers. I've not eaten this well in years, if ever."

"I love cooking," she said. "Do you know that book about love languages? I think the author found five. But he should have added a sixth in a section all on its own. Cooking."

Tony laughed. "I'm by no means fluent in that particular language, but I'd love you one day to teach me."

"I will," she said. "Cooking can get quite magical sometimes, the way ingredients flow together unexpectedly, the reactions the flavours produce in others. My mother had the gift. She said I did too. That's why she named me Tita."

"I don't follow."

"It's from a romantic story by Laura Esquivel, about a girl called Tita who falls in love with a guy called Pedro, but her mother won't let her marry him. He marries her sister just to be near his true love. Meanwhile, she uses the magic in her meals to try and orchestrate it so they can at last be together."

"I'll have to watch what I eat," Tony said.

He finished his dinner and took a sip of claret. Wiping his lips with a napkin, he set his glass down and looked at her. "You look tired," he said. "Shall we have an early night?"

"I'd like a bath."

"I'll run one for you."

"Come and sit with me," she said. "I'll tell you where I've got to with my research."

Tony headed upstairs and ran the taps of the old enamel bath, adding a scented bath bomb.

"I love it!" Tita cried.

The next minute, she was lying on her back, her eyes closed, stroking the water and suds over her soft skin.

"There's all kinds of correspondence in the bundle," she

said. "Most of it is love letters from a man called Robert, who clearly courted Mary, Catherine's daughter, when she was about eighteen years of age. They're in English, although it's Tudor English of course, rather rustic, and not that easy to read."

"What did you learn about him?"

"Only what he reveals of himself in his eighteen letters. He seems to have been someone who worked hard in the grounds, maybe a gardener. He speaks of picking apples and bringing them into the kitchen and handing them to Mary. He tells her that the very sight of her causes his heart to burn within him."

"Was she in love with him too?"

"Very much so. You can tell by the way he quotes back some of the things she has been writing to him. She wrote that she longs to rest her head upon his chest and feel his arms around her."

"What happened to them?"

"I'm not sure. Robert's letters stop abruptly. I cannot tell if this was because he died, or moved away, or maybe married her. After all, there would be no need to write letters anymore if the two of them were living together as man and wife."

"So, we are in the dark."

"Not as much as we were before. There are other revealing letters. There is one from Queen Catherine which she must have dictated. It seems she knew she was dying and shared her message with John Parkhurst. Then she signed it. She must have been very ill. Her signature is verry erratic, though recognizably hers."

"What did she say?"

"That she loved Mary more than all the finest words from the most refined languages of the world could ever express, that she was deeply sorry she would not see her grow up to become a young woman, that she hoped that she would find faith in her Saviour, and that she would discover true love in the arms of a trustworthy and self-giving man. She told her to be like Almighty God, who does not look upon the outward appearance, but upon the heart, and she encouraged her never to forget that she was the daughter of a queen, and therefore a princess, but always to remember that true virtue is seen in humility, not in pomp and ceremony, especially in matters of religion."

Tony moved a stray strand of dark hair from her forehead and said, "That is very touching."

Tony started to rub Tita's shoulders.

"There were also letters from Mary's father, Thomas Seymour, including one written from the Tower, the night before his execution. It's hard to read when you know what kind of a man he was, but at the same time he must have loved her."

Tony kissed Tita on the forehead. "Thank you for doing all this. It's a real labour of love."

"I'm not finished yet," she said.

"Are there more documents?"

"Some, but that's not really the issue."

"What do you mean?"

"I mean that I can read, translate, and study all the rest of the documents in the box, but I'm not sure they will answer the one big question that won't stop nagging me."

"Which is?"

"Why now?"

"What do you mean?"

"Why did Lady Mary Seymour appear to *you*, Tony, five hundred years after the original house was built?"

"I can't answer that."

"Has she appeared to anyone else?"

"The historian told me that she'd been seen by a few people over the course of the centuries. But he seemed very interested when I told him she'd appeared to me."

"Why do you think that was?"

"I have no idea."

"Tony, there's something I don't understand. And yet I feel like it's on the tip of my tongue. We've found the casket and we've discovered some of the secrets that have been buried. But there's something else. Its secrets seem to be even deeper, bigger still."

Tony continued to rub her neck.

She concluded, "Those secrets are bound to the one big question I have. Why is Lady Mary, dressed in her kitchen clothes, appearing to you now, and only you?"

54

THE INVASION

Three hours later, just after midnight, Tony was rudely awakened by Tiger's long cold nose. The dog seemed agitated.

Tony climbed out of bed, careful not to waken Tita. Thinking that Tiger would run downstairs towards the front door, he slid on his slippers, preparing to let the hound out.

But Tiger did not turn towards the staircase. He headed to Tony's study a few doors down and stood there, staring at the handle, his tail stationary, his attention unwavering.

"You want to go in?" he whispered.

The dog's tail swished.

Just once.

Tony opened the door.

A soft, silvery light from the half-formed moon filled the room. Tony could see the casket on the desk where Tita had left it. Tiger trotted to the desk chair and sniffed at the old box. At first, Tony thought he wanted him to open it. But then he rose on his haunches and started looking towards the ancient panes in the arched and stone-framed window. His sniffing turned into a low-level growl. His nose twitched as he unfurled his gums and revealed his teeth.

"Something out there, Tiger?"

He tilted his head towards Tony and grinned. Wagging his tail, he nudged him.

"All right! I get the hint."

Tony climbed onto the stone shelf and leaned against the left-hand side of the archway. None of the newly installed security lights had been activated. The only illumination was from the moon, but it was enough to afford a measure of visibility.

Tony studied the gravel drive.

Nothing.

Then the gates and the cob wall.

Nothing.

Then the lawn.

He wiped his eyes.

There was someone there.

Why had the lights not been triggered?

As Tony squinted, he began to form a clearer impression. Seconds later, he knew who it was. The height. The paunch. The gait. The beret. It was Maul. And he was carrying something.

Tony refocused.

Then he saw it.

A large jerrycan.

He had come with one purpose.

To burn the house down.

The house that had become Tony's refuge.

His haven.

His retreat.

The house whose address Maul had somehow discovered.

Even though Tony had made every effort to conceal it.

Tony was about to race downstairs and confront the intruder when curiosity got the better of him. What was he doing standing there on the grass? Why was he not pouring the petrol on the house?

Maul was on the lawn now, intrigued by the pit, looking down into its depths. He stood at the house-end of the dig and stared into the darkness, trying to fathom its significance. Maybe, like a green-eyed mercenary, he detected the scent of treasure. Maybe he was just being nosey, trying to find out what his nemesis was doing. Whatever his reasoning, and he alone knew, he activated the torch on his phone and made as if to step down into the pit.

And then it happened.

He stopped in his tracks.

The phone spilled out of his hand.

Its torchlight now muted by the grass beneath the screen.

He was staring.

Pale-faced.

Gawping.

As a figure began to emerge from the hole.

Not so much walking.

Floating.

Head bowed.

Looking down.

Tony knew who it was even before she raised her face to meet his eyes. It was Mary, the kitchen maid, the daughter of the Dowager Queen of England, Ireland, and France.

Lady Mary Seymour.

The ghost in the garden.

Only she was not there to curtsy.

She was there to terrify.

And she was wearing an intricate coronet of bluish fire, not simple ribbons of white cotton.

Maul took a step back.

She rose to her full height, as tall as the apple tree.

Her face was not welcoming, as before.

It was fierce.

Shining like the moon.

Becoming ever brighter.

Her eyes became enraged.

Her hair came loose from her crown.

Each strand seemed to be alive.

Phosphorescent.

Charged by a preternatural energy.

Maul dropped the jerrycan on the ground. He tried to bend down and pick up his phone, but he was too frightened by the figure looming above him. His arms were flailing. Rabid. Incoherent. Like the wild waving of a drowning man.

"Get away from me!" he screamed.

Tiger barked and bounded downstairs.

Tita ran into the study.

"What is it?"

"See for yourself!"

She leapt onto the desk in one athletic movement. Tony made room for her on the stone sill.

"Madre de Dios!"

Tita seized Tony's arm.

"Is that her?"

"Yes, but not as I have ever seen her before."

"Who's that standing at the pit?"

"Maul."

"What's he doing?"

"He was about to burn the house down."

"He could have killed us!"

"I don't think he cares."

"Bastard!"

Maul struggled to his feet and tried to maintain his balance beside the pit. He was swaying.

The arms of the spectre now reached towards him.

Her fingers seemed to be elongated.

They started to grasp Maul's neck.

And then came a scream.

One neither Tita nor Tony would ever forget.

Long.

Piercing.

High-pitched.

Abject terror in a single note.

And when the keening stopped and the phantom vanished, the intruder turned towards the gravel and staggered towards the gates, tripping every light in the area, until he was out onto the road, revving his engine, his tyres screeching as he drove away, while the muffled light of his phone glowed in the wet grass of the lawn.

They watched as the ghost returned to her normal proportions. She looked up at them and smiled. Then, in one sweet motion, she curtsied again, her hand drifting over the edge of the pit, pointing to the darkness below, a look of joy on her face.

She disappeared.

"Do you think you'll ever see her again?" Tita asked.

"I don't know. I hope so. I can't imagine this place without her. The house and the ghost ... they're bound together. Her history, its history. All part of the same rich tapestry."

"And what about that ugly man?"

"You think he's ugly?"

"He's so ugly he would make onions cry."

Tony laughed.

"He won't ever come back."

Tita jumped down from the desk. She looked back at him and said, "His torch is still on."

"So?"

"So, if he's left his phone on, maybe we will be able to access its contents and find proof of his intentions. You know how I love evidence. This could be perfect."

Tony followed her down the stairs and ran out with her and Tiger onto the grass.

Tita picked up the phone.

"We're in!" she cried.

55

THE KIPPER

It was the sound of the digger outside that wakened Tony. He turned to his right to talk to Tita, but she was gone. Tiger was lying in her space, his body the full length of the bed. It was obvious to Tony that this was Tita's doing. She had tucked him in so well that he was visible only from the neck up, and she had positioned her pillow so that the dog's hairy head was resting right in its centre.

"Out of here!" Tony barked.

The dog groaned.

The hound slowly stood with the duvet draped over him, like the canvas of a tent being lifted off its poles.

"Downstairs!"

Tony found Tita in the kitchen with Maul's phone connected by a lead to her laptop.

"This is amazing!" she cried.

"Tell me more."

"He's a complete *gilipollas...*"

"I don't know what that means, but I can guess. Something

like 'asshole' or 'dickhead'?"

"You got it, babe!"

"I agree, but why?"

"He's got the most inflated ego I've ever come across, and believe me, I've met a few. He thinks he's a great writer. Hard done by, but one of the greats. He's completely deceived. His writing is average at best. The reviews on Amazon, they're mostly very damning. The poor deluded fool sees himself as the last coke in the desert."

Tony smiled.

"Have you found any incriminating evidence?"

"Plenty. There are all the emails he sent to his lawyer about you and about the settlement. There are emails to some dodgy character who seems to be a forger..."

"He must have helped him fake that document!" Tony cried.

"And there's other stuff too. Emails in which he makes enquiries to various estate agents, obviously trying to track down this house. He then seems to have contacted a private investigator..."

"Did he employ one?"

"Man called Roger Brandon. From what I've read so far, I think he's the PI who found your address."

"He'll be getting a strongly worded email," Tony said.

"I hope you'll let me write it."

Tony laughed.

"I will. It'll be fun."

"Is there anything else of interest?"

"That's it really," she said. "I've been sending all the documents to your printer so they should be in the tray. I'm sure your lawyer will find them interesting."

"I hope this time it's really over," Tony said.

"What do you mean?"

"After my lawyer found Maul's ex, I thought I'd finished him, but he's kept coming for me."

"This time it's over," she said, standing up and placing her arms around his neck. "He now knows you have two terrifying *perras* on your side, and one is a ghost."

"*Perras*?"

"Bitches," she said.

Tony smiled.

"How long have you been up?" he asked.

"Since 6.00 am."

"Don't you ever sleep?"

"Not when I'm like Tiger."

"What do you mean?"

"Weren't these dogs bred for hunting?"

"They were."

"Well, I hunt too."

"Hunt what?"

"The truth."

"I guess you do."

"Have you ever read Lucretius?" she asked.

"I've heard of him."

"He encouraged pupils to be like dogs that roam over mountains and sniff out where the wild beasts hide. He told them to track down the secret places and draw the truth from them."

"That reminds me," Tony said. "We should go out and say goodbye to the team. They must be filling in the pit. But first, let me make you some breakfast. I've got some kippers."

"Kippers?"

"They're delicious."

Tita did not find them at all delicious. She spat out the first morsel, much to Tony's amusement.

When she had finished drinking her coffee, Tita looked down at the staring eye of the pale, golden fish. Picking the creature up by its tail, she said, "This thing reminds me of Maul."

Tony coughed out some coffee. Wiping his wet beard, he said, "You're going to have explain."

"In Spanish, we have a saying. *Que te folle un pez!*"

"I hesitate to ask, but what does that mean?"

"It means 'I hope you get f*!#ed by a fish'."

She placed the kipper on her side plate.

Tony laughed. He said, "I don't understand you, Tita. One minute you're quoting Lucretius, the next you're talking about someone being abused by a kipper."

She smiled. "I'm complex."

While they were embracing, their new dog appeared at the side of the table. Tiger was so tall and so stealthy that neither of them saw his nose until it was too late. He had taken the kipper by its tail and then, with a toss of his head, flipped it in the air and into his jaws where it was efficiently sawed and then swallowed. And, like Maul, the wide-eyed kipper was never seen again.

56

THE INVITATIONS

After the entire excavation team had left, and Tony had thanked Ella, it was time for a light lunch.

Tita spoke first. "I need to leave next week."

They both felt the sadness of it.

Keenly.

"I have two requests," she said. "Firstly, I would like you to ask the historian to come round to the house. I need to meet him before I go. I think he may have some interesting things to share."

"I can arrange that."

"The second may sound strange to your ears, *mi amor*, but I want something to remind me of you when I'm back in California. Something I can put in this..." She produced a locket on a golden chain. "It belonged to my grandmother."

"What's on your mind?"

"It's something on *your* mind," she said pointing to his head.

"A locket of my hair?"

"Precisely."

"That's very old school, Tita."

"I'm a bit of an old-fashioned romantic."

Tita walked to a drawer and withdrew a pair of scissors which she then opened over Tony's head.

"How much are you thinking of taking?" He asked, gawping at the yawning blades.

She laughed.

"Only a little."

True to her word, she snipped a couple of what she called "stray hairs" from the back of his head and locked them away. "There," she said, hanging the locket over her chest. "You'll be close to my heart, even when I'm far away."

"I have a request to make to you," Tony said.

"Name it."

"I'd like you to come back for Christmas."

"I'd love to."

"Good."

"Just so long as you let me buy Christmas decorations and make your house look festive."

Tony nodded, feigning grumpiness. He said, "I want to have a party for all the people who've helped me over the last year, especially those who've helped... how is it Shree puts it? ... helped to restore the soul of my house and the house of my soul."

"I love that!" Tita said. "Shree sounds amazing. I can't wait to meet her. Isn't her partner Japanese?"

"She is."

"We are going to get on like a house on fire." Tita paused, then said, "Sorry. I shouldn't have said that."

"It's okay. You don't need to tiptoe around my heart."

"That's good," she said, squeezing his hand. "Who's on the guest list? I'll make notes on my phone."

"Well, there's you and me."

"You mean Lord and Lady Lawson…"

"There's you and me," he said, ignoring the promotion. "Then there's Shree and Aya. Yinka, Nadiya, Hamish, and partners. The archaeological team. Ditto with the painters, decorators, and builders. Rakesh and his family from Chelsea. And Naomi Marsh."

"What about Ella?"

"Definitely. Ella plus one."

"And the historian, Con?"

"Yes."

"Does he have someone?"

"He lives alone, I think."

"Anyone else?"

"Ms Macready, the estate agent."

"Does she have a plus one?"

"I hope so."

Tita thought for a moment. She said, "Let me organise this party. I'd like to give it a Mexican theme."

"Okay, but why?"

"Most English people don't realise how much their Christmas traditions are dictated by America. In Mexico, we have very different Christmas customs. I'd love to introduce all your friends to them, especially their children."

"Children?"

"Yes, Tony. We must invite all their kids. Christmas isn't Christmas without the kids."

"What have you in mind?"

"You'll see. I'll email you nearer the time. But I'll need

to borrow Ella and maybe a couple of others too, the day before the party. They can help me set up a few things in the garden."

"When are you coming over?"

"December 14th," she said. "Is that okay?"

"Sure. But why then?"

"It's the day before our nine-day festival in Mexico."

"We're not having a party that long!"

She laughed. "No, let's have it the Saturday before Christmas. 4pm. When it's getting dark."

"Okay, but I really want you by my side as well - to introduce you to the most important people in my life."

"Of course, Tony." She looked back down at her list. "Will any of these guests be staying over?"

"A few. Shree and her partner. Possibly Yinka and his wife. Let's ask and see if they want to stay here. And I'd like Jimmy, my godson, to stay the weekend if he can."

She added his name to the list.

Tony paused, then added, "I think I should invite Renée and her new feller. Maybe it's time to say sorry."

"Peace on earth," she said.

"Season of good will," Tony added.

"It's the right thing, baby. You can't start a new thing healthily unless you end the old thing healthily as well. And I'm sure Shree would agree with that."

"That's true. Speaking of starting a new thing..."

"Yes?"

"Should we let people know our relationship status?"

Tita shook her head. "Listen, Tony. True love isn't like a ladder, with each stage given a name and a ceremony. True love is gravitational. It's not about climbing. It's about falling."

"So, when we stand together at our Christmas party," Tony said, "you're saying we shouldn't let anyone know that we're dating, or whatever the case may be by then."

"Tony!" There was fire in her eyes now. "It's about showing, not telling. We're too old for labels. Let's just be who we are and what we are, and let our friends see the falling."

Tony was still unsure, so she turned around and pointed to the stone hearth in the kitchen.

"When you light a fire in winter, people come and stand around it to get warm. It's the same with romance. When two people are ablaze with love, people come and watch you burn. Even Renée may end up warming her hands at our hearth."

"Renée is a cold one," Tony said. "But maybe that, and a genuine apology from yours truly, will help to thaw her a little. You never know, Nick may even have cause to thank me."

"Nick?"

"Her new man. I think they could be very happy if she just lightened up and laughed a little."

Tita said, "Okay. If you give me the email addresses, I'll send them all a save-the-date. Right now, I need to get back to the study. There are still some documents to read. I can't help thinking there's something I'm missing. Maybe Con can help us."

"Okay, girlfriend," Tony said.

Tita punched his shoulder on her way past. "No labels!" She cried, before swinging back and kissing Tony on the lips.

57

THE LIBRARY

Two days later Tony was sitting on a sofa in the drawing room keeping watch, along with Tiger, over the fire in the grate. Tita walked in carrying two large leather-bound books.

"New editions to your library," she said.

"What have you bought now?"

"Reverend John Hutchins's History of Dorset. It's a first edition, 1774. There's a section on this village, the church, and on this house, although you may know most of it. It's the county's standard work of reference to this day. Have a look."

She handed over the two heavy volumes, full of engravings, and an old map of the county in the first. Tony skim-read the section on the village, the church, and the Rectory. She was right. There was little they had not already discovered.

"This must have taken him ages," Tony said.

"Remember, Tony, rectors in those days had plenty of leisure time to write. That said, it's a true labour of love all the same. Hutchins nearly lost his manuscript in a ..."

She paused as a log splintered.

"In a fire?"

"The house with all his papers burned to the ground while Hutchins was away conducting a service. A careless maid caused the blaze which destroyed a third of the town. The author's wife ran in and rescued most of his manuscript, clutching under both arms twenty years of her husband's work."

"She sounds amazing!"

"She was. People remember her standing in the river with the papers over her head. The fire was so intense, it was the only safe place she could find. But that's not all."

"Tell me."

"Anne was the daughter of Thomas Stephens. Do you remember who he was?"

"He was the rector here when the Tudor original of this house burned to the ground."

"Yes, and do you recall who rescued his papers?"

"His daughter Anne." Then it hit him. "Not the same Anne who salvaged these volumes?"

"The same! Poor Anne endured two devastating house fires. One at the start of her life. The other towards the end. And in both cases, she proved to be a heroic saviour of books."

Tita walked over to Tony and opened the first volume. "Do you see the quotation on the title page?"

"It's in Latin," he said.

"*Reliquiae Troia ex ardente receptae*,' she read.

"I don't know what that means," Tony said, "but it sounds really sexy when you say it."

"Thank you *carino*. It means 'relics rescued from the fire.' You know where that's from?"

"You're the academic."

"It's from Virgil's *Aeneid*, the epic poem that was translated by another rector who lived here, Christopher Pitt. I'm looking for first editions of that for your library as well."

"Maybe you should calm down ..."

"No, *mi amor*. I also have another book I need to find and then I promise I'll calm down, as you say. It's by George Bingham, the longest serving rector who lived in this house. He helped Hutchins to research and write the two-volume work in your lap. But he wrote his own book too, a tribute to Hutchins called *Biographical Anecdotes of the Rev. John Hutchins, M.A.* It was published in 1785."

"Another writer cleric then," Tony said.

She said, "You told me his beloved wife passed away while he was living in this house, and she died of what sounds like the same cause of death that afflicted Queen Catherine."

"That's right, and he also lost one of his sons in a drowning accident. His surviving son wrote a memoir about his father, prefixed to George Bingham's *Dissertations, Essays and Sermons ...*"

With a coy smile, Tita interjected. "I am going to buy a first edition of that book too. It is an important volume, *carino*. Not as expensive as Hutchins ..."

"How much did these cost me?"

"A lady never tells."

"Over a thousand?"

"Maybe," she said, even more coy now.

Tony sighed.

It was a long, exaggerated exhalation.

Tita came and sat next to him on the sofa. "See," she said, touching the gilt-panelled boards of the books. "These writers have all died, and yet they continue to live through their words."

Tony nodded.

"Do you not think there is something magical about owning a library that lives?"

"You believe dead authors still live through their books?"

"Of course, *mi amor*. Does not Queen Catherine continue to speak through her four volumes?"

Tony nodded. Mention of Queen Catherine prompted his next question. "Have you found out anything about Mary's death? I know about the start of her life, but not about its ending."

"I am forming a picture. There are various letters in the casket that suggest something."

"Care to share?"

"I can't yet. My research isn't finished."

Tony leaned back into the sofa and looked at the rows of books that were filling the shelves. Many of them were related to the history of the house. Most were written by people who had lived there, and their names seemed to glow on the spines. Some were still well known, like Charles Kingsley. Some had been well known in their day, like Christopher Pitt. Others had been less famous both then and now, and yet from their pens the words that had burned within their hearts were branded forever on the pages of their books.

"I feel like writing again," Tony said.

Tita squealed. "*Mi amor!*"

"This place inspires me."

Tita took hold of Tony's arm. "What kind of book will you write?"

"Maybe a memoir. But with a record of my dreams. Those I've had since the day I first set eyes on this house."

"And what will it be called?"

"*The House of the Soul.*"

"It will be a bestseller. I prophesy it!"

"Maybe. But that isn't why I'm writing it."

"Why then?"

"Partly therapy."

"What else?"

"Legacy."

"What do you mean by legacy?"

"Well, look at Queen Catherine. She has left a great mark on the world. She campaigned for religious freedom, and she was the first woman to get her name on the cover of a book. You and I are excited about her impact."

Tita looked into his eyes. "I sense there's more on that theme that we will soon discover."

58

THE EMPTYING

Before they were due to part, Tony and Tita took a day trip into London. Tita went off to order Christmas decorations for the party while Tony headed for Harley Street to see Shree.

"Any more revelations?" Shree asked.

"Tita is still working on the casket. She says there may be more in the letters we need to unpack. We're having Con, our eccentric historian, round for drinks tonight, so we're hoping he'll help us. We will need to hand everything over to the coroner soon."

"So, the clock's ticking."

"It is."

"Are things good with Tita?"

"Couldn't be better."

"And how are you feeling after our last session?"

"Purged."

"Of what?"

"Childhood pain."

"Can you be more specific?"

"I'll try. What I mean is that I've now confronted the trauma I'd buried for decades. I've been honest. Real. Transparent with myself for the first time, especially about losing my parents."

"And this trauma turned you into what?"

"An orphan, I guess."

"Have you ever worked with orphans?"

"No. Why?"

"Orphans perform to earn the love and affection they miss. They are driven to succeed because they believe this will give them the honour they didn't receive from their parents."

"You're saying I'm a performer."

"I'm not judging you, Tony. I'm saying that this is what orphans do. Deep down, the lie they believe about themselves is 'I am worthless.' So, they become overachievers or super-achievers as a compensation, in the hope that they will succeed enough to swap the lie, 'I am worthless,' for the truth, 'I am worthy'."

"So, how do I get shot of this mindset?"

"That's where psychologists differ."

"In what way?"

"Well, most opt for a cognitive approach..."

"Cognitive?"

"Their therapy consists of you replacing the negative things you've believed about yourself with positive beliefs. In other words, they encourage you to replace lies with truths."

"Sounds helpful."

"It is and it isn't. Most people who come to me have had

a negative experience. Call it trauma if you like. If you adopt a cognitive approach to trauma, then what you're trying to do is to displace a negative experience with a new way of thinking."

"What's wrong with that?"

"It doesn't ultimately work."

"Why not?"

"Because only a positive *experience* can displace it. Standing in front of a mirror and stating 'I am worthy' only works if your heart has first been impacted by a positive experience. That's why I believe in an *affective* model of therapy, not just a cognitive one."

"Affective?"

"One that impacts your feelings, not just your thoughts. If you want it in the language of neuroscience, one that transforms the limbic system not just the frontal cortex."

"But what does that mean for me?"

"What it means is that you need to be open to an epiphany, to enlightenment, to revelation. To something so luminous that it not only changes the way you feel. It also changes the way you think. It makes positive beliefs believable."

"What does that actually look like?"

"Everyone's different, but what you're looking for is a positive experience about who and what you really are."

"I don't follow."

"Well, look at the ghost in the garden. At first, you thought she was a lowly kitchen maid. Turns out she's a princess. That's the great secret in the soul of the house. You need something similar now in the house of your soul. An epiphany. An experience."

"Yes, but how does that happen?"

"Love, Tony. Love."

"You mean, the love of someone like Tita."

"Can be, yes. If she genuinely and demonstrably loves you, then her love is a positive experience of affection. It will help to displace the negative experience of abandonment. That way, you can start standing in front of the mirror and declaring, 'I am worthy of love. I am worthy of belonging. I am worthy, full stop'."

"How do you know this stuff, Shree?"

"How do you think?"

"You were orphaned?"

"Precisely. And it's taken me decades to learn what I've shared. All I can say is this, cultivate a mindful attitude. Raise your levels when it comes to consciousness. Be aware enough to experience epiphanies when they come to you. They will change your sense of identity from false to true, from toxic to healthy."

"I'll try."

"I'll send you some links to articles of mine."

"Thanks."

"Just be open to moments of discovery, Tony. And be patient. These things take time. We're all on a journey of healing. Including me. So, don't push it. Don't try to control it. Just let it come in its own way and in its own time."

"I'm not the most patient person."

"Then consider your house. You told me it's five hundred years old. It's taken all that time for you to come into its world, find the secret casket, and to restore its sense of wellbeing."

"The house does feel more peaceful," Tony said.

"Have you been having any more dreams?"

"Funny you should mention that. I haven't had a dream since the casket was found."

"See?" Shree said. "The house was waiting for one special person and one special moment. It was patient."

Tony nodded.

"You're waiting for a moment of clarity in which you feel differently about your identity – about the true you. Most of us, we can either denigrate, tolerate, or celebrate who we are. You're in a process leading to celebration..."

"Speaking of which..."

"What?"

"Of celebrating."

Shree looked confused.

"Tita's sending you a save-the-date message for a party at the new house. I'm killing two birds with one stone. Saying thank you to people like you who have helped me and giving a house-warming party. It's plus one, so bring Aya."

"We'll be there!" Shree said. "I can't wait to see what you've done to the house and gardens."

"The dig's been filled. We're pretty well finished."

"That's actually a really helpful picture," Shree said.

"How so?"

"Healing involves emptying and filling. The first I call *kenosis*. You've got rid of all the muck and dirt, the detritus of the wounded self. The key for you, Tony, is not to neglect the second stage, the process of discovery and filling."

"Sounds a bit like my bank account, at least the way I'm spending money on the house."

Shree smiled.

"That reminds me," he said. "Tita is shopping for Christmas decorations for our celebration."

"It's a bit early for that!"

"She's going back to the States in two days."

"How long will she be gone?"

"She's coming back on the 14th of December."

"That's good. Not too long then."

"Long enough!"

Shree held onto Tony's hand when he shook hers. "The worst is over, Tony. But you may still need some ongoing aftercare. Just call me or text me whenever you need to talk."

"Thank you, Shree. It's been worth every minute, and every penny too."

With that, he left to rescue his credit card.

59

THE INTERROGATION

Back from London, the first thing Tony and Tita did was take Tiger out for a run. They left the Queen's Walk and headed towards the top of a nearby hill. After half an hour, they arrived at a clump of trees where they sheltered from the light rain. They let Tiger off the lead and watched him accelerate to top speed through the ploughed fields. Flushing a hare out of hiding, he chased it until the creature disappeared through a tiny gap in a long, tall hedge. He returned and stood panting beside them as they looked down at the Old Rectory.

"It will look beautiful this Christmas," Tita said. "When the tree is up and the white lights are on in the gardens and around the house, it will be like a beacon."

"I can't wait for you to return," Tony said.

"Me too, *mi amor*. Me too"

Tony sighed.

"I'm sorry I need to leave tomorrow. Work calls. But I'll be back. I promise I'll be back."

"I'll miss you," he said.

Just then, Tiger sneezed. Not a quiet sneeze. Nor one with a preamble to warn them. Instead, a deafening, sudden sound that jolted Tony out of his sadness.

"Con will be here soon," he said.

They marched down the hill towards the house, arriving just as Con appeared at the front door.

"I'd like to introduce you to Tita," Tony said.

"The pleasure is all mine," Con said, taking her hand, raising it to his lips, and kissing it.

"Let's get inside," Tony said. "I'll light a fire."

Tita dried Tiger while Tony ushered Con into the drawing room. While he sat in an armchair, Tony cleaned the hearth, loaded some kindling and paper, then ignited several firelighters. The flames rose without any encouragement. Within minutes, three dry logs were perched on the sticks, each one crackling.

Tony offered Con a drink just as Tita returned. As the wood hissed and snapped, they sat and sipped sherry while Tiger reclined facing the fire, his forelegs crossed.

"He looks so regal when he lies like that," Tita said.

Con said, "Gervase Markham once declared that greyhounds 'are of all dogs whatsoever the most noble and princely, strong, nimble, swift and valiant; and though of slender and very fine proportions, yet so well knit and coupled together, and so seconded with spirit and mettle, that they are master of all other dogs'..."

Tony chuckled.

Tita asked, "Are you an academic, Con?"

The man nodded.

"A professor?"

"Retired."

"Where did you teach?"

"Zurich. I started my career as a lecturer in theology, but then I narrowed my interests, focusing on time. So, you could say I became a Professor of Horology."

"Time may be a narrower field than theology, but it's still a huge subject," Tita said.

Con smiled. "You are right. I have specialised in a branch of my subject called *kairology*."

"What's that?" Tony asked.

Tita answered. "There are two ancient Greek words for time. *Chronos*, meaning ordinary, finite, chronological time. And then *Kairos*, which refers to extraordinary, infinite, unique moments of time. Isn't that correct, Professor?"

"That's certainly the traditional translation."

"Well, how do *you* translate them?"

"I have been developing an already existing theory of time," he said. "For me, *Chronos* represents dilated time, time that runs at a slower speed. *Kairos*, on the other hand, signifies contracted time. Time that moves faster."

"Your research is theoretical, then?"

"In the sense that Einstein's proposals about time were theoretical, yes. But it's based on actual measurements too."

"So, would I be right in saying you have abandoned theology for physics?" Tita asked.

"Not at all. In fact, I believe that astrophysics and metaphysics are like heavenly twins."

"I must look you up when I get back to the States," she said. "What's your surname?"

Tony intervened. "You're turning this into an interrogation!"

Tita apologised.

"It's all right," Con said. "My name was changed when I was a child. I was born with a German surname but my mother's brother, trying to be funny, replaced it."

"Why?" Tony asked.

Con looked at Tiger. "Your greyhound and I, we have something in common. Nature endowed us with extravagantly elongated snouts. My uncle renamed me Conrad the Pelican. That stuck. Became abbreviated. Then contracted to Conrad Pelican. I have never like it and I have been in servitude to its nuances ever since, which is why I rarely tell anyone my full name in these or any parts."

"I'm sorry to hear that," Tony said.

"But you should not feel ashamed of it," Tita said. Her tone was softer, kinder now. "In Tudor times, the pelican was regarded as a noble bird because it made sacrifices for its young, even to the point of shedding its blood."

Con smiled.

"And if memory serves me," she said. "King Henry VIII changed Cranmer's coat of arms from three cranes to three pelicans, because he said something to the effect that Cranmer was a man prepared to lay down his life for others."

"The king's exact words," Con said, "were that Cranmer should be ready, as the pelican is, to shed his blood for his young ones brought up in the faith of Christ."

"Well then, Professor, that means that you already know your name speaks of that greater love, the love that lays down its life for others. There can be no nobler theme than that."

Con looked at Tony. "Your lady is very kind, and a very wise and a very able student of Tudor history."

"That is what I teach in America," she said. "In fact, I'm

writing a book about Queen Catherine Parr…"

Con coughed.

"Are you alright?" Tony asked as Tiger turned to look.

"It went down the wrong way," he said.

He placed his sherry glass on a side table and wiped his lips with a white, silk handkerchief from his jacket pocket.

When he recovered, Tita said. "About Catherine Parr, we found a treasure chest under the lawn."

Con coughed again.

"Pardon?" he said, recovering.

Tony answered. "We have excavated the lawn since I last saw you, Con. We discovered the original kitchens. Underneath them, we found a cellar. And within the cellar, a casket."

Con's lips quivered. "What did it contain?"

"Some jewels, books, and letters," Tita said. "I have been studying them all. They were clearly gifts from Queen Catherine Parr. Gifts given to her daughter…"

"Her daughter?"

"Yes, Lady Mary Seymour, the only child of Queen Catherine and Sir Thomas Seymour. She disappears from the records of history aged two, but we believe the casket proves that she lived here as a humble cook, never revealing her identity."

"Have you discovered anything else?"

Tony took over. "We know that she was the ward of John Parkhurst, the rector appointed here at the time of the Queen's death. The rector whose name is not recorded on the list in the church, just as you once showed me."

"I remember it as if it was yesterday," he said.

"You pointed out to me that his name was missing because

you already suspected that he needed to be protected against prying eyes and his existence remain hidden."

"I did," Con said.

"And what more do you know?" Tita asked.

"I know only what is contained in the casket."

"But how?" Tita asked. "It's been buried for five hundred years! There's no way you could know its contents."

"Bring it to me," he said.

Tita looked at Tony who nodded. She left to retrieve it from the study. "I have returned everything to it," she said. "Tony has to hand it over to the coroner very soon."

Con looked at the chest. "I have known about this for a long time," he said. "Ever since I received into my possession a letter that no one else has seen, from Mister John Parkhurst, describing what he had done for little Mary. It is a most poignant piece of writing. I can rarely bring myself to read it."

"I would like to see it," Tita said.

"It is in Latin, I'm afraid."

"That won't be a problem."

"You read Latin?"

She nodded.

"Just like Queen Catherine," he murmured. "I may show it you one day, my dear."

Con opened the first till of the chest and studied the jewels, holding them up to the light of the fire. Opening the second till, he read several pages of each of the ornate books, concentrating mainly on the hand-written dedications. Finally, he perused the letters before placing them back in the drawers of the third till.

"And this is all you have discovered?"

They nodded.

"But it is not everything," he said.

"What do you mean?" Tita asked.

Con laid the chest down on the rush mat and withdrew each of the tills once again.

"It is like a little house with many rooms, no?"

Then, when the box was empty, he leaned over the empty floor of the casket and pressed down on one corner. The board sprung up and away from the mechanism that had held it in place. Tony saw what lay beneath. More documents. Not many. Maybe four or five. All flat, like pressed flowers in an old book.

"Even this little house has a cellar," he said.

"What are those?" Tony asked.

"Your lady will need to study and translate them. They are in Latin. But they will contain more treasure. Not tangible gems, like these in the first level of the chest, but less visible and more spiritual ones. The true treasure in the casket."

Con took out his pocket watch.

"Goodness me," he cried. "Is that the time?"

"Are you sure you have to leave so soon?" Tita asked. "I have so many more questions."

"Maybe another time," he said.

They followed Con out into the hallway.

"Before you go," Tita said. "I have an invitation for you. We are having a house-warming party here just before Christmas. We would love you to come. May I have your address?"

"How charming. Just send me the details. Tony has my contact information."

"Can't you give us your address? Tony can walk round

with Tiger and deliver the invitation."

"It's better this way. You'd never find it, my dear."

Before the old historian left, he turned to them both and said, "This has been a true example of *Kairos*. Its impact, I'm sure, will be felt for many years to come."

Con reached out his arms and embraced Tita, kissing her on both cheeks, pausing after the second kiss.

When he was gone, Tita said, "I'll take photos of the new documents. Make sure you get a press embargo on the findings, Tony. The story should be yours to tell."

"Ours," he said.

Tita smiled. "I'll cook dinner. After that, I have a little game I want to play called family trees."

"What's that?"

"Just a way of getting to know each other better. It'll encourage us to share memories of those who came before us."

Tony sighed and said, "Okay."

60

THE PARTING

The next morning, they said little as Tony drove them from the West Country to the airport. Only as they navigated their way from country lanes onto the motorway did Tony break the silence.

"What did you think of him?"

"Who, *mi amor*?"

"Con."

"I'm not sure I can give a simple answer. But my impression is he's totally unique. He's one of those very rare people that deserves the adjective 'unreal'."

"In what sense?"

"In the sense that I'm not sure he's quite real."

"You think he's dishonest?"

"I don't mean 'unreal' as in a con artist. I mean I'm not sure he's what he appears to be."

"I don't follow."

"While you were snoring last night..."

"I was not!"

"You were, *bebé*. But it doesn't matter."

Tony sighed.

"Anyway, back to the point, while you were asleep last night, I started a search on my phone. I was convinced I had heard his name before, and I was right."

She paused.

"Go on," Tony said.

"I can only find one academic called Conrad Pelican. The name is sometimes spelt with a K instead of a C, both in the first name and surname. But there's only one I can find who started out as a lecturer in theology, and whose country of origin is Switzerland."

"Who is that?"

"Are you ready for this?"

"Of course!"

"Then here it is. The only man who fits the bill is someone who started life as a Franciscan priest, then became a lecturer in theology in Zurich, and became a well-respected mentor to young theologians who went onto be influential scholars. He had an extremely long nose, as a few rare pictures of him confirm."

"I don't see any controversy there," I said.

"You may when I tell you that he lived between 1478 and 1556 and would therefore be over 450 years old."

"Are you serious?"

"I am. He's the closest fit."

"But that's impossible to accept. He seems... well... so physical, so tangible, so solid."

"I agree. But think about it. The accounts of Christ's resurrection indicate that he rose from the grave in bodily form. I'm not saying I believe these stories, but Pelican obviously did."

"Okay, but Con isn't Christ."

"I agree but consider how elusive he's been. He wouldn't give his address last night. I know people protect their privacy, but what if this is because he doesn't have an address. Have you ever seen his house? Has anyone? People know he exists, but they don't know any more than that. People receive messages from him, but that's it."

"True."

"And, Tony, you live in *La Casa Dos Espiritus*, the house of the spirits. You have seen Mary curtseying on the lawn. You have seen the Three who built the Tudor Manor House."

"That's true too."

"Most of all, he behaves as if he was around at the time we have been investigating. He speaks as if he knew and loved some of those we mention, like Queen Catherine Parr."

"And John Parkhurst," Tony added.

"And above all, Mary," she concluded.

"And look at the way he dresses," Tony said. "His clothes are otherworldly. Or at least from a different time. And speaking about time, he is always looking at that golden pocket watch. He behaves as if it's a kind of stopwatch."

Tita frowned. "He has very original views about time. Did you not find it strange how he redefined *kairos* and *chronos*?"

"I didn't quite understand that."

"You need to read Carlo Rovelli's *The Order of Time*."

"I'm not aware of it."

"Rovelli says that you can set two watches to the same time then put one in your attic and the other in your cellar. When you collect them again after a few weeks, you'll find that the one in the attic has run faster than the one in the cellar."

"How can that be?"

"Rovelli claims that the greater your gravitational environment, the slower time runs. So, a twin who lives at sea level will experience time more slowly than the twin who lives at the top of a mountain. When they meet after say forty years, the twin who's been living in the lower environment..."

"Where gravity is stronger," Tony said.

"Exactly... That twin will say to the mountain-dwelling sibling, 'My, you've aged more than me.' This is because gravity is stronger nearer to the earth and weaker at the top of the mountain."

"So, you're saying that Con has somehow been living at a far slower speed than the rest of us."

"That's a possibility. He's been living in dilated rather than contracted time. When he visits us, maybe he comes out of dilated time into contracted time. In contracted time, he ages much more quickly but these are the moments where significant things happen. These are the *kairos* moments, the ones that affect history."

"So, there's a scientific reason for him being so old."

"Perhaps, yes. Rovelli hypothesises that a person in a spaceship at the edge of a black hole will experience the passing of a small amount of time, maybe seconds. But when he arrives back on earth, he will find that years have gone by. It's all to do with the black hole being the strongest gravitational environment in the universe."

"Sounds like Narnia," Tony said, adding, "maybe Con stumbled on a gravitational anomaly somewhere in the locality and he's been aging far more slowly than us."

"Or maybe he really is a ghost," Tita said.

As the signs for the airport began to appear more often, Tita said, "Right at this moment, I hate time. It always goes so quickly when you don't want it to." She held Tony's hand

and whispered, "*Mi amor...*" Tony could tell she was crying.

Five minutes later, Tony was standing outside the clubhouse embracing her as if it was the first time. He wanted the kiss, so strong and deep, to last forever. And he wanted Einstein to be right, that a minute with a pretty girl feels like an hour.

But it felt like a minute.

Less than a minute.

And before he knew it, Tita was heading towards the glass doors of the lobby, turning with flooded eyes, lifting the locket from her chest, kissing it before she disappeared.

61

THE WRITING

The day after he handed over the casket to the coroner, Tony began to write again. He had over two months to fill before Tita returned and was determined to redeem the time. There were plenty of spaces in his schedule between October and December. Most of his meetings were by video, including appointments with his agent and publishers, discussing the plans for *The House of the Soul*. They were as excited as he was that he had his writing mojo back.

In a message to Tita, he told her what he was doing. She replied that he was becoming like the rectors of old. A gentleman of leisure. With plenty of time to sit at his desk.

He smiled and said that he might be a gentleman of leisure, but he was not a man of the cloth. Tita had not heard that expression before, so he had to explain it.

Whenever Tony sat at his father's desk, the writing was easy not arduous. Thoughts flowed without interruption. From time to time, he would look through the old Tudor window and stare at the lawn. He would smile when he thought of the princess who became a kitchen maid. He was grateful to her. In his eyes, she had become his Muse, stimulating his thoughts, guiding his hand.

After seven weeks of writing, his agent Sarah came to visit the Old Rectory. The last time they had seen each other was in New York, at the beginning of his stay there.

"Sarah Bernstein," Tony said opening the door and his arms. "Welcome to my new abode."

"This place is peaceful," she said.

Tony took her coat and a heavy food box.

"Would you like tea?" he asked. "Or something stronger?"

"Has the sun set?"

"It has."

"Then Hanukah has begun. So, something stronger, please. Maybe a glass of red wine?"

"I'll bring it to you."

She headed left and stood in front of the roaring fire. As Tony walked to the kitchen, he caught sight of her bending down to stroke Tiger's head, then reach out for a taper at the fireside.

When he returned, Sarah was lighting a large candle on the mantlepiece. Her head was bowed.

"Sorry to disturb," he whispered.

She turned and beckoned him to come and stand beside her. Tiger leaned his head on Tony's foot.

"I'm just saying a prayer." She looked at him. "Do you want me to say it out loud?"

"Be my guest."

She lit the candle and said, "*Baruch atah, Adonai Eloheinu, Melech haolam, asher kid'shanu b'mitzvotav v'tsivanu l'hadlik ner shel Hanukkah.*" As the ancient Hebrew words filled the room, it felt to Tony as if every timber shivered, every stone trembled. Sarah began to translate. "Blessed are You, Lord our God, King of the universe, who has sanctified us with His commandments, and commanded us to kindle the Hanukkah light."

"Thank you," Tony said.

"Happy holiday," she said.

"Happy holiday," he replied.

Tony handed Sarah her glass of wine. She sat near the fire while he decanted some bourbon.

"I love it," Sarah said.

"What?"

"The house."

"It's enchanting, isn't it?"

"It really is. I love the way you've decorated the interior with Victorian furniture. It's so elegant. Regal almost. Looks like a set from *Downton Abbey*."

Tony laughed. "Maybe one day people will use this as a location for a period drama."

"You know something else I love?"

"What?"

"The new book."

"Thank you."

"It's so fresh, Tony. I think it's because you're telling the story of the healing journey you've been on. You've been so honest. So real. And it all feels so relatable."

"I was worried it was a bit too, I don't know, bourgeois. I enjoy so many privileges that others don't."

"But Tony, everyone needs healing. And everyone dreams. It doesn't make any difference whether you're in a palace or a rented flat, everyone is interested. Everyone!"

"But it's been so long. Will people read it after so many years without us publishing anything?"

"I don't think you realise how interested people are. You have an incredible understanding of dreams. And your ability to interpret them ... I've said it before, and I'll say it again. You're like Joseph, like Daniel. You have *hochma*..."

"What's that?"

"Wisdom. Not ordinary wisdom either."

"Thank you."

"No, don't thank me. I have seen it so many times when you're on stage or in a TV show. When people tell you their dreams, you interpret them in a unique way. Almost spiritual. Scary even. And now, with what you're currently writing, you've gone to a whole new level. People are going to absolutely love it."

"You're sure? I've had writer's block for so long, what with the divorce and the legal battles ..."

"I know, Tony. I know. But it sounds like you're entering new beginnings. In fact, I'm going to give you something to remind you daily of that fact."

She stood.

Tiger stirred.

She removed a necklace and brought it to Tony.

She pointed to the pendant. "See this?"

"Looks like a gate," he said.

"It's the Hebrew letter which represents the number eight. Seven is the number of perfection and completion. Eight starts a new sequence so is the number of new beginnings. It looks like a gate, yes, because it symbolises a portal to new things."

She draped it over his head.

"Whenever you look at it, remember it's the time of new things, including in your relationships."

"Thank you," he said.

Tony began to share about his new beginnings with Tita.

Sarah clapped her hands. "Do you think that's why you've started writing again?"

"Partly, yes." He took a sip of Bourbon. "I don't think I've ever really understood the 'you've got be miserable if you want to write' argument. What about the happy writer? Surely, it's joy that releases the water from the well, not misery..."

"And joy," she said, "comes from love."

"Exactly!"

"So, you're saying Tita is responsible."

"Not only Tita. This house too."

"It is perfect, Tony. Such solitude. Such atmosphere. It's magical. I'm so happy for you."

"It's just me and Tiger," he said. "And our ghosts."

"Ghosts?"

"Yes, I have some otherworldly friends."

"Do they haunt you?"

"Not at all. They are here to heal, not to haunt, except when they see someone like Maul."

"What happened to him?"

Tony told her.

"He's the son of a dog."

Tiger stirred and looked at her.

"Sorry," she said, leaning down to pat him.

Turning back to Tony, she said, "I presume you've informed Yinka about Maul's antics."

"I sent him the video from the surveillance cameras, as

well as Maul's phone. Yinka's informed Maul's lawyer that if he ever so much as texts me these will all be handed to the police, and he will be arrested for trespass and attempted arson."

"Then it's over," she said.

"It's over."

"So, tell me more about Tita."

"She's very, very clever. An academic. Lecturer in Tudor History in the States. She's writing two books. One about Queen Catherine Parr. The other about the Queen's lost daughter."

"Sounds fascinating. Does she have an agent?"

"Her agent has just retired."

"If she's looking for a new one, perhaps she'd like me to consider repping her."

"I'll ask her if you like."

"I would like."

"Consider it done."

Sarah excused herself and headed into the hallway. She picked up her food box and paused in the doorway.

"Working dinner," she said.

Tony stood, took the box off her, and led her to the kitchen. Tiger followed them, his nose drawn to the smells from the container. Tony sat at the table while Sarah served the food. She lit another candle then broke some freshly baked pretzel buns.

She announced what she called the main event.

"Potato latkes," she said. She served more portions. "With slow-cooked brisket. Roasted carrots and sprouts."

"It looks and smells sensational," Tony exclaimed.

"Don't overdo it," she said. "There's homemade

cinnamon apple cake for dessert."

"Are these Hanukah recipes?"

"They are."

"Perhaps I need to convert."

Sarah laughed.

An hour later, they had finished their discussions and dessert. The publication date for *The House of the Soul*, which Sarah insisted was a "working title," would be September the following year, in time for the Christmas book sales. The publisher's marketing department had already spoken with Sarah about their plans. A big push was on the cards, with a host of TV interviews and broadsheet reviews.

Tony suggested a toast. "To new beginnings."

"To new beginnings," Sarah replied.

At eight o'clock, exactly at the time Sarah had said, she made for the front door with her food box, much lighter now. Tiger followed the box all the way, his long snout twitching.

As Tony helped Sarah on with her coat, he said, "Tita will be sending you a housewarming invitation. Saturday before Christmas. Save the date. We'd love you to be there."

"Wouldn't miss it for the world," she said. "I'll bring a framed copy of the *Birkat HaBayat*, the traditional Jewish blessing for the home. The words are stunningly beautiful. It would be a lovely picture beside the door just here."

"I don't know it."

"I'll give you an English version this time."

"*Let no sadness pass through this portal,*

Let no trouble come to this home.

Let no fear come over this threshold.

Let no conflicts occur in this space.

Let this home be filled with blessing,
With love,
And shalom."

Sarah walked to her car.

While Tony watched her leave, he held the tiny golden gate she had given him, turning it in his hand.

It truly was time for a fresh start.

62

THE SHELTER

By the time Tita returned, Tony had more than just a few chapters to show her. He had three quarters of his first draft.

"It's mesmerising," she said on the morning of the party. "I can't express how much I love it. It's even deeper and richer than *Dreamers*. I can't wait to see how it ends."

"Thank you."

"You'll have it finished in no time, Tony."

"Speaking of time," he said, "Five hours until the housewarming. How are you getting on?"

"Ella and I have finished building the nativity. No one is to see it until the unveiling, and that includes you, my love. She's also helping me with the lights and the sound."

"Can't wait!"

That afternoon, as the sun went down, the guests started arriving, including Jimmy, Tony's godson. Earlier, at midday, the professional caterers had brought a portable firepit into the garden and started roasting the biggest turkey Tony had ever seen. Twelve children were among the guests. These boys and girls, aged four to fourteen, were standing near the bronzing meat, watching with wide-eyed fascination as the fat dripped from the smoking flesh.

When most of the guests had arrived, Tony asked Jimmy to whistle with his fingers and usher the party, numbering forty-nine, towards the front door. When they had assembled there, he thanked them for coming and explained that they would be outside for the eating of a turkey dinner in a short while.

"But first," he said, "I want to introduce you to Tita. She's asked if she could give us a flavour of a Mexican Christmas. You don't have to join in, but please do if you want to."

Tita stepped forward and encouraged the children, whose parents waved them on, to gather round. Drawn by her appealing eyes, they did not hesitate. When they were all within a foot of her, she bent down to their level. The adults drew closer too.

"This is a very special day," Tita said, her voice hushed as if she was standing in a sanctuary. "In Mexico, where I grew up, there are nine special days, from December 16th to Christmas Day. These are called *Las Posadas*. Can anyone tell me what that means?"

Several guesses followed.

"*Las Pasados* means shelters. It reminds us of a particular shelter. Can anyone tell me which?"

A boy started jumping up and down.

Tita nodded.

"The inn where Jesus was born."

"Very good!" Tita shouted. "You get the first go at hitting the Christmas pinata a little later!"

The boy seemed very happy about that.

"In Mexico, we spend nine days walking through neighbourhoods and streets and paying our respects at shelters constructed for Christmas to celebrate the birth of Jesus."

A little girl raised her hand.

Tita nodded.

"Have you built a shelter?"

"We have. It's hidden somewhere in the garden. Would you like to come with me and visit it?"

The child clapped her gloved hands.

"Well, in that case, I need you to get ready. You see, children, this is a very special shelter, so we need to walk there in a special way. Will you practice with me?"

They all nodded.

Tita spent the next five minutes teaching the children to follow her and imitate her moves. This consisted of a choreographed short-step march. The children copied her.

"Right!" Tita said. "You've done well. I think you are ready. Remember, the wise men followed a star to the shelter where Jesus lay. We need lights too."

Tita raised a hand.

A score of lanterns appeared in the trees. The children gasped. The grownups clapped.

"We call these in Mexico *las luces de Belén*, the Lights of Bethlehem," she said.

Tita raised her hand again.

The sound of marching music began.

"Time to get behind me!" she said, draping a small drum over her shoulders.

As she led the children towards the Bethlehem lights, she started to hit the drum with her sticks, tapping softly at first. They followed in her footsteps, their eyes focused on her movements, their faces illuminated by the lanterns in the trees.

Then the singing came through the speakers hidden and fixed in the branches. Tony recognised the tune. It was the Little Drummer Boy.

"*El camino que lleva a Belén*," Tita shouted. "It means the road that leads to Bethlehem. It is what they are singing about. They are talking about a drummer boy walking with the little shepherds to meet Jesus in the shelter."

For the next three to four minutes, Tita marched with the children around the Queen's Walk, following the lanterns to the oldest yew tree. When she arrived, the music stopped and she pulled aside some lowering branches, revealing a full-size nativity scene.

The troupe of children gasped at the shelter. Music began to play from inside the space - Andrea Bocelli singing *Noche de Paz* through invisible speakers while a soft, golden light glowed in the heart of the scene, just where the baby lay.

"Do you see Joseph?" Tita asked.

"There's Mary," a young girl said.

"And the baby Jesus," a boy said.

"In the manger," the youngest cried.

Several parents wiped their eyes.

"In Spanish, we call the baby *El Nino Dios*, the Child God. He did not know he was the prince of heaven, but Mary would one day tell him this great secret. It is a beautiful story."

She looked at the children, "Others may think you are very small and very ordinary," she said. "But in God's kind eyes, you are all princes and princesses. Never forget it."

A strange silence fell on the crowd. The adults, who had drawn in behind the children, felt it too.

Tony sensed it.

Standing there.

Watching Tita.

Listening to her words.

Fighting his scepticism about the unashamed sentimentalism, and at the same time marvelling at how she held the guests so spellbound. Held *him* so spellbound.

"So," she said, lifting her head and her voice. "We have a lot to celebrate. Let's sing Happy Christmas."

The children clapped.

"*Feliz Navidad!* Can you all say that with me?"

Everyone had a go.

"That sounded amazing!" she said. "Now we are going to sing it as we head back to the house."

No sooner had she said the words than the song began to play through the speakers.

"You can dance however you want as you go back to the front of the house!" she shouted.

And they did.

The children went wild.

The adults attempted dance-like movements. Some showed a semblance of skill, but most made awkward movements, lurching in the direction of the front door.

Tita shook her head.

When the last *Feliz Navidad* had been sung, a huge, star-shaped pinata was lowered by Jimmy from the Tudor window. Tita gave each of the children a plastic tube that looked like a light sabre. One-by-one they tried to beat the candy out of the gaudy coloured star. In the end, it was left to the tallest boy to do the honours. When the sweets spilled onto the ground, Tita gathered them in two baskets, one for older children, the other for the youngest.

When all the sweets had been distributed, Tita nodded to Tony. Tony announced that everyone was to head to the outdoor tables where the caterers would serve them turkey tacos and sweet potato enchiladas. He stayed at the front door with his arm around Tita, watching the hungry guests taking napkins and food in their cupped hands, before heading to other tables and benches with heated lamps above their heads. There they were served Mexican hot chocolate.

"That was wonderful," he said.

"Thank you. Did you see their little faces when I told them how special they are?"

"I'll never forget it."

They stood for a while without talking, watching the children's wordless wows as they tasted the food, enjoying the odour of the meat, listening to the carols flowing from the trees. They held each other, keeping one another warm.

Tony would have stayed like this for a long time had Tita not jolted him out of his bliss.

"Who are they?" She asked.

"Where?"

"Over there!"

Tony followed the direction of her gaze.

Then he saw them.

They were standing next to the shelter, the branches of the huge yew tree draping over their shoulders.

Two men and one woman.

Glowing.

Smiling.

"They are the three," he said.

Then, without warning, some words from way back, from the years at his prep school, poured out of his mouth.

"As it was in the beginning, is now and ever shall be …"

The three smiled again and disappeared.

63

THE GREETING

Once the guests had eaten their churros, a light snow started to fall. Tony found Shree among the guests warming themselves around the firepit. She introduced him to her partner Aya.

"And this is Tita," Tony said.

"I have been looking forward to meeting you," Aya said, her tone soft, her words enunciated in a measured tempo. "I have been told that you are half Japanese."

"That's right," Tita said. "My mother was Mexican and my father Japanese. His family came from Hatsukaichi. They migrated to the United States in the 1950s."

"That's such a pretty little town," Aya said. "I will never forget passing through the floating gate."

Tita turned to Tony and said, "In Japan, these gates open onto some of the most sacred shrines."

"When we go through them," Aya said, "we make a transition from the ordinary world to a special and sacred world. It is quite beautiful, quite unique."

Tony touched the front of his jumper, pressing his fingers against the pendant Sarah had given.

He said, "Shree once told me that you believe in greeting and thanking a house when you enter it."

"It is a practice that I learned from my wonderful mentor. I owe so much to her."

"It would be a great honour for us if you would do it here," Tony said. "I know the house would appreciate ..."

"You know?" she said.

"Yes, I know."

"How do you know?"

"I have had many dreams in which the house and I become one. In one of my dreams, I saw through the house's eyes a chaplain blessing the halls, and I felt the effects of that."

"What did you feel?"

"Immersed."

"In what?"

"In love."

She smiled. "You are a most unusual man, Mister Lawson."

"Please, call me Tony."

"You are a most unusual man, Tony."

She bowed.

"Not many people in the West have the sensitivity to connect at such depth with their homes."

Now it was Tony's turn to bow.

Aya continued. "In answer to your question, yes. I would be honoured. It feels to me even from out here that it has a sweet, sweet soul, one that has found a deep peace."

Tita ushered all the guests inside and told them to wait in the hallway and up the staircase, anywhere they could see what was about to happen. She also told the children that if they wanted to join in and copy what Aya was doing, they could.

A minute later, everyone was indoors. The front door shut out the cold behind their backs.

Tony joined Tita who was at the top of the stairs, standing and watching on the landing.

Aya remained in front of Shree in the hall below.

She stood still for about ten seconds.

As soon as everyone laid eyes on Aya, they fell silent. There was something about her. She would not have pretended to be a holy woman, but that is how she appeared. Her movements were slow and elegant. Her words, whenever they were uttered, were few. It was as if a priestess had crossed the threshold.

"And now," she said, removing her coat. "I am going to greet and thank this house."

Shree stepped aside.

Clothed in a white dress that covered almost the full length of her short frame, Aya descended to the floor and rested her tiny torso on her knees. She did this with the ease of someone who was well practiced in the lost art of genuflection.

There was the sound of movement.

In response to Aya, everyone in the house fell to their knees, the children first.

Aya closed her eyes.

She took slow, deep breaths.

Her hands dropped slowly by her side.

She lowered them to the ground.

Palms down.

Fingers facing backwards.

Connecting with the ground beside and in front of her.

"Almost a curtsy," Tony whispered to Tita.

Aya's lips were twitching.

Greeting the house.

Thanking it.

Tony closed his eyes.

"Thank you," he said beneath his breath.

He knew the house felt the goodness of it.

His body trembled.

And the house did too.

He opened his eyes.

Aya was leaning forward, her head low, her hands stretched out behind her, like a swan.

The benediction was over.

Aya was on her diminutive feet again, her pale skin shining, her eyes sparkling, a smile so warm that it melted even the frostiest heart. And then everyone in the house was heading for her, their voices soft, thanking her for what she had just done, their faces still glowing from the sanctity and rarity of it all.

Several minutes later, the house was filled with laughter.

Tony found Aya and thanked her.

She said, "One of my tasks is to help transform a home into a sacred space."

She paused.

Looked up at him.

Smiling.

"But I find, Tony, that your house is already transformed, already sacred. There is a powerful energy here. And there is so little clutter! Everything is so tidy."

"Even in here?" Tony said, leading her into the drawing

room, showing her the shelves Tita was filling.

"Yes, in here too," she said.

"But I thought your mentor was very strict about the number of books we should own."

"She was not talking about people who have a great love and respect for books, who want to keep them because they are living treasures. She was talking about people who fill their houses with books they have no joy in keeping."

Tita, overhearing these remarks, said, "That's right, Tony. See? These books bring joy."

He smiled.

"I can see that you two have teamed up against me!"

Tony was about to laugh when he felt a rush of cold wind.

The front door had opened.

Renée had just arrived.

64

THE APOLOGY

Tony fetched Renée and her partner Nick a drink. He asked whether they wanted some food, but Renée declined on their behalf, insisting that they would not be staying long.

"Then I'd like to borrow you for a few minutes and talk to you in private," Tony said, looking at Renée.

"What's this all about?" she asked.

"A Christmas present," Tony said.

Renée looked far from convinced.

Tony cast a glance at Tita. "Could you look after Nick?"

Tita took Nick by the arm and started introducing him to some of the guests in the corridor.

Tony escorted Renée into the snug beyond the kitchen.

"Make it quick," she said as he closed the door.

Tony poured himself a Bourbon.

He took a sip and began to speak.

"I have an apology to make to you, Renée. I'm giving it completely without strings attached. I'm not up to anything, so you don't need your guard up. What I'm about to say is long overdue."

"I'm waiting," she said.

"You know I've been in therapy."

"Yes. Must be costing a fortune."

"It is."

"So?"

"So, something surfaced during the sessions, something that's been wrong with me for a long time, something I have used to great destruction in our years together."

Renée for once was quiet.

"I was always very straight with you about being sent away to boarding school at eight."

"You were."

"And I was always clear that something terrible happened during my early days there."

She nodded.

"What I didn't realise was that both of these events were deeply traumatic, that they damaged me deeply and permanently, and that I buried the emotions around them."

"You mean you became detached."

"Yes."

"Well, that's no great revelation."

"But I think it is. I see now that I survived by disengaging my emotions. And the problem with that is that I continued to use this survival strategy when I became an adult."

"Including in our marriage," she said.

"Exactly. In shutting down my emotions to cope with my abandonment, I didn't have a clue how to reengage them when I got married to you. That's why I was often physically present but emotionally absent."

"I'd say *always*, not often."

"Okay, always then. But here's the point. Switching off my emotions was fine for surviving boarding school, but it was totally counterproductive for thriving in our marriage. I basically weaponised that tactic against you and against us."

Renée looked down.

"I never gave our marriage a chance," Tony continued. His eyes were watering now. "And I'm so deeply sorry. I robbed you ... I gave you apathy when you needed empathy."

"That's okay," she said, her voice softer now.

"But it's not okay. I sabotaged our relationship. I didn't give us a chance. I'm not asking to get back together. We've both moved on. This is not about the future. It's about the past. Owning my mistakes. Saying sorry. Asking for your forgiveness."

Renée reached across the sofa and held Tony's hand.

"Just tell me one thing."

"What?"

"All I need to know is that you're going to be okay. I've known for a long, long time that you have buried everything, and I've also known that that it's done you no favours."

Tony nodded.

"So, are you going to be okay now?"

"I really am. I've switched my emotions back on after all these years, as you can probably see."

Tony wiped his eyes.

"Well, that's much healthier," Renée said, withdrawing her hand and sitting on the edge of the sofa.

"I'm not asking for your forgiveness right now, Renée. I know there's a lot of hurt and I'm thoroughly guilty, as charged. But the French have a saying that may help..."

She raised her eyebrows. "Are you, an Englishman, about

to share a French proverb with a French woman?"

"I am."

"I suppose I'm going to have to hear it."

She showed the first hint of a grin.

Tony said, "To understand all is to forgive all."

There was a full smile now.

Tony sensed the old warmth and affection she had shown during the days of their engagement.

"Look, Tony, I can't give you my forgiveness now. I need some time. I'm not saying I won't give it. I'm just saying... well, forgiveness is not an easy thing. But I will try."

"Thank you. That's all I can ask."

"Now, where's this Christmas present you were talking about?" she said, looking around the snug.

"You've already had it."

Renée smiled. "I know. I'm just kidding. And I'm grateful, Tony. As Christmas presents go, your apology is right up there."

"Thank you."

She stood.

"I like the house, and what you've done to it. And the gardens too. Very pretty."

"I'm glad."

"Tita is pretty too," she said. "She seems lovely. And you both look very happy together. I'm pleased for you, Tony. Truly I am. You've got your magic back."

Tony escorted her back to the party.

She found Nick and took a glass of champagne from a silver tray that was bound for someone else.

Tony smiled.

He smiled again hours later, when Renée and her new

man were among the last to leave.
Maybe a great thaw had begun.

65

THE ADIEU

Con arrived at the stroke of midnight. Only those who were sleeping over had remained.

"Do you want some turkey?" Tony asked.

"No food for me, thank you. I just came to bid you farewell."

"Are you leaving us?"

"I have some things I'd like to share," he said. "In private. I won't keep you long."

Once they were sitting in the dining room, Con looked at Tita. "You have discovered who I am, no?"

Tita drew a folded piece of paper from her pocket. She straightened it, then showed it to Con. It was a line drawing of a Reformation theologian with a long nose.

"It's you. Isn't it?"

The likeness was unmistakable.

Same curly hair.

Pronounced chin.

Big eyes.

And the trademark snout.

Tita put the paper away and said, "It's not *who* you are, so much as *what* you are that intrigues me."

"What do you think I am?"

"The obvious answer is that you are a ghost," Tony said. "You wouldn't be the first we've seen here. But at the same time, the other ghosts have not interacted with us as you have, and they have not appeared in such a tangible form either."

"So, what am I then?"

"You're an anomaly," Tony said. "You should not be here at all. You're five hundred years old."

"Then *how* am I here?"

"And *why* are you here?" Tita said.

"You know why."

Con was looking at Tita.

She nodded.

Con took her hand and kissed it. "The story you now have is beautiful, no?"

"You still haven't told us what you are!" Tony cried. "Have you been resurrected, like Christ?"

"I would not be worthy."

"I think I know," Tita said.

Con smiled.

"Tell us then!" Tony said.

"Somehow, you have been existing for five hundred years in a location where the gravity is unusually strong, and where time moves much more slowly."

"Go on, my dear."

"I think you'd call this *chronos*," she said.

"Maybe I would."

"And every time you come here, to this house, or to the church, you enter a reality where gravity is much weaker and in which time moves much faster."

"Maybe I do," he said.

"Call it *kairos*," she said. "The downside is that you grow older much more quickly, but the upside is you are able to interact with this house and leave your mark on its occupants."

His big eyes widened.

"Wait a minute," Tony said. "So, you're saying there is a scientific explanation for Con's slow aging."

"Not everything is magical," Tita said. "Some mysteries may have a perfectly scientific cause."

"Some," Con agreed. "But not all."

"And then there's mysteries that defy scientific explanation," she said. "Are they magical? Or are they miraculous?"

Con nodded, and then asked, "Do you remember the introduction to Queen Catherine's book, *The Lamentation of a Sinner*? It was written by William Cecil."

"You'll have to remind me," Tita said.

"He wrote about the Queen's experience of the divine, saying that some would perhaps regard it as the mystery of magic or the practice of alchemy. But he said the proper explanation was that it was a spiritual enchantment of the grace of God."

"A spiritual enchantment," Tita repeated. "I like that."

"So do I, my dear. So do I."

Con glanced at his timepiece.

"Hang on!" Tony said. "Let's say your great age really can be explained scientifically. That just makes me want to press you for more answers. If you come from a realm of slow time, where is it? What do you do there? And how do you get here? And how can gravity be so much stronger in a place where it's weaker everywhere else?"

"I don't think he'll tell us," Tita said.

"Your lady is right, as she is about so many things. All you need to know is that the task my friend John Parkhurst entrusted to me has been fulfilled. And let me say with a sincere heart that all the years of sacrifice have been worth it."

There were tears in Con's eyes.

He withdrew his timepiece one last time.

Tita sighed. "We won't see you again, will we?"

He shook his head.

"Why?" Tony asked.

"You don't need me anymore."

"Maybe not as a historian," Tony said, "but what about as a friend? What if I told you that I like your company, that I have come to be fond of you, and that you are welcome to stay?"

"But Tony!" Tita protested. "If he stays, time will move fast for him. He will age rapidly. And he will die."

"Isn't that better than living alone?"

"I am not alone."

"There are others?"

"I am not alone. I have never been alone."

"We need to let him go," Tita said.

Con made to leave. When he reached the door, he turned and spoke some ancient words.

"*Nunc dimittis servum tuum, Domine, secundum verbum tuum in pace.*" Tony recognised them from his school chapel. He muttered, "Now, Lord, let your servant depart in peace."

Con smiled and left.

Tita walked over to Tony and hugged him.

"He's not abandoning you," she whispered.

"I know."

"You'll never be alone again."

"What do you mean?"

"I'd like to live with you here, *mi amor*. I can pursue my writing career in this beautiful house. I really can't think of anywhere more appropriate, more... peaceful."

Tita took a step back while still holding onto Tony's hands.

"You are so much more extraordinary than you know," she said.

Tony pulled her back into his arms.

He whispered "yes."

"Yes, what?"

"Yes, I'd love you to live here."

66

A DREAM

That night, Tony dreamt he was sitting on the sill in his study, looking down on the gravel drive. He was aware of two things. First, the simple fact that he was dreaming. Second, that he was seeing events from his own life, not from the house's history.

It was midday and the sun was high in a bright blue and cloudless sky. The air felt balmy and warm, more fitting for a summer's day. The leaves on the trees, which were plentiful and vivid, were motionless. So were the rhododendrons that lined the road from the olive-green gates to the front door of the house.

Although nothing was happening, there was a sense of expectancy, as if something significant was about to occur.

Tony was not afraid.

Just vigilant.

He heard something.

Car tyres crushing the gravel.

When it appeared, Tony was shocked. It was the light-blue-and-white VW campervan that used to belong to his parents. The one they drove to holiday destinations in the school breaks. The one they used to carry him, his teddy, and his black Mossman trunk to his prep school when he was just eight years old.

As the van stopped, he saw them. Mum and Dad were both sitting in the front two seats. They were leaning forward, peering through the front window screen, looking up at the façade of the Old Rectory, straining their eyes and looking for something.

They saw him.

They waved.

There was joy and excitement in his mother's eyes, and a look of measured pleasure on his father's face.

Then it hit him.

This was the scene that he had longed for all his life, the moment when his parents returned to take him home. Except that even in the dream he knew that it was all a fiction, a visual manifestation of something so deep it would take a submersible to find it in the dark trenches of his mind.

Tony remembered what Shree once told him about lucid dreams, that he could influence and even control the narrative. He was no longer a passive observer and recorder of events. He was not only immersed in the world he saw. He was involved in it too. And not only involved but interacting with it if he chose to do so.

And he did choose.

He chose to change the narrative.

In his dream, he climbed down from the sill.

He paused to look in the long mirror at the end of the landing as he headed to the top of the stairs. In the mirror, he was eight years old. Dressed in grey shorts, navy jumper, light blue shirt, navy tie, and a cloth cap emblazoned by the prep school logo. He expected to see himself looking frail, exhausted by the endless nights of languishing under the bedsheets, muffling the sound of his sobbing. But he was surprised. He looked strong. Healthy. Alive.

He went down the stairs.

Walking to begin with, then running.

He reached the front door and ran to the van.

Dad and Mum were still sitting in the front.

They were the same age as when Tony last saw them before the inferno took them from him. And not only his parents, but his home. His hope. His life.

Dad wound down the window. He said, "Where's your trunk and your teddy, my son?"

Tony smiled.

"I'm not bringing them."

Mum leaned over. "Why not?"

Tony's smile disappeared. This was the gate he had been waiting to pass through for a long, long time. He gazed at them, and they gazed at him. There was sadness in their eyes.

The sun disappeared and the sky grew grey.

The fallacy struck Tony as pathetic even while it served to remind him that all this was a contrivance.

A healing fiction, yes.

But still a fiction.

Tony observed them with such an intensity of love he thought his eyes were going to burst.

"I'm not coming," he said.

Rain started to fall.

Light rain at first.

Then heavy.

Tony found it hard to distinguish between the rivulets on the window screen and the tears streaming down his mother's face. Even his father's eyes were filling.

"Why not?" Dad asked, in a voice that suggested he already knew the answer before he asked.

"Because you don't exist. Not like this. Not like you used to. This is a memory. An opportunity."

"An opportunity for what, sweetie?" Mum asked.

"To say goodbye." The words were out of Tony's mouth before he even had a chance to filter them.

"What do you mean goodbye?" Mum asked. The pain was etched on her brow with thick, dark lines.

"We never had the chance," Tony said. "Over forty years ago, you drove out the school gates and never came back. You promised you would. That you would bring me home for the holidays. But you never did, and I have been waiting for you ever since."

"What on earth happened?" Dad asked, his voice tentative, as if he wanted and didn't want to know at the same time.

"Our house burned down," Tony said. Mum was crying again. "You didn't make it," he added.

"I'm so sorry, son."

"Don't be, Dad. I've had help. I'm getting over it."

"But I broke my promise," Dad said. "And dads should never do that. And so, I say again, I'm sorry, my son."

"I forgive you," Tony said.

"Really?" Mum asked.

"Unconditionally."

With that, the clouds began to race away. The skies brightened. The sun made a new appearance. The rain on the campervan began to evaporate. The paintwork was gleaming, as if new.

"Is this goodbye?" Mum asked.

"It is."

"I'm proud of you, my son," Dad said.

He reached out to Tony through the open window, his shirt sleeve wet from his leaning. Mum reached too.

Tony held their hands. They were grasping his, their knuckles white from the clinging.

Then he stepped away from the car.

"I need to hear you say something," he said.

"What?" Dad asked.

"That you love me, but you're not coming back."

They looked at each other. Mum sobbed. Dad comforted her. Then he whispered something in her ear, and she wiped her red cheeks with her sleeve and forced a smile.

"We love you," they said in unison, trying to be strong. "But we're not coming back."

"That's good," Tony said.

"Good?" Dad said.

"How can it be good?" Mum asked.

"Because I have been robbed for far too long of my ability to appreciate the present. I have lived trapped in the past. And I've waited for something in the future that was just a dream, a fantasy. And I cannot live like this anymore."

"Then you are right, my son. It is good."

"Mum," Tony said. She looked at him with such desperation that he thought her heart was going to break. "Dad," he added, looking into his father's already grieving eyes. "I need to turn around and head to the front door. I'm going to do that without looking back. Don't try to stop me. You need to leave too."

Tony heard his mum's muffled, "No!"

But he did not look back.

He fixed his eyes on the door to the house.

As he walked there, he heard the engine starting.

The door of his house opened.

He was in the hallway.

The house was humming like a hive.

There was a sweet honey-like scent in the air.

A warm glowing balm started to pass down his throat into the deepest part of his stomach.

Its light seems golden to him.

He was glowing from the inside out.

Tony took a deep breath.

He climbed up to the landing.

He stared at himself in the mirror.

He was over fifty and in his regular clothes.

In the dream, he made an inner vow, that he would no longer be obsessed with his history or anxious about his destiny. He would be content in the present. Grateful for every single second of happiness. No longer groping for impossibilities. But counting every transient blessing. Savouring each one to the full.

As he concluded the covenant, he turned around, facing away from the mirror.

He knelt.

He stretched out his hands behind him, just as Ana had done at the party the night before.

He bowed low to the floor.

And he uttered two words to the house in whose chambers and grounds he had found such sweet freedom.

Thank you.

67

THE HART

Jimmy had stayed on after the party. Before he left, Tony went for a walk with him. They headed with Tiger along the Queen's Walk and up the hill behind the house. As they approached the coppice, Jimmy asked how Tony had coped with his boarding school experiences. He listened without commenting as Tony summarised what he had learned from his sessions with Shree. He recounted the dream from the previous night, the dream in which he had passed through the gate of forever farewells and found himself at peace with his past.

They reached the clump of trees at the summit and turned back to face the Old Rectory. The sun was going down and the Christmas lights that Tita had promised to install were shining like luminous gems on the neck of a noble queen.

"I think boarding school has damaged me too," Jimmy said.

"In what ways?"

"It's filled my head with knowledge, but it's done that at

the expense of my heart."

"What do you mean?"

"My dad is so stubborn. He's got this view that a private education makes me a more rounded person. I keep telling him it can't be that rounded if your head gets filled with information while your heart gets broken. But he doesn't seem to hear me."

"You know why that is?"

Jimmy shook his head.

"If he admits you're right, then he'll have to admit he was wounded by it too. And that's hard for someone who's spent their whole lives believing they ought to be grateful."

"I guess so."

"The thing you need to see is that your father is also a victim. His father inflicted the wound because the wound was inflicted on him by his own father. And so, the damage is passed on until someone is brave enough to say this far and no more."

They walked deeper and deeper into the clutch of trees, savouring the odour of leaves washed by the recent rain. Tiger walked by Tony's side on his lead.

"We are very alike," Tony said.

"We are and we aren't," Jimmy replied.

"What do you mean?"

"Not everyone reacts in the same way when they're abandoned at boarding school."

Tony turned to look at Jimmy.

"Explain."

"You once told me that your response to trauma was to stop feeling. I get that, I really do. And I also get that this is probably the normal way of surviving. But it hasn't been true for me."

Jimmy looked down at the ground.

"My problem is that I have reacted in exactly the opposite way. I haven't stopped feeling. I feel more than ever. It's as if being sent away to school has upped the levels of my empathy to an almost unbearable level. I think that's why I spend so much time painting. Trying to express and externalise all my feelings."

"You're right. That's very unlike me," Tony said. "It must be really hard to live at such an intense level."

There were tears in Jimmy's eyes. "It is. All I want to do is help the boys around me who are going to sleep at night in tears, dreaming of home, longing to be in their own beds."

Tony nodded.

"Then I remember there are kids who are far worse off. Foster kids. Adopted kids. Trafficked kids. Kids everywhere who feel robbed of their dreams. At least we have our privilege to fall back on. They have nothing. There's no safety net for them."

He looked away towards the fields the far side of the hill.

"We should do something for them," he said.

"What do you have in mind?"

"I keep having a dream," Jimmy said. "It won't go away. It's about centres for young people whose dreams have been stolen. I call them Dream Houses."

Tony felt goosebumps on his arms.

"That's a brilliant idea. And the best thing about it is that it's yours. It's your vision. Your dream. Your concept. And I'm going to help you make it happen."

"I'd love you to be involved, godfather."

"I'd love that too."

"What do I need to do to get started?"

"You need to decide whether to stay at boarding school."

"What do you think I should do?"

"I think you should be happy."

"Then I'm going to tell Dad I'm leaving."

"If you do that, Jimmy, you ought to identify the subjects you most need to study to fulfil your dream. Then you need to find somewhere that doesn't require you to board, somewhere you can get some further education – the kind that gives you the practical skills you'll need for starting and running your Dream Houses."

Jimmy threw his arms around his godfather. "I feel such a weight lifted off my shoulders," he cried.

Then, without warning, he froze.

"Don't move," he said. "And keep Tiger on the lead."

"What is it?"

"Turn very slowly."

Tony moved his head.

"Do you see it?"

"Where?"

"Down there. In the fields. By the furthest wall."

Only when the creature moved its antlered head did he see it. A white hart. Tall and bright in the dimming light. Chewing and staring. Looking in their direction.

"It's like a ghost," Jimmy whispered.

"It's also upwind."

Even as Tony spoke, the creature sniffed the breeze and cast a glance to the left and right.

"It looks like the one I've seen before. In a dream."

"What dream?"

"I dreamed about Henry VIII. He was trying to hunt and

kill a white hart here in the 1540s. It eluded him. He was very angry about it. I was extremely happy."

"How long do you think it's been here?"

"Potentially, a long time. It's no coincidence that the white hart is associated with extreme longevity."

"And with Jesus," Jimmy added.

"Come again?"

"St Eustace. He was a Roman soldier. Apparently, he encountered a white hart that spoke to him. Told him he was Jesus, and that Eustace had been hunting him."

"How on earth do you know that?"

"We have a very eccentric RE teacher."

Tony motioned to Jimmy to follow him back to the slope leading down to the Old Rectory. Whisps of smoke were fleeing from its chimneys, like an expulsion of ghosts. Neither said a word. Both were thinking of the white hart. All Tony could think of was Ms Macready. She had dreamed of a white hart. He had told her that the animal was a symbol of royalty, and that she must be a very special person to be deserving of such a vision. He told Jimmy the story, adding that seeing the white hart meant he was special too.

"How do you know it was for me?"

"What?"

"The appearance of the white hart. You say it appeared because I'm special. But what if it was really appearing to say that to you? What if you're the chosen one?"

"I'm just an orphan who got lucky in life," Tony said.

"You're a hell of a lot more than that."

As they arrived at the house, Tony took Jimmy by the arm and said, "Let's talk some more at our January jolly about your vision for Dream Houses. It's ignited something in me.

I really think you're onto something. Couldn't be prouder of you. And I know Tita is going to absolutely love the vision."

Jimmy blushed.

"And don't forget, if it ever gets too tough at school, you can always talk to me. And as for this place...." They looked up at the façade. "As Tita would say, my house is your house."

68

THE PRESENT

When Tony woke on Christmas morning, Tiger was lying next to him wearing a red collar embroidered with holly leaves. He had suffered the further ignominy of having golden tinsel wound around the inside and outside of his collar. When he saw Tony open his eyes, he uttered a long and exasperated sigh. Tony laughed, patted him on the head, before wishing him a happy Christmas.

Downstairs, Tita was already preparing breakfast. When Tony arrived, *Feliz Navidad* was playing. She led him in a dance while Tiger padded around them on the flagstone floor.

When the tune was done, Tita poured him some strong coffee and said, "Time for your present!"

"I don't see it."

"That's because it's invisible."

"Invisible?"

"Come with me, *mi amore*."

Tony followed Tita into the drawing room. She had

already lit a fire and the logs were crackling in the hearth. She gestured to him to sit on the sofa while she headed for the bookshelves. She pulled out a volume in half-red leather, one of a set of twelve.

"I don't remember seeing those," Tony muttered.

"They're new."

"Did you buy them?"

"All twelve volumes."

"They look expensive."

"Don't be grumpy. It's Christmas Day."

Tony gulped some coffee.

"In any case," she continued. "You can blame this purchase on Con. He was the one who suggested it."

"When?"

"When he said goodbye for the last time. He hugged me, kissing me on both cheeks. After the second kiss, he whispered one word in my ear. It was a name."

Tony waited.

"Strickland," she said.

"I don't know it."

"Agnes Strickland and her sister Elizabeth published the twelve volumes that we have just bought..."

"You have just bought."

"All right, grumpy. I have just bought. The title is *Lives of the Queens of England: From the Norman Conquest.* These volumes were published between 1840 and 1848."

"And how is this relevant to my present?"

"You'll see."

Tita opened one of the books.

"Before I read this, I need you to know something. Don't be mad at me, but I have kept a secret since my last visit here.

When Con triggered the mechanism at the bottom of the casket, there was an official document among the papers. I did not want to get you excited so I took some unusual measures..."

"What unusual measures?"

"Enough questions! Just let me tell the story. It's worth waiting for, I promise you!"

Tony sighed.

"I had to wait until the results from these measures could be made known to me. Only then, when I was sure, could I share with you the real treasure in the casket."

"What treasure?"

Tita sat next to Tony with the book. The lightly faded spine read Volume III. She opened the marbled boards and turned to a page she had saved with a bookmark.

"Agnes Strickland was a great fan of Queen Catherine Parr, about whom she writes admiringly. She called her the intellectual model of the women of England and said that she also earned the respect of the most learned men in Europe."

"We share that admiration," Tony said.

"We do. But what I'm about to read to you is not about Catherine as a woman of letters, nor as a Reformation theologian. This is about her as a mother. It's to do with her daughter and a theory proposed by the two sisters, Agnes and Elizabeth Strickland."

"Did they find something?"

"Yes, they did. It seems that they had access to some descendants of Queen Catherine Parr, and to unseen documents, documents that contained a secret."

"What secret?"

"These sisters discovered that little Lady Mary Seymour did not die but lived, just as you and I learned from the contents of the casket. She married her suitor, and they had children. The Strickland sisters met the descendants of this union."

She looked down at the page.

"The sisters say that they were privy to information about Catherine Parr from two brothers, one in Clevedon, the other in Hereford. These two men were the sons of a rector in Kent who later became a dean in Sussex. These brothers produced documentation proving that the Lady Mary Seymour lived, became a mother, and that her children were their ancestors."

"That's fascinating."

"It's even more fascinating when you see their surname."

Tony scanned the printed words.

He focused on a single paragraph.

Strickland claimed that she had been 'favoured.'

There was a list describing those who had granted her favour.

John Lawson of Clevedon.

Henry Lawson of Hereford.

The sons of the late very Reverend Johnson Lawson.

These men afforded presumptive evidence that they derived their descent from Lady Mary Seymour.

"What were they called, Tony?"

"Lawson," he said.

He wiped his eyes.

Checked that he had not been dreaming.

"Lawson!" he cried.

"Your surname!"

"But..."

"Tony, do you remember this locket?" She opened the cover, revealing a strand of his hair.

He nodded.

"And do you remember the game we played the night before I left for the States?"

"Some nonsense about ancestors," he said.

"It wasn't nonsense though, was it?"

Then it hit him. "You were using the game to find out about my family tree!"

"And I've been examining your DNA using your hair."

"You're very devious, Tita," he said with a frown. "And what have you unearthed?"

Her face became serious. "You, Tony Lawson, are a direct descendant of Lady Mary Seymour, which means you are descended from the Queen of England, Ireland and France, the Queen who once resided here."

He shook his head.

"That can't be true!"

Tita laughed.

"I told you that you are an extraordinary man, Tony. You came to this house by appointment not by accident."

His head was spinning now.

Images flashed across his mind.

Seeing the chimneys of the house peeping above the cobbed wall on the day of his divorce.

Feeling drawn to the gates.

The dreams.

The Professor.

And above all, the ghost in the garden.

"She curtseyed...." he whispered.

"Pardon?"

"Lady Mary. She curtseyed."

"Of course, she did, my darling. She knew who you are. And she knew what you are. You are not only worthy of living in this house. You are worthy of honour too."

Tita walked to the drinks cabinet and poured a Bourbon. Handing it to him she said, "Everything in that casket, especially the official marriage documentation, proves that this is the real secret, and that you were always meant to discover it."

Tony took a gulp.

"How does it make you feel?" she asked.

"Well, the cynical part of me says I've done nothing to deserve this, that this is inherited privilege, something my political self would normally despise. But the emotional part of me... well... that's different. I really do feel amazed. It's like an epiphany..."

He paused.

"Are you all right, *mi amor*?"

"Something Shree told me."

"What did she say?"

"She said that I had been emptied, but that I would be filled."

"I don't understand."

"She predicted that after being emptied of shame I would be filled with honour. She taught me that a negative experience, like trauma, can only be displaced by a positive one."

"Like a revelation?"

"Exactly."

"Well, you have that now."

"I'm descended from Queen Catherine," he said.

"Don't forget little Mary," Tita cried. "She's been forgotten for five hundred years. But she's not going to be forgotten any more. We are both going to write about her."

Tony took another gulp.

"Thank you for my present," he said.

"You're welcome, my darling."

"It's the best ever."

69

THE PROPOSAL

How long they held each other on the sofa Tony could not say, but after some while Tiger entered the room to check on them. He put his head on Tony's lap and looked up at his master.

"Even he senses it," Tita said.

"What?"

"Who you really are?"

"How do you know?"

"Because he's a royal dog..."

Tony said. "*Rex Canorum*. King of the dogs!"

They both laughed.

"We should let him out," she said.

They walked to the front door, put on long coats and slippers, and headed out onto the gravel. The air was cold, and the ground powdered with a light dusting of pure white snow. But the skies were blue, the sun bright and golden.

"The perfect combination for Christmas Day," Tony said.

Tiger cantered over the lawn and disappeared to do his

business, just as he always did.

"He's a very discrete fellow," Tony said.

"The old boy's a gentleman just like you, Tony."

They laughed again.

Wandering over to the old yew tree, Tita parted the snow-burdened branches to reveal the nativity scene from the Christmas party. As they stared at the sacred figures, the church bells began to summon the Christmas worshippers across the lane.

"Do you think we should go?"

Tony shook his head. "I don't deny I'm on a bit of a journey, but I'm not there yet. One day. Maybe."

Turning back towards the house, they paused on the lawn, now covered in half an inch of snow.

"You know, I was anxious when we dug here," he said.

"Why?"

"I kept thinking of Edgar Allan Poe. Two of his short stories. One about a chest of treasure..."

"Ah, yes, 'The Gold-Bug'."

"Precisely."

"And the other?"

"'The Cask of Amontillado'."

Tita shuddered. "You didn't expect to find a prisoner buried here?" she asked.

"I did not know what to expect. My imagination was going wild. I was daydreaming all the time, trying to picture what might lie beneath this stretch of grass."

"The cave and the cellar," she said. "They have yielded many treasures, more than we could have imagined."

"It's like Blanchard wrote," Tony said. "When it comes to excavated ground, dreams have no limit."

"Not just excavated ground," Tita said.

"What do you mean?"

"I mean the house. Its grounds. All of it. We have no idea what dreams are yet to come from this extraordinary place. Maybe they will have no limit too."

Tony nodded.

They walked from the lawn to the drive and then towards the entrance. Tony looked up at the flintstone façade and the Tudor window. As the light snow touched his face, he said with a sigh, "I'm so very grateful for this house."

"The house knows it," Tita said. "Now that a descendant of Lady Mary Seymour is the owner, I think it's going to feel like a very peaceful and happy home."

"Whenever I look at it," Tony said, "and whenever I'm walking through the rooms, I think of some lines I have always loved by Poe, lines that I have often quoted."

"What, my darling?"

"Something about a holy dream that cheers me like a lovely beam, this lonely spirit guiding."

"Do you feel lonely?"

"Not anymore."

"I'm so glad we'll be enjoying it together," she said.

"Me too!"

As they held each other, Tony looked over Tita's shoulder at the gardens. He imagined the three looking at them. Smiling. Dancing. Singing with the Christmas Day joy of it all.

He pictured the ghost in the garden, his ancestor Lady Mary Seymour, curtseying low on the lawn as she saw them embracing under the eaves of the great house.

And he smiled.

They walked through the front door and entered the warm hallway. Tiger followed, his snow-dappled tail swishing as he headed off to the kitchen to his bed in front of the aga.

As they took off their coats, Tony said, "Exactly a year ago, I was on my own in a soulless box of a house in Chelsea. Today, I'm enjoying Christmas Day with the woman I love."

"So much has happened, *mi amor*," she said. "You and I, we have received so much. Now, all we need to do is work out how to give it away to those who are less fortunate. Isn't that what Queen Catherine would have wanted?"

"Jimmy wants to help us with that."

Tita smiled.

"He has a kind soul, that boy."

"He does. He wants to set up Dream Houses in the poorest areas of the country. I'm very proud of him. And I've told him that we'll be involved, and that we'll support him."

Tita clapped.

"Let's talk some more about it after lunch," she said. "Speaking of which, what have you in store for us?"

"I'm making a traditional Christmas dinner," Tony said. "Turkey with all the trimmings."

"What fun!"

Tita was about to head into the drawing room when Tony held her back.

He knelt.

"I have something to say."

He took out a small velvet-covered box.

"I've been very remiss. I haven't given you your Christmas present yet, have I?"

Tita shook her head.

Tears were forming in her eyes.

He opened the miniature casket and lifted a diamond ring.

"Will you marry me?"

She put her hands to her mouth.

When she had composed herself, Tita took the ring from its cushion and placed it on her finger.

"My answer is yes!"

70

THE EPITAPH

After lunch, Tony and Tita left with their cheerful greyhound for a walk in the fields around the village. When the light began to fade and the snow thicken, they made their way home.

"Let's go through the churchyard," Tita said. "I have something I want to show you."

"You're being very mysterious."

"One last Christmas surprise," she said.

As they walked through the lychgate, Tita pointed to the corner of the cemetery. "It's over there."

Tony followed her.

"You need to see this."

She pushed away a low-hanging branch, releasing a tiny avalanche of snow through her fingers onto the flat, marble surface of an old grave. As she cleared the debris, Tony could see that someone had been cleaning it. There was a lighter, clearer space in the middle of the slab, untarnished by moss and grime.

"Did you do that?"

"I came here the other day on a walk with Tiger. Brought a high-powered granite and stone-cleaning spray. It took me a while, but I managed to clear it up a little."

"I can see some words."

"I think you'll find them interesting," Tita said as she removed a small object from her pocket.

"Hey! That's my beard brush!"

"Sorry, darling," she said. "May I?"

"I suppose."

She swept the marble and picked away at some recent accretions. "There!" she cried.

Tony saw a capitalised word.

"That looks like Latin."

"It is."

"Seems to say *viator*."

"It does."

"My Latin's a bit rusty. I presume *via* means way or road. But I'm not sure of the rest."

"*Viator* means wayfarer or traveller."

Tita brushed some more stray snow from her gloves and sleeves. When she turned to Tony, she was like one of Lucretius's hounds. Searching. Hungry. Eager.

"I know what this is," she said.

Tita was trembling, but Tony could not work out whether it was the cold or the chase.

"Tell me."

"When we were in the car one time, coming back from the airport, I read out an epitaph that John Parkhurst wrote in Latin. The one he composed to protect little Mary. The one where he gave the impression that Mary had died. Do you remember?"

"Of course."

"He wanted to put people off the scent. Didn't want them coming down here, sniffing around the old Tudor Manor House, trying to find Queen Catherine's child."

"I recall you reading me the English translation," Tony said. "It was a bit unusual. Spoken from the dead child's perspective. Quite odd. Made it sound like she was still alive."

"Yes, that's right. She said that she wished she'd been alive to show off her mother's attributes."

"It was a sad sentiment," Tony said.

"It was, except that Mary did not die when she was two years old. John Parkhurst knew that and shared the secret with his wife Margaret and at least one other."

"You mean Con."

"Con, yes, but also the rector at the time of Parkhurst's return from exile. Parkhurst confided in him and instructed him to pass it down to his successor, until the time of Mary's death."

"How do you know?"

"Because his instructions are in one of the documents we found at the bottom of the casket."

"So, you're saying the rector at the time of Mary's death..."

"John White," Tita interrupted.

"You're saying that John White buried Mary here, knowing full well who she was."

"Not only that," Tita said, "But he used the money that Parkhurst had left for digging Mary's grave, so that she could have a carved inscription. This one right here."

Tita brushed away some more snow.

"Every word you see on this grave was chosen by Parkhurst. And his successor, John White, made sure the old chaplain's wishes were honoured and the message recorded faithfully."

"So, this is a riddle."

"Precisely."

Tita pointed to the top of the stone. "This Latin word *viator*, for example. It was a common metaphor in Renaissance and Tudor times, describing the pilgrim travelling between two worlds, this world and the world to come."

"You mean people like us," Tony said.

"Exactly. There are many instances of Roman tombs where the inscription addresses the passer by as *viator*. It was a way of saying, 'Watch out! Your turn is coming'."

"Scrooge's tombstone," Tony muttered.

"Yes, but that's not the only reason." Tita started picking at some grime from the tiny carved channels in the marble. "It's also the same word used in Parkhurst's epitaph for baby Mary, the one which he wrote to make people think she was dead."

"You're saying *viator* is a code, not just a cliché."

"Yes. It connects the two epitaphs."

"What about the rest of it?"

"If you look closely," Tita said, "it says *inclyta filia sub hoc marmore dormit*."

Tony tried to remember back to his Latin lessons at school, but he was unable to get past *inclyta*.

"The first two words *inclyta filia* mean much-praised daughter," Tita said. "Can you translate the rest?"

Tony shook his head.

"The whole thing reads *a much-praised daughter sleeps*

under this marble," she said.

"I'm sure I've heard this before," Tony said.

"That's because they're straight from Parkhurst's epitaph."

Tony frowned. "Like *viator.*"

"That's right. Everything here is a kind of cryptic code. Parkhurst's original epitaph had little Mary speaking to the passing *viator*, saying that she slept under the marble."

Tita took hold of Tony's arm.

"She's been here all along."

Tony shook his head.

As he stood in the snow-covered garden, a single word rose from the buried treasure in his soul.

"Mary!" he said.

As Tony spoke her name, he remembered the ghost in his garden - the Tudor maid with the plain grey dress, the old black keys, and the elegant yet enigmatic curtsey. He thought of all the years she had spent as a humble maid in the kitchens of the Tudor house, dull decades of anonymity and humility. Royal blood had coursed through her veins – the blood of one of England's queens. She had been a princess and yet she had lived as a pauper. No one had come to rescue her. Her mother had died. Her father had been executed. There had been no fairy-tale ending. Just a silent descent into obscurity.

"There's one more thing," Tita said, brushing some snow-powdered leaves from the gravestone.

Tony rubbed his eyes.

There was a name.

Clear even in the fading light.

"Mary Lawson!" he whispered.

Tony fell to his knees.

"Are you okay, Tony?"

"She's here," he said. "I can feel it."

"Sleeping," Tita said.

"Not all the time."

Tita nodded.

"Are we the only ones who know about this?"

"There is another," Tita whispered.

"Who?"

"Con."

And then Tony remembered. What was it Con had said to him when his eyes had felt drawn to this very space nearly a year ago? "God knows who lies there."

God knew, yes.

But God had not been the only one.

Con had known too.

"This is the end of my royal road," he said.

"The end and also the beginning," Tita replied as she helped Tony to his feet and headed back to the Old Rectory.

They removed their hats and scarves in the hallway and crossed the threshold into the drawing room. Tony stoked the coals in the grate and the flames began to reach towards the flue.

"What did you mean by the beginning?" he asked.

"I mean it's the beginning of another story - one that will be published as a book and stand with all these other books about the history of this extraordinary house."

Tony took her in his arms.

"I'm so glad you're in it," he whispered.

Before she had a chance to answer, he leant forward and kissed her. When his lips and hers became one, Tony thought of Queen Catherine and Sir Thomas Seymour, embracing five hundred years before. He thought of all the others who had been warmed and enlivened by the fire of love – a fire that had ignited a longing to leave a legacy with ink and parchment, pen and page.

As Tony took a step back, he noticed Tiger lying on the rug at his feet, staring at the flames in the grate. Holding Tita's hand, he lowered himself to the floor and sat next to the dog. Tiger moved his long snout and rested it on Tony's thigh while Tita laid her head on Tony's shoulder. Together, the three gazed at the fire.

A familiar and endearing yawn from the greyhound roused Tony from his dreamlike state.

He stood, helping Tita to her feet.

Together, they walked over to the window looking out onto the lawn where he had first seen Mary.

"She's there!" Tita whispered.

Sure enough, there was the ghost of Tony's ancestor, no longer in a maid's simple dress, but in the far more noble attire of a Tudor princess. The look on her face was one of unbridled happiness. Her eyes sparkled as brightly as the diamonds around her neck.

Just then a strong wind blew through the yew trees, causing a flurry of snow to move like a murmuration of snowbirds towards the top right corner of the garden.

The princess looked to where the snowflakes fell.

As did the couple watching from the house.

Out of the gloom a figure left the Queen's Walk and started moving across the grass towards the apple tree nearby. The outline was shadowy at first. But whoever it was, their steps were slow, rhythmic, measured, like the start of an ancient dance.

It was only as they approached the ghostly princess on the lawn that the two observers saw who it was.

It was a lady.

In Tudor dress.

A crown upon her head.

As she neared the princess, her entire being began to glow with the same phosphorescence that Tony and Tita had seen the night the intruder had tried to destroy the house.

The princess responded in kind.

With light.

Warmth.

Joy.

This time, the colour of their bodies was not a lunar blue, as on the night of the intruder, but purple, the colour of royalty, and their faces were an incandescent and transcendent gold, more lovely than the treasures in the casket once buried beneath their feet.

As the two stood face-to-face, they studied each other before falling into each other's arms.

"Mama!" the princess sighed, a new gust of wind bearing that single word on its unseen wings to every corner of the ancient house and its walled gardens.

As the mother took a step back, Tiger stirred from his resting place before the hearth and hurried to the window.

Raising his front paws, he barked twice, his tail wagging furiously, his lips forming into a broad smile.

The Queen and her daughter looked towards the house.

Seeing the greyhound, they laughed.

Then, seeing the couple standing behind, they smiled, curtseyed, and mouthed two simple words before they faded away into the yew trees behind and beyond.

"Thank you."

AUTHOR'S NOTE

I'm often asked about the house in this novel. Is it imaginary or real? It's real, yet it also has something magical about it which is why it's proven an ideal setting for a work of magical realism.

The idea for my story began during a visit to an Old Rectory in Dorset with my wife Cherith. One night sleeping within its walls and my imagination went into overdrive.

The tale goes like this. I had been asked by a landlord in the West Country to come to his pub and give a talk. The pub was called 'The Farquharson Arms'. The landlords – Nev and Lesley Green – are old friends. They saw some posts of mine on social media about the TV series *The Walking Dead*. "Come and give some of our customers a talk about the show," they said. I agreed. My wife and I duly travelled with our Black Labrador Bella to Dorset.

I will confess that the talk itself was poorly attended and utterly unremarkable. What was remarkable, however, was the house where Nev and Lesley put us up for the night. Yes, an old rectory. *The* Old Rectory. As I stepped into its unfamiliar world, I felt at the time that this was a providential moment, a *liminal* moment if you will - a moment when you cross a threshold from your ordinary world into a special world. It seemed to me that there was something serendipitous, something *meant* about all this. When we started chatting with the owners - Hugh and Miranda - it turned out that Hugh and I had been neighbours growing up decades before in North Norfolk. Our homes were a stone's throw away from each other. Our respective families were friends. Hugh and I had not seen each other for over forty years but after several conversations about books, accompanied by some more-than-decent glasses of wine, we celebrated our shared background.

That night, after giving my forgettable talk in the pub, I found myself lying awake thinking about the house. My hosts had shared that King Henry VIII (whose coat of arms I had noticed above the front door) had given the original version of the house to Queen Catherine Parr, and that after the King's death, Sir Thomas Seymour had met the queen there. That piece of information was enough to hook me. When I returned to Kent the next day, I began my own research into the house. The list of the rectors who had occupied the property turned out to contain some well-known names, at least to anyone who has studied literature. One of them was Charles Kingsley, the famous Darwinian cleric who wrote one of the world's most popular and endearing children's stories, *The Water Babies*. He was just one of an impressive line of rectors who had written their books in this magical house. What if I wrote a story about a contemporary writer who wanted to buy the house and continue the tradition?

From the start, there was one writing resident who stood above them all - someone who I didn't even know had written books (four, to be precise). I'm referring to Queen Catherine Parr herself. She had used the Tudor version of the property as a bolthole where she found refuge from the often-censorious eyes of the courtiers in London. Here she wrote at least some parts of her four books. When these works were published, they had an enormous impact. Not only did she provide the roadmap for a simple, personal faith in God – one unhampered by the influence of coercive religious systems – but she was also in many ways a pioneer for women's rights. She was the first female author in the history of English Literature to have her name – rather than a male pseudonym – on the cover of her books. In both feminism and faith, Queen Catherine Parr was therefore an emancipator as well as an educator.

Once I had picked up this trail in my research, I began to find more and more treasures hidden in the history of the house. For example, I wrote to Lady Susan Hussey, wife of the late Marmaduke Hussey (formerly chairman of the BBC) whose grandfather had been one of the rectors there. She pointed me to her late husband's memoir in which he wrote about the impact that the Old Rectory had on him during a visit to the house very late in his life. It was the one time when he felt a sense of true homecoming. As he stood in the bedroom once occupied by his father (when his father had been a child), Hussey had felt a strong sense of connection with his past. Walking into the church of St Peter's nearby, he spied a kneeler with his grandfather's name embroidered on it. He knelt on it and felt that same sense of history and home that is so critical both to our sense of who we are (our identity) and where we've come from (our history). That was an experience I wanted my hero Tony Lawson to have as well.

I have therefore had many significant moments writing

this novel - moments of convergence when the past and the present have fused to create an impression of patterning and providence. When I wrote to Lady Susan Hussey, she was the principal lady in waiting to Queen Elizabeth II. It struck me then, as it does now, how fitting it is that I should be writing to someone so close to the Queen at a time when I was writing about Catherine Parr.

As I now look back on my writing journey, I recognise that I owe a debt of gratitude to Hugh and Miranda for giving me their blessing to write a novel with their magnificent and magical house as a primary character and setting. I have so appreciated their hospitality whenever my wife and I have visited. I'm deeply grateful.

But there are others too.

I am grateful to Rachel Hassal, archivist at the Old Shirburnian Society, for photocopying pages from John Hutchins's history of Dorset and sending them to me. I am especially grateful to Carolyn Pepper for helping me understand the finer legal issues and processes that my hero would have been forced to confront in his battles with Matt Maul on matters to do with copyright law.

I am also grateful to Juliette Coffey for her advice on psychotherapeutic issues, and to Rachel Kitchen and Rachel Wilkinson for reading and commenting on a draft of my story.

I especially want to thank Cherith and Bella, not only for accompanying me into the special world of the house six years or so ago, but for supporting me ever since, encouraging me to keep dreaming and writing, a bit like Tony Lawson himself. Without them, I would be so much less than I am, and I doubt this novel would ever have been written. Cherith's comments on the final draft, as well as her constant cheering me on, have been key for me.

Cherith and I share the same values in so many things, not least in our attitudes to our home. We - and our dog - occupy a tiny, rented property in a remote village in Kent. On almost a daily basis, we tell each other how much we love our home and the glorious countryside that surrounds it. This constant expression of gratitude for both our material abode and its context is something perhaps we all need to rediscover. When we welcome and thank our home, we are effectively giving a blessing to our surroundings. In doing that, we not only enhance the spiritual atmosphere. We also transform the attitudes we conceal within us, turning negativity to positivity, denigration to celebration. In this regard, we start to undo the damage done by the fragmenting tendencies in our intellectual evolution, and we do that by reconnecting the material to the spiritual, the spiritual to the material.

That is why I want my final thanks to go to houses. This may seem a strange place to land, but I feel we need to learn from cultures and traditions in which homes are not just regarded as material places but as mystical spaces – spaces where we rediscover the art of dreaming, whether by day or by night. Wherever you live, I hope you'll be able to say, "Bless this house!"

Mark Stibbe
September 2023

TIMELINE

BEFORE THE FIRE

1530 The Tudor Manor House is built

1543 Catherine Parr marries King Henry VIII

1543 Catherine Parr is given the house by King Henry VIII

1547 Death of King Henry VIII

1547 Catherine Parr marries Thomas Seymour

1547 John Parkhurst becomes Rector

1547 Catherine Parr publishes *The Lamentations of a Sinner*

1548 Catherine Parr dies after childbirth

1549 Thomas Seymour is beheaded

1553 John and Margaret Parkhurst become Marian exiles

1701 Thomas Stephens becomes Rector

1703 The Tudor house burns down

AFTER THE FIRE

1712 Rectory is built using stonework from the Tudor House

1722 Poet Christopher Pitt becomes Rector

1740 Pitt publishes his translation of *The Aeneid* in two volumes

1748 George Bingham, longest-serving Rector, is appointed
1756 George Bingham's wife, Sarah, dies after childbirth
1806 Thomas Wyndham becomes Rector
1844 Charles Kingsley (*The Water Babies*) is Curate
1862 William Bury becomes Rector
1886 James Hussey becomes Rector
1873 Lord Portman refurbishes the church and the Rectory
1998 Marmaduke Hussey visits the Old Rectory

Printed in Great Britain
by Amazon

30962046R00245